Praise for *ZOMBURBIA*

"If you haven't read *Zomburbia,* you haven't read about zombies. This is a new take and it is scary, freaky, and original. Gallardo resets the zombie bar and it's sky-high. Get this book!"
—**Nancy Holder,** *New York Times* bestselling author of *The Wicked Saga*

"*Zomburbia* combines deliciously dark humor with genuine moments of gut-wrenching horror. Courtney Hart experiences the undead uprising with all of the malaise of a bored suburban teenager. Adam Gallardo's world building is innovative and fascinating, turning the typical vision of post-zombie survival on its rotting ear. *Zomburbia* is sick and twisted and unexpectedly touching. I only put it down long enough to check that my zombie-apocalypse closet was well stocked."
—**Molly Harper White,** author of the Naked Werewolf series

"What if the zombie apocalypse didn't get all that apocalyptic? What if life went on pretty much as normal for most kids, except it was incredibly dangerous just getting to and from high school? What would it be like to grow up in a weird but eerily familiar Zomburbia? Meet Courtney, a flawed but spunky teen, and her misfit pals, who are trying to find their places in a world where death lurks around every corner. Readers are guaranteed plenty of mayhem and romance, laughter and heartbreak in Adam Gallardo's accomplished debut novel."
—**James Patrick Kelly,** Hugo, Nebula, and Locus award-winning author

ZOMBURBIA

ADAM GALLARDO

Teen

KENSINGTON PUBLISHING CORP.
www.kensingtonbooks.com

KTEEN BOOKS are published by

Kensington Publishing Corp.
119 West 40th Street
New York, NY 10018

ISBN-13: 978-1-61773-098-6
ISBN-10: 1-61773-098-X

First Trade Paperback Printing: September 2014

10 9 8 7 6 5 4 3 2 1

Printed in the United States of America

First electronic edition: September 2014

ISBN-13: 978-1-61773-099-3
ISBN-10: 1-61773-099-8

To my wife, Melissa,
and boys, Oscar and Gus,
who had to live with me as I wrote this.

CHAPTER ONE
Good Times at Bully Burger

The night shifts at Bully Burger are the absolute worst. It's like sitting through a five-hour History lecture from Mr. Chanders, only you have to wear a festively colored polyester uniform while you do it. Maybe a car an hour comes through the drive-thru, and you really get tired of that fearful look people have in their eyes after dark.

The Bully Burger—whose mascot, I swear to God, is a cartoon of Teddy Roosevelt holding a hamburger—is a minor big deal in these parts. Six stores that sprouted up back at the dawn of time. People around here are crazy proud of this homegrown franchise. This particular store, the last one to be built, is at the far end of a developed strip out on Commercial Street. That nicely named strip is where the town started to shove all the franchises and big-box stores in the late '70s and, as you can imagine, it looks like one long stretch of hell. It's all Walmarts and Mickey D's as far as the eye can see. Depressing.

There are no other stores really close to the Bully Burger, so we don't share a fence with anyone. We've got a sturdy chain-link that runs all around the lot with a motor-controlled gate facing the street. All of the parking is in the front of the shack and the drive-thru runs around back where our patrons get a lovely view of the shed that holds our Dumpster and incinerator.

Despite the fact that TR is our mascot, our color scheme is a rip-off of every other burger chain in existence. It's all red and orange and yellow. I doubt very much that our twenty-sixth president really dug on these colors much. Not that anyone asked my opinion before settling on the decor.

Inside it's as cheerless as you might imagine. Hard plastic seats molded for the average 1970s fanny, which means that today's super-size variety hardly fits in them. Not that there were many butts in seats the night this story starts. There was only one, in fact: that of our security guard, Chacho.

I suspected that was not his real name. Even though it was on his name badge and all, it was in quotes, so I think there was some subterfuge going on at some level. Besides this attempt to hide his identity, he was a pretty cool dude. He was ancient, maybe forty, a big Latino guy with a shaved head and a long mustache. Like a Mongol warlord, you know? If Chacho worked the afternoon shifts, he stationed himself by the gates the whole time to make sure no undesirables—no shufflers—got on the property, but if he worked a night shift, even though he should've been outside, everyone looked the other way and he sat inside with his newspaper and his armor all piled up on the seat next to him. He could throw that shit on in about ten seconds flat if something slipped through the gate that shouldn't. It seemed like a weird way to make a living, beating the crap out of shufflers. I guess someone had to do it.

Behind the counter were me and my friend Sherri. Sherri and I had been friends since the womb practically. We went all the way through school together, and we were gonna graduate together next year and then screw off to New York together. I had a plan that extended past that—including saving the world—but I doubted that Sherri did.

Sherri was shorter than me, maybe five-five? And she'd always been more athletic than me, not that she played sports or anything. Playing sports would be trying just a little too hard, if you get my drift. She wore her black hair cropped really close to her head and she was pretty in a butch sort of way. Actually, her looks started causing whispers about us being lesbians ever since our classmates figured out what lesbians were. Which we were totally not. Lesbians, I mean. That night, she wore her company-mandated clown shirt unbuttoned over a T-shirt that was made to look like it had handwriting on it, though it was screen printed or something. YES, I'M A ZOMBIE, WHAT'S YOUR EXCUSE? it said. Many raised eyebrows from customers when she helped them at the counter. Which was rarely at night. Mostly she ran the grill.

If there had been any manager besides Mr. Philips on duty, Sherri would have buttoned the shirt. But Mr. Philips had just been a shift grunt named Ted until a couple of weeks before, and Sherri felt like he'd not yet earned her, or anyone's, respect. So, the shirt was to remain unbuttoned for the foreseeable future. Ted spent most of his shifts back in the manager's office on the phone with his girlfriend or surfing the web for porn. Apparently he'd figured out a way to erase all traces of where he'd been online and he wouldn't tell any of us how to do it, too.

I worked the drive-thru window that night. I say "worked" but mostly what I did was talk to Sherri, and run my side business.

"Okay," she said from the front counter, "top three people you'd like to see have their brains eaten by hordes of zombies."

I didn't have to think about this list for very long.

"One," I said, "Mr. Chanders—"

Sherri cut me off with a slicing motion of her hand.

"You know, Courtney," she said, "we should call this game 'top three people you'd like to see have their brains eaten by hordes of zombies who aren't Mr. Chanders since he's so obvious.' "

"You didn't say that, though," I said. "So, number one, Mr. Chanders.

"Two: Lori Caldwell."

"For serious?" Sherri asked. She looked at me totally not believing it. "I'm going to need some justification."

"She completely hates me," I said, ticking things off on my fingers as I went. "She thinks she's so great, even though she's got that lazy eye, and she ruined my grade point average by not letting me borrow her notes for our last AP English test."

Sherri looked at me with narrowed eyes.

"That's sort of lame, but I'll allow it," she said. "Give with number three."

"My mom," I said with no hesitation.

Sherri did a long, drama-queen-y sigh and shook her head.

"So obvious," she said. "If this was a TV movie, you'd be forced to come to terms with your tumultuous feelings about her. Also, you'd be played by a second-tier Disney starlet."

"Let's hear yours," I told her, ignoring the jibe.

Before she could get to it, we heard three sharp car-horn blasts.

A car sat in the median lane waiting for us to open the gate.

"Open 'er up," I shouted at Sherri, my head outside the drive-thru window. Almost immediately I heard the electric motor hum to life and then the rattle of the chain-link gate sliding open. The car waited until the gap was just big enough to let it through and then it sputtered to life and drove into the lot.

"Okay," I said, pulling my head in, "close it."

I noticed that the third member of our crew, Phil, had come up from the back where he'd been cleaning. He stood there waiting to see if we'd need his help with this order or if he could go back and keep prepping to close. Phil was pretty unremarkable—average height, average short brown hair, average medium build, average—the only other thing you need to know is that he was a year younger than Sherri and me and he was in our grade as well as in two of my AP classes, and in my Journalism class where he mostly draws incomprehensible editorial cartoons. This classified him as annoying in the extreme.

"Back to the bog, Gollum," Sherri said to Phil.

He slowly turned his head and just stared at her in his creepy way for a second before answering.

"Gollum lived in a lake in a cave," he said.

"Whatever," she said, shooing him away with her hands. "Go and get cleaning; I want to get out of here before eleven."

He blinked again, then turned and disappeared into the depths of the store.

A tone sounded in my headset, and I hit the button that lets me talk to the customers out at the order board.

"Welcome to Bully Burger," I said as fast as I could, "where we're bully about service. How may I help you?"

I winced a little. That slogan was so dumb, I was convinced it killed my soul a little bit every time I said it.

I heard whispering over my headset. No matter how much I strained, I couldn't make out what anyone was saying.

"Can . . . can I get, um, two Whoppers?" the voice on the other end said.

"We don't serve Whoppers here, sir," I answered, and

shot a look at Sherri. She purposefully avoided eye contact but made sure I could see her frowning at me. Her back stiffened, too. I ignored her. "Is there anything else I can get you?"

"Sure," the voice said. "How about, uh, two Bully Meals, extra-large, one with curly fries. Both with Coke."

I punched it into the register.

"That'll be thirteen-ninety-six at the window," I said. "Please pull forward."

Sherri chucked some frozen patties on the grill.

The car sat under the window as I threw it open and looked out at my customer. A rat-faced little guy with a knit cap pulled down over his ears sat behind the wheel of an old beat-up Escort. He smiled up at me expectantly. It looked like he hadn't shaved in a few days and hadn't bathed in even longer. Another, equally rat-faced, guy sat next to him, his leg bouncing up and down. The passenger craned his neck to look up into the window.

I glanced around behind me to see if anyone was paying attention. No one was.

"You wanted Whoppers?" I asked.

The first dude's head bobbed up and down on his pipe-cleaner neck.

"Fifty dollars," I whispered.

The guy frowned and did this involuntary head shake. I thought he might argue with me, but then the passenger leaned over and said something. The driver shot me a look and then dug cash out of his pocket and counted out fifty dollars.

"And thirteen-ninety-six for the burgers," I said.

If looks could kill, there'd have been an empty seat in Mrs. Callow's homeroom the next day. But I didn't change my expression; I just waited. He counted out a few more notes and handed them to me.

"Thanks," I said as brightly as I could. Fifty bucks went into my pocket and fourteen went into the register. I didn't bother with the four pennies I owed him.

And before you start to get all judgmental on me, just don't, okay? Yes, I sold Vitamin Z, but I wasn't really a drug dealer, you know? And, before you ask, it's true; Vitamin Z *is* made from actual zombie brains, but I'm not going to get all judgmental about what people put in their bodies. It might have been a rationalization, but I only sold to asshats like the two ferret brothers. I mean, Jesus, those guys were going to find a fix somewhere and I might as well have been the one to get their money.

Also—and this may be way self-serving—I needed the money if I was going to escape Salem and go away to school in New York. My dad had offered to pay my way but only if I agreed to go to a school in-state. Ideally, he'd have liked me to spend the first two years at the community college where he taught. That way it'd all be free. However, community college in a no-horse town in Oregon was not going to advance my plan to help rid the world of the undead. Also, I have to tell you, the thought of another two years stuck in Salem made me want to blow my brains out.

So I'd been saving up every penny I could to get out of Dodge. That's why I originally took the job at Bully Burger. Soon after, it became clear I wouldn't make the dosh fast enough, so I started looking for another way to make money. And I found it. I figured the rate I was going, I'd have four years at most any school wired. Especially if I got scholarships. Which I totally would.

Sherri brought a bag full of food and a cardboard tray with two drinks over to the window. The smell of grease wafted up and hit me in the nose. How people could eat this garbage I would never know. I shoved in a handful of ketchup packets and napkins. Then I slipped my hand into my apron and pulled out two small Ziploc bags full of shiny black powder. Those Ziplocs went into the bag, too. I handed the whole mess out the window to Ratzo. He immediately ripped open the bag and seemed to relax when he saw the two baggies sitting on top of the burgers.

"Thanks for choosing Bully Burger," I said.

The guy tore off without saying anything. In fact, I barely got my arm out of the car before he screeched away.

"Come again!" I yelled out at the car that was now waiting for the gate to open.

"Brothers?" Sherri asked in my ear. I didn't know she was still standing there. "Or dad and son?" She had her arms crossed on her chest as she looked out the drive-thru window at the car. "Or, given the strong genetic markers, both?"

"Not really interested," I said. "Already forgotten."

"Hmm . . ." was all Sherri said.

She pushed the button, and the gate started to slowly close and the lights from the beater receded. Another car in the turn lane was trying to get in the gate before it closed. They slammed on their brakes when it became obvious they wouldn't make it.

"Hey," I shouted, "we got another car! Open it up again."

The gate shuddered as it came to a stop and back open again. The car pulled through.

Chacho stowed away his paper for the moment since the car parked in the lot. The owner frowned on customers seeing the security guard wasting time like that. Three guys in letterman jackets got out of the car and walked toward the door.

"Great," Sherri hissed, "like these dopes don't know we're supposed to close in half an hour."

"Relax," I told her. "With the monkey in back catching up on cleaning, we'll still get out of here early."

She didn't look at all relieved by this and practiced her best sneer to sling at the a-holes who were just now coming through the door.

The trio filed in, all of them high-fiving and laughing that too-loud, we-are-dudes laugh. God, I was just glad that Sherri had front counter.

I moved to the grill and waited for their order to show up on the monitor. As I was waiting, staring at the screen, I became aware that I could hear something over the hiss of my headphones that didn't sound like ordering.

Sherri scowled at me. Then my eyes slid over to the guys in front of the counter. There was a six-foot pile of blond hair and flashing white teeth speaking to me. I slowly pulled the headset off my ears.

"Hey," the guy said, "hey, aren't you Courtney?"

Oh, my God, one of these trolls knew me.

"Yeah?" I asked, unsure of protocol when spoken to by someone so clearly outside my social station.

"Brandon," the guy said like that explained it all. After a second or two of blankness from me, he pointed at himself. "Brandon Ikaros," he said.

It slowly dawned on me. Brandon Ikaros. He was in my Journalism class. Not an AP class. He played a bunch of sports and mostly wrote human interest pieces for the *Quotidian*—which is a stupid name since the paper comes out once a week. Sometimes Mrs. Johnson even lets him write movie reviews despite the fact that he'd seen and liked all the *Transformer* movies.

Also, I'd never done anything to make him aware of me, ever.

"Right," I said, "Brandon."

"Yeah," he said. "I just wanted to say hi, because," he

hesitated and smiled at me and I did my best to deflect it. "Because I didn't know you worked here."

"Okay," I said. "Hi."

Why was Sherri not taking their orders? Why was she not breaking this up and saving me from this terribly awkward situation? If I was on fire, she'd put me out, right? Actually, I might have to think about that one.

"Listen, Brandon," I said, "it's great to see you, but," I waved my hands over the grill to indicate I had other, more important matters to attend to, "I have to get back to work."

"Sure," he said, nodding his head. "No problem. I'll see you in class tomorrow."

Rather than reply, I just nodded and then shot daggers at Sherri as Brandon turned away from me and faced her, ready to give his order. Maybe if I stared at her hard enough, her head would explode all over Brandon's letterman jacket.

The cream of the school's jocktocracy was about to give their orders to Sherri when I heard a voice behind me.

"Hey, there's someone outside."

Phil stood behind me. He stared past us all and into the parking lot. The rest of us turned and looked.

He was right: there was someone out there who hadn't come in with the rest of the football team. This someone shuffled awkwardly, slowly, dragging one leg behind. His shoulder hitched in a weird way with every step.

One of the boys said, "Shit."

Chacho moved fast for a big guy. He sprang up out of his bright plastic seat and started throwing on his body armor. The knee pads and shin guards were already on, so he got on his elbow pads and the pads for his forearms. He ignored the high-necked body armor and just put on the helmet. Then he scooped up his clear plastic shield and his club and he sprinted out the door.

Sherri and I ran from behind the counter and stationed ourselves next to the picture window closest to the action. Phil was close behind us and the jocks came up more slowly; maybe they felt like they shouldn't be watching this. But, really, how could they not?

It was totally a zombie, a pretty fresh one, too. It was a dude, maybe my age, maybe a little older. He wore jeans and a MELVINS T-shirt. He wore one Dr. Martens boot. The foot missing the shoe looked like it had been chewed on pretty well. Also, except for half of his face being gone, he was probably pretty good looking when he was alive.

"If I were a zombie," I whispered to Sherri without taking my eyes off the scene, "I'd totally go with him."

"Uh-huh," she said.

When the shuffler moved into the light, I saw that he had a death grip on a bloody stump of a leg. Someone somewhere was missing everything below the left knee. I shivered when I noticed that the foot was wearing a pink Chuck Taylor. Then I wondered if I knew anyone who owned shoes like that. I couldn't think of anyone.

Out in the parking lot, Chacho approached the shuffler. Zombies are slow and all that, but they can move surprisingly quickly when you least expect it. Chacho had been trained to deal with them, so he knew that better than most folks. He kept his shield in front of him and his club ready to swing.

As soon as the undead kid saw him, he went into Classic Zombie mode—arms up like he wanted to give Chacho a hug, and he started groaning. He dropped the leg he'd been gnawing on. It lay there forgotten as the zombie eyed fresh meat. Something black and thick dribbled out of his mouth. Maybe he wasn't as cute as I originally thought . . .

Chacho shouted at the thing. I couldn't hear what he

was saying. Probably cursing at him in Spanish. I'd heard it before; it was pretty entertaining.

When it got close enough, Chacho did a pretty good head feint to the left and when the zombie moved that way, he slammed into it with his whole body, the shield between them. The shuffler stumbled back, grunting in surprise, and then Chacho brought his club up and over from behind the shield. There was a dull crack we could hear even through the glass and then the kid's head was barely attached to his body. It hung there at a weird angle that made me feel sick. But, of course, the kid already being dead, that didn't stop him. So Chacho swung his club again and caught the kid on the other side of his head. That drove him to the ground.

Chacho dropped his shield onto the thing's chest and then put all his weight on top of it. He left the head exposed, though, so he could go to town on it with the club, which he raised and brought down again and again. Pretty soon it went from a cracking sound to something like sucking mud every time he did it.

After a while, Chacho stood up and the zombie kid didn't even twitch. Chacho stood over him, bent over with his hands on his knees, and breathed hard. After a few seconds, he took off his helmet and wiped his forehead. He placed his gear on the ground next to the body and grabbed the kid's legs. He started to drag it toward the incinerator that lives in the back of the store. A wet trail snaked behind him from the kid's shattered melon.

I realized that I hadn't breathed in a while, so I took a deep breath. Sherri and a few others did the same thing. I turned and smiled at Sherri, though it felt forced. She didn't say anything if she noticed.

"Good times at Bully Burger," she said, and she sounded a little shaky.

"Yeah," was all I could say.

We turned and made our way back behind the counter. Phil held the kitchen door open for us, and Sherri must have been feeling generous because she didn't snarl at him or order him back to the depths of the store, she just mumbled a thanks and returned to the register.

Brandon and his friends were up at the counter then, Sherri at the register ready to take their order. I stood in front of the grill and Phil was in the back of the store. The only sound I heard was Chacho outside banging open the incinerator door.

We all stood like that for what seemed like a long time.

"Welcome to Bully Burger," Sherri said finally. "How can I help you?"

I shuddered and I thought, for the millionth time, that I needed to get the hell out of this town.

CHAPTER TWO
A Topic for Casual Conversation

I was totally young on the Day the Dead Came Back. Like three or four? The point being, I don't remember it at all. Okay, maybe that's an exaggeration. But only barely. I remember being scared, mostly because Mom and Dad were scared, and that was something that'd never happened before.

I have a few concrete memories that I can call up. I remember my dad buying a gun. A shotgun. Now I know it was a cheap pump action from Walmart, but at the time I'd never seen a shotgun, or a gun of any kind, really, except on TV, and I was pretty fascinated by it. I wanted to look at it and hold it. My dad got, like, red-in-the-face mad at me for even bringing it up.

"This is very bad and dangerous," he told me as he put it in his closet and then locked the door with a key. There'd never been a lock on it before he brought home the shotgun. "This is only to keep our family safe," he said as he carried me out of the room. I remember being confused that something so dangerous would keep us safe.

The only other thing I remember well is sitting on the living room floor in front of the TV. Mom and Dad were behind me on the couch. We all watched the news, which I never really cared about. I sat on the floor playing with Legos or toy ponies or something else stupid little kids do.

Then I heard the dude on the TV say something about the dead coming back.

"Does that mean Grandma is coming back?" I asked.

Usually when I made these kinds of, what do you call them? Intuitive leaps, right? When I did that, there were two possible reactions. One: Get patted on the head and told that I was right and, gee, wasn't I smart. Two: Get patted on the head and told that I was wrong and, gee, wasn't I cute. This time though, Mom just started bawling and Dad looked at me like I'd just taken a crap in his shoe. Not at all what I was expecting.

So, there you go. My only memories of the event that defined our whole life, more or less. Not real great, huh?

But anyone that's interested in learning about those times just has to turn on their TVs most any night and they'll see some made-for-TV movie or Discovery Channel re-enactment about it.

And, weird, zombie movies are a big hit now. Especially old ones. They're kind of thought of the same way sci-fi movies from the '50s used to be viewed: quaint in how wrong they showed a future the makers could only barely imagine.

Because here's what all the George Romeros in Hollywood got exactly wrong: The zombie infestation didn't cause the world to come to an end. Sure, things were real shitty for a while—in a lot of places, especially big cities, they still are—but for the most part, things recovered.

Okay, yes, there are whole countries where you can't go anymore because they're overrun by hordes of ghouls. That's pretty uncommon, though, and those are places you wouldn't want to go anyway. Places in, like Africa and China. Those places weren't cool to begin with so it's not too big a loss, right?

A lot of people in America live in gated communities now, and those who can't afford that—people like me and

Sherri and most of the kids we go to school with—all have chain-link fences around their houses. Shufflers are not big on manual dexterity so things as simple as gate locks, doorknobs, and flights of stairs can hold 'em back. Of course, a chain-link fence won't stop a whole herd of the undead. Not that there have been big roving groups of them since right after they came back.

Cities are mostly abandoned since the zombies like to gather there. This means, of course, that everyone lives in the freaking suburbs.

And it was the suburbs north of Bully Burger that I was riding through with Sherri and our friend Willie. I say "friend." He's got a car. Okay, I'm being unfair; I've known Willie almost as long as I've known Sherri. Somehow, though, he's always felt like he's on the fringe of our little group of just three people.

Willie is tall—like, six feet at least—and kind of big. Husky. The ungenerous would call him "fat." He's always been this way. When we were kids, he was the boy who wouldn't take off his shirt to go swimming. You know that kid, right? When he grew up, he dressed all in black with his dyed-black hair swept up into a really outrageous '50s-style pompadour. I totally respect his hair. The thing about Willie is, I think he'd be kind of good looking if he wasn't, you know, big boned? It's kind of how a movie star lets himself go when he starts to get older. You look at him and you can still see the thin, sexy guy he used to be. Willie is like that, only he was never ever thin or sexy.

I might be able to look past all of that, except for one thing. Please believe me that I feel sort of mean and petty when I say this: Willie is not all that smart. I mean, he's not in a single AP class, for Pete's sake! Me dating him would be like M. Curie dating the guy who cleaned up her lab. Right?

His redeeming feature was that he absolutely had a car. And what a car.

Besides being huge—probably too big to be on the road—the defining characteristic of the land boat was that it had a custom front bumper. One day the previous year, Willie and his dad beefed up the front suspension and swapped out the factory-installed bumper—a bumper that thousands of people were perfectly happy with, I might add—and replaced it with a freaking railroad tie. A huge six-foot length of seven-by-nine-inch, creosote-soaked wood. Sometimes the car felt like it rode funny because the back tires barely touched the ground, but that bumper came in handy every once in a while.

As we drove along, Sherri told Willie about the shuffler from earlier in the night. He couldn't seem to get past the part of the story where I talked to Brandon Ikaros. He kept asking questions about this aspect of the narrative, trying to divine if I had feelings for the aforementioned jock. Let me state emphatically that I did *not* have any feelings for Brandon.

I should also mention what you may have already figured out: Willie had feelings for *me*. Not to worry, however. Deflecting the advances of unworthy boys is something a girl learns to do early in her life. Like hiding the fact that you're on your period.

I rode up front next to Willie; Sherri kept up a running commentary from the backseat. I mostly stared out the window. We were headed north on Winthrop Road, which is a sort of main road that borders the town; the west side of Winthrop is pretty much woods and the east is houses. All the houses out here have chain-link fences, the gates all shut up tight. We'd seen what we thought were a couple of zombies about a mile back. I guess they could have been just people walking along, though most people don't

go out walking alone—especially after dark. *Especially* in
the woods on the edge of town. Zombies kind of congre-
gate there. There's been talk for years about developing
that land, knocking the trees back to give the shufflers
fewer places to hide. No one really has the money to do it.

All I know is, I'd hate to live out there. You probably
have to deal with a lot of undead trespassers out this way.

"So, how well do you know this guy?" Willie asked.
Again.

"Jesus, Willie," I said without turning from the view
outside the car. "I hardly know him.

"I'm just boning him, is all."

Willie said, "Ha, ha," real slow and sarcastic. In the
backseat, Sherri let out a real laugh.

"Oh, yeah, Willie," she said, "you could feel the chemistry. It was like Sid and Nancy."

"Ike and Tina," I added.

"Probably more like . . ." Willie's voice trailed off. It
was obvious he couldn't think of anything to say. I felt a
little bad for him. We needle him a lot and sometimes it
was just a bit too much. I hoped that Sherri would let it
lie.

"Nice . . . one," came from the backseat, and I grimaced.
Then I turned away from the window. Willie made a
point of keeping his gaze straight ahead.

"There's nothing going on, Willie," I told him. "I neither know, nor like, the guy. He's of the ruling class and
therefore repugnant."

"Yeah?" Willie asked, sneaking a sidelong glance at me.

"Yeah," I said.

I heard Sherri muttering from the backseat, which was
fine—it's her favorite pastime, really, being generally unhappy with the state of things. I'm sure she wished I'd destroyed Willie by proclaiming my love for Brandon, and I

usually would have, but I just wasn't in the mood at that moment. Being nice to Willie felt like atonement for something. I wasn't sure what.

"Before your mouth becomes otherwise engaged up there, Courtney," Sherri said, "tell me if you're working tomorrow night."

"Not again until Friday," I said.

Sherri immediately went into a full-blown fit.

"Does that mean you won't be at my party?" she yelled. "Why didn't you tell me, you bitch!"

I spoke to her like you'd talk to a dog or a really slow kid.

"I am only scheduled until ten," I said. "I should be there before eleven." I turned and looked at her. "Unless you think it'll be over by then."

"Hell, no," she said. "We're not shutting it down until someone calls the cops!"

"Right," I said, and sat back. Our parties almost always involve a bunch of us sitting around, drinking whatever booze we could convince our older brothers and sisters to buy for us, listening to terrible music, and talking Olympic-level amounts of B.S. Really, the booze was the only thing that distinguished our parties from our daily lives.

"Saaaay," Sherri drawled, "why don't you bring along your new boyfriend?"

Both Willie and I cringed. I decided not to answer, as any response would just feed the fire.

"How's your sister doing, Willie?" I asked him as a diversionary tactic. It is well known that the only member of Willie's mutant family he can stand is his little sister, Julie. She has mild Down syndrome, and she is, by general consensus, the sweetest kid in the whole world.

"She's great," Willie said, "despite everything my mom

does." His mom refused to accept that Julie was different from other kids at all and insisted that she be put into regular classes and stuff. So, instead of getting the help she needed to thrive, she was always behind and confused and upset. Willie's mom believed she was doing what was best for her daughter, even though anyone who wasn't an ass could see she was doing just the opposite.

That's the way it was with most parents.

"She read a story to me the other night," Willie said, and he smiled, which didn't happen very often. "It took a while and I had to help her a few times. Still . . ." He trailed off and left it hanging, like he didn't know how to talk about stuff that made him happy. That was probably the case, actually.

The car rumbled through the night and we all fell silent. I could tell by the way the woods thinned out that we were close to my neighborhood. I sank a little lower down in my seat.

"I don't have to take you home," Willie said. He was actually pretty good at reading my moods, not that it was too hard where my house was concerned.

"And where would you take her, Willie," Sherri asked. "*Your* house? And what would you do with her there?"

There was what I can only describe as a dramatic pause.

"Maybe you could finally deflower her and do us all a big favor," Sherri squealed.

"Jesus, Sherri!" As fast as I could, I turned around in the seat and slapped at her. She was laughing and swatting me away.

"I thought you didn't care who knew the status of your hymen," Sherri managed between giggles.

"That doesn't mean it's a topic for casual conversation," I said as I sat back down. Truth be told, I may have huffed. "Bitch," I added.

We drove on in silence for a few moments. Thank God.

"Good times," Willie said as he turned the car into my subdivision. "We should do this more often."

Little houses with chest-high chain-link fences lined either side of the street. This late, most of the houses were dark. Light attracts the shufflers. The living room light was on in my house. I hoped Dad just left it on for me and had gone to bed.

After another minute of silence, Sherri spoke up.

"Sorry," she said.

"Whatever," I said like it was no big deal. No way was I going to let her know it bothered me.

"Here we are," Willie said, and pulled over to the curb. He parked so that I was the shortest possible distance from the gate into my yard.

"Clear this way," he said, looking forward to make sure there were no zombies.

"Ditto in back," Sherri said.

"Thanks for the ride, Willie," I said, and climbed out.

"And good night, Sherri," Sherri yelled at me from the backseat. "I'm sure that's what you meant to say."

I covered the distance from the car to the gate in no time, opened it, stepped in, and closed it all in one motion.

The car started to pull away from the curb and the passenger-side window cranked down. The *front* passenger-side window. Sherri must have climbed over the seat. Her head stuck out of the window as the car continued on its way.

"You should have forgiven me," she yelled, her hands cupped around her mouth. "What if something happens to me and you never have another chance to be nice to me? Isn't there something you want to say?"

I flipped her my middle finger and she fell back into the car, cackling, as it turned the corner and drove out of sight.

Sherri *can* be a total bitch, but she can do it in a way that eventually makes you laugh, and I guess that counts for something.

I turned and walked up the short path to the front door, digging my key out of my bag as I went.

As soon as I opened the door, I heard the TV. I groaned a little. My hopes that Dad had gone to bed were dashed. I took a deep breath and walked into the house, closing and locking the door behind me.

"Hey, kiddo," Dad said from the couch.

I avoided eye contact, hoping I could just slip on past.

"Hey," I said, and started walking down the hall to my room.

"Why don't you sit down and tell me about your day?" he asked.

I grimaced, then put my bland face back on by the time I'd turned around.

I heard him mute the TV.

"Sure," I said, and walked over to the couch.

Dad sat there, a ratty old robe wrapped around him, his skinny little legs poking out the bottom. I guess he could have been handsome once. Now he looks too sad and defeated to be good looking. His face is kind of pinched up, and his hair is really thin and straggly. I guess it's a good thing he wasn't interested in finding a replacement for my mom.

I sat on the far side of the couch and scooted over when he patted the spot next to him. He flashed me a weak smile. I don't think he's very used to smiling.

"I thought you'd be in bed all ready," I said.

"Not without checking in with my favorite girl," he said, and patted my arm. "So, how was your day?"

"Pretty uneventful," I told him. I thought about Chacho taking on that zombie earlier. I didn't say anything.

"That's it?" he asked. " 'Uneventful'?"

I shrugged. "Come on," I said, "I'm a high school student, how much exciting stuff could there be in my life?"

He nodded. "Sure," he said. "Sure."

He smiled. "You know you can talk to me about anything, right?" he asked.

I thought again about Chacho taking on the zombie earlier and the sick feeling in my gut when he knocked it on the head with his club. Again I didn't say anything. We both turned and concentrated on the TV because that's easier sometimes.

"What are you watching?" I asked.

Dad waved his hand dismissively. "One of those late-night talk shows," he said. "This wacko thinks we should be trying to talk to the Returned."

I groaned. I've always hated the term "Returned" for the zombies. It's got this slightly religious flavor like a cool-ranch communion wafer or something. But then, Dad always had a flair for the dramatic. For instance, whenever he talks about my mom, he makes people believe that she died in a zombie attack, when the real reason she's gone is because she left to go live up in Seattle with her Pilates instructor. Honestly, though, I was happy to think of her as dead, too.

"Huh," was my only response. Best to nip these things in the bud.

"Well," he said as he stood up, "I'm going to hit the hay. Don't stay up too late, huh?"

He shuffled off down the hallway, and a second later I heard his bedroom door close.

I turned my attention to the TV.

Two middle-aged white guys in suits sat across a table. If it weren't for the titles that appeared beneath them on the screen, I wouldn't be able to tell them apart. The zombie talker was a professor somewhere and he was mildly annoyed. Probably because the host was barely containing his derision as he spoke to the dude. Being a high school student, I can discern even the best-hidden condescension. I'm sure the professor was used to this since the host made a point of saying how many people thought his ideas were total crap. Though he used nicer words than that.

The prof didn't take any of the host's shit, which made me like him. He sat forward, looked the guy right in the eyes, and told him he didn't care what others thought of his theories.

"The world of academia changes course so slowly in response to changes in the world, they make the *Titanic* look like a race car," he said, and then gave a hint of a smile. I thought about my teachers and smiled, too.

"The truth is," he said, "there is a great deal of interest in this subject in the general population. These creatures have come back, that's undeniable, and now it's up to us to figure out what that means. I simply don't understand why," he said, "despite the fact that these creatures were once human, no one has tried to communicate with them. Literally no one. Once spotted, the immediate response is to kill them."

The host turned to the camera and practically rolled his eyes. "Yes," he said. "Why would we ever kill flesh-eating monsters bent on our destruction?"

There were lots of guffaws from the audience.

Before the guest could say anything in his defense, the host jumped in again.

"What do you think these things could possibly tell us," he asked, "provided you could get one to talk?"

"What they have to tell us may be nothing less than how to save the world," the guest answered.

The host turned and mugged for the camera.

"Only if the answer is, 'braaiins . . .' " he said.

All of the goons in the audience laughed like hyenas. The guest sat there and stared at the host. I'm sure he was wondering why he ever agreed to be on the show and talk with this douche bag.

"That's all the time we have tonight," the host went on. I could hear the guest in the background trying to get a word in. The host just steamrollered over him. "I'd like to thank our guest tonight, Professor Richard Keller. Good night and we'll see you again tomorrow." The lights dimmed and the camera showed the two of them. This is the part of the show where the guest and host pretend to carry on the conversation even though the audience can't hear it and the credits roll up. The professor—Keller— wasn't playing along. He was on his feet and trying to get the mic off his lapel so he could leave. The host was look- ing off camera, probably at his producer, and probably waiting for advice on what to do. After a few seconds, the screen went black.

I turned it off before another crappy program had a chance to come on and suck me in. The remote clattered on the coffee table where I threw it and I got up to get ready for bed.

As I washed my face and brushed my teeth, I thought about Professor Keller. I suddenly realized I was happy that Sherri wasn't here—which was really weird to feel. If she'd been here she'd be making fun of the guy and I'd feel the need to jump in and make fun, too. I didn't know if I be- lieved what the guy was saying. I wanted to contemplate it for a while. If I decided the guy was full of it, then I'd bring it up to Sherri and Willie. If I decided there was something to what he said, I'd probably keep it to myself. It felt good to have something that was just for me.

On the way back down the hall, I paused in front of the door to my dad's room. I held my breath, listened, and heard faint snoring. I tiptoed back to my room and closed the door behind me.

I pulled a wad of bills out of my backpack—$600, not a

bad night—and hid them in my underwear drawer. That drawer has a false bottom that Willie helped me make. Or that Willie made, if you want to be entirely accurate. My dad said he wouldn't go through my room without permission, but I still worried about it. If he ever did decide to violate my Fourth Amendment rights, the one place he'd never dig into is my underwear drawer. Pawing my delicates would be too creepy. I hoped.

Right before I turned off the light, I took a small revolver from my bag. It's a pretty compact Smith & Wesson .38. It's nickel-plated and cute. My dad gave it to me after I started working nights at Bully Burger. He's come a long way since he freaked out about me wanting to look at the family shotgun. I removed the rounds from the cylinder and put them in one drawer of my nightstand and put the pistol in another. I'd clean it in the morning before school.

That last bit of business taken care of, it was time to hit the hay.

I crawled into bed and turned off the lamp on the bedside table.

I drifted off thinking about what kind of conversation I would have with a zombie. It would probably be a lot like talking to my dad or my teachers.

CHAPTER THREE
Zomburbia

My dad taught an early class every day, which meant he left to prepare for it before I woke up. He was on the faculty at the community college. Psychology. Whenever I think about my dad being a psychologist, I think of that old saying, *The cobbler's children always go unshod.* Though, in my case, I guess it would be, *The psychologist's children always go around complete emotional wrecks.* Not as catchy, but true.

After I showered, I got into my uniform for the day. Jeans, oversized flannel shirt, black Chuck Taylors, minimal makeup but heavy on the mascara. Basically, I look like the world's tiniest emo lumberjack—which does not help with the "Courtney and Sherri are lesbian" rumors. I grabbed my backpack, the pistol once again tucked into the front pocket, and headed out the door.

Willie's land boat idled at the curb. The street was free of shufflers, so I opened the gate and jumped into the battered old Buick. I barely had the door closed before Willie gassed it and we were out of there.

"Hey," he said. I barely heard him over the squeal of the passenger door closing.

"'Morning," I said as I did up the seat belt. The way Willie drives, the seat belt is necessary even if it separates my boobs and makes them look all wonky.

After I turned the radio to an appropriate, listenable station rather than the ear-bleed sonata Willie had chosen, I settled back in the seat.

"You up for a Portland run this weekend?" I asked. For the last few months, Willie had been driving me up to meet with the guy that sells me Vitamin Z. Sherri used to do it, but then she decided to become Ms. Morals about the whole deal.

"Sure," Willie said. "Just let me know when."

"Can do," I said.

Silence filled the car as Willie threw us around corners. Thursdays were always kind of a mixed blessing. Sherri had a late start, so I got a break from her constant critiques of everything in the entire world. On the downside, I was stuck all alone in a confined space with Willie.

He's a great guy and all—as great as a guy can be, anyway—but his crush on me was a little hard to take sometimes. He refused to admit it and so he acted weird all the time. If he'd just get it out in the open, I could shoot him down and crush his dreams and we'd move on from there, you know?

We rode along a little while without saying anything. I never know what to say to Willie when we're alone. But I've learned that you have to fire off the first salvo in any conversation or else he'll start it and then you're stuck talking about Danish hard-core bands or his latest D&D adventures for the entire ride to school.

I saw him open his mouth to speak, so I plunged ahead.

"So I saw this crazy guy on TV last night," I said in a rush.

I winced. Just last night I'd told myself I wouldn't bring this up to Willie or Sherri until I was sure it was bunk. But here I was, blabbing away about it. Next I'd be telling him about my sexual fantasies. I really sucked sometimes.

I sat and waited to see if Willie was going to bite.

He raised an eyebrow.

"Crazy how?" he asked.

"He thinks we need to start trying to talk to the UDs," I said. I kept my voice neutral.

Willie considered this as we drove.

"Like the *Pro-Deathers*," he said. "It sort of makes sense."

The Pro-Deathers are a group of kids on campus who think we shouldn't be killing zombies on sight. Most of them are religious, I hate to say. And most of them have also had family members or loved ones turned by the virus. They argue that destroying the shufflers is like killing them twice. Needless to say, this outlook is not a popular one.

Willie surprised me sometimes. I expected him to mock the idea, and maybe he would have if Sherri had been there. Right then he was open to it.

"It sort of does, huh?" I asked.

"What's that kid doing in the road?" he asked, and pointed out the windshield. Maybe a hundred yards ahead, a kid was walking beside the road. You never see anyone out on foot, or alone, anymore. At most you see packs of kids on bikes.

"I don't know," I said, "maybe he missed the bus. Wanna offer him a ride?"

"Sure," Willie said. "Okay, so what were you saying?"

"Right," I said, "this guy, this *professor*, figured that zombies used to be human, right? So maybe we'd be able to communicate with them if someone could figure out how to, you know, speak their language."

"Okay," Willie said.

"The host of the show was sort of a tool," I went on. "He didn't give the guy much of a chance to talk. I was thinking about it this morning, and I was wondering what sorts of things they could tell us."

"Besides 'braaaaains'?" Willie asked.

"That's the same joke the tool of a host made last night," I said. "I'm being serious."

Willie grunted.

We got closer to the kid. With every step, his leg hitched up in a weird way, like he'd hurt his hip.

Willie slowed the car and I rolled down the window.

"I mean, what if they could tell us how to cure the zombie plague?" I asked. Then I stuck my head out the window.

"Hey, dude!" I yelled at the kid. "Do you need a ride to school?"

He looked up at the sound of my voice. The front of his shirt was torn open and his guts—what was left of them— hung down around his knees.

"Oh, shit!" I said, and reeled back into the car and rolled the window up as fast as I could.

Calm as anything, Willie slammed on the brakes, then threw the boat into reverse.

"Maybe the shufflers could tell us things like what happens after we die," he said as he turned to look out the back window.

By now, the zombie had turned toward us, his eyes glinting. I told myself that I didn't recognize him.

"Since they're dead, they might know all kinds of stuff about being alive," Willie said as he brought the car to another screeching halt. He sat forward and put the car in drive, then he revved the engine a couple of times.

Willie turned to look at me and smiled.

"It's like how, if you're in the forest, you can't really describe it too well."

He stomped on the gas and the car shot forward, pushing me back into my seat.

"You have to be outside of it to really get a good look at it, you know?" Willie asked.

The kid stood in the middle of the road and he threw up his arms in a grabbing gesture—classic zombie—and opened his mouth greedily.

Willie swerved at the last minute so that just the edge of that huge bumper caught the kid. The car lurched a bit, but that was all. The kid flew over us, barely grazing the roof as he went.

I turned in my seat and watched him land on his head and neck. I imagined the sound it must have made and winced. I watched for a few seconds. The thing just lay there unmoving.

I sat forward.

"I think that guy might be onto something," Willie said. "I hope people start to listen to him."

I got to spend the rest of the ride to school listening to Willie go on about a band called der Wankendoomen, or something else just as equally depressing and Nordic, that he'd just discovered on the Internet.

I don't know what schools were like before the dead came back. I'm guessing they didn't look like maximum-security prisons. My high school featured chain-link fences topped with razor wire, towers with snipers, and guards roaming the grounds with shotguns. It didn't do much for school spirit, though it did cut down on on-campus violence.

A grim-faced guard dressed in full riot gear and carrying a scatter gun—seriously, this guy made Chacho look positively cuddly—checked our student IDs and waved us through the gate; all the while, his partner scanned the surrounding area with his own shotgun.

Things had gotten really bad since one of the PE teachers, Ms. Sawyer, went missing a couple of weeks ago. The rumor mill said her empty car was found in the parking lot and that the front gate wasn't closed properly. I guess getting caught being lousy at their jobs gave the guards itchy trigger fingers.

We moored the boat and got out. There was always this awkward moment when Willie and I parted where I thought he was going to go in for a hug. That day he settled for chucking me on the shoulder—for real!—and then we went to our classes on opposite sides of the school.

I sleepwalked my way through Homeroom and AP English. At one point Mrs. Hamburger called on me and asked if I did the reading because I wasn't joining the discussion. I controlled myself and did not roll my eyes. *Of course I did the reading.* I just didn't feel much like talking. I kept thinking about that professor from last night, and Willie that morning running over that UD. I also felt like there was something else, like a dream I couldn't remember. Does that ever happen to you? You wake up feeling bad—scared maybe, or angry, and you know you had a bad dream, but you can't remember it.

Things picked up in Health and Hygiene. Mostly that's because it was the only class I had with Sherri and she kept up a steady stream of derisive comments about everything Mr. Souza told us. H&H was really just a nice name for the class they teach us *every year* about how to identify zombies and make sure we don't get infected. Basically the second part all boils down to not being bitten or scratched by one. The virus, whatever else it might be, is wicked communicable. Doctors have seen it transmitted in scratches that don't even draw blood. Thank God it's not airborne, you know? The government forces the school to teach the class to us every year. Really, there's a limited amount of information on all of this so they tend to review the same stuff over and over again. And again. Maybe it worked, though, because I heard that cases of zombie-ism were down lately. Maybe it was clearing up altogether and we'd be able to move back into the cities. That'd be nice. Living in the suburbs was just killing me.

The only cool thing about suburbs before the undead popped up is that you could visit the city any time you wanted to. But now all the cities have been abandoned to the shufflers and the military keeps those of us with pulses out. Mostly, anyway. It was like the worst of both worlds.

Sherri started calling where we live Zomburbia, and that sounds just about right. Lately, she says the whole world feels like Zomburbia. "Every city that ever mattered is closed 'cause of the shufflers," she said, "so now the whole world lives in the freaking suburbs."

We made it through Mr. Souza's endless drone and headed out into the halls along with everyone else in the school. We used the ten minutes between classes to stand there confirming our plans.

"See you at lunch?" Sherri asked. "The tables behind the school, over by Cancer Corner?"

"Sounds good," I said. It should have sounded good; it's been the plan every day since we started high school.

We were just about to break up and go our separate ways when there was a big commotion down the hall. Naturally, we headed that way to see what was what.

A crowd gathered in the middle of the main hall, and everyone had carved out a space in the center to watch a couple of jocktoids pushing around a Goth kid. I didn't know the jocks' names. The Goth kid was named Chris. He and I used to be friends back in grade school. We drifted apart around the time he bought a floor-length leather duster.

Life wasn't too easy for the darkwave kids. Regular folks were touchy about the whole undead thing, and wearing white fright makeup wasn't exactly endearing. I had to admit that as antisocial as I tried to be, they made me uncomfortable, too. Still, I didn't condone beating them up.

Apparently the jocks did not have the same generous outlook as me. They gleefully took turns slamming Chris up against some lockers. No one stepped in to help. Not even other Goths. They have a pretty strict code that basically boils down to, "You're on your own." I've never met a Goth who didn't delight in showing you the scars they'd received just because they were enamored with the undead. For instance, I could see the unofficial head of the group, their Dark Prince—a kid I'd known all my life as Ray Simmons, but who now probably went by the name Reginald Bloodsbane—standing in the back of the crowd watching the whole thing without emotion. He sported a huge neck brace that disappeared under his floor-length black coat.

I don't even remember what the juicers said as they bounced the kid around—I'm sure it was your standard "You're different from us and so worthy of our scorn and derision, not to mention our thinly veiled homoerotic aggression."

A security guard watched the melee, his shotgun slung over his shoulder, the visor of his helmet raised for a better view. He seemed to be enjoying the show. Popular rumor around the schools was that the folks patrolling our halls all wanted to be prison guards but couldn't pass the Psych exam.

After Chris's head bounced off the locker for the third time, I heard a man's voice booming down the hall.

"*Move* it, people!" he shouted. "Pretend you're at a sale at Hot Topic!"

Mr. Santori, who is a moving five-and-a-half-foot-tall wall of muscle and anger, plowed through the group of kids. He didn't seem to mind that he actually knocked over at least one guy.

The two jocks stopped using Chris as a human punching bag and tried to straighten his torn clothes. For his part, Chris just stood, embarrassed.

"Jock A" opened his mouth to start defending himself, but Mr. Santori cut him off with a quick hand gesture.

"Shut your pie-hole, Mitchell!" he said, and even I cringed. "And if you're smart, you'll keep it shut until we get to Principal Ibrahim's office."

Then I remembered—Kim Mitchell. He was probably overcompensating for the fact that his parents gave him a girl's name. Either that or he was currying favor with the upper echelons of the varsity elite since he was a junior and only on the JV football team.

"Are you okay, Chris?" Mr. Santori asked. Chris sort of shrugged. He tried to play it cool—a feat that would have been easier if blood wasn't leaking out of his nose and covering his top lip.

"Okay," the teacher said. "Regardless, you're going to have to come along to Ms. Ibrahim's, too."

Mr. Santori turned his gaze on the ranks of us gathered around.

"I think you all have classes to get to," he said.

We all kind of evaporated like smoke.

As Sherri and I walked away, I heard Mr. Santori's voice again.

"And you," he said. "What the hell do we pay you to guard, exactly?"

He said this to the guard, who now had his face shield down and his shotgun in his hands, I might add. Mr. Santori didn't seem intimidated at all. Not even by the fact that the guard was like a half-foot taller and kind of towered over him.

"Far as I could tell," the guard said through the face mask, "all of those kids had a pulse."

"That's brilliant," Mr. Santori said. "Just . . . lovely." He studied the dude's badge. "I'll be talking to my principal about you, *Officer* Daniels. We'll see how long *your* pulse holds out."

He started to turn, and I hightailed it out of there before he caught me lollygagging.

Sherri waited for me by our lockers again. Even though the bell had rung, a ton of people still milled around talking about what they'd seen, so we felt safe in our truancy.

"Mr. Santori is a badass," Sherri said. "Did you see him stare down the guy with the assault rifle?"

"I totally get dibs on him for my side in the coming zombie apocalypse," I said. "And it's not an assault rifle, it's a shotgun."

"Because that's important right now," Sherri said.

"It's important to be precise," I said with a straight face.

"It's important for you to smooch my pucker."

"Hmm," I said. "That's an image that's gonna stay with me. Unfortunately."

"Yeah," Sherri said, "I guess I'd better get to Home Ec. Those cookies aren't going to bake themselves."

"See you at lunch," I said.

Sherri walked off, careful to avoid a pod of popular girls who were also rushing to class.

I started off down the hall in the other direction, then stopped. There was a big spot of Chris's bright red blood on the white tile floor. I stared at it until the final bell rang, then I ran to class.

CHAPTER FOUR
Very Diesel Indeed

Later that day, a group of us—me, Sherri, Willie, and a few others—sat eating our lunches in the commons area near the school's designated smoking zone, Cancer Corner.

We weren't talking about anything really important, just shooting the breeze. Sometimes we seem to really think we're like junior Oscar Wildes or something. However, actually recalling our conversations makes me cringe.

Case in point: Brandi Edwards looked down at her tray of industrial-strength goop, what passed for lunch in our school district, and said, "Sometimes I really envy you guys."

There was a moment of silence before I bit. "How's that, Brandi?"

"If I was a welfare case, I'd have a sack lunch, too, and not this crap," she said. She stirred her food and pouted.

"That's funny," said Sherri, a bright smile on her face. "Not as funny as the alignment of your bottom teeth, but still . . ."

Brandi isn't that bad—and she certainly isn't ugly—but in our group, any complimentary statements are seen as highly suspect. Sometimes it feels like being mean to each other is a kind of sport. I mentioned it once at a party and I thought I was going to be run out of town on a rail. A huge, sarcastic rail. For weeks I kept finding travel-size tissues in my bag and in my locker, and people kept offering me a hankie. "You look like you're about to squirt a few, Courtney, do you need this?"

Like I said before, we're all the most hilarious.

"I have a new piece of business to bring up with the group," Sherri said. She waved her fork around like a drunken judge might wave her gavel. Everyone looked up at her, expectant. "It seems that our little Courtney has attracted the attention of one of the men-folk 'round these parts."

Oh, Jesus. I groaned and hid my face in my hands. I really did not need this to become common knowledge.

"Who is it?" asked Brandi.

"A member of the jocktocracy," Sherri answered, dragging it out. "Yes, Courtney has managed to catch the eye of a member of the date-rape set."

"Again," said Brandi, "I ask: who is it?"

Sherri could hear the encroaching boredom in Brandi's voice just as well as I could. If she didn't stop playing it out, she'd lose her audience.

"Brandon Ikaros," she said.

There were a lot of murmurs and guffaws. I did my best to tune it out. Seriously, I could give a shit what those people thought about something that Sherri just made up anyway. Then one voice cut through the clamor of chimpanzee chatter.

"I know Brandon," the voice said. "He's a good guy."

The ensuing silence was almost a physical presence. I looked up from my hands to see who had made such a grave breach of bitchy etiquette. Elsa Roberts met my gaze, a half-smile on her lips. I liked Elsa. As much as I liked anyone I hung out with, anyway. She's kind of quiet and more than a little frumpy. She's also the most consistently positive of all of us. Why she hangs out with us is sort of a mystery, actually.

"He lives in the same neighborhood as me," she went on as everyone gawked at her. "And he's helped me out with my Calculus homework."

Calculus and not Trigonometry, I caught myself thinking. Jesus, I could be a real bitch.

Sherri glared at Elsa and went on in an icy voice, "Thank you for a dissenting opinion, Elsa."

"No," Brandi interrupted, "Brandon *is* pretty nice. Even for a jock." She looked me up and down. "*You* could certainly do a lot worse."

"Thank you, Brandi," I said.

Sherri could tell she'd lost control of this talking point, and she needed to steer the conversation somewhere else or it might fall on some shortcoming of hers.

"Well," she said, "that might be true," her gaze shifted to Willie, "but I know someone who isn't so happy that Courtney's got herself a fella!"

The pack rode that wave for a good half-hour before everyone started drifting away to classes. I felt bad for Willie, bad enough that I only made a couple of jabs—and not even my best ones!

Sherri was the last to go and she asked if I was going to stay. That was the plan, and I told her so. We had a substitute for AP History, so I planned to skip and work on my assignment for Journalism class later in the day. She left and I sat there wondering how I'd fill the blank piece of paper that sat in front of me.

It felt like someone was watching me, but the only kids out there besides me were the Goths smoking over in Cancer Corner. I shook my head. Again I wondered why the Goths thought it was worth all the crap they took just so they could wear lots of pancake makeup and black clothes. I know I liked to play at being an outsider, but those kids took it to a whole other level. They carried their battle scars with pride. I saw Ray Simmons standing there among a small clutch of black-clad Lolitas. They must have thought his neck brace was sexy as hell. He got the brace after some drunk guys in town took a disliking to his pale skin and dark eye makeup. The fact that he didn't pee all over himself and stood up to them hadn't helped. At least that's the way he told the story.

Anyway, the Goths only had eyes for each other.

I went back to my paper and tried to ignore the feeling of being watched. Every few seconds I'd scan the school yard. I checked the guard towers, too. Sometimes you'll catch a guard perving and watching you through the scope of his rifle. It's creepy on a few different levels. Despite how much I liked to think ill of the guards, they were all doing their jobs that day.

Finally, I looked out at the fence that surrounds the school. For the most part, it's a double fence: one that completely surrounds the campus and one about six feet beyond that *should also* surround us. They ran out of money while they were building it, and none of our city's lovely taxpayers wanted to pony up the dough to complete it. Because, you know, we were their children and it was just our lives at stake. Along the back of the school there's a section about fifty feet long where it's just a single layer of fencing. The two open ends were closed off to prevent any shufflers from getting in. They could still theoretically get right up next to the school yard, though.

Some movement out along the tree line caught my eye. I looked deeper into the woods, trying to see what was out there. A patch of shadows removed itself from another patch of shadows, and the zombie came into view. He was a skinny blond kid, or at least he had been. I felt myself blush when I realized he was naked below the waist. Then

I felt stupid when I noticed everything that might make me blush had been eaten away. His top half looked pretty complete. He wore a pink polo shirt with a popped collar. A preppie zombie. It seemed redundant to call him that.

He swayed back and forth gently, as if he was underwater and the current was pushing him back and forth.

After a moment I realized I'd been holding my breath, and I let the air out of my lungs. It sounded too loud for some reason. I couldn't take my eyes off him. He wasn't the first zombie I'd seen, not by a long shot. I'd seen plenty, and a couple a whole lot closer, but there was just something about him. Or maybe it wasn't him. Maybe that stupid talk show from the night before had affected me more than I wanted to admit.

I waited for him to either move closer to the fence and get zapped by the guards in the towers, or else disappear back into the trees. If I didn't know any better, I'd have sworn he was looking back at me. But I don't think that could be right. If he had seen me, or sensed me, or whatever the hell it is zombies do, he'd have charged the fence and tried to get at me.

I was suddenly filled with the urge to get up and approach the fence myself. I wanted to force him to do something, not to just stand there like a dummy. I was just rising from the bench when a hand clamped down on my shoulder. A tiny shriek escaped from my throat, and I recoiled back onto the bench.

I looked up at Astrid Milne, who stood over me giving me this weird half-smile.

"Hey, are you okay?" she asked.

I busied myself with arranging my papers, papers that I still hadn't touched. I glanced at the trees. The kid was nowhere to be seen. Where had he gone?

Astrid still had that weird half-smile. She seemed unsure

if I was safe or certifiable. Astrid was a senior, a year older than me, and she used to be sort of pretty. Maybe a little plump, but pretty. The girl who stood over me now was no longer either of those things. She was rail thin, her eyes bloodshot. Acne bloomed all over her face. She flashed that smile at me again and exposed gray teeth. They looked dead. What the hell happened to her?

The prep zombie was no longer out by the trees. Had I imagined him? I returned Astrid's smile. I'm sure it looked fake.

"I'm fine, Astrid," I said. "What's up?"

She glanced back over her shoulder, making sure no one could hear her. For some reason this made me feel uneasy. "I heard you might be holding some Z," she said. For a second I thought I was going to be sick.

Of course that's what it was. It totally explained how this plump, pretty girl had become a skinny, blown-out skank.

That wasn't the worst of it. The worst of it was that she had approached me *at school* to ask if I was selling. If she knew, or suspected, who else knew? My mind spun at a million miles an hour, trying to think this through. Any way I sliced it, I was dicked.

"I don't know what you mean, Astrid," I said slowly.

"Hey, listen," she started to say, a pleading tone creeping into her voice, "I just heard that I could maybe—"

I cut her off. "No, you need to listen," I said. "I don't know who you heard that from, though I'd be very interested to find that out, but I don't sell drugs. Even if I did, *I certainly wouldn't sell them on school grounds.*"

Tears welled up in her bloodshot eyes.

"C'mon . . ." she said. This time the pleading tone didn't just creep in, it danced out front and center.

"No, I'm sorry," I said. "You've got the wrong girl."

Before she could start to outright beg, I gathered up my

stuff and hurried off to my next class. I forgot all about the zombie out there.

Journalism class didn't have desks; it had tables that sat two people each. I moaned a little when I got into class because (1) I was late, which I loathe—I always gave the stink-eye to people who walk into class late—and (2) the only seat available was next to Brandon Ikaros. The expectant smile that lit up his face did not make me feel any better. I was definitely starting to pick up a serial killer vibe from him. Why else would he turn his attention on me?

"Courtney, so nice of you to join us." Mrs. Johnson stood up at the chalkboard and watched me make my way to my seat. Normally I'd have said something sarcastic—*Well, I didn't have anything else better going on right now*—today all I managed was to mouth the word, "Sorry."

Every sound seemed amplified. The scraping of the chair against the floor filled the room, my bag's zipper was as loud as a jet taking off. I swear I felt every eye on me as Mrs. Johnson resumed writing on the board at the head of the class. She'd written, STORY IDEAS. When I read that, I groaned again. I was supposed to have written down my ideas for next week's issue of the *Quotidian* before I got to class. Watching that stupid zombie and talking to even more stupid Astrid had distracted me from doing my homework.

"Are you okay?" It was Brandon. He was looking at me with real concern. *Jesus.*

"I'm fine," I whispered. "I just forgot to generate any story ideas."

He pushed his notebook in my direction. "You can use some of mine," he said. "I came up with more than we had to."

The first item on his list read: *Cover the pep rally from the perspective of Sully.* Sully being our school's mascot, a huge seagull. Or, more accurately, a poor misfit sophomore who didn't make it onto the cheer leading squad and was offered the chance to wear a sweltering seagull costume to sporting events. I think that story could only be of interest to furries or those with a sweat fetish.

"Thanks, Brandon," I said. "I think I'll just scribble down some ideas of my own."

Mrs. Johnson put down her chalk and faced the class. "Okay, let's hear what you've come up with. Who's first?"

The Journalism class often took a while to get started. We could be a little cutthroat so people didn't like to offer themselves up for sacrifice early in the running. Once ideas were being thrown around, it became easier to speak up. I started racking my brain, because I knew that if no one volunteered soon, Mrs. Johnson would call on someone. The law of my shitty life would demand she pick me.

I sat hunched over, trying my best to be inconspicuous, while also trying to be a creative genius.

"No one has any ideas?" Mrs. Johnson asked. "Okay, Courtney, what do you have?"

Damn. Shit. Damn.

I sat up and gave her a tight-lipped smile.

"What about the fence?" I heard myself ask.

"What about it?" Mrs. Johnson asked right back.

I cleared my throat. "Well," I said, "it's supposed to be a double fence to keep us safe, and they never finished it." I started to warm to the topic. "The, uh, district says there's no money to finish it, yet the uh . . . the football team just got a bunch of money for next year to buy all new uniforms and equipment." I shrugged at Brandon. *Sorry, dude.*

Mrs. Johnson nodded. "Sure," she said. "Who were you thinking of talking to?"

"You could talk to Principal Ibrahim and the coach—"

"Coach Amara," Brandon chimed in. "Sure, he'd give you some choice quotes."

"My mom knows one of the school board members," I heard someone add. It must have been Elsa. "We could probably use her to get an interview."

Several students, and Mrs. Johnson, were all throwing ideas back and forth. Talking about the angle to use and who to talk to. I sat back, relieved. Finally, Mrs. Johnson cut it short.

"I like it, Courtney," she said. "I want you to work with Elsa and Brandon on this; you take point. Lara, you'll get us some photos—the fence, the team in their new uniforms, okay? What else have we got?"

I sighed. Bullet dodged.

I was unaware of Brandon leaning over to whisper to me until I felt his warm breath on the side of my face.

"Nice job, Courtney," he said. "Way to come through in the clutch."

Hating myself as it happened, I felt my cheeks grow hot as I blushed. I tried to play it off casually, you know, no big deal.

"Yeah," I said, "well, that's how I roll."

Real smooth, I thought. I should have just flashed him some gang sign and poured a forty on the ground to prove how uncool and white I was.

Well, I did want Brandon to stop paying attention to me. Keep this up and that was guaranteed.

Trying to pretend I no longer existed, I put my head down and started working on my amazing made-up story.

After class, I gathered my stuff and headed down the hall toward Trig. I wanted to get to class early to go over my homework before I handed it in. I'd spent a lot of time on it already, but Ms. Kay had a real hard-on about neatness and legibility. I figured I'd give it one last once-over to make it as clean as possible.

Someone called my name. Brandon waved at me from down the hallway. I considered making a run for it, then decided it would be easiest just to stand my ground.

He came loping—yes, loping—up to me. He flashed me a smile that must have cost as much as my dad's car.

"Hey, Courtney," he said, "mind if I walk with you? You're on your way to Trig, right?"

"Totally," I said. Brandon apparently had the ability to make me sound like an idiot. It must have been his super-power—or he was my kryptonite. I needed to think about it later when he wasn't in the immediate area.

"I was thinking we should get together," he said to me, and my jaw fell open. He quickly followed up with "You know: you, me, Elsa. To talk about the story."

Right. The story. The one that I made up on the spur of the moment and wasn't really interested in writing. That story.

"Okay," I said, trying to sound noncommittal. "It'll have to be tonight or on the weekend, though. Tomorrow I work and then there's a party at Sherri's."

"Sherri's throwing a party?" he asked, and smiled. This news should not have generated that level of excitement. I stifled a groan. Why had I mentioned the party?

"Not so much a party as an informal get-together," I said. I wanted to downplay any aspects of the evening that might sound fun. "It's going to be pretty boring, really."

"No, it sounds chill," Brandon said. "Do you think Sherri would mind if me and a couple of guys came over?"

I tried to imagine the apocalyptic scene that would ensue should members of the football team show up at Sherri's place. I'm sure she'd throw an epic hissy fit. Come to think of it, it might be worth it to see that.

"Well," I said, deciding to err on the side of caution, "I

don't know if . . ." I let my voice trail off so that he could fill in the blanks himself.

He seemed to get it because this embarrassed grin spread across his face.

"Oh, man," he said, "that's rude, isn't it, me inviting myself along?"

I started to relax.

"I should ask Sherri personally if it's okay for us to come along, right?" he asked.

Relaxation evaporated.

"No, don't!" I said louder than was warranted in a school hallway. Several kids stopped to look at us. I gave a blanket dirty look to the gawkers, and they all went back to their business.

"I'm Sherri's friend," I said. "Why don't I ask her for you? I'm sure it'll be fine."

"That'd be diesel," Brandon said, and flashed that perfect orthodontia again. *Diesel?*

"Yes," I said in reply, "very diesel indeed."

"And what about studying? Tonight would work best for me."

I agreed that tonight would be best for me, too. Brandon said he could talk to Elsa and clear the plan with her.

"So can I get your phone number?" Brandon asked me. After a very long pause, he followed up with "so we can figure out when and where exactly."

So there I stood, in the middle of the hall, exchanging phone numbers with this weird boy. A boy who, by all the laws of high school social hierarchy I'd ever learned, should have done his level best to pretend I was invisible. I really needed to get a handle on this situation, to somehow gain the upper hand. Be decisive, Courtney!

"So, I'll call you," Brandon said.

"Great!" Ugh.

He trotted off and left me standing in the hall to contemplate what exactly had happened to me and to the situation and to wonder exactly how I was going to break it
to Sherri that Brandon and his friends might be showing
up at her party. Maybe I could remind her she'd told me to
invite him? Or maybe she'd have a stroke and I wouldn't
have to worry about it at all.

I headed off to class and consoled myself with the
thought that I might well be eaten by zombies before I had
to talk to Sherri again.

CHAPTER FIVE

Now That We've Broken the Ice

I swear to Jebus that I was going to tell Sherri about The Brandon Fiasco while we were on the way home from school. Willie drove us as always. Sherri in back, me in the front, and we kept up a steady stream of inane chatter. I'll spare you the details.

Anyway, Sherri had just delivered a droll bon mot about her farts and I decided to use the ensuing silence to introduce a clever conversational tactic that would end with Sherri thinking it was *her* idea to invite the steroid brigade to her wingding. I never got the chance. Just as I was about to launch my offensive, Willie slowed the car and pointed off to our left.

"What do you think's going on?"

The front door stood wide open on the little house on the corner of the street. That wasn't so strange, but the fact that the chain-link fence out front had been knocked down really got my imagination going.

"I know who lives here," I said.

"You know them? Who is it?" Sherri asked.

"I don't *know* know them, but it's an old lady and her dog." I could see her in my mind. A little woman who looked like she was born old. She walked around during the day in a baby blue jogging suit and led her equally ancient corgi around the neighborhood. She also wore a huge pistol in a shoulder holster, which is the reason I re-membered her in the first place. I told all of this to the guys.

"What should we do?" Willie asked.

"Call the cops," Sherri said. "Let them deal with this."

"Park," I said. "I want to check on her."

"Is what someone would say if they were retarded," Sherri said. She stopped when Willie stiffened behind the wheel. "Oh, shit, Willie. I didn't mean it. But, listen, stop-ping is a very bad idea."

Willie didn't say anything as he pulled the car to the curb and shut off the engine. In the backseat, Sherri started in with a steady stream of swears. Willie and I ig-nored her and climbed out of the car. I made sure to grab my pistol.

Sherri rolled down the window. "I am not going with you. No way am I getting eaten for someone I don't even know!"

"Call nine-one-one," I said. "And no one is getting eaten. We're gonna shag ass out of there if it looks hinky, right, Willie?"

"Yep," he said. I loved that he was just coming along without making a big deal about it. And without trying to convince me to stay put.

"Say hi to the zombies," Sherri said. Then she pulled out her phone and started dialing.

It took some effort to control my breath as we walked up to the house.

"Maybe it was dogs or something," I said.

"I don't think so," Willie said. He pointed to a couple of loose fingers that lay near the fence. Great. What the hell were we doing?

Despite the fallen chain-link, we went through the gate. Manners. I held the pistol in a two-hand grip as we walked up to the door. I was careful to keep my finger on the trigger guard and not the trigger itself. It would really suck to shoot Willie—or myself—in a moment of panic.

"Hello?" Willie called into the house. "Anyone there? Ma'am?" He motioned with his head to me. I guess since I had the gun, I had to go first. I pushed the door open with my shoulder and stepped inside. Since I was in the lead now, I raised the pistol.

As soon as I stepped into the house, I knew we wouldn't find anything good. It smelled like someone's butt and spoiled meat. A table by the entryway lay on the ground and a cabinet in the living room had been knocked down. It didn't look like the place had been ransacked, more like some clumsy person had staggered through the house.

"Go down the hall," Willie said, and I nearly jumped out of my goddamned skin. I'd practically forgotten he was there.

"Sure," I said, and I tried my best to sound calm. My heart beat fast in my chest and I heard the blood rushing in my ears.

We made our slow way down the hall, looking into the rooms we passed as we went. A sewing room; the cleanest bathroom I'd ever seen; a little office, its desk cluttered with knickknacks. Then I saw the bloody footprint in the middle of the otherwise spotless hall carpet.

My hands were sweaty and I had a hard time gripping the gun. My dad sent me to a gun safety course every summer since I got the thing—the way other parents send their kids to camp—but I still got nervous every time I thought I might have to use it. Especially since Willie was with me.

The door at the end of the hall stood ajar. I paused before going any farther, terrified what I'd find. What if the room was chock-full of UDs? Could Willie and I make it out of the house before they got to us? I wasn't sure if I could go on.

"I'll go," Willie said, and that settled it. I shook my head and stepped forward.

After just a couple of steps I could see into the room. The furniture was overturned, the blankets stripped off the bed. The zombies must have cornered the old lady in there, and she put up a fight. Good for her. I was about to tell Willie that I didn't see her—maybe they carried her away—then I saw a frail arm sticking out of the heap of blankets. One of the fingers had been gnawed off.

"Shit," I said. "They ate her."

"No zombies?"

"Nope," I said.

"Okay." Willie stepped forward and pulled the door shut. "We can't do anything else here. Let's get outside, okay?"

Then he grimaced.

"What?" I asked, but didn't look back in the room.

"They got the dog, too," he said.

I'm not sure why, but that made me even more sad than thinking about the old lady getting eaten.

"Let's get out of here," I said.

I let him lead the way. By the time we got to the front step, we heard sirens getting closer. Sherri sat in the car, her arms crossed over her chest. She looked pissed. Maybe she was angry that neither of us had been eaten along with the old lady. She only got out when we told her there were no zombies around.

The cops arrived as we were leaving the yard and we spent the next half-hour answering questions. The guy who interviewed us never came out and said it, but I could tell he thought we were idiots for walking into a potential un-dead buffet.

At one point, we heard a gunshot come from inside the house. I jumped.

"Standard operating procedure for anyone who dies by

zombie attack," he said. He said it the same way I imagined he explained to drivers why it was dangerous to exceed the speed limit. A little while later, two EMTs carried out a full body bag on a stretcher.

"But she had a fence," Sherri said, echoing what I was thinking.

"Well, that'll stop one or two," Officer Insensitive said, "but a big group of them will just push it right over." He stopped and took a moment to collect himself. "You kids should get on home," he said, "and be safe."

"Thanks, officer," Willie said, "we will."

We climbed back into the car and Willie eased us away, leaving the cop to stand in the middle of the street.

We all jumped when my phone beeped. I scrambled through my bag to find it. The screen displayed a number I didn't recognize. I hit the button to read the message.

Meet my place at 6
Put UR name on list at gate
Call if U cant make it

That was followed by an address and a link that I guessed would take me to a map of how to get to Brandon's house. I put my phone away.

"Who was that?" Sherri asked.

"My dad," I said. "He's going to be home late."

We drove on in silence after that because there really wasn't anything else to say.

After I dropped off a bunch of my stuff at home and left a note for my dad, I rode my bike to Brandon's place. I could have asked Willie to give me a ride over there, but that would have led to a lot of questions I didn't want to answer. I know that a lot of you are shaking your heads at this point and asking, "What the hell was she thinking? She just found out a kindly, old grandmother was brutally murdered practically next door and now she's going to ride her bike through the streets?" What can I say? I was young and stupid. Also, even someone as inept as me at bike riding should be able to avoid a group of shufflers during the daytime. I'd just have to hope that our little study group got done before the sun went down.

Brandon's place was only about two miles from my house. In a lot of ways, though, it was a whole other world. I rode down Commercial Street to get there. I hate riding on such a busy road, but the fact that there were so many cars on it made it safer in terms of the undead hordes. Brandon's subdivision was to my left off Commercial, which means I had to walk my bike across the street. I am not one of those bicycle ninjas who can do things like ride along with the cars on the road and take left turns. Once I got to the correct side of the street, I realized that my legs felt pretty rubbery, and I couldn't imagine climbing back up on the bike, so I just pushed it the last hundred yards or so.

All of this means that I was a sweaty, heavily panting mess by the time I got to the gates that led into Brandon's subdivision. The sub was called—believe it or not—Elysian Fields. Doesn't that sound like the name of a cemetery? Don't you think that in this day and age developers would name a place to live something a bit more *lively*? The guard added to the funereal atmosphere. He looked a little like a walking corpse with a riot gun strapped across his back. I couldn't tell if he was taking his sweet time to get to me or if he was really walking as fast as his arthritic legs would carry him. Either way I had lots of time to stand in the sun. Unless Brandon had a thing for really sweaty girls, I think me showing up on his doorstep soaking wet would put a stake in the heart of his seeming obsession with me.

The World's Oldest Guard (WOG) finally reached the

gate and squinted at me like I was there to commit some high-dollar-value vandalism. A safe bet any other time, actually.

"Yes?" he said.

"I'm here to visit Brandon Ikaros," I told him, and gave him the address.

"Name?"

"Courtney Hart," I said, keeping the exasperation out of my voice.

"You on the list?" he asked.

My resolve was slipping and I could hear the annoyance ratcheting up as I answered him. "Brandon said he'd put me on the list."

He eyed me for a moment, trying to figure out if I was giving him guff. Finally, he turned and toddled off toward the guard booth because he *did not have the list on him.* Actually carrying the list with him to the gate would have been too much trouble, I guess. I gritted my teeth to keep my mouth shut. I could see WOG in the booth. His head was down, consulting the list, I'm sure, then he looked back up and met my eyes. I could tell he was debating whether or not to let me in even though he'd found my name. He frowned deeply and hit a button. The gate rumbled to life. I heaved my leg over the bike's crossbar and made my wobbly way down the street.

WOG tried to say something to me as I rode past— probably the subdivision's rules of conduct or the Geneva Convention or something—but I ignored him and kept riding. One can only spare so much of one's time to annoying people.

The houses in the subdivision were nice, not too vomit-inducing. They all seemed to just skirt the McMansion designation. Brandon's place was no exception. It was a two-story job with columns in front. Though it looked nice, it did lose points because there was a monster pickup in the driveway. It was raised so high, I'm sure I would need a ladder to climb into it. Not that I ever would.

I did note with approval, however, that there was a gun rack in the back window that was loaded up with a couple of shotguns. I couldn't tell from my vantage point what types of shotguns they were. I guessed that, based on the income-level in evidence, they'd be top-of-the-line.

I didn't bother chaining up my bike. I can't imagine anyone in this neighborhood would deign to steal it. They'd be more likely to have it removed as an eyesore.

I mopped my face as best I could and rang the doorbell. Brandon opened the door a few seconds later, and I got goose bumps as I felt the twin effects of the house's full-bore air-conditioning and his high-voltage smile.

"You're here," he said. "Great!" And he moved aside so I could enter.

Elsa already sat at the large dining room table with a glass of soda in front of her. She looked mildly disappointed that I'd shown. Probably wanted the boy all to herself. I'd have to let her know she was welcome to him. I sat down and started to arrange my stuff, and Brandon offered to get me a soda, too. I asked for a diet.

"Doesn't look like you need it," he called as he went into the kitchen. I exchanged a look with Elsa, neither of us able to believe he'd said that.

Brandon came back with my soda—diet, despite the fact that I'm apparently rail thin—and we got down to business. It only took about an hour to figure everything out. We weren't blowing the lid off Watergate, after all. Afterward, I could feel us shifting into the part of the evening where we socialize. I was trying to calculate how quickly I could leave without looking like I'd been raised by a pack of ill-socialized badgers.

Actually, it wasn't that bad. Elsa talked about rehearsals

for the spring play. The drama club was putting on the umpteenth production of *The Diary of Anne Frank*. This year, however, the director, Mr. Richland, was trying to make the play edgy and relevant by having the Frank family terrorized not by Nazis. His grand theatrical vision was to have the family terrorized by *zombies*. It must have taken five whole minutes to come up with that bit of genius. When it was Brandon's turn to introduce a conversation starter, he brought up some volunteer work he did with his Scout troop at an old folks' home. Yes, Brandon was seventeen and still a Scout, an Eagle Scout, actually. I refrained from making any Brownshirt jokes; I didn't think they'd go down very well. This topic actually generated a fair bit of talk since Elsa has a minor phobia about old people and I wanted details about their bathroom habits. What can I say? My interests are many and varied.

It fell to me to bring up something next. I couldn't think of anything Nazi-related so I started telling them about the scene that Sherri, Willie, and I had come across earlier: the lady who'd been attacked by zombies in broad daylight. I meant it just as a story to tell. Certainly not funny or anything. Not too serious, either. I mean, odds were good that none of us knew the woman and besides, attacks like that happen all the time. Taking any one too seriously would be like getting all het up every time it rained or something. I could tell that Brandon really was affected, though. His cheeks were all red and he was kind of snorting. His mouth was a straight line. I'd never seen him angry before, but I'd be willing to bet money that he was angry now.

"Are you okay?" Elsa asked him. I'm glad she took point on that one.

He took a moment to answer, and when he did, his voice was low and strained. "I'm fine," he said. "It's just that stories like that . . . they get to me, you know." I found myself nodding, just like Elsa, even though I didn't think I did quite get it.

"It's just that," he paused and looked down at his hands. "It's just that my mom . . ."

Oh, Christ. Now I felt like an ass. I mean, I didn't know he'd lost his mom in a zombie attack. Really, am I supposed to go around all the time never saying anything because I'm going to rub some sensitive jerk the wrong way? It's not like I did it on purpose.

None of that made me feel like less of an ass, of course. Now I felt sorry for Brandon, and that was definitely not how I wanted to feel about him.

"I'm sorry," I finally said, my own voice sounding pathetic in my ears. "I didn't know." *Stellar performance, Courtney. You are one top-notch human being.*

A really loud silence followed that. I heard the kitchen clock ticking away in the other room. The ice cracking in my glass sounded like a gunshot.

Brandon steepled his fingers together and looked down at the table.

"Well," he said, "now that we've broken the ice . . ."

I giggled nervously until he looked up and I saw his grin. Then I giggled for real. He and Elsa joined in, and I felt something go out of the room. It felt better. We actually started to talk after that— not just waiting for our turn to say something. A real conversation. It was nice. For a while. Until it was time to leave.

Elsa looked at the time on her phone and frowned. "I have to get going, guys," she said. "My folks are expecting me back."

"Me, too, I guess," I said.

We all stood and started to move toward the door.

"Okay, you two," Brandon said, "drive safe."

Elsa said she would, and I must have had one of those looks on my face. It would have been easy enough for me to say okay, too, even though I hadn't driven. To be honest, there's a part of me that never wants to miss an opportunity to correct someone.

"What?" Brandon asked.

"Well," I said, "I'll *ride safely*. I rode my bike."

"Oh," Brandon said, "you should let me give you a ride."

"No, that's okay," I said, "I don't live far from here and I don't want to leave my bike."

"It's not okay," Brandon said. "I can't let you ride your bike home."

"Excuse me," I said. "You *can't let me*?"

We were between Elsa and the door. I shot her a look, and I could tell she wanted to be anywhere other than where she was.

"What the hell does that mean?" I asked.

"It's dark out, Courtney," Brandon said, and I could tell he was as frustrated with me as I was with him. "And you told that story about the lady who got attacked today!"

"First of all," I said, "I can take care of myself. Second, even if I couldn't, *you* are not who I'd run to to save me. So, please, take your macho, chauvinistic bullshit and cram it!" I threw the door open and checked Brandon as hard as I could with my shoulder. Granted, he barely moved. I heard footsteps on the driveway behind me and turned to see Elsa getting her keys out of her purse. Thank God Brandon hadn't come after me.

I hopped on my bike and was about to ride away when she spoke to me. "You know," she said, "he was just trying to be nice."

"Yeah, well," I said, "he was being kind of a dick about it."

She shrugged. "Maybe," she said. "Do you want a ride? We could probably put your bike in the trunk."

"No," I said, "but thanks. I don't have far to go."

"Okay," she said, and climbed into her car and pulled out onto the street.

I made my own way behind her. It was a lot easier getting out of the subdivision than it had been getting in. The security guard seemed eager to have me leave. That made two of us.

I heard the gate clang shut behind me and I rode out into the darkness on my way home.

CHAPTER SIX
This Is Too Much

I'm going to admit right up front that turning down that ride from Brandon was not one of my best ideas. Or, to put it another way: I was stupid to ride my bike home in the dark. The first mile or so was fine since I had to ride up Commercial Street with all of its traffic streaming by. The passing cars and the well-lit parking lots made me feel safe. Hell, I almost forgot that it was dark outside.

Almost, that is, until I turned off the main drag onto Madrona Street and slowly left the halogen lights of the parking lots behind. Madrona is a really steep hill at that point, and, because I refused to get off and walk my bike up the incline, I was a sweaty, huffy pile of humanity by the time I crested the hill. It's not even like it goes down after that, it just levels out. But believe me, after that climb it felt like I was coasting. I realized that the hard work of climbing the hill had actually held back any fear I might have felt. Once I could breathe normally, that feeling started to creep in on the edges.

I turned down 12th Street toward my part of town, and the streetlights were few and far between. A lot of those had been busted out. I found myself riding from one insubstantial puddle of light to the next. The occasional car that did pass me wasn't reassuring at all; their lights created weird swaths of shadow where anything could be hiding.

For the most part, I rode in the middle of the street where, theoretically, it would be easiest for me to avoid any attacking undead. My heart rate spiked every time I had to swerve to the sidewalk because of a passing car.

Because my mind is a bitch and likes to conspire against me, I started to think about every zombie attack I'd ever seen, whether it was real or not. Real life scenes started to get mixed up in my mind with stuff I'd seen in horror movies. Dead, gray hands reaching out of the dark, rigor-mortised lips pulled back from hungry teeth. It didn't matter if the shuffler coming after you was a complete stranger or your best friend or your mom when they had been alive, because after they'd been turned, all that mattered was their unending hunger for live flesh. Nothing was going to stop them till they got their teeth into you.

I found myself panting again even though I was on flat ground. I was tempted to stop there in the middle of the street and grab my pistol out of my bag and maybe shove it in my waistband like some TV show cop. Somehow the thought of stopping there in the dark was even worse than the thought that my gun was so hard to get to, which meant I was unprotected.

I shuddered as my mind flashed on the image of a pair of zombies crouching over a still-screaming woman and feasting on her guts. At least that was a scene from a movie. Thank God. I needed to get a grip on myself. I needed something else to occupy my stupid brain.

I started thinking about how I would tell off Brandon the next time I saw him. I'd start by pointing out I was very much alive and intact and in no way eaten by any stupid shufflers. Then I'd ask where he got off assuming I couldn't take care of myself. I've probably been through more attacks than him and could handle myself better—

I nearly let out a scream when I rounded a corner and saw someone on the sidewalk. I was just a few blocks from home by that point and was really not expecting anyone to be out, especially not on foot. It was a woman and I relaxed a little when I saw she had her hands on her swollen belly. Jeez, what was a pregnant lady doing out here by herself after dark?

"Hey," I called out, "are you okay?"

I swerved the bike toward the curb, and she turned more swiftly than I thought possible, her yellow teeth bared, her desiccated hands outstretched. I tried to maneuver the bike away from her, overcorrected, and toppled over. The next thing I knew, my cheek was pressed against the asphalt—that was gonna hurt like a bitch later. If there was a later. My legs tangled in the bike and I felt panic setting in, my breath coming fast and shallow.

I forced myself to slow down my breathing and to actually look at my legs. It only took a second after that to get them free and under me. By that time the zombie had made it out into the street and bore down on me. I swung my bag around and tore at the zipper. My pistol. I needed my pistol. I could hear the zombie right behind me, her shuffling steps so loud despite my ragged breath. There wasn't enough time. Why did I have so much crap in my bag? Why couldn't I find the pistol? It was the only gun-shaped object in there!

I became dimly aware of a rustling from the bushes behind me. Great, the expectant shuffler brought friends, probably her baby-daddy.

My hand wrapped around the pistol's grip—just as I felt the zombie's hand fall on my shoulder.

I heard a loud thud and felt a jolt travel up the zombie's arm. Her grip dropped away from my shoulder and she fell to the ground beside me. A couple of guys in camo and face paint stood there with homemade weapons.

"Phil?" I yelled as I stood and backed away from the quivering zombie. I kept the pistol trained on her, even

though my hands shook. My mind refused to accept this. Phil was the troll who lived in the back of the Bully Burger and washed dishes; he wasn't the guy who came to my rescue.

Phil looked at me for a moment, like he was considering whether or not he should have saved me. Then, very swiftly, he raised his weapon—a baseball bat with nails driven through it—and brought it down on the shuffler's face. She stopped quivering.

"Hey, Courtney," he said as he straightened. "What are you doing out here?"

"Me?" I nearly screamed. "What the hell are you and Junior G.I. Joe doing out here?"

He shrugged. "Saving your ass, I guess."

Fair enough.

"Who's your buddy?" I asked.

Phil pointed with his bat. The end of which was covered in black zombie-brain-stuff. Nice.

"Cody," he said. "Cody, Courtney. We work together."

Cody gave me a chin nod. "Hey," he said.

"Hey," I said back.

"So, you know it's not a good idea to be out joyriding by yourself after dark, right?" Phil asked.

Joyriding? "Jesus, am I going to have to take crap from you tonight, too?"

"Well, you have to admit it was a pretty bad idea," Phil said.

"Hey, guys?" Cody started to say. I cut him off.

"For your information, douche," I snapped at Phil, "I was doing fine!" I brandished the pistol.

Phil looked unimpressed. "Yeah," he said, "from the looks of things, that undead bitch was about to take that thing away and shove it up your butt. Then she was set to chow down."

"Go to hell, Phil," I said, not really having an answer to what was basically the truth. "I didn't need—"

"Hey, guys," Cody said again, this time urgently.

Out of his black face paint, Cody's eyes were huge and too-white.

"What is it?" Phil asked. But Cody didn't say anything, he just pointed down at the for-real-dead zombie.

All I noticed was the place where her face used to be. Thank God her matted hair covered the worst of it. I couldn't see what freaked out Cody. I was ready to ask him what his beef was, but then I caught Phil's expression. His face contorted into this horrified mask, his mouth open in a kind of disgusted grimace.

"You have to be shitting me," he said in a husky voice.

The zombie's swollen belly was moving. It looked like a puppy playing under a blanket. Of course, that's not what it was. I couldn't process what I saw. My mind felt blank—a long, silent scream filled it. The baby. It was still inside her and it wanted to get out and get at us. I could imagine its empty eyes and its gaping toothless mouth. I thought I was going to puke.

I looked back at the boys. They were right there with me.

"This is too much," I said, and my voice croaked out of my throat. Cody nodded.

"We have to kill it," Phil said.

I started to back away slowly. I wanted to back out of this whole stupid night.

"We can't leave it," he said. "It's going to get out soon." I looked at the zombie's belly. A tiny hand pushed against the skin, its little fingers very distinct. He was right, the mother's desiccated flesh wouldn't hold up for long.

"Call the police," I said, "it's *their* job." Even to me, that sounded lame.

"It could get out by the time they get here," he said. "*We* have to do it."

Cody shook his head and turned away. He looked ashamed. Phil pointed at what I held in my hand. "You have a gun," he said. "You could make it quick."

I cradled the gun to my chest. There was no way I could kill a baby, even if it was a zombie baby. My cheeks burned and I was glad at least for the fact that it was dark. Phil couldn't see me blushing.

"No?" he said to both me and Cody. "Well, I guess I'll have to do it then." He hefted his nail-studded bat over his shoulder. He hesitated and looked right at me. I couldn't read the look. I'm sure it was hate or disgust. He swung the bat with a grunt.

I turned away just in time, though I still heard the sound of its making contact. A wet thump followed by a kind of sucking sound as he pulled the nails out. I know it took more than one blow to get the job done, but I didn't hear anymore after that. I was too occupied with throwing up to hear much of anything besides my own retching.

I felt a hand on my shoulder as I finished dry-heaving. Phil stood over me and offered me a bandanna. I wondered how long it had been riding around in his pocket. I went ahead and wiped my mouth and tongue with it anyway.

"Thanks," I said.

"C'mon," he said, "we'll walk you home." I didn't say anything, just started my feet moving.

Phil walked beside me with my bike. Cody held back a little and carried their weapons. We walked in silence for a minute, our feet on the pavement the only sound.

"Is this something you do?" I asked. "Saving people from shufflers?"

"This is only the third time we've gone out like this,"

Phil answered. "And this is the first time we've even seen one of the undead."

One of the undead. There was something in the phrase Phil used, but I left it alone. I didn't have the energy or brain capacity to think about it.

"Well, thanks," I said, "you're right, I'd've been toast if you two hadn't come along."

"Sure," was all he said.

I became aware of a distant buzzing sound.

"Is that your phone?" Phil asked.

I started digging through my bag, looking for my cell. It was probably my dad—*oh, shit, my dad!*—I was supposed to call him when I was done at Brandon's house. I found the phone and looked at the caller ID. Sherri. I groaned; I didn't have the strength to talk to her right now. I let it go to voice mail. I then checked for messages from my dad. He'd called from work and left me two voice mails and three texts. The last message said that if he didn't hear from me in half an hour, he was coming home to look for me. He'd left it twenty minutes ago. I texted him right away and apologized for not getting back to him. I lied and said I'd been somewhere without service and I stressed that I was fine. I felt my chin and cheek throbbing and I let my dad know I wrecked my bike so he wouldn't freak out the next time he saw me.

By the time I finished typing the message, we stood in front of my house. Cody opened the gate and Phil pushed the bike into the yard. I walked to the front door and let myself in. Phil and Cody waited outside the fence to make sure I got in okay, and I waved to them as I closed the door. They waved back silently, and there was something so crazy about these two guys in camo and face paint, both holding weapons—one of them covered in gore—waving good night to me that I got the giggles. I couldn't help it, and I couldn't stop it. I stood at the door, racked with laughter until I realized that it had somehow become sobs. I sat on the floor and just let myself cry and cry. I wasn't even sure why I was crying, but, God, it felt good.

Phil and Cody stood there looking awkward. I waved them away, and they looked almost relieved to hightail it out of there.

When the episode passed, I went inside and cleaned up. Being covered in snot and tears when my dad got home, I'd have no choice but to engage him in conversation. I needed to head off that situation.

I took a shower and picked gravel out of my chin and both my palms. I hadn't even noticed the damage to my hands what with the nearly dying. I dressed for bed: boy's boxers and a T-shirt. Before I got under the covers, I figured I could use a pick-me-up so I decided to look on the web for news of the army retaking New York City. The latest gossip was that the city would be open by the beginning of the new year. I tried to not look it up too often because that led to heartache. I had a feeling that tonight had been so shitty, there just had to be good news to counteract its sheer lousiness.

I fired up my Mac—my dad got a wicked good discount at the college's bookstore—and logged onto my Google homepage. I had a filter set that automatically sent me stories about the NYC situation. The first headline made me groan. PLAN TO RETAKE NYC MEETS SETBACKS. Long story short, the Army was looking at next spring before they'd try to take the city back from the mass of shufflers. My plan to save the world from the zombie hordes was going to shit the bed if the U.S. military didn't get on the stick. This was a situation so massively screwed it demanded I update my Facebook status.

I opened a new tab and logged onto the site. *Is it wrong to take global events as a personal insult?* I typed and hit SEND.

I was about to log off when a chat window popped up. It was Sherri. Damn.

Sherriberri: hey courtney!

I considered just logging off and telling her in the morning that I hadn't seen her message. I hovered the mouse over the LOGOUT button for a few seconds before I decided to bite the bullet and answer.

Currently Courtney: Wassup?

SherriBerri: o nothing

SherriBerri: just had a great chat with elsa roberts

My heart sank. Why the hell would Elsa be talking to Sherri? This could only be bad.

Currently Courtney: Yeah? What about?

SherriBerri: well let's see . . . she called to make sure it was okay if she came over to my party.

SherriBerri: how do you think she heard about my party?

Currently Courtney: I couldn't guess, Sherri, but I think you're going to tell me.

SherriBerri: turns out brandon told her about it and she wanted to be all polite and ask me if it was okay for her to come over.

SherriBerri: and i'm pretty sure you KNOW how brandon heard about the party.

Currently Courtney: Sherri

SherriBerri: YOU ARE A COMPLETE BITCH COURTNEY!

SherriBerri: inviting this boy you supposedly don't like to MY party? That's balls, courtney.

I stared at the screen, not sure how to respond. Not sure if I even wanted to respond.

SherriBerri: WELL . . . ?

Currently Courtney: Well, for now, Sherri, I'm going to bed. If you want to yell at me tomorrow, feel free. But I had a royal shitty night and want to put it behind me as fast as I can.

Currently Courtney: Toodles.

SherriBerri: DON'T YOU DARE SIGN OFF COURTNEY HART!

She might have kept on typing, threatening me in all caps. I didn't see any of it, however. I closed the screen on the laptop, turned off my light, and crawled into bed.

I decided I needed to be optimistic. Tomorrow was another chance to not mess up my life too completely. I rolled over and went to sleep.

CHAPTER SEVEN
You're Talking About the Wrong Girl

The next day was one episode of avoiding Brandon after another. Maybe he wanted to apologize or whatever. I was not interested. I swear that every time I turned around he was standing there scanning the halls for me. He was like the human equivalent of herpes—every time I thought I'd shaken him, he'd turn up again.

The worst was Journalism. I walked in only to see Brandon sitting there practically wagging his tail. He moved his bag off the chair next to him. He'd obviously been saving it. Ugh. A quick scan of the room revealed that the only other empty seat was next to Monty Rusk. Monty is the student managing editor of the paper, and he and soap are not really on speaking terms. On the plus side, I knew Monty wouldn't try to engage me in a discussion of our various emotions. My choice was clear.

Monty grunted a hello as I sat down and scooted my chair as far from him as possible as a way of saying "howdy" right back. I could feel—*feel*—Brandon staring at the back of my neck. I did my best to ignore him and concentrate on whatever was being discussed by the class.

I finally raised my hand and told Mrs. Johnson I'd like to be excused to the library to work on my story. People writing stories can often get away with this on Fridays, paste-up days. She eyed me skeptically and finally wrote out a pass. Some days I'd pull this stunt so I could leave campus, but today I planned to actually go to the library and work. Anything to get out of the same room as Brandon.

While I sat in the Brandon-free environs of the library, I realized I hadn't seen Sherri all day. We only have the one class together, and she has been known to skip, so it wouldn't be out of the question for us to not see each other. Though we almost always make a point to track each other down. I guess she wasn't interested in finding me today. I was starting to get wound up about it until I realized that I hadn't exactly mounted a mission to find her, either. Fine, we'd let the situation cool down today and see what happened tonight at the party. If she let me in, that is.

After school, Willie gave me a ride to Bully Burger. He seemed suitably appreciative of the road rash on my chin. Not wanting to be social at all, I'd texted him early that morning and told him I'd take the bus to school but that I'd appreciate a ride to work. When we got to the burger joint, I had more than an hour before I had to start my shift, so I bought us both Bully Meals and we sat there talking. It was sort of pathetic how much Willie seemed to appreciate the meal I bought him. Or maybe he appreciated the fact that we could talk without Sherri around.

We talked about his sister, avoided talking about his parents. Classes. Willie is in as many shop classes as the school would let him. I think he takes basic English, pre-Algebra, second-year Spanish (for the second year in a row), and four shop classes. But Willie is really good in shop. He can fix just about anything, and if he can't fix it, odds are he can build you something to replace it. His face lit up when he talked about his shop classes. Almost as much as when he talked about his sister. I liked seeing him all happy. I wasn't even tempted to call him a fag and spoil the mood.

And then, right in the middle of our little love-fest, Willie sprung his trap.

"You should come over to my place for dinner tomorrow," he said.

"Oh, um . . ." I said. Damn me for lowering my ironic defensive shields. Tomorrow was Saturday, and while I didn't have anything planned, that is an important day to leave open when one is an eligible young lady. Or a young punk who might get invited somewhere to drink until you puke. I was searching for a reason to say no when I looked at Willie's big, stupid, hopeful face. I gave up on that idea.

"That'd be great, Willie," I said. "Just let me check with my dad. I'm sure it'll be fine."

And after that Willie just wouldn't stop smiling and laughing. I decided I liked Willie best when he was happy, and I vowed to do what I could to make him that way more often. As long as I didn't have to swap bodily fluids with him to do it.

Willie left when it was time for my shift to start. The franchise owner, Mr. Washington, was working that night, which meant everyone had to be on their best behavior. Ted wasn't in the back office playing five-knuckle shuffle, and I had my uniform shirt buttoned and my hair tucked under my hat. Phil worked the fry station, a kid named Jamal was at the grill, and two sisters, twins named Mary Kate and Ashley—for real—worked the cash registers at the front. A thirty-year-old, ex-con-looking dude named Barry was a floater/greeter/whatever. Barry was on the schedule for the drive-thru window, but he knows about my side business and lets me do it as long as I give him a discount on Vitamin Z. Chacho was out in the parking lot in his full armor.

Phil barely made eye contact with me, which I thought was weird. On the other hand, I found going out at night in camouflage and killing zombies to be weird, too. I wanted to thank him again, but decided not to if he was going to have a stick up his butt for some unknown reason.

It was a pretty good night, both for Bully Burger and me. Although, to be honest, I'm sure I made a lot more than the drive-thru did. I actually sold everything I was holding. I'd have to go back to Buddha, my source, and get more.

After our shifts were over, anyone without a car could get a ride home from Chacho. It's part of his duties as a security guy. I'm sure I could have gotten a ride with anyone else that night. The problem was, I wanted to go to the party and I didn't want to invite along yet more people on Sherri's list of undesirables. I'm pretty sure Chacho wouldn't want to come party with us, and if he did, I think I'd have scored some points with Sherri because of it.

I was the only one riding with Chacho that night. We climbed into the big SUV that the company provided him for just this reason, and it rumbled to life with the push of a button. I usually hate these oversized hunks of crap as a rule, though I had to admit that I liked the feeling of contained power as Chacho stepped on the gas and I was pressed back into my seat. He fiddled with what looked like a TV remote with just one button, and the gate opened for us. We turned left out of the lot and he hit the same button. The gate closed behind us.

"You're north of Madrona, aren't you?" Chacho asked me absently as he got the radio and air going. Something with lots of drums and guitars started coming out of the speakers.

"Who's this?" I asked.

"Big Star," he said like I should have already known. "You know, Alex Chilton . . ." he tried again.

"Are they new?" I asked. "They sound new."

He laughed. "New?" he asked. "No. They broke up when I was, like, two or something."

I rolled my eyes. "Oh," I said, "so they're ancient. Why would I know them?"

Chacho shrugged. "You just seem like you'd know them, is all. You seem like you know more than the other kids at The Bully."

"Oh," I said, and I turned toward the window and smiled to myself. I didn't think Chacho had ever thought anything about me, let alone that I might know this old band he thought was cool. Note to self: Look into Big Star.

"So, up past Madrona, right?" Chacho asked.

I turned back from the window and gave him a sheep-ish smile. "Well," I said, "that *is* where I live, but I was wondering if you'd take me to Sherri's place instead."

"Nope," he said. "Company rules are I can only take you home. You know what kind of liability I'd be exposed to if I took you over there and something happened to you?"

"If something happens," I said, "which it won't, just tell them you took me home and you have no idea what I did after that."

"Okay, forget the liability," Chacho said. "What about how lousy I'd feel?"

"And how lousy would you feel if something happened to me while I rode my bike over to Sherri's because you wouldn't give me a ride?" I knew I was being unfair. I just really *did not* want to ride my bike in the dark again. I knew that once I got to the party I'd be able to beg a ride home from someone.

Chacho mumbled under his breath. Something in Spanish, probably a curse.

"This one time, Courtney," he said, "one time. I don't like being put on the spot."

"Totally," I agreed. "I'm sorry, Chacho, I didn't think it'd be a big deal. It won't happen again."

I think I did a lousy job concealing my joy because Chacho glared at me and muttered in Spanish some more. I tried to get him to talk. He just wasn't interested. So we just sat there and listened to Big Star and didn't talk until we got to Sherri's place.

Toward the end of the trip, I gave him directions to Sherri's, but as we pulled up in front, I wondered if we'd made a wrong turn. Past experience with Sherri's parties led me to expect three or four cars on the street and a somber group of sad sacks gathered in the living room listening to music and bitching.

What greeted me were cars lining both sides of the street. People flowed out of the house and into the yard, and music pounded out so loud I could hear it through the windows of the SUV. Every light in the house shone out into the night. Man, it was like they were doing everything they could to attract a zombie horde, short of hanging a banner on top of the house that read ALL-YOU-CAN-EAT BUFFET.

"I thought you told me once that you guys's parties were pretty tame." Chacho said as he peered out at the scene.

"I think the term I used was 'lame,' " I said, "not tame. And I'm not really sure what's going on here." Except that I did have an idea what it was.

I thanked Chacho and climbed out of the SUV. I approached the house and was struck by the surreal nature of all of these faces hanging out at Sherri's place. Jocks, cheerleaders, popular kids. It was like seeing British royalty hanging around in front of a strip club. Not that I would be making that analogy to Sherri.

I said hi to a few people as I walked into the house. I didn't linger and talk to anyone. I needed to find our lovely hostess. I maneuvered through the crowd, doing my best to not have any drinks spilled on me.

I spotted Brandi Edwards and Carol Langworthy sitting on the couch staring sullenly at everything going on around them. They projected such an aura of contempt that no one else tried to sit on the empty cushions.

"Hey," I shouted above the din of the music and got a frown in response. "Either of you seen Sherri?"

Brandi shouted something that I couldn't hear. I shook my head and pointed to my ears. Finally she just pointed toward the kitchen. I gave her a thumbs-up and set about moving through the thirty feet of space that lay between where I was and where I wanted to be. Thirty feet otherwise occupied by hormonally unbalanced teenagers.

After many stepped-on toes and shoulder-checked bodies, I made it to the kitchen. More people. And a keg. Someone had brought a keg to Sherri's party. I didn't see any faces I recognized so I couldn't ask after her whereabouts. I passed through the living room for a second time, and I felt my phone vibrating in my pants pocket. I fished it out and saw I'd received a message.

LOOK UP.

I looked up the stairs and there was Sherri, phone in hand, grimace plastered on her face. She was in her standard party garb: all black pocket-T, skirt, and leggings, and her knee-high Dr. Marten knockoffs. She raised her hand

and wagged her finger for me to join her. I took a deep breath and did just that, winding my way up the stairs past knots of people.

When I reached the top of the stairs, Sherri turned and stomped off down the hall toward her parents' room. I followed, of course. We got inside and she slammed the door, then stalked over and sat on the edge of the bed.

"Do you know why we're in my folks' room?" she asked.

"Because this is where you always stay when they're out—" I started. She cut me off.

"Because there are people humping in *my* room!" she shouted. "If anyone was going to hump in my room, it should be me."

I didn't bother to point out that she had no boyfriend at the moment and that there was probably no one at the party that she liked, so really the humping issue was moot.

"Do you know who's to blame for all of this?" she asked. Her voice was very controlled, very even. I knew I had to be careful.

"I guess that Brandon told everyone," I said.

"You, you stupid cow," she said calmly. "I blame you."

"You blame me," I said, and I felt my cheeks growing hot.

"It's because of your fat mouth that all of these losers are in my house right now," she said, her voice growing shrill. She was losing her cool finally. Good, so was I.

"I really need to apologize," I said. "How horrible of me to make your party an actual, you know, party." I felt my voice rising and I was talking faster and faster. "I know you wanted it to be what your parties always are—a bunch of lame-asses sitting around being miserable."

"Maybe that's the way we like it!"

"Well, guess what?" I asked. "If that's what you want, you can still have it. Brandi and all the rest of our lame friends are sitting on the couch downstairs looking like they sucked on a turd. The fact that all these people are here makes it even easier for you to act alienated. Have a goddamned ball!"

She stood up and I wondered if she was going to throw a punch at me. That might have been better, maybe.

"Is this all because you think you're better than me?" she asked, her eyes narrowed.

I took a step back from her, recoiled like she had slapped me.

"What the hell—?"

"Don't pretend," she said. "You know you think it. Sometimes I think you only hang out with us so you can feel superior."

She paused, probably giving me a chance to defend myself. But all I could do was stand there and look at her. All my anger, so righteous just a minute ago, was completely gone. She nodded to herself.

"You never miss a chance to point out the AP classes you're in, or to correct us if we get something wrong—grammar or some stupid saying that doesn't mean anything." She took another step toward me, closed the gap between us. "The only people at school who know about your little side business are us, a bunch of loser kids who aren't smart enough to screw it up for you and who envy all the cash it brings in."

I finally found my voice. "I—I'm not doing it to make you feel small," I said.

"No," she said, and headed toward the door. "You're doing it so you have enough money to ditch us one day."

"You're going to go to New York with me," I said. My voice sounded hollow.

"You and I both know that's never going to happen, Courtney," Sherri said. "You might get out some day, but I'm stuck here."

She stopped, her hand on the doorknob. She didn't look angry anymore. Contemptuous, maybe, not angry.

"Maybe you should go find your new friend," she said, "and the two of you can enjoy his party together." She opened the door and disappeared behind a wall of music and laughter. She closed the door behind her and left me alone in the sudden silence.

I just stood there for a minute. I tried to convince myself that she was a stupid bitch who didn't know what she was talking about. The moment I thought the word "bitch" I burst into tears. I wiped frantically at my face. There was no way I'd give Sherri the satisfaction of seeing me like this. I blew my nose on the sleeve of my sweatshirt and walked out of the room. I needed to get out of there. If I couldn't get a ride home, I'd walk. The zombies could go screw themselves.

I made my way through all of the people in the hall and walked down the stairs. I got some glares and dirty looks since I was stepping on more toes than usual. I didn't care. I needed to get outside, get some air in my lungs, and get away from this constant noise before I went crazy, threw up, or started crying again.

I made it through the front door, pushed my way past the smokers on the porch and down the steps. Finally, I was relatively alone on the front yard. I took a deep shaky breath and closed my eyes, trying to soak in the feeling of being alone. That's when I heard Brandon's voice behind me.

"Courtney," he said, "is everything okay?"

Son of a bitch. I turned around and caught sight of his open, simpering face. I didn't need this right then.

"Just go away, Brandon," I told him. "I just need to be by myself right now."

"Yeah, but, I saw you and Sherri go into that room," he pressed on, and I could hear the sincerity and concern dripping from his voice. "Then I saw her come out and you came out a minute later and it looked like you were crying."

"Thanks for the recap, Brandon," I spat back at him. "And what were you doing, spying on me? What kind of creep are you?"

"I wasn't spying," he said. "I was just up there talking with Tori and Kyle and some others, and I saw you. I wasn't spying."

"If you must know," I said, "Sherri was mad because of how many people showed up to her party."

He stopped and thought for a second and then a pained look spread across his face. "Did Sherri blame you for that? Because that is totally *my* fault. I'll go find her and tell her what's really going on."

He turned to head back to the house. I'd had too much.

"Stop," I shouted. "Just stop! What the hell, Brandon?"

"I don't know what you mean." He looked so perfectly, puppy-dog-with-his-head-tilted-to-the-side confused that I would have thought it was hilarious if I wasn't furious with him.

"I mean what the hell is up with you?" I said. I noticed that people on the porch were looking at us. I didn't care. "Up until a week ago, you were content to ignore me— which was, actually, freakin' awesome. Then you come into the Bully Burger, you're there every time I turn around in the halls, you're saving seats for me in class. Now you're being Mr. Gallant. So, one last time, Brandon. What. The. Hell?"

"I just like you."

The answer was so unexpected and his face so serious, I broke out laughing. It was either that or lose my F'ing mind. The pained look on Brandon's face that followed my little outburst just made me laugh harder.

"What?" I said when I'd regained some control. "You

like me? When have I ever given you cause to like me, you spaz?"

Things on the porch started to quiet down as more people caught on to the drama playing out in the front yard. Brandon became aware of it and seemed to draw into himself a little. Let's see how much he liked me when he had to proclaim it in front of the whole party.

"You're interesting," he said, and I stopped chuckling. I wanted to gauge the reactions of the folks on the porch. They were all backlit and I couldn't see their faces. "You're really smart—smarter than me," he went on, "and you're funny. When you don't feel like you have to be the toughest girl on the playground, you're really nice, too.

"Listen," he went on, and took a step closer to me. "When I say 'like' I mean that, I don't mean 'love' or 'lust' or anything else. I mean that I like you and I'd like to get to know you better. That's what I mean.'

I backed up and bumped up against a tree in the yard. I tried to make it look like I meant to do that and leaned against the tree for support.

The crowd on the porch was frozen. Still life with red party cups. Though none of them was actually looking in our direction.

"And how long has this been going on?" I asked.

He shrugged. "I don't know. Most of the year, I guess. Since we've been in Journalism together."

I tried to think back and examine my behavior over the past year. What had I done that would have encouraged this boy to like me? I thought I'd done a pretty good job of being uniformly rotten. Obviously, I should have stepped up my game.

"I think you're talking about the wrong girl."

He shook his head and looked a little angry maybe. "No," he said, "that's what you want me to think—what you want everyone to think. I don't think that's true. That's not who you are."

"Thank you so much for telling me who I am and am not," I said, tired of arguing, tired of talking, tired of being. "Listen. Give me a ride home, will you? I don't think I can stand being here tonight."

"I'm sorry all of these people are here and they spoiled Sherri's thing. I swear I only told a few people." He paused and frowned. "I guess they told a few others."

"Among the growing list of things I can't stand," I said, "is you apologizing."

He opened his mouth—I'm sure to say "sorry"—but then closed it again.

I pressed on, maybe looking for him to tell me to go screw myself.

"And I'll only let you drive me home if you promise not to talk to me along the way. Okay?"

"Can I ask one thing before my restraining order goes into effect?" he asked.

"What?"

"What happened to your face?" He touched my chin, and I felt an electric thrill go through me and settle in a place that young ladies don't talk about.

"I crashed my bike this morning," I lied. "Now can we begin our silent voyage home?"

He nodded, didn't speak. Good boy.

He led me to the ridiculous truck I'd seen parked in front of his house. He helped me up into the cab. While he walked around to the driver's side, I checked out the shotguns in the gun rack in the window. The one on top was a Browning Citori over and under double barrel. It was pretty but not exactly practical when it comes to fending off hordes of shufflers. But the other one was the real deal. A Benelli M4 twelve gauge with a pistol grip. It's gas powered and it's the same model that the Marines use in combat. It's a pretty serious piece of weaponry. I was impressed.

Brandon climbed behind the wheel and keyed the truck to life. It rumbled softly beneath me. I got that same feeling of restrained power I got from the rig Chacho drove. It was comforting. As we drove, Brandon leaned over and turned on the stereo. I was prepared to jump out of the truck if Big Star came out of the speakers. Thankfully I could keep my seat belt on. A girl sang about being held captive by a guy and loathing him and wanting him to touch her hand all at the same time. I could relate.

"Who's this?" I asked.

Brandon checked to see if he had permission to speak. I nodded.

"Her name is Jenny Owen Youngs," he said. "She's out of New Jersey, I think."

"I didn't have you pegged as a fan of girl-power-singer-songwriters."

"Within me I contain multitudes, you know?" he said, "I'm not just one thing."

"I said no conversation," I said, and turned toward the window. I know I asked him a question, but I had to let him know I was in charge. Also, what was up with the Whitman quote? The real question, of course, was whether Brandon knew who he was quoting, or if he was just spouting something he'd read in a quote-a-day calendar. I'd have to investigate further some other time. For now I was enjoying riding along listening to Brandon's mix tape. After the Youngs girl, a semi-local band from Portland came on: The Thermals. They were really cool until the lead singer Hutch or Hitch something got turned into a zombie during an attack during a show. They had just signed with a big label, and I remember hearing at the time that the label suits tried to figure out a way to still get him to perform. The other band members wouldn't have anything to do with their zombified pal, though, and the band broke up.

We pulled up in front of my house, actually right up in front. Brandon jumped the curb and stopped so I had literally two steps to the gate into my yard. I climbed down and was about to swing the door shut when Brandon called out to me.

"Hey, Courtney," he said, "I assume since we're not driving anymore that I can talk to you." I didn't say anything, and he took that for agreement. "I want to call you sometime and hang out. You know, to see if I really like you or not."

I thought about it for a minute. As they say all the time in one of my favorite movies, *The Wild Bunch,* why not?

"You already have my number," I said. "I can't stop you from calling me." I closed the door before he had a chance to say anything else.

I guess I got home late enough that my dad was already in bed. That was good. I didn't have it in me to have one more conversation about my feelings or whatever.

I crept into my room and stowed the cash from my second job. I wanted to read ahead in my AP English class, so I took Camus's *The Stranger* to bed with me.

I was asleep in about thirty seconds.

CHAPTER EIGHT
Ilsa of the SS

I gained consciousness knowing I wanted to murder someone. I had just closed my eyes and now my cell phone chirped away somewhere. I pulled the pillow off my head and squeezed my eyes shut against the light pouring in through my window—that couldn't be right, could it? Groping blindly on my bedside table, I finally found the phone and brought it to my ear.

"What?" I demanded. My voice sounded thick, like it belonged to someone who wasn't me. Someone who'd been smoking nonstop for the last twenty years.

"Did I wake you up? Were you still asleep?" A boy's voice. Who? It sounded familiar.

"What time is it?"

"Just past eleven," the voice said. Awareness started to leak in past the wall of sleep in my brain. The voice was cheerful. Who did I know that was (a) a boy and (b) cheerful in the morning?

"Brandon?" I asked.

"Good morning!" he said. He'd passed cheerful and gone right on to chipper. "Are you surprised I'm calling so soon?"

"Well," I said, my wits finally coming back to me, "I don't think calling a girl the day after she tells you to is really the cool guy thing to do."

"Or maybe it's *exactly* what the cool guy would do."

"I'll take that under advisement," I said. "What's up, Brandon?"

"Me and some friends are going to hang out today," he said. "Do you want to come along?"

I was wide awake. I sat up and pulled the phone away from my ear and looked at it suspiciously. Maybe it was on the fritz and it was somehow misinterpreting what Brandon was saying.

"You want me to hang out with you and your friends."

"Me, Ken Leung, Crystal Beals," he said, rattling off the names of kids in the school's upper echelons. "Maybe a few others—it depends."

"I see," I said. There was a silence as I tried to figure out what to do next. My first instinct was to hang up and run. Then I discovered, with no small feeling of horror, that there was a part of me that wanted to take him up on his invitation. If nothing else, it would be an interesting sociological outing.

"Do you have plans today?" he asked, and I could hear, for the first time in the conversation, a note of doubt creep into his voice.

"Um, no, no plans today," I said. Then I swallowed hard and said, "Sure, let's hang out. When and where?"

I could hear his grin beaming down into my phone from a miles-high satellite. "That's diesel! I'll pick you up about two, if that's okay."

"Two'll be great," I said. "See you then."

He promised he'd see me then, and he rang off. I flipped my phone closed and looked at it again. What the hell was I doing? Hanging out with Brandon and the high-five crowd? Was I getting in over my head? I wished I could call Sherri and talk to her about this. Unfortunately, I had a feeling that she probably still wouldn't want to know I was alive.

I showered and got dressed. Cutoff jeans, black tights,

my black-and-white chucks, a flannel shirt over white T.
I put on even more makeup than usual—black eye liner,
eyelash stuff, red lipstick, concealer on the road rash on
my chin. It felt like a protective mask.

As I put on the finishing touches, I smelled bacon cooking. Interesting. I finished up what I was doing and looked
out into the hallway. The unmistakable smell of bacon was
accompanied by a sizzling sound. Someone out there was
definitely cooking breakfast. At noon. I say "someone"
because it couldn't be my dad; the most he did at breakfast was microwave instant oatmeal. Most mornings it was
cold cereal or—horror—untoasted bagels.

I came down the hall and into the kitchen, and I
thought I was having a full-blown aneurysm. Not only
was my dad cooking breakfast, he was doing it in his boxers and T-shirt. I wondered for a second why he wasn't
wearing his robe. I guess the strange blonde woman sitting
at the kitchen table needed to wear something, right? Piles
of probably-not-natural blond hair framed her heart-
shaped face. She was a bigger woman—what you might
call "thick"—and my dad's robe barely wrapped around
her. I had to admit that the look worked for her if she was
going for slightly older, cougar/sex kitten. I marveled that
she was in my kitchen looking at my father in a suspiciously satisfied way.

I considered backing out of the kitchen quietly and hiding in my room until all of this resolved itself. My dad
looked up just then, and a huge smile broke out across his
face.

"Hey, Pumpkin," he said. "Come on in here. There's
someone I want you to meet." *Pumpkin? Really?*

I took a tentative step into the kitchen and pretended to
see her for the first time. *Oh, my, is there someone else in here
with you?* The smile on my face hurt the corners of my
mouth.

"This is Bev," my dad said. "Beverly."

She stood up and rearranged the robe around herself. She barely got that thing around her rack and her hips. The wave of sexual energy coming off of this woman nearly knocked me back. She was a five-and-a-half-foot sexual dynamo, and she had obviously spent the night with my dad. What little sense there had been in my world quickly drained away.

"You must be Courtney," she said in a deep voice. She smiled again, and it dazzled me for a moment. I smiled and nodded. "Your father has told me so much about you." *Really, when?*

"Come in here and sit down," she said. Being invited to sit at my own kitchen table felt odd. She sat down, too. She sat there looking at me for a long time. It made me nervous as hell, and I was about to say the first thing that came into my head just to break the tension when she finally did it for me.

"You know, you sure are a pretty girl," she said, "but you'd be a whole lot prettier without all that eye makeup."

I felt my cheeks grow hot. I'm sure she couldn't see me blush through all that makeup. My dad just chuckled and flipped over some bacon. Obviously I'd get no support from him.

"I tell her the same thing all the time," he said.

"Well," I said, louder than I'd meant, but not as loud as the scream that had been welling up inside of me, "how did you two meet?"

Dad chuckled again. I really wished he'd stop. "Now that's sort of a funny story."

"We met at the college," Bev said. *Community college,* I corrected her in my head.

"So you teach out there, too?" I asked.

"No, no," my dad said, "Bev is a security guard out there."

I looked at her again. I tried to picture her body encased in one of the pseudo-police uniforms the guards out at the community college wear. I could totally see why my dad was acting like a goofy kid. My mind flashed on the hand-cuffs the guards wear, and I shuddered.

"Well, last night after I was done correcting some papers, I walked out to my car," my dad said as he dished up plates of eggs and bacon. "I was parked in the South lot."

"It's so dark back there," Bev broke in. She said it for me, even if she never took her eyes off Dad.

"Right," he agreed, "it's really dark. Anyway, I'm trying to juggle my papers and my bag and get my car keys out of my pocket."

"But that's not important," Bev said, and I flashed her a narrow-eyed glare. Which she didn't see.

Dad sat down, and I thought for a terrifying second that he was going to sit in Bev's lap. Trauma was averted, how-ever, and he just sat *very* close to her.

"I'm just trying to set the mood, honey." *Honey?* "I drop my keys and while I'm bending down to pick them up, I notice someone walking toward me. Now, I thought it was one of my students who wanted to talk to me."

"They must be all over you, Fred." Bev stroked his arm as she said this. All I could do was smile and nod. Most of Dad's students can barely make it through his lectures. None of them is going to seek him out after hours to have him expound even more on the brilliance of the Skinner box. I could already guess who, or what, had been walk-ing up to him.

"My God, Dad," I said, "are you okay?"

"I'm fine," he said, and waved his hand like he was swatting a bug, like my concern for him didn't matter. "But that's only because of Bev here." And he beamed at her.

He turned away and started serving up the breakfast.

She turned toward me for the first time since this conversation started, and her eyes were wide with excitement. Her teeth flashed as she talked, and I feared I'd become hypnotized.

"It was the luckiest thing," she said, her husky voice even more breathless than usual. "I was driving the cart to the physical plant, and I thought I heard someone screaming." Dad blushed, though he still looked adoringly at Lady Serpico.

"It was pretty damned scary," he confided in me.

"Well," Bev went on, "I wheeled that sucker around, shot up the path to the South lot, and there's your dad, running away from that danged bloodsucker."

"Bloodsucker?" I asked. "Aren't those vampires?"

She went on like she didn't hear. "Your dad is lucky that it was me and not someone like Karl Maynard shooting at that thing. They'd have like to blown his head off before they ever got to the zombie." They shared a laugh over that and, excuse me, I couldn't see the humor in my dad potentially dying.

"I took your dad back to the office to calm down a little," Bev went on, "and we got to talking."

"Talking led to dinner . . ." Dad said, "and dinner led here." He looked at me sheepishly as he set a plate in front of me. For drama's sake, I wish I could have refused to eat. The truth was I was hungry as hell, so I started to eat the eggs and bacon. I'm not sure why Dad was acting all shy around me. I'd been telling him for a couple of years to go out and find a woman. Now that he'd done it, he should take that at face value—even if I was having a hard time doing the same thing.

I wolfed down my food as fast as I could and told them I had homework to do. I got up, rinsed off my plate, and hurried out of the kitchen. Not before I saw my dad and Bev kissing, though. Ugh.

Both Elsa and Brandon had e-mailed me their pieces of the fence article, so I worked on that for a while. Afterward, I tackled some pretty atrocious Organic Chemistry. There was a knock on my bedroom door. Dad poked his head in.

"Hey, Courtney, mind if I come in?"

"Sure?" I said. It came out a question.

He took his time and looked around the room as he walked over to sit on the bed. He told me more than once that he only came in when I was there and had given him permission. The way he gawked at everything like a tourist made me believe him. The bed creaked underneath him. I swiveled my chair around. After a second, he leaned forward with his hands on his knees. He had on his serious dad face.

"I, um, just wanted to come in and check with you about Bev," he said. "To see if you're okay with her being here."

"Well, it's a little late to ask me now, isn't it?" I asked, and I hated myself for saying it. It just freaked me out to find Ilsa of the SS in my kitchen first thing in the morning.

"Oh, I see," Dad said, and he sat back on the bed and pushed his glasses up his nose. "I'm sorry it upset you."

"How would you feel if you walked into the kitchen first thing in the morning and there was a boy sitting there in nothing but my robe?"

"First, eleven isn't first thing in the morning," he said, and when I opened my mouth to say that wasn't the point, he raised his hand to stop me. "But I get what you're saying. There are differences, of course. I'm an adult and can have . . ." *Please don't say lovers, please don't say lovers!* ". . . partners if I want.

"However, you live here with me and I need to respect that. I should have told you I was going to have a guest over last night," he said.

"A *guest*?" I asked. "Is that what it's called these days?"

"Please stop being snarky, Courtney," he said. "I know you're upset, but walling yourself off with sarcasm isn't the answer."

I just looked at him. He knows I hate it when he starts using his jargon mumbo jumbo on me. He sighed and hung his head for a second and then looked up at me.

"Listen," he said, "I'd really like you to give Beverly a chance. We're going in to town to catch a movie, maybe some gelato. You should come with us."

"Sorry," I said in a voice calculated to let him know I wasn't. "I already made plans with some friends today."

His frown deepened. It did really unattractive things to the lines on either side of his mouth. That made me happy.

"It's not Sherri and Willie," I said.

"Oh," he said, brighter, "who is it?"

"You don't know him," I said. Then, before he could ask, I said, "His name is Brandon Ikaros. He's in my Journalism class. Crystal Beals and some others will be there, too."

"I remember Crystal," he said. "I haven't seen her around here in a while."

Not since sixth grade when she figured out how uncool I was.

"And what are you going to do?" he asked.

"Hanging out was mentioned."

Dad stood up and thrust his hands in his pockets. Having me admit to hanging out with anyone other than the reprobate twins was tantamount to a victory, and he needed to get out before anything happened to mess it up.

"Okay, please don't be too late," he told me. "And I want you to think about getting to know Beverly. I really do think you'd like her." He headed toward the door.

"I'll think about it," I said. "'Bye."

"I love you," Dad said as he closed the door.

"'Bye," I yelled after him. He could be so needy sometimes. I thought that having a new sex toy running around the house would mean I could escape any displays of emotion whatsoever.

I kept working on my paper while I heard Dad and Bev getting ready to go. I put on my headphones when I realized that no matter what room Bev was in, her voice cut through the house and it sounded like she was standing next to me having a very loud conversation.

I finally saw my dad's Volvo back out of the driveway and putter down the street. I was safe. I finished up the chem homework, then I set about waiting for Brandon to show up for our journey into class differential.

I found myself constantly checking my phone while I waited. Was Sherri going to call me? If she wasn't mad at me, she'd at least call to give me a hard time for not sticking around to help her clean up last night. I even went on to Gmail and Facebook to see if she was logged on. She was maintaining strict radio silence, apparently.

Fine. Let her sulk. I really didn't feel like I'd done anything wrong. As if she'd never told someone I didn't like about a party. Hell, it was because of her that I had to invite Lori Caldwell to my birthday party two years ago. That was way worse than telling Brandon about her stupid get-together last night.

I finally worked myself up enough that I decided Sherri could go screw herself. She was totally wrong about this whole situation. I grabbed my phone and thumbed the power button. Let her try to get a hold of me now. I hoped she called all day needing to talk to me. I fantasized about her trying to call to apologize and not reaching me. I hoped she'd wallow in guilt for being such a bitch to me. I'd talk to *her* when *I* was damned good and ready.

I threw my phone into my bag and got up as I heard the sound of an engine rumbling up to the front of the house.

I parted the curtains and looked out into the street. The truck came to a stop right in front of our gate, and Brandon hopped out. Two people sat in the back of the king cab. I couldn't tell who they were. Brandon opened the gate and entered the yard. I took that as my cue to grab my bag, check my makeup one last time, and scoot toward the door. I opened it just as the bell ding-donged.

The look of shock on his face made me burst out laughing. He was only confused for a second before he laughed, too. "Have you been standing there all day?" he asked.

"Only since noon," I said, and then laughed again as he tried to figure out whether or not I was serious. "I saw you pull up and grabbed my stuff and came out to meet you."

"Gotcha," he said. "So, I guess you're ready?" He looked me up and down. He was subtle about it, but I could tell.

A million thoughts raced through my brain. Was he silently judging me? I mean, I know he was, but was the verdict negative? Should I have toned it down for a first date? Christ, was this a date? We'd never actually used that word. "Date." I worried I might start hyperventilating if I didn't get the situation under control. I needed to say something to zero in on how he felt about my ensemble. Something subtle.

"Is how I'm dressed okay?" *Goddammit!*

"Oh, sure," he said. "I was just asking."

I decided to give him the benefit of the doubt. I checked to make sure I had my house keys and closed the door. He just grinned at me for a moment.

"Okay," he said, "let's get back to the truck. The others'll be wondering what's taking so long."

Suddenly it felt like there was a hot rock in my stomach. In all of our rom-com banter, I forgot others were involved in this scenario. Other people who probably weren't as nice or cool as Brandon seemed. As we walked toward the gate I started wondering again what the hell I was doing. Why was I dressed like this? I should have dressed more normal, or put on less makeup. Why was I even thinking things like this? What did I care what anyone thought about me? God, I felt like I was going crazy. I should probably just go back to the house and go to bed until this case of hormonal insanity passed.

Then Brandon opened the gate for me and it was too late. He also opened the door to the truck and gave me a hand up. He closed it and went around to the other side.

"Hi, Courtney," said a voice from the backseat. Crystal Beals sat back there looking cute. She was a tiny brunette girl with long hair and sharp features. She always reminded me of the elves in *Lord of the Rings*. I told her that once when we were in sixth grade and it made her so happy. I called her elf girl all the rest of that year. I'd probably still call her that if we were still friends. She wore an orange T-shirt and tan capri pants. She looked good. Summery.

"Hi, Crystal," I said, "how are you?"

"I've been really good?" she said. She had a habit of making most her sentences sound like questions. "I'm gearing up to take the SATs next month?"

"Yeah," I said, "I took them a couple of months ago. I haven't got my scores yet."

The driver's side door opened and Brandon hopped in. He closed the door and turned to look at all of us.

"You guys know each other?" he asked.

"Me and Crystal go way back," I said.

"We used to play together all the time," she agreed.

"Nice, well, this is Ken Leung," Brandon said, and tilted his head toward the guy sitting next to Crystal. He hadn't said anything to me, and I couldn't even tell if he was looking at me because his eyes were hidden behind huge aviator glasses. His short black hair was gelled so it stood straight up, and he wore a baby blue polo shirt with a popped collar. Everything about him screamed, "Douche!"

I nodded at him.

"Yeah," he said, "hi."

I turned back around. "So what are we doing?"

Brandon gave the truck some gas and steered it into the street. "My dad has a cabin out on Silver Creek Reservoir, so I thought we'd go hang out there," he said. "We can swim, there's a grill out there, and my dad stocks the fridge with beer."

"That's what I'm talking about," Ken said even though he hadn't actually been talking about it.

"Swimming is great?" Crystal said.

I knew I wasn't dressed for it and hadn't brought a suit. Why the hell didn't Brandon mention it so I could prepare? I had a feeling this is how the whole day was going to go—one small annoyance after another. I forced a smile, however, because I like to maintain a sunny disposition.

"Yeah," I said, "let's do it."

Brandon gave an honest-to-God whoop and stepped on the gas. "Yes," he said, "this is going to be fun."

And as we headed out on our little adventure, I just hoped he was right.

CHAPTER NINE
Not a Great First Date

I had to admit that the drive out to the reservoir was a pretty nice one. You drove out on Highway 22 through a town called Aumsville and then to the reservoir. Along the way, farmland lined the old highway. My dad said it was nicer before all the pieces of land were surrounded by barbed wire and electric fences. I can only take his word for it.

As we drove, Ken and Brandon kept up a steady conversation about the football team—who would make first string next year (they were both certain they would); what sorts of punishing exercises their coaches devise; what would the schedule of games be, et-kill-me-cetera.

Crystal tried to start a conversation with me, but we couldn't really talk over the two knuckleheads. When they weren't talking, Brandon focused straight ahead. Which is probably what he should have done since he was driving. He was also quiet and licked his lips a lot. If I didn't know better, I'd have said he was nervous.

I was content to sit back and watch the scenery. Lots of rolling hills and rows of one kind of plants or another. I don't know. I heard they grow a lot of grapes for wine out here. Maybe if wine didn't taste like ass, I'd have cared more about it. Really, I might have been able to see myself living out there one day. You know, when I'm old and boring.

The farmland became more and more sparse and was replaced by lots of trees—spruce and pine and, here and there, a cedar. The air coming in through my cracked-open window felt noticeably cooler. I started to think that it might be too cold to actually go swimming. For now, it felt good, refreshing. The road narrowed and Brandon dropped our speed because it also became rougher.

The barbed-wire fences were replaced with some split-rail ones. You could see the occasional side road disappearing up into the woods, each one with a gate of some kind across the road. Brandon eventually pulled into one of these and stopped, letting the engine idle. The gate across the entrance to the property had a heavy chain locking it closed. Brandon turned and handed a set of keys to Ken in the backseat.

"Want to unlock it, dude?" he asked.

Ken looked like he was going to put up an argument, then he took the keys and got out of the truck. His movements were quick and precise. He opened the gate for the truck and then swung it shut again as soon as we'd passed through. Brandon stopped and let him climb in again.

"Thanks, man," Brandon told him as he took the keys from him.

"De nada," Ken said. I rolled my eyes.

We drove on for another fifteen minutes down this one-lane dirt road. The light barely reached us through the thick forest. I started to creep myself out thinking about what could be out there. I mean, you could only see a few feet past the tree line. People are always talking about how zombies don't come into Salem anymore because they're all hiding out in the woods now.

As soon as we got to the reservoir itself, it was different.

A clearing surrounded the water, and the sun beat down on the cabin there. Well, Brandon called it a cabin. When I heard that word, I thought of something out of a Jack London story—something big enough for maybe two people and held together with bailing wire and prayers. This was a pretty massive building with a porch and everything. Even though it was built out of logs, I don't know if "cabin" was the right term for it.

"Your dad owns this?" I asked.

Brandon looked a little sheepish. "Yeah, this and the property for a few acres on either side."

"Is your dad a bank robber?" I asked. *Or a drug dealer,* I thought.

Brandon laughed and threw open the door to climb out. "Nope. He was a session musician in LA before the dead came back. He wrote some hit songs for other musicians. That's what paid for all of this."

I sort of regretted giving up on piano lessons when I was twelve.

We unloaded the truck—a cooler, blankets and towels, and some lawn chairs. Brandon and Ken grabbed the shotguns out of the rack and slung them over their shoulders. Brandon took the Benelli. The way they handled the guns, I was glad I'd brought my pistol in my purse. If there was trouble, I wouldn't want to rely on those two amateurs to save me.

We walked down to the shore, which was just a few yards past the house. The sun beat directly on us here, and I started to feel hot. I was going to need to get these leggings off soon. We arranged the chairs and blankets and sat down. Brandon headed back to the house to start some music—his dad had outdoor speakers wired up. Ken went with him. They left the double-barrel with us girls.

After they were gone, Crystal smiled at me and asked, "So, are you and Brandon a thing?"

"I don't think so," I said, and then thought about it a moment. We weren't. I turned back to her. "Mind if we don't talk about it?"

"God, no," she said. "Boy talk is boring. It's just that sometimes I feel, you know . . ."

"Obligated?"

She nodded.

"Sure." I said.

Then she asked about my folks and got embarrassed when she remembered that my mom wasn't on the scene. I assured her it was okay. I was about to ask about her parents, when the music started up. It was something funky, maybe George Clinton. It didn't matter, really; it was fun.

The boys came out of the house then, each carrying a bottle and some plastic tumblers. Uh-oh. Brandon grinned as he brandished his bottle. "Rum," he said, "and Ken has vodka. I don't think my dad'll miss them." Ken held up his bottle. Apparently, smiling was too pedestrian for him.

"There's juice in the cooler," Brandon said, "and beer, too."

I decided to go with OJ and vodka, the drink of choice for juvenile delinquents everywhere. After everyone got their drinks—Crystal just took juice I noticed—we sat around and sunned ourselves and talked about stuff other than football. Grades and after-school jobs (everyone but Brandon had one and, no, I didn't mention my second job); music and movies; Ken talked about a video series he wanted to write, direct, and star in, which he would post to YouTube and that I thought sounded like it would suck ass. I didn't say that.

I made the boys turn around so I could take off my shorts and strip off my leggings—it was way too hot now for that sort of nonsense. I asked if anyone wanted to get in the water, and Crystal was the only one who seemed interested, so I grabbed her hand and dragged her down the shore and into the reservoir. Before we got in, Crystal stripped off her capris to reveal a black bikini bottom. I dived into the water. I screamed, it was so cold at first. It felt like all the air was crushed out of my chest for a second by the frigid water. Then I got used to it and it felt really nice. I was glad the sun was so hot that day—it would make climbing out again bearable. I floated on my back while Crystal swam lazy circles around me and we talked some more. I guess the boys couldn't resist our wet siren call, and they came running into the water. They acted like boys for a while and shouted and splashed and drew attention to themselves. When Crystal and I failed to react, they calmed down and waded or swam or floated. It became really quiet, and, as I floated on my back in the water, my ears below the water line, I heard my heart beating. I timed my breath with my heartbeats and stared up into the sky. Wispy cumulus clouds hung up there, and I fought against the feeling that I was falling up into the sky.

The others got out of the reservoir and mixed new drinks. I followed and had more OJ and vodka. After being in the sun and water, the drink hit me kind of hard. I definitely felt light-headed. Great. A joke came to mind: What's the cheerleader mating call? I'm so drunk! Ooh, I was going to have to apologize to Crystal for even thinking that. She was so nice—I shouldn't have thought bad things about her chosen lifestyle.

And then I was struck by a sudden need to pee.

"Are there toilets in that rustic, pioneer structure?" I asked Brandon, and I tried to enunciate as carefully as possible so no one would suspect I was feeling tipsy.

Brandon flashed me a weird grin and then he nodded. "There are toilets, yep," he said. "They flush and everything. Go inside, down the hall, and it's on your right."

I stood up and halted my swaying and headed off toward the cabin.

Crystal called out behind me. "I'll come with you." I almost asked why, but dropped it. I just hoped she wouldn't want to come in with me while I peed. We left the boys behind making jokes about how women were incapable of going to the bathrooms by themselves. Very funny material circa 1960.

The rough grain of the wooden porch felt good beneath my feet. Inside the cabin the air was noticeably cooler. Little goose bumps raised on my arms. It made my head feel better. The interior of the cabin was beautiful. It was mostly an open space with a loft above the living area. The kitchen sat in the far corner, and a big dining room table—that looked like it was carved out of a single gigantic slab of wood— added to the feeling that I didn't belong there. Everything was either wood or stone. There were lots of rugs and cushy furniture so it didn't feel cold. This place is what Land's End catalogs were trying to look like. And failing.

"You've never been out here?" Crystal asked. My awe must have been written all over my face. I needed to rein that in.

"Yeah," I told her. "You have?"

"Sure," she said. "Brandon's had parties out here before. His dad's cool with it. The bathroom's down there." She pointed down the hallway.

"Thanks," I said, and scooted away.

The bathroom was nice, but nothing like the rest of the house. Functional. I closed the door and as I turned toward the mirror, I caught a look at myself. All of my carefully applied makeup—my mascara and eyeliner—had spread out so I looked like the world's biggest, saddest raccoon. I burst out laughing and then immediately tried to stifle it.

A second later, Crystal knocked on the door and asked if I was okay. She said it sounded like I'd screamed. Doing my best to hold back new peals of laughter, I told her I was fine. I got it under control and sat on the toilet and pissed for about an hour. I needed to cut back on the alcohol.

I finished up and washed my hands and then scrubbed my face until I couldn't take it anymore. My skin was all pink when I was done, but that was better than what it looked like before. When I left the bathroom, I found Crystal looking at a shelf that practically groaned under the weight of all the books on it.

"I love looking at all of Mr. Ikaros's books whenever I'm out here," she said without looking up at me, then she turned and smiled. She was really pretty when she smiled. I mean, she was always pretty. Especially when she smiled. When I didn't say anything, she turned back to the books. "He has a ton of books by journalists. *All the President's Men, Black Hawk Down.*"

She took a book down from the shelf. "Wow," she said, "this one is brand new. *The Black Flower;* it's a book about that zombie drug, Vitamin Z. I can't believe he's already got it out here."

"Is that something you're interested in?"

"Journalism?" she asked. "Oh, yeah."

"That's great," I said. I'd meant was she interested in Vitamin Z, and I was relieved to hear that she wasn't.

"Yeah, I want to study it when I get to college." She put the book back on the shelf and stood up. "How about you?"

"Me?" I asked.

"In college," she said. "What do you want to do?"

"Oh, epidemiology," I said. We started to head back outside. "You know, studying how diseases spread. Why aren't you on the school's newspaper?" I asked her.

"I had some core classes I needed to get out of the way this year," she said, "you know, before I send off college applications. I figured I'd join the paper next year—if I can get in. Why do you want to study diseases?"

We were out on the porch and I was about to tell Crystal the broad outlines of my master plan. She stopped and looked off toward the shore.

"Where are the boys?" she asked.

I looked to where we'd been sunning ourselves. Brandon and Ken were nowhere to be seen. I scanned the shoreline and still didn't see them. Next to me, Crystal shivered and hugged herself.

"I bet they're just being dicks," she said, "trying to scare us or whatever?"

I might have agreed with her, but I noticed that the double-barreled shotgun was gone. This was officially bad news.

"I'm going to go back into the house and lock the doors until they come back," Crystal said, and she started to do just that.

"I'll be right behind you. First, I have to get something out of my bag," I told her.

"No, wait," she said, "don't go. What the hell do you need out of your bag?" Her eyes were big and her lips quivered a little. I tried not to feel as scared as she looked.

"I have a gun in there."

Her eyes narrowed. "Okay," she said, like I needed her permission. "But I'm going down with you. No way do I want to be alone."

I understood, but didn't say anything. I headed down the path toward my bag. Crystal followed right behind. Behind me, I became dimly aware that a new song started up on the stereo. Pink Floyd, I think, something with a woman bellowing wordlessly into the mic. It was eerie as hell and I wish I'd thought to turn the damned thing off.

As we reached our towels, a shotgun blast roared out of

the woods. We both jumped and Crystal gave a little shriek. "What is going on?" she demanded, her voice shaky.

"I don't know," I said, and bent down to rummage through my bag. Dammit! I either needed a smaller bag or I needed to rig up some kind of holster so I could get a hold of the F'ing pistol when I wanted it. I shoved aside my mp3 player, and my hand found the checkered wood grip. I'm always amazed at how comforted I am by holding that thing. I get why teenaged boys love guns.

"Is that them?" Crystal asked, and I looked where she pointed. Shadows moved along back in the tree line to our left. They became more distinct; I saw there were three shapes.

"That's not them," I said. "Let's get back to the house."

"But maybe someone else—" she stopped cold when the two zombies shuffled out of the woods. A girl and a guy. Even though they were all naked, there was nothing even close to sexy about them. Major parts of their bodies were gone. The guy was missing his face.

I heard Crystal talking to herself under her breath behind me. I couldn't make out what she was saying. Probably trying to calm herself down. I could have used some of that, too. I felt like my heart was beating up in my throat.

The UDs started to walk toward us with purpose. As much purpose as dead folks can have, anyway.

I grabbed Crystal's hand and she started. She seemed to calm a little bit when I smiled at her. "Let's just walk to the house," I told her. "They can't walk as fast as us." I started to lead her that way.

Everything seemed like it was going really well. Until I noticed that a fourth zombie had come out of the woods on the opposite side of the clearing and now stood between us and the house. We both froze. Even though I had the gun in my hand, I felt like I couldn't walk on, couldn't get closer to this new zombie. Where the hell had she come from anyway? Was she the David Blaine of zombies, just appearing out of thin air? She looked fresher than the other three; still had on her bikini and no bite marks that I could see. So, maybe she was the David-Blaine-zombie's assistant.

I got my courage up—still being a little drunk helped, and was about to prod Crystal into action when she lost her shit.

She screamed and tore her hand out of my grip and ran to the house. Bikini zombie rushed to meet—way faster than I'd ever seen a zombie move. The monster got its hands on her arms and opened its mouth as it pulled her close. Crystal fought back, thank God.

She bought me time enough to run after her and get so close that I put the muzzle of the pistol right up against the dead bitch's forehead. The shot was incredibly loud, and I felt the shock of it all the way up my arm since I hadn't taken time to prepare myself for it. The zombie and Crystal both fell to the ground, and I kicked at the finally dead thing until it let go and Crystal could crawl some distance away. Crystal sat there panting, and I leaned over her, asking if she was okay. She screamed again, this time right in my ear. It was louder than the loudest concert I'd ever been to.

The shufflers were nearly on us. Rather than try to get Crystal up and into the house, I assumed a kneeling stance, pistol held out in front of me with both hands. I sighted down the barrel, squeezed the trigger, let out my breath, and squeezed it some more. I was ready for the recoil this time. Too bad I missed. I squeezed the trigger again and this time scored a hit—in the boy's chest. Damndamndamn. I didn't have time for this. I fired the pistol again, and the boy dropped as a small dot appeared in his forehead.

I was lining up my next shot when a loud boom sounded behind me. The girl on the left had her middle section evaporated by the shotgun blast. I dove into the sand and covered my head, afraid to be hit by any stray buckshot.

Another shot boomed out, and then Crystal started screaming again. *What now?* I thought. I didn't want to open my eyes again. Then I figured I'd better check out what was going on. Good thing I did. The top half of the blown-apart zombie crawled toward me; was nearly on top of me. She was so close that I was able to reach out and stick the pistol in her mouth. If I were in an action movie, I'd have said something clever. The truth was I was too scared and tired. I pulled the trigger, and the top of her head disappeared. She lay on the ground right next to me, quivering. I rolled over and, as discreetly as I could in front of my new friends, barfed until I nearly passed out.

Brandon helped me up and walked me toward the cabin. Ken tried to help Crystal. She didn't want him to touch her. I understood. I glanced at the pile of bodies and wondered what their brains would be worth to my dealer. I started to laugh, and the effect on my throat nearly made me hurl again. No more of that. Inside, Brandon got me a glass of water and asked what had happened.

"I was going to ask you that," I said. My throat felt raw from spewing and my voice was all crackly.

"While you guys were in here, Ken saw someone in the trees," Brandon said. "We grabbed the guns and went to see what was up."

"We thought we'd be back by the time you got back," Ken said. He sat on a chair across from Crystal. It looked like he wanted to reach out and comfort her since she was obviously still freaking out. Unfortunately for him, she was also giving a clear *"no touch"* vibe.

"Yeah," Brandon said, "but when we got in there, we didn't see anyone, so we went in deeper and . . . ," he blushed, "and we got sort of lost."

"Lost?" Crystal said. Hysteria didn't just creep into her voice, it moved right in and set up house.

"It's easy to do," Brandon said, defensive, "even just a few yards into the woods and you can lose sight of where you walked into them."

"And we did find a zombie," Ken put in.

"Yeah, you probably heard us shoot it," Brandon said.

"You found a zombie?" Crystal asked, her voice shrill. "Well we found some zombies, too, you asshats!" She was up out of her chair, the tendons on the sides of her neck bulging out as she screamed at the boys. "If it hadn't been for Dead-Eye Lolita over there, we'd be dead!"

"It's okay, Crystal," I said, and she seemed to calm down when I spoke to her. She sat down at least. "We got through it."

Brandon started to apologize. "I am really—"

"Don't," Crystal said, and she drew back into herself on the chair.

Brandon looked to me for support, and I shrugged. I had no interest in leading our group therapy session. But there *was* something that needed to be done.

"Hey, Crystal," I said as soothingly as possible given the fact that I sounded a lot like Cookie Monster at the moment.

"What?" she asked, not bothering to make eye contact.

"We need to check you out."

"What does that mean?" she asked. Her voice was weak; she knew what I meant. I had to say it for Brandon and Ken, though.

"That thing got a hold of you," I said. The boys shifted their focus from me to her. "We need to look you over to make sure it didn't scratch you or anything. If it did, we'll have to take you to the hospital. Shit, we'll probably all have to be quarantined."

Ken started to say that he could check her out. Crystal shook her head. "I want Courtney to do it."

"Okay," I said, and stood up. My legs felt pretty rubbery, but I thought I could make it. Crystal followed me into the bathroom, and she closed and locked the door behind her.

I sat on the toilet, and then she and I stared at each other for a second. It was starting to feel pretty awkward, when she suddenly stripped off her shirt. That didn't really help with the awkward feeling. I just needed to do what I'd come in there to do. Crystal wore a black bikini top, though she probably could have gotten away without wearing anything up there. I was impressed with her stomach muscles. She had a definite six-pack going on. I concentrated on her arms, since that's where the thing had grabbed her. I didn't see any claw marks. I did see row after row of straight cuts running the length of her upper arms. Some were old and nearly faded, some were obviously fresh.

I looked away from her arms and into her face. She didn't blink, defiant. "Those aren't from the zombie," she said.

"No," I said, "I guessed that. Let me look at the other side." She held up her arms. No marks of any kind on the backs of them. Maybe they were too hard to reach with a razor. I gave her torso and neck a quick once-over. The zombie hadn't given her as much as a scratch.

I stood up and she put her shirt back on, covering her arms.

"You know, Crystal," I said, fumbling for what to say, "if you ever want to talk . . ."

"I appreciate that, Courtney. I won't want to. Thanks,

though." She walked out of the bathroom and I followed. We found the boys lounging on the couch, not saying much.

Crystal asked if we could go, and no one argued. We gathered up our things from the shore, packed them into the truck, and then climbed in ourselves and drove away. The ride back was mostly silent. Brandon played his mix CD quietly and everyone seemed locked in their own heads.

When we passed through Aumsville, Brandon asked if we could stop at a Thai place he likes, and none of us could muster the strength to say no. The Drunken Noodles were great, but I didn't have much of an appetite. I was sure I'd eat the leftovers the next day for lunch. We all got back in the truck after we were done eating—or after Brandon was done I guess I should say—and drove on home without stopping again.

We dropped Crystal off first, and she got out of the car and left without saying good-bye. As we pulled away from her house, Ken sighed a huge theatrical sigh. "Not a great first date," he said. I grimaced. It was a first date for him, too, and it was shitty to boot. We had so much in common.

Ken lived in the same gated suburb as Crystal, so he got dropped off next. He and Brandon did a complicated handshake thing, which I'm sure they thought was very street, and then he left without saying good-bye to me. Maybe no one was going to acknowledge leaving my presence ever again.

By the time we reached my hovel, it was nearly eight o'clock. The sky was darkening and a slim crescent moon already hung in the sky. Brandon parked right in front of the gate and shut the truck down. He turned to look at me and was Very Serious.

"I'm really sorry about this afternoon, Courtney," he

said. "I feel like an ass for leaving the two of you alone like that."

"Well, don't," I said. "Everything turned out fine."

"Yeah. It's just the thought of something happening to you . . ."

"Honestly, Brandon," I said, "don't worry about it."

"I just don't want you to hate me," he said, and he looked so sincere and forlorn that it short-circuited my sarcasm response.

"I don't hate you," I said, "honest. We should hang out again. No zombie-infested reservoir next time, okay?"

"Okay," he said, "I promise."

"Great," I said, "and now I need to go to bed and sleep for one million years."

"Sure, have a good night."

"You, too, Brandon," I said, and I climbed out of the truck and through the gate. I heard him start up the truck and pull away as I walked into my house.

I found Dad and Bev snuggling on the couch watching TV when I entered. Just great, as if I hadn't seen enough horrors for one day. Dad had his arm around her shoulders and she had her legs thrown over his. They both turned and smiled at me.

"Hey, you're home earlier than I expected," Dad said. "How was hanging out?"

"Not great," I said, "but we're going to give it another shot sometime."

"Atta girl," Bev chimed in. "You've got to keep on trying."

"Anything you want to talk about?" Dad asked.

"No," I said, "right now I just want to clean up and go to bed."

I headed down the hall toward safety, and my dad called out after me.

"Say, did William get a hold of you?"

I stopped dead, an icy ball in the pit of my stomach. "Willie called?" I asked.

"Sure," Dad said, "a few times. You should call him in the morning."

Willie had been calling me all day while I frolicked with Brandon. Right then I wished I had been eaten by those stupid shufflers because at least then I wouldn't have to call Willie and apologize for standing him up for dinner.

CHAPTER TEN
A Rictus Smile

Willie wasn't online anywhere. Facebook, Gmail, Tumblr, none of the weird message boards he frequents. He didn't have a cell phone—I mean, c'mon, who doesn't have a cell phone?—and it was too late to call his house. If I tried it, all I'd get would be his mom screeching into the phone demanding to know if I knew what time it was—and his dad in the background yelling at her to stop yelling for God's sake. It was already ten o'clock because, okay, I'd put off trying to contact him until it was too late to call. I had to admit that I sucked. The only way I could get ahold of him would be on the Internet, and he was definitely off line. Dammit, he was *never* off line. I guessed he was doing to me right now what I'd done to Sherri earlier. Made himself unavailable so I couldn't reach out and apologize to him. He wanted to stew.

I looked at my bag for a while. Tried to gird myself for listening to his messages. Damn. Damn. Damn. Why did I have to turn off my stupid phone? If I'd left it on, I'd have remembered to go to his place and none of that zombie crap would have happened.

I turned it back on and it buzzed a bunch of times as new messages loaded. I noticed that they were all from Willie; Sherri still hadn't tried to contact me. I gritted my teeth and hit the button to play my voice mails.

It was worse than I thought it would be. In the first message Willie sounded all cheery, reminding me about dinner and making some dumb joke about not bringing anything with me but my appetite, ha ha ha! He called back during the afternoon, wondering why I hadn't called back. He was still trying to sound upbeat and not managing it very well. In the third message, left right after Willie had come over to the house and knocked on the door, he sounded depressed as all get out. He hoped everything was okay, wondered where I was, and asked me to call when I got in. I could still come over and eat if I wanted.

The last message was left just about a half-hour before I came home. I could hear his mom yelling something at him in the background. His voice barely registered. "Hey," he said, "so I guess you're not gonna come over tonight. I wish you'd called me . . ." He said something I couldn't catch. "Anyway, yeah, I'll talk to you later, or something . . ." And he hung up.

Looking at the phone, I saw that he'd called about ten times besides the four times he left a message. I threw the phone away and slumped into the bed. I couldn't believe I'd done that to Willie. Just yesterday I was thinking how I wanted to be better to him. Why did I suck so much? In the morning I would have to call and beg him to forgive me. Maybe make him some baked goods? Buy him some porn? I didn't know. I needed to think of something.

I turned off the light. I hadn't washed my face or brushed my teeth and I didn't care. I just wanted to go to sleep and make this day be over. I'd screwed it up so bad that I had to do a better job of things tomorrow, right?

I dreamed I was talking to one of the zombies from that afternoon. The bikini-girl, the one I shot in the head. She wasn't dead in the dream. She was alive, tanned and bright-eyed and plump, which really worked for her in that suit. She looked really good, actually, except for the pair of holes in her head. She had a small, star-shaped hole in her right temple where I shot her—a small line of blood trickled from it. A crater about the size of a fist was on the other side of her head. Despite that, she smiled at me.

We stood on the shore of the reservoir. I crossed my arms over my chest, trying to keep warm. Bikini-girl didn't seem to notice. She told me a long story about what happened to her after she was turned into a zombie. After a while I realized I couldn't understand what she said to me. I strained to hear. Nothing was overpowering her voice; it was just that I couldn't make out the words.

I kept leaning closer and closer to her, trying to catch what she said. I knew it was really important. I finally got so close that I could feel her breath on my neck. I wrinkled my nose at the smell—rotten meat, garbage, turned peaches.

She finally said something I could understand: "Courtney."

I turned to glance at her and she was a zombie again— eyes glassy with cataracts, lips pulled back in a rictus smile. She opened her mouth impossibly wide and I just stood there, waiting, as she slowly pulled me closer.

I woke up, my heart racing, my legs tangled in my sheet and blankets. *What the hell was that all about?* More than likely it was the fault of that talk show with the zombie whisperer. I could tell him what the result would have been yesterday if I'd tried to open lines of communication with those shufflers on the reservoir.

I sat up and rubbed my eyes and scratched my head. Tried to get the cobwebs out. I picked up my phone and looked at the time. 9:30. Why was I up so early? I put the phone back on my bedside table.

The phone. Oh, hell. There's nothing worse than that

moment after you wake up, when your brain spins up to speed and you remember what happened the day before and you face the crushing realization that you're a shit.

I started thinking of all the things I could do right now instead of call Willie's house. I could clean my room, do my accounting before I went to meet my dealer, read ahead in my homework, clean my pistol, slit my F'ing wrists. Ugh. I just needed to cowboy up and call him.

Before I could talk myself out of it, I picked up my phone, flipped it open, and hit the speed-dial for Willie's place. He's number 2 right after Sherri.

Three rings and I started to have hope that no one would pick up. Maybe they'd gone out to breakfast or something, and I could just leave a message and I'd be off the hook!

"Hello," said Willie's mom on the other end. Suck.

"Hello, Mrs. Luunder," I said.

"Oh," she said brightly, setting my nerves on end, "it's the amazing disappearing girl! No, wait, I'm wrong—you would have to show up first to be able to disappear."

"I'm sorry about last night, Mrs. Luunder," I said lamely.

"Well, I'm sure you have a good reason for making my son mope around the house like the world's biggest infant." Jesus, this was worse than taking shit from one of my friends. I decided not to play along.

"Is Willie home, ma'am?" I asked.

"I'm sure he is, Courtney" she said, "since he's been waiting since about four in the afternoon yesterday for you to call. Just a moment."

There was a pause and then I heard her bellow out, "William, it's your so-called friend on the line. She deigned to call you." I heard her husband yell something but couldn't make out what.

I listened to the hiss of the empty phone line and then heard a muffled clumping sound as Willie walked to the phone. There was a conversation as Willie's mom handed it over. I couldn't hear what they were saying. I did hear her rising voice, shrill even though he must have had his hand over the mouthpiece.

I knew he was on the line because I heard a huge Charlie-Brown sigh. "Hey, Courtney," he said.

"Hi, Willie," I said. "I'm really sorry about last night. I'm a total douche."

"No," he said, "that's okay . . ." At this I heard his mom in the background calling him the human welcome mat.

"Can I make it up to you?" I asked, trying to speak over her. "Let's get together for lunch—my treat!" I could afford to dip into my second income to make Willie feel better. "And I'll tell you about what happened to me yesterday." I'd just need to figure out a way to leave out any mention of Brandon.

"I don't know if I can," Willie said. "I have a bunch of chores to do today."

"And you should get to them," his mom said. She sounded like she was standing right over his shoulder. Which she probably was. "You left all that fish out last night—you know, the fish we made for *dinner?* Now it stinks to high heaven."

"But it's a great story," I said. "It involves nearly being eaten by a zombie and everything!"

"Oh, who were you out with?" he asked, and my heart sank. It was bad enough that I ditched him; hearing that I was out with Brandon would kill him.

"Just some people," I said. "Ken Leung, Crystal Beals."

"Is that all?" he asked.

"No," I said. "Brandon Ikaros, too."

There was a long silence on Willie's end of the phone.

Long enough to make me wonder if he had hung up or just left the phone to dangle on its cord on the kitchen wall. "Willie?" I asked.

"Brandon Ikaros?" he asked, and there was something in his voice that scared me.

"Yeah," I said, trying to sound casual about it, dismissive. "It was totally not a big deal. He called me spur of the moment . . ."

"Do you like him?" Willie asked. I could hear his mom in the background again, harping on him about the fish and how it wasn't going to throw itself away.

"I guess I like him," I said, and then added quickly, "but, hey, I like you, too, buddy!"

"But you don't like me the same way you like him, right?" he asked.

I really thought about what to say to him next. I could lie, but that wouldn't be fair. I could tell him I didn't have any feelings for Brandon, which I didn't think was true. Or I could tell him that I liked him in the same way as I liked Brandon—I was confused is all. I knew that it was going to hurt him to tell him the truth. Telling him anything else would hurt even worse.

"I'm not exactly sure how I feel about Brandon yet, Willie," I said. "I know that I like you as a friend. One of my best friends."

"That's what I thought," he said, and then there was a long pause. I could hear his parents still yelling in the background. God, why wouldn't they just shut the hell up? Then his mom must have walked closer to the phone because I heard her say, plain as day, "Are you crying?" Oh, man, this was going from bad to worse. Willie screamed at her to get out of there, and she demanded to know what I had said to him and to hand her the phone— which Willie did not, thank God.

By this time, *I* was crying; my cheeks were wet with tears because I was breaking the heart of this big, dumb guy who was stupid enough to have a crush on me.

"Willie." I tried calling to him. I knew that he couldn't hear me over him and his mom yelling.

He finally put the phone to his ear long enough to say in a voice choked with tears, "I have to go, Courtney. I don't blame you, you know. It's not your fault." And still his mom yelled on and on. Then there was silence from his end of the line.

I chucked the phone away from me and buried my head in my pillow and sobbed. Why did Willie have to have such a horrible mom? Why did he have to like me? And why couldn't I like him back in return? None of it seemed fair, and none of it made sense.

The one person in the world I never wished any harm was Willie, and here I'd just taken a huge dump all over his heart.

Someone sat beside me on the bed and started to stroke my hair and back. I hadn't heard anyone come in. I looked up long enough to see my dad sitting there, looking down at me wearing his worried face. He made a soft shushing noise as he petted me. My first reaction was to pull away from him, to give in to the misery I felt and deny myself the chance to feel better, and my dad's efforts to help. Instead, I made myself scoot closer to him and wrapped my body around him like a cat. My sobs slackened, but I was still crying. He didn't say anything, didn't ask what was wrong—he just sat there for a long time and tried his best to comfort me. Maybe he sensed that trying to get me to talk about it would drive me away. Maybe he was smarter and better at his job than I ever gave him credit for.

After a while, even the tears ebbed away and I lay there against my dad, completely limp from the exertion.

He brushed the hair from my face. I heard someone

else creep in, Bev, and then creep out again. Dad pressed a cool cloth to my face and started to wipe it along my cheeks and over my eyes. Bev must have brought him that cloth without being asked. God, why was I such a bitch? Had I misjudged every single person in my life?

"Do you want to talk about it?" Dad asked.

"No," I said, and I hated the whine in my voice.

"Maybe later?"

I nodded. Right then all I wanted was to stay curled around him and have him pet me. I felt like I was eight years old again and he was trying to explain to me why my mom wasn't home anymore. He let me stay there. It was maybe twenty or thirty minutes later before I sat up and sat away from him, my back against the wall. I wiped my eyes and my nose on my shirt. Dad winced at that, but he didn't say anything.

"Still don't want to tell me about it?" he asked.

I wanted to tell him *everything*. I wanted to tell him about what happened yesterday at the reservoir. I wanted to tell him about how I maybe liked Brandon even though I had my doubts about him. I wanted to tell him about how I hurt Willie and I made Sherri mad at me, all because of this stupid boy. I wanted to tell him about selling drugs because I wanted out of Salem so bad I could scream. I wanted to tell him that I never blamed him for my mom leaving even though I think he blamed himself; and I was glad that he'd found Bev even if he didn't end up staying with her forever.

"Not right now," I said. I let my head fall back and thump against the wall behind me.

"Okay," he said. "I hate to leave you alone. It's just that I need to take Bev home and then I have to go to my office to prepare some things for tomorrow."

"I'll be okay," I told him. "I'm going to clean up and then call Sherri. I need to apologize for some stuff."

He raised his eyebrows at that, but didn't press it. He stood up and arched his back. I heard his spine popping. Then he leaned over and kissed me on the cheek. I couldn't remember the last time he'd done that, or the last time I'd let him.

"Thanks, Dad," I said.

"We should have dinner tonight," he said. "Just the two of us."

I said that would be nice and he left. I heard him and Bev talking in the hallway. She asked if I was okay and sounded really concerned. Ugh. I guess I was going to be nice to her from now on. Nicer. Not completely nice, just nicer.

I actually pried my ass out of the bed and showered. It felt good to no longer smell myself. I decided I'd call Sherri before I got dressed. I figured that if she chewed me out or refused to talk to me, then there was no point in getting dressed since I'd just spend the day in bed thinking about how sorry everyone would be if I got run over by a truck. I hunted down my phone from where I'd thrown it and pressed the 1 key to speed-dial Sherri.

She picked up on the first ring, like she'd been waiting for my call.

"Oh, my God," she said too loud and too excited, "is this South's Queen of the Jocks calling little ol' Sherri Temple?"

"Can we not do this, Sherri?" I asked. "I'm calling to grovel and apologize."

She must have heard something in my voice because she dialed it down. "I'm not sure how nice I want to be to you right now," she said. "You were a royal dick the other night."

"That is true," I said, "so let me make it up to you."

There was a long pause. "Well, now that you mention

it, I still haven't cleaned up around here and my folks get home tonight."

I groaned and she pounced. "Hey, if that's too much to do to, you know, earn my forgiveness . . ."

"No," I said, "I'll be right over. Let me just get dressed."

"Bring something to eat," she said by way of good-bye.

I rolled my eyes. There was nowhere to get food between my house and hers, and I was on my bike. It was so typical of her to make demands that were impossible to follow through on. I smiled because it was evidence she wasn't really mad at me anymore.

I threw on some black jeans with ripped-out knees, black T, and my Dr. Martens boots. A black hoodie went into my backpack in case it got cold later, then I was on my bike and headed toward Sherri's place.

I felt like I was on high-alert since being attacked yesterday in full daylight. Also, there was that old lady who got attacked a couple of days ago. That sort of stuff never used to happen—attacks in the daytime. I checked out every shadow, rode around every object behind which a zombie could be lurking. I didn't see anything. I was still pretty jumpy by the time I got to Sherri's.

She was waiting on the front step, dressed almost identical to me, and she smiled a sort of evil smile at me when I got off my bike and said hi. I asked her what was going on and in response she just got up and opened the door to the house.

Using the word "trashed" would do a disservice to the house and the pain it had gone through. It looked like a prison riot had taken place. It reeked of spilled beer and there was a slight hint of vomit. Nearly empty bottles were everywhere, furniture had been overturned. Food had been spilled and then ground into the carpet as people walked over it all night long.

"And you decided to wait until today to start cleaning, why?" I asked.

"Well, I was pretty hungover all day yesterday," Sherri said, "and I was pretty sure you'd call groveling and offering to help me clean up."

"Well played," I said.

"I already started in the kitchen. You get to start in the bathroom." She pointed down the hall. "Cleaning stuff is already in there. Good luck."

I imagine there are cleaner bathrooms in Bangkok strip clubs. I saw that Sherri left me rubber gloves to wear. What I really wanted was one of those full-body containment suits that I'd seen CDC types wear when they care for people who may have been bitten by a zombie. I put on the gloves, took a deep breath, and got to work.

The only real break we took was to sit on the porch and drink the last beers in the fridge, and eat the chips and salsa I'd bought at the 7-Eleven that's *six blocks* out of the way. I told Sherri about what happened the day before. Meeting up with Brandon, going to the reservoir, getting attacked. I hesitated and then told her about Willie, too—ditching him and then breaking his big, stupid heart.

She eyed me for a minute and then drew on her beer.

"That's kind of a dick move, Courtney," she said. "You killed Willie's dreams the same way you offed those zombies. Sort of a hat trick of death."

"I came to you with this because I knew you'd be so understanding," I said.

"Did you want me to pat your hand and say, 'There, there, you're all forgiven'? Because that's not really my style."

"I do feel like a bitch," I said, "but I thought I was doing the right thing by telling Willie the truth. He had to know that I'm not into him."

She nodded and took another swig of beer. "While I

agree that his crush for you had to nipped in the bud, I also think you could have found a less harsh way to do it. Despite his size, I think his ego is smaller than a walnut. Minus the shell."

I just drank my beer. Which tasted bitter now. More bitter. Why was I drinking this?

"But, yeah," she went on, "ultimately you did what you had to."

"Then why do I feel so awful?" I asked.

"Because it's an awful thing, even if it had to be done. God, I'm just glad he didn't have a crush on *me*."

I killed off my beer and set the bottle beside me on the porch. "I can just picture his big round face," I said, "all teary and sad. Oh, *God*."

"Yeah, it's rough," Sherri said, and she killed her beer. She slapped my knee hard enough that I heard a sharp firecracker retort. "Let's get inside and keep cleaning before this conversation turns any more gay."

She stood up and walked back into the house.

After about four hours, we sat at Sherri's kitchen table and ate a frozen pizza she'd thrown in the oven, and we drank some off-brand cola. I was totally exhausted. I felt good, too. Happy to have helped clean up the mess I was responsible for. A couple of times throughout I apologized for all of the people who ended up coming over to the party. She waved it away. Like it didn't matter anymore or something. She took a sick interest in the fact that my dad had a girlfriend.

"Have you walked in on them doing it?" she asked.

"No," I said, "as evidenced by the fact that I have not clawed the eyes out of my head."

"I would totally try to walk in on them," she said. I shuddered. Scraping a big pile of vomit off the linoleum in the bathroom hadn't made me sick. The thought of seeing

my dad's pasty naked butt going up and down while he
gave Bev the business, however, made me queasy.

"Change of subject," I said.

"Okay," Sherri said. "Brandon What's-his-name: What
in the hell?"

I put down the piece of pizza I'd been eating; this new
topic killed off whatever bit of appetite the last one had
left standing.

"What?" I said.

"I'm sorry we have to have this Kotex-commercial-
moment conversation," Sherri said, "but really, what's going on with you, re: him."

I thought about it for a minute before saying anything.

"He's nice," I said.

Sherri sat back and groaned. "Nice? Nice is what you
say about a puppy or, or a freaking . . . I don't know.
Something really bland. 'This is a very nice dish of bland
vanilla ice cream.' "

I felt my cheeks getting hot. "I guess I should stick with
boys from our social circle who think it's the height of hi-
larity to fart at each other."

"Courtney," Sherri said very patiently, like she was my
therapist. "Think: Why would a guy outside our"—here
she raised her hands and made air quotes—" 'social circle'
want to date someone like you?" She caught the look in
my eye. "Or *me*? He's got to have an interior motive,
right?"

Ulterior, you stupid sow, I thought. I sat back and leaned
the chair away, trying to get as far from her as possible. I
crossed my arms over my chest.

"Maybe you didn't hear me mentioning that Brandon
is nice. Maybe he doesn't have an 'interior motive.' " I
picked up my glass to take a swig of soda.

She narrowed her eyes at me. "I'm sure he's just awe-
struck by your sparkling personality."

I nearly did a spit take. Soda sloshed out of the glass as I slammed it on the table.

"And is that so beyond the realm of imagination, Sherri?" I asked. She sat back, a little wide-eyed. I think she knew she'd crossed a line.

"I'm just saying, Courtney, that I don't trust anyone from his circle," she said, not looking me in the eye. "I don't want to generalize, but I've never met a jock worth a shit."

"That's probably because you never met a jock," I said. "You just sit back and silently judge them."

"And they're not doing the same thing to me?"

"Right," I said, "and instead of trying to be the bigger person, it should be a race to the bottom of the tolerance barrel."

"Hey," she nearly shouted, "I'm the suppressed minority in this situation, and I'm an acknowledged pain in the ass! I don't think anyone can really expect me to be all Nelson Mandela here."

Sherri was starting to get het up now, too. I knew I had to nip this little chat in the bud if we were going to finish out the day on speaking terms.

"I think we're going to have to agree to disagree about Brandon's motives," I said, "and you have to accept that I like him. I do reserve the right to hate him if he screws me over, though."

"If he does, I get to say 'I told you so,' but I'll also help you get revenge."

"Great," I said, "now let's change the subject."

Sherri sat forward, her elbows on the table. She picked up her glass and swirled her ice.

"Okay," she said, "new subject. I don't know how much you'll like this one, either."

I braced myself for what was coming next.

"Are you going to tell Brandon you're a drug dealer?"

I leaned forward so fast that the chair slammed onto the linoleum—a muted gunshot sound.

"Jesus Christ, Sherri," I said, "I *am not* a drug dealer."

She didn't say anything in return. She stared at me. Silent. Judging.

"Saying I'm a drug dealer makes me sound like freaking Omar from *The Wire* or something," I said. "I sell drugs sometimes because I'm trying to get money for college." I winced because it sounded like a piss-poor excuse even to me.

"Right," said Sherri. "So, when are you going to tell Brandon that you *sell drugs*? *Sometimes*."

"I don't see why I *should* tell him."

"Because you like him," Sherri said, "and you don't want to start a relationship based on filthy lies, and because he'll start to ask questions eventually—I'm assuming he's not stupid if you like him."

I started to say something and she cut me off.

"Also, if you don't tell him, I will."

"What the hell are you talking about?" I asked. "Why would you do that?"

She leaned back in her chair and smiled at me.

"Because I hate that you do it," she said, "and I'll do whatever I have to to make you stop. Short of telling the cops and getting you thrown in jail."

"Thanks for nothing."

"You're welcome."

"You realize I hate you right now, right?" I asked.

"Sure."

I sat there seething. What right did she have to screw with my life like that? I stared straight ahead. That meant looking at her and her smug, smiling face. I scooted back and got up from the table. I walked away through the house and out onto the front steps. I sat down and decided to have a nice, long pout.

After a few minutes, Sherri came out, too. She sat down and handed me a refilled glass of cheap-ass soda.

"Thanks," I said.

"Courtney," she said, "I like you. I like you enough to risk being sincere with you. What you're doing is wrong, really, really wrong.

"You're selling a drug made out of zombie brains. It's a drug that makes people *act* like zombies. Jesus, some people think that using it too much can *turn you into* a zombie. How are you okay with that?"

"I just never think about it," I said. I looked off down the street. I couldn't stand to look at her right now. There's no way I could admit to her that I think about it a lot. I hate the thought of helping people throw their lives away. If I didn't want to improve my own life so badly, I'd never even consider it. "I never sell to people we know."

"So, you're not selling to people we know," Sherri said. "You're still messing up somebody's life."

I looked at her then, and I tried to hold back the tears I could feel welling up in my eyes.

"I just want to get out of this place so damned bad," I said. "Sometimes I think there isn't anything I wouldn't do to get out."

Sherri nodded. "I get that. I do. And I get that you have this weird quest to clean up your mom's past mistakes. Whatever. If you're so willing to get out of Dodge, then you must be willing to work at something legit to earn the money."

I didn't say anything. It felt like there was nothing to say.

"I'll stop trying to convince you," Sherri said, "but what I said about telling Brandon still stands."

When I didn't answer, she stood and held her hand out to me.

"C'mon," she said, "I have about a million dollars in empties to take back to the store. I'll let you do the glass bottles. I know how much you like the sound of them breaking."

I took her hand and let her pull me up. It meant a lot to me that she was trying to make me feel a little better. Even if she was being a jerk otherwise.

After we were done at the store, we went back to Sherri's. I climbed on my bike and rode home. My dad was there. He told me he'd ordered a pizza and I feigned enthusiasm. You can't have too much pizza, right?

I worried he was going to ask me about my spazzing earlier that day. All he did was ask if I was okay. I told him I was on the way there and he seemed satisfied. We just sat and watched TV and ate our pizza. Despite it being time I spent with my dad, I did have a good time.

I guess weirder things have happened.

CHAPTER ELEVEN
Too Much Eyeliner

I sat on the front porch and looked at my watch again. 8:30. I'd been sitting there for twenty minutes already, waiting for Willie to come get me. He was never late, and if he couldn't get me, he always called. Great. He must have been really pissed at me.

I took out my phone and dialed his house. Again. No answer. I didn't expect one, really. I'd already called twice before and not gotten ahold of anyone. Which was sort of weird when I thought about it. His mom didn't have to leave the house until it was time to take Julie to school. I was sure she'd pick up just for the chance to berate whoever was on the other end of the line.

I hung up and dialed Sherri. She answered on the first ring.

"Am I sitting here waiting for Willie to come pick me up because of you?" she demanded.

"Good morning," I said full of false chipperness. "So he didn't pick you up, either, huh?"

"Nope," she said. "Any chance your dad can give us a ride? We've already missed the bus."

"He's left already," I said. "What about borrowing the Beater?"

"That'll mean speaking to my dad," she said, "and more

than likely having to promise to perform some sort of chore."

"If that's the case, I'll help with whatever it is."

"You'd better," she said. "Let me go talk to him." She said she'd call if she couldn't get the Beater, what we called her parents' spare BMW. Usually parents would never give their kid the keys to such a car, especially an avowed delinquent like Sherri. It was because the car was about a million years old and looked like the only thing holding it together was Bondo, which is why they felt okay about letting Sherri behind the wheel.

While I waited for Sherri to show up, I basically sat there and fretted. I couldn't believe that Willie was so mad that he'd just not come get us *and* not call. He'd been picking us up ever since he could drive—most of last year and all of this one. Those early morning drives in together were the closest thing to a school tradition we had between the three of us. The thought that I'd messed that up with my carelessness made my stomach sour. Was sixteen too young to develop an ulcer?

Sherri saved me from my thoughts by pulling up to the curb and laying on the horn even though she could see me sitting there waiting for her. I hurried as fast as I could and got in the car so she'd stop. She screeched the tires as she pulled away.

We didn't talk much. I didn't feel like it and I think Sherri was tired of chastising me about how I'd treated Willie. Lucky me.

"Want the radio?" Sherri asked. I told her sure. The Beater doesn't have a CD, just an old cassette player. As Sherri and I would not lower ourselves to buy a cassette, we were stuck with the radio. Which was stuck on NPR. God.

The voices droned on in the background, barely audi-

ble over the sound of the engine laboring to pull us along
on perfectly level ground. It was kind of hypnotic. The
sound of the engine and the voices just on the edge of
hearing. I leaned my head against the door and closed my
eyes. I thought I'd get a few Zs before we got to school.

I was nodding off when I heard something on the radio
that jerked me awake. I sat up suddenly and startled Sherri.
The car swerved as she reacted.

"What the hell, Courtney?"

"Shut up a minute," I said, and reached over to crank up
the radio. Normally telling her to shut up and touching
the radio are two big no-nos. She must have heard something in my voice that made her keep quiet.

The news guy's voice came in mid-story.

". . . Police suspect the fire to have been deliberately
set. Professor Keller's belief that the undead can be com-
municated with had sparked controversy. He has received
more than a dozen death threats in the past several weeks
following an appearance on a late-night talk show. Four
undead humans were destroyed in the attack, which left
Professor Keller in critical but stable condition. No other
living humans were harmed in the fire. The FBI is currently following up on several leads.

"In international news . . ."

I switched off the radio and sat back in the seat. I let out
a breath I hadn't realized I'd been holding.

"Is that the guy you saw on that show?" Sherri asked.
"Willie told me you told him."

"Yeah," I said.

"The zombie-whisperer, right?"

"That's him," I said.

"People suck, dude," she said, but without a lot of feeling. I agreed with her.

I wasn't sure why news of this guy's being attacked affected me. I felt really sad, though. God, I'd barely thought about the guy since I'd talked to Willie the day after I saw the show. I'd meant to Google him, maybe even write him an e-mail. I just hadn't gotten around to it. I mean, I thought his idea was interesting. I just couldn't even decide if I thought he was crazy or not.

"You okay over there?" Sherri asked.

"I'm fine."

"It's not like you knew the guy, Courtney. He's not even dead."

"I said, 'I'm fine,' " I said.

"Yes," she said, "everyone who's fine says so in a monotone." But she let it drop after that and we got to school just a few minutes later. Thankfully, she couldn't talk as she navigated security to get into the parking lot. After she parked, we climbed out of the car and walked toward the building. We had to split up before reaching the doors.

"I have Willie in pre-Algebra," she said. "I'll kick him in the ass for the both of us."

"Go easy on him," I told her. "I think he had a rough weekend."

"If I went easy on him," she said, "he'd think that *I* didn't love him, too!" She ran away before I could take a swing at her. I had to admit it did make me smile despite myself.

I was distracted during my homeroom and AP English class, still worried about Willie. As the day went on, I thought about him less and less. Being able to concentrate on school despite whatever crap was going on in my life was sort of a survival technique.

I didn't see Sherri again until lunch, and I really expected Willie to be with her. When he wasn't, I again felt a hot rock in the pit of my stomach. As she approached, Sherri shook her head.

"He was a no-show in PA," she said. "I even tried to

call him while Saunders was explaining radical equations. No answer."

"Dammit," I said, "it's not like him to go all silent-treat-ment-y."

She sat and opened up her lunch bag. She started to pull Tupperware dishes full of weird-looking food out and set it on the table. Sherri's mom is full-blood Hungarian and a lot of her leftovers look like science experiments gone horribly awry.

"I think it's a good sign," Sherri said as she tucked into something blood red and stringy. "I think it's a sign that he's growing a backbone."

"What the hell are you talking about?"

"Of course, we don't want him to get too uppity," she said around a mouthful of food. "We'll have to make sure he knows his place in our little hierarchy."

I was about to accuse her of being mentally deficient when a voice spoke up behind us.

"Can I join you?"

We both turned—Sherri with a forkful of food halfway to her mouth. Brandon stood there looking at us expec-tantly. I wondered what horror was about to pop out of Sherri's mouth. She placed the fork back in its plastic re-ceptacle and she smiled. I winced.

"Brandon," she said, "it would be lovely if you would join us."

Oh, dear God, I thought, *please let me die of something really fast right this instant.*

It was further proof that there was no God when I lived to see Brandon plant himself on the bench opposite us.

For several moments, we all just sort of stared at one an-other. Maybe this situation was so awkward we'd all be rendered speechless. It was a scene of biblical awfulness, so maybe God stepped in and, in a reverse Tower-of-Babel sort of thing, he'd taken away our ability to speak.

"You're Sherri, right?" Brandon asked, dashing my hopes. "I'm Brandon. I didn't get a chance to meet you Friday night. I guess I owe you an apology."

Sherri looked at me before turning to Brandon and giving him a toothy smile. "And why's that, Brandon?" she asked.

"Well, it's because of me that all of those people showed up," he said. He really did look sorry. I looked over at Sherri to see if she was buying it. She was still pulling her I-don't-know-what-you're-talking-about act. "I just hope it wasn't too much of a problem for you to have them there," Brandon said.

"Well, it *was* unexpected, Brandon," she said, "but, you know, no harm meant, right?"

"God, no," Brandon said.

"Then don't sweat it," she said.

I wouldn't have been surprised if she'd laid into him, made him storm away from the table with her berating. I'd seen it happen before. Honestly, the nice act made me even more uneasy.

"I'm so glad you see it that way," Brandon said.

Sherri just nodded and took a big bite out of her whatever. Brandon turned his smile on me.

"How are you doing?" he asked. "Better since Saturday?"

"I'm fine," I said more quietly than I'd meant.

"That's good; you seemed pretty shaken up," he said, and then looked to Sherri. "Did Courtney tell you about Saturday?" he asked her.

"Oh, I know all about Saturday," Sherri said, and something about her tone caught Brandon's attention. He paused a moment before going on.

"Um, yeah," he said. "It was crazy. Courtney handled herself like a champ."

I felt myself blush. Which was stupid. I knew I'd handled myself well. Why would Brandon's saying so matter?

"Mind if I change the subject?" Sherri asked.

"No, of course not," Brandon said.

Sherri nodded and frowned a little bit, like she was considering something important.

"Let me ask you, Brandon," she said. "What do you think about drugs?"

I was only barely able to keep myself from gasping. That's why she was being nice to Brandon. It wasn't him she wanted to punish, it was *me*!

Brandon looked at me uncertainly and then back to Sherri. He gave her a nervous grin.

"Drugs?" he asked.

Sherri nodded, encouraging him. "Yeah, you know what drugs are."

"Yeah, sure I do," he said. "I guess I've smoked pot a couple of times. It's not a habit or anything." He added that last bit faster than he needed to and it made me wonder. Whatever.

"Sure, sure," she said, nodding sagely. "But what about other drugs, harder drugs? Narcotics?"

"What's this about?" Brandon asked.

"It's nothing," I said, and shot Sherri a glare that she chose to ignore.

"It's just something that Courtney and I were talking about earlier," she said. Brandon shot me another look. "So what do you think about harder drugs?"

"I don't know," he said, "I . . . I guess they're not for me . . . I don't know? They can mess people up pretty bad."

"They can mess people up pretty bad," Sherri said. She said it in a tone of voice like the thought had never occurred to her. "They can. Can't they, Courtney?"

"Not as bad as some other things," I hissed at her.

"And what about people who sell drugs, Brandon, you know, *drug dealers*?"

Again he looked between the two of us. I'm sure he wondered what the hell was going on.

"I suppose they'd be responsible for anyone that got hurt doing drugs," he said slowly.

Sherri nodded again, another revelation! She turned to me. "That makes sense, doesn't it, Courtney?"

"Sure," I said, and I tried to hate her to death.

Sherri stood up and gathered her things.

"I should go away," she said. "Brandon, it was really swell getting to know you better. I hope we can talk more later. Toodles, Courtney."

I didn't say anything, just glared at her back as she walked away. When I turned back to Brandon, he looked at me funny.

"Don't mind her," I said. "She has deep emotional flaws."

Brandon gave me a courtesy laugh. "Yeah, that was my strangest conversation in a long while. I guess I'm just glad she's not mad at me."

"Oh, she's not mad at *you*," I said.

"I guess you're today's lucky winner," he said.

"Oh, yeah."

"How come?"

I thought about that for a bit, wondering if this was when I should have my Oprah moment with him. I decided it wasn't.

"Any number of reasons," I said.

"Sure," he said doubtfully.

We sat there for a minute just sort of staring at each other. I started to eat my sandwich again. No reason the awkward tension should keep me from eating. I might need something in my stomach to throw up if things got worse.

"I actually wanted to check in with you about how you're doing," Brandon said, "after, you know, Saturday."

"Oh, I know," I said, "and I'm okay."

"Yeah?"

"Yeah," I said, "I was more upset about the next day."

"What did I do yesterday?" Brandon asked.

"Paranoid much?" I asked. "I wasn't upset at you, I was upset with myself. Still *am* upset, really. I let down one of my friends and I think he's still mad at me."

"He?" Brandon asked too quickly. He must have thought I was discussing some potential competition.

"Yeah," I said, "my friend Willie."

"Is he the big guy with the hair?"

"That about sums him up," I said.

"So, is he . . . ?"

"He's just a friend, Brandon," I said, "or at least I hope he still is. I need to talk to him. He's not answering when I call his house."

"That's rough," Brandon said, and I parsed his response to see if he was being sarcastic or insincere. The amount of genuineness in his reply surprised me.

After a minute, Brandon rapped his knuckles against the table. I looked up at him.

"We should do something, go get some burgers or something, and invite him along," Brandon said. "You know, make it up to him and make him feel included."

"I think he probably needs some alone time with me," I said, "but I appreciate you thinking of him." And I meant it.

"Okay," he said. He looked at his watch and stood up. "I guess we should be getting to class. Can I walk you?"

"Um, yeah," I said. No boy in the history of History had ever asked to walk me to class. Was he going to ask to carry my books? Lay his coat over any puddles we came across? Hunt and gather something for me?

We walked across the back field and into the school. The crowds already thinned out as the beginning of class approached. More than one head turned as people saw Brandon and me walk down the hall together. Was I about to become an item of high school gossip? We could be a blind item in the school's paper: *Item: What first-string quarterback was seen canoodling in the halls with a certain loser female who may or may not be a lesbian?*

"You have really pretty eyes," Brandon said, and I stopped dead in my tracks. "But you know what would bring them out even more? If you toned down on the . . ." he made circular motions around his own eyes ". . . black eye makeup stuff."

"My eyeliner?" I said.

"Yeah, your eyeliner."

"Gee, thanks for the advice, Mr. Blackwell," I said.

"I don't know who that is," Brandon said, "but it looks like you want to hide how nice your eyes are or something."

"That is the shittiest delivery of a compliment I've ever heard, Brandon," I said.

"What?" He looked seriously in the dark.

"Nothing," I said. "It's too early to be complimenting me anyway."

"What does that mean?" he asked. " 'Too early for compliments'?"

"It means I don't know you well enough for that yet," I said, "and it makes me suspicious that you're throwing around I-like-your-eyes comments already."

"Suspicious?"

"Yes," I said. I noticed again that people were watching us, which annoyed the hell out of me. I pitched my voice lower when I spoke. "And I have to tell you, Brandon, that I can't believe I have to bring this up to you. It's like you weren't socialized in the American co-educational system or something."

"I didn't mean to make you suspicious," he said, desperate, "I just, you know, like you and wanted to say something nice. And see if you liked me, too."

"I like you fine," I said, and then paused. "Or I will like you. I am on the road to liking you. Just take it down a notch, okay?"

Now it was Brandon's turn to be frustrated. "Maybe there's a website you can point me to that has a timeline of appropriate behavior, Courtney."

The class bell rang and the last few stragglers made their way to class.

"Listen," I said, "we don't have time for an Oprah-style talk right now. Don't worry; you're doing fine, okay?"

"Okay," he said, doubtful, still a little pissed.

"Let's just go to class and we'll talk later," I said.

He nodded and we walked on.

I couldn't believe this was happening. Not only did a boy outside my social genus and species like me, now I was having to coach him about how to behave in the situation. I headed toward AP Chemistry.

As we walked past the school's trophy case, I caught a look at myself and paused for a second. I found myself wondering if I did wear too much eyeliner.

Goddammit.

CHAPTER TWELVE
Their Slate of Sins

It's always weird to be called into the office from class. There are two ways it can happen. One is the intercom. You'll be sitting there taking notes or writing on the board and suddenly there's a loud hiss of static and then the voice of God, or Mrs. Schoen, the school's secretary, comes on and announces that you're wanted in the office. Everyone else in class snickers and points and makes "oooh" sounds. It's all very public and somewhat humiliating. I guess it's better than the alternative.

The alternative is when Mrs. Schoen quietly enters your class with a folded piece of paper in her little hands. A hush spreads across the room as people catch sight of her and she approaches the teacher and hands them the slip. The teacher opens it and reads and there's always this moment before the teacher announces whose name is on the slip and everyone gets to sit and silently assess their slate of sins. Have I done anything office-visit worthy; is it me? It's all very *Hunger Games* as we sit and wonder if we'll be this year's tribute . . . No one laughs or whispers to the person sitting next to them. Everyone watches in silence as the condemned gathers his things and skulks out of the room followed closely by that five-foot-tall-in-heels executioner, Mrs. Schoen.

It's even worse when you really have been involved in some major-league bad shit. You know, like when you sell drugs in your off-hours. That's what happened as I sat in AP Chem class (AP Biology would come next year), writing a short essay about ionic equilibria in aqueous solutions and the door to the room opened. There was Mrs. Schoen. She looked a little sad, resigned to serve as the principal's henchman. She handed Mrs. Ellis the slip. My heart began to drum. I thought back to Friday and my run-in with Astrid. Had she said something to campus security because I'd refused to sell her any Z? That vindictive bitch.

I told myself to calm down, odds were that the note was for someone else. I was really careful. I never sold on campus. Heck, I'd never even sold to a fellow student out at the Bully Burger as far as I could tell.

I knew I was in the clear.

"Courtney," Mrs. Ellis said as she looked up from the note. "Would you go with Mrs. Schoen to the office, please?"

I kept my gaze straight ahead as I put my books and pen in my bag. My heart beat so loud in my ears, I wondered if the others heard it. I stood and approached the secretary. She gave me a sad half-smile and opened the door for me. We stepped out into the hall.

I kept my head down and I watched my feet making their way across the floor. Beside me, I saw Mrs. Schoen's tiny steps racing to keep up with me. I chanced a look up at her.

"Do you know what Mrs. Ibrahim wants with me?"

She gave me another sad smile. "Sorry, hon, I don't."

I went back to looking at my shoes.

I reviewed every move I'd made in the last few days. Who had I sold to? Had I revealed anything when I talked to Astrid? Maybe my dad found my stash of money . . . I felt like I was going to be sick.

When we got into the office, I finally tore my gaze away from my shoes and looked through Mrs. Ibrahim's opened door and I saw a Salem city policeman in there with her. My head swam.

"Are you okay?" Mrs. Schoen asked.

Of course I wasn't. Even as barely socialized as I am, I knew I couldn't say that. "I'm fine," I said. It was becoming my personal mantra.

She nodded like she understood. "Well, go ahead on in." She motioned me toward the door to the office. Almost against my will, I shuffled in that direction.

Mrs. Ibrahim motioned for me to sit down as soon as I entered. The cop, who had been standing behind her desk, walked around and closed the door as I slumped into the chair. He walked back and stood with his arms crossed over his chest. He held a manila envelope in one hand. I stole quick glances at him. Tall and beefy, with dark hair that stood up like a brush, he also had one of those ridiculous cop molestaches. Is it a rule that you have to have one before you join the force? Do women officers and those with a testosterone deficiency get waivers? He met my gaze and I went back to staring at the floor.

I needed to think of something to say when they confronted me about the drugs. Maybe I could claim I didn't know that Vitamin Z was illegal? Would they buy that?

"Courtney," Mrs. Ibrahim said, and paused. I caught my breath and looked up at her. She looked so sad. She must have been so disappointed in me. "This is Officer Rey, Courtney, and he needs to speak to you."

They shared a look. Oh, man, he looked really unhappy, too. I would've thought he'd be super-psyched to bust a teenage drug dealer, like he'd get a bonus that month or something.

He cleared his throat. "Hi, Courtney," he said. I was surprised by how high his voice was. "Were you friends with William Luunder?"

I sat up straight. This wasn't about me? This was about . . . ?

"Do you mean Willie?"

He looked at whatever he had in the folder and frowned, then he made a note with the pen from his breast pocket.

"We didn't know he had also been called Willie, but yes, that's him."

I tried to conceal my sigh as I sat back in the chair. This wasn't about me and my second job. This was about Willie. What had Willie done to get himself in trouble?

"Wait a minute," I said as things began to sink in. "Did you say, 'were you'?"

Mrs. Ibrahim blanched and coughed. The cop frowned even more deeply.

"That's right," he said. "I'm really sorry to tell you this, Courtney. William, Willie, died in a zombie attack sometime last night."

"That can't be right," I said. "I talked to him just yesterday morning." I felt like I couldn't draw a deep enough breath.

"You talked to him this morning?" Rey asked. "Monday morning?"

"No," I said, "yesterday. Sunday."

He exchanged a glance with the principal. Then he turned back and cleared his throat again.

"Right," he said, "and the incident I'm describing happened sometime last night. Or early this morning.

"You said you spoke with him yesterday?"

I was too busy concentrating on the word "incident." I sometimes made fun of Willie, but he wasn't dumb enough to get caught up in some damned *incident.* Officer Rey had to ask me again.

"Uh, yeah," I answered. "I talked to him yesterday around, like, nine in the morning."

"Did he seem depressed to you?"

That stopped me short. Depressed? Yeah, he was depressed as hell. But I didn't get what him feeling mopey had to do with anything. I asked why that was important.

"We have reason to believe that William's death was a suicide."

I actually felt my mouth fall open. That made no sense whatsoever. It just couldn't be true. I tried to say that, and my voice refused to work.

"A murder-suicide, actually," Officer Rey said. "His mother and father also died in the attack."

My head swam. I dropped my books and I think I started to slump forward because the next thing I knew, the cop was kneeling right next to me and Mrs. Ibrahim stood behind her desk.

"Should I get the school nurse?" she asked Rey.

"I think she'll be okay," he told her, and I wondered if that was the truth. I felt tears welling up in my eyes and there was no way I wanted to cry in front of these two. Unfortunately, I didn't think I had a choice.

"That's so crazy," I said through a constricted throat. "Why would you even think that? Willie would never hurt himself like that. Why are you telling me like this?" The last bit came out in a whine. It felt so unfair. They were torturing me for no reason. Were they going to do this to all of Willie's friends?

"Courtney, we're almost positive it was suicide," Rey

said. In response to my hysteria, he seemed to be growing more calm. God, I wanted to smash him in the face for being so collected. "He left a note. The reason we have you in here," he went on, "is because the note is addressed to you."

I squeezed my eyes shut against the tears and shook my head back and forth. I started to chant, "No, no, no," but I knew it must be true. Willie somehow killed himself and his parents and he got some zombies to do it. I stopped as something occurred to me. My sudden stillness startled Officer Rey.

"What about his sister?"

"She's fine, Courtney," he said, calm again. "Willie made sure that she was safe."

The thought of Julie all alone in the world really opened the floodgates. I started to openly sob. Huge gasping breaths tore through me. I heard Officer Rey ask for the nurse then, and soon she was there trying to give me a sedative. Normally the school doesn't hand out so much as an aspirin, so they must have been really freaked out.

I started to feel more calm. No, that's not right. There was a part of me that still screamed inside. I just felt more distant from it. Like I could watch that part of me and it didn't affect me personally. If that makes sense.

As I got my shit together, Officer Rey sat in a chair next to me and Mrs. Ibrahim sat back down.

"Courtney," Rey went on, "if you feel up to it, I need you to tell us what you two talked about. It might have some bearing on what happened."

Through the fog of whatever it was they gave me, I told them about having plans with Willie and blowing him off accidentally. I told them about hanging with Brandon and his friends and calling Willie on Sunday and the talk we had. When I got to the part about Willie's mom harping on about the fish, Officer Rey got a weird look on his face, but he didn't say anything.

I told them everything that happened Saturday through Sunday morning. I even told them about all of us drinking up at Brandon's dad's cabin and the zombie attack.

When I finished talking, the two adults were silent. I don't know what they thought. The cop probably wanted to fit all this new information into his theory about the *incident*. I bet Mrs. Ibrahim wondered if she should pursue my admission that we'd been drinking illegally. Whatever. It didn't matter to me just then.

"The part about the fish makes sense." Rey scribbled into a little reporter's notebook.

It took a lot of concentration to turn my head and look at him.

"What?" I asked.

"We think that William attracted the zombies into his home somehow," Rey said. "The smell of rotten fish might have done it."

So now zombies were like goddamned raccoons? This situation was reaching a level of absurdity that threatened to make me puke. What next? The shufflers also dug up his yard and knocked over the trash cans? I needed to get out of that room.

"Do you think, based on your conversation, that William was despondent enough to kill himself?"

I didn't have to think it; it was obvious he was since he went ahead and killed himself! I didn't say that. Instead, my foggy mind clutched at something the officer said earlier.

"You said there was a note?"

"Um, yes."

"I want to read it," I said. Rey exchanged a look with Mrs. Ibrahim.

"I don't know," Rey said.

Mrs. Ibrahim cleared her throat. "He wrote it to her," she said, "she should be able to read it."

Rey nodded and rooted around through the notes in his file. He handed me a photocopy of a piece of ruled notebook paper, like Willie had been writing a school report instead of a suicide note.

Courtney,

I don't want you to think that what I'm going to do is because of you, okay? And don't be too mad at me. It's just hard, you know? Too hard. I look around me and I don't see a way out of all of this shit.

I feel stupid and ugly and like I'll never get out of this town. Not like you. The worst part is my mom is always reminding me about this stuff so it's not even like I could forget, even though I try. I think about her and how she treats me and Julie and my dad and I just feel crazy. Especially Julie. She's the best thing in this ugly world. She's like sunshine when everything else is dark. And mom is trying her best to ecstingwish that light, you know?

Like I said don't blame yourself. I've been thinking about this for a long time. I couldn't do it myself, meaning I couldn't pull the trigger or whatever, but I think I know a way. I saw some shufflers out near Parker's field across the street. I might be able to get them over here. Over—

I was thinking about what we talked about the other day. About that doctor guy who wants to talk to the zombies. Maybe if I get these ones inside, I'll try and talk to them before they do there thing. Or maybe, if I come back as a zombie, then you could talk to me. It would be nice to talk to you one more time, Courtney.

*I love you, you know. I should of said that to you
before now.*

Willie

I read through the note a couple of times. He said not
to blame myself. Come on, how could I not? And don't
be angry? I was furious! What the hell was he thinking? If
he had talked to me again, we could have figured something out. Now we'd never have the chance to do that, to
talk, to figure stuff out.

Tears streamed down my face. The pill they gave me
earlier was keeping me from flipping out, but it couldn't
keep back all of what I felt. Through all of the frustration,
anger, and sorrow, what I felt was a gaping hollow space
where Willie used to be. Big, dumb Willie. Willie who was
always there without me having to think about it. Well,
that just wasn't true anymore.

"I think that's enough, don't you, Officer Rey?" Mrs.
Ibrahim looked like she was crying, too, and somehow
that helped. I wanted the whole world to feel as bad as me
right then.

"Of course," he said, and he stood up. After fumbling
through his pockets for a second, he handed me a hankie.
Jesus. Him being nice to me just made me cry even
harder.

"Will you be okay?" he asked. I didn't answer.

"We have a grief counselor on staff," the principal
said. I wasn't sure if she was talking to him or to me.
"For now we're going to take you to the nurse's office,
Courtney. We'll call your father to come and take you
home."

The nurse came in again and I let her lead me to her office. I lay down on the cot and she put a thin, scratchy
blanket over me. She turned off the lights and I drifted in

and out of sleep for a while. I came to at one point and my dad sat on the bed beside me, stroking my hair. We didn't say anything for a long time.

He told me he had to talk to the principal before we could leave, and he'd be back soon to take me home.

Even worse than finding out one of my best friends killed himself and thinking I was partly to blame was that kids were between classes when I emerged from the nurse's office. I walked out on my dad's arm and every face turned to watch us as we passed. I wasn't sure how long I was in the office. It must have been more than an hour. Word of what happened started to spread through the school. I knew from experience what I looked like after a crying jag, what with me wearing too much eyeliner and all.

Heads came together and whispers were exchanged. Eyes followed us. For someone who made it their mission to pass through their school years invisible, it was pretty traumatizing.

My dad must have picked up on my anxiety. He snaked his arm from me and wrapped it around my shoulders instead. He squeezed me tight.

We finally emerged into the bright sunlight outside. There were fewer kids out there, which made it a bit easier. Dad poured me into our car and he pulled through the gates.

We drove on in silence for a while, Dad trying to give me my space. He cleared his throat after a bit.

"Your principal says you can take a few days off, if you'd like." He gave me a weak smile. "The whole week, if you want."

I didn't respond, just sat and stared out the window at the passing houses.

"We'll get home and we can do whatever you'd like," he said. "Rent a movie or get dinner from Muchas Gracias. Or you can just rest if that's what you want."

Without turning, I said, "I might want to just rest."

"Sure, sure. I have more sedatives at home if you need them. Whatever you need to make you feel better, okay, sweetie?"

I nodded, still looking out the window. I didn't know how to tell him that I felt like I'd never feel better again.

CHAPTER THIRTEEN
Back in the Land of the Living

The next few days passed by in a fog. I took Dad up on his offer to feed me pills to sleep. I sort of hate taking drugs of any kind, even prescriptions—which is one reason I've never been tempted to try any of the product I sell. The other reason, of course, is because it's a drug made out of *zombie brains*. I guess I just felt being asleep was better than being awake right then. Dad came into my room periodically to check on me and tell me if people called or something. He'd arranged for my homework to be gathered. More than once, he stopped in to say that Brandon or Sherri had called. I barely roused myself out of my stupor of self-pity to acknowledge what he told me. I didn't really care that they, especially Sherri, were trying to deal with all of this, too. It was pretty pathetic. Put me in a wedding dress and I could have played Emily Grierson in a high school adaptation of *A Rose for Emily*.

I kept waking up from bad dreams that I didn't remember. I was just left with the feeling like I needed a shower. Which I didn't take. I rolled over and went back to sleep. When I finally got up from the bed, burning the sheets would be a priority.

Extracting myself from the bed finally happened on Thursday night. More than seventy-two hours after escaping into my room. I sat up and placed my feet on the rug next to my bed. After so long in bed, my whole body felt raw—even the bottoms of my feet resting on the long shag.

I reached for my phone to see what messages and texts I'd missed. A bunch from Sherri and Brandon, a couple from the school—probably the grief counselor—and one text from a number I didn't recognize right away. I thumbed the message to life: *Call Me,* it said.

Call me? Who the . . . ? And then it hit me. It didn't come up in my caller ID because I have strict instructions not to store it. It was from Buddha, the guy who sold me Vitamin Z. If Sherri thinks I'm a drug dealer, it's just because she hasn't met Buddha, who is the real deal. He'd sent the message on Wednesday during the day. He probably wondered why I hadn't called back. I should have already gone back to him for some new product. I needed to make time to call him tonight.

First things first, though; time to let Dad know I was still among the living.

He and Beverly snuggled on the couch. Her legs draped across his and he rubbed them idly. I felt so grateful for the way Dad had been treating me that I couldn't even muster the reserves to feel gross about their PDA.

Personal displays of affection aside, Dad started to get up when I came into the room. I told him not to. I sat in a chair next to the couch. I didn't want the lovebirds to have to move.

"How are you, hon?" Bev asked.

"I'm fine, thanks."

"Are you?" Dad asked. He looked skeptical.

I shrugged. What was I supposed to say?

"I'm okay, I think."

Dad accepted this and said that they'd ordered takeout from Kim Huong's. They were going to leave in a few minutes to go and get it. He'd ordered plenty for me. If I didn't want that, there were three days of leftovers in the fridge. Dad had kept making or ordering enough for me at every meal, hoping that I'd eventually join them. I told him Vietnamese would be great. I was starved like you wouldn't believe. I'd pretty much only had water for the three days I was in bed.

Everyone's attention drifted to the TV. They watched some lame sit-com. *Undead and in Love* or something equally horrid. The makeup on the star of the show looked completely fake. I noticed my dad was looking at me.

"Do you think you'll wait until Monday to go back to school?"

I thought about it. "I'll go back to school tomorrow."

"Only if you think you're ready." He raised his eyebrow at me. He probably thought he looked like Mr. Spock when he did it. He actually looked like he had an uncontrollable facial tic.

"I'm ready," I said, "and if I'm not, I can always come home, right?"

"Of course."

"Besides," I said, "all I need is to fall even further behind."

I thought about the stack of homework on the desk in my room. I'd start in on it tonight and stay in all weekend if I had to to get it done. I couldn't fall too far behind. If I screwed up my grades, I wouldn't get accepted to an out-of-state school no matter how much money I had.

And then, without meaning to, I was thinking about Willie. Tomorrow, Friday, he would have had Auto Shop, his favorite. He'd been so good at those vocational classes. Even if he hadn't been too bright, he'd always been really good with his hands. He could have made his way in life using the skills he picked up. At least that's what I always suspected. Now I'd never find out if I was right because he was gone. Gone because I'd blown him off and hurt his feelings. I didn't care what he said in his stupid note, I knew that on some level I was responsible. I felt tears welling up in my eyes.

"Where'd you go?" my dad asked. He and Bev were looking at me with real concern.

"I just started thinking about . . ."

My dad took up when I trailed off. "It's normal to think about the dead when you least expect it," Dad said. "The one thing you can't do is to let yourself feel guilty—"

"For surviving, yeah I know," I said.

"Well, it's true."

What about feeling guilty because you think you're responsible for the person's death?

"Hey, shouldn't you guys go get the food?" I asked. "I'm starving."

"Okay," Dad said. "Want to come with?"

I said I didn't and they got up and headed for the door. Bev stopped and looked at me, her eyes wet.

"Are you sure you're gonna be okay, Courtney?"

I resisted the urge to be flip and just said I would. Then I shooed them out the door. They wouldn't be gone long and I wanted to call Buddha before they returned.

Buddha's deep voice sounded genuinely happy when I called.

"Courtney, I thought I was never going to hear from you again."

"Things here have been pretty crazy, Buddha," I said. "Crazy and shitty."

"I hope you're okay."

"A friend of mine killed himself," I said, and a lump formed in my throat.

"I'm sorry to hear that," he said. "I don't want to keep you long, and I'm really sorry to bother you with business. I just thought I would have seen you again by now."

"Sure," I said, "I don't know if I can come see you till Saturday."

"Saturday would be fine," he said, and then something crept into his voice that I couldn't quite place, but that I didn't like. "That is, if you still want to come and see me . . ."

"I have to, Buddha," I said, trying to sound reassuring. "I need to give you some money and pick up some more . . . stuff from you."

"Well, then I'll be expecting you Saturday," he said, "and I am sorry to hear about your friend. Take care, Courtney."

"You, too, dude," I said. He hung up.

What did he mean by, "if I wanted to come see him"? Did he think I was considering running out on what I owed him? He'd never threatened me or anything, but even I knew it would be a bad idea to cross a drug dealer. Zombies aren't the only thing in the world that can kill you.

Dad and Bev came home and I ate with them as we watched TV. They tried to talk to me a little. I was so busy cramming cabbage rolls into my face I couldn't answer and they gave up after a while. My belly swelled as I ate and ate and ate. I looked like a teen mom by the time I was done—the memory of the preggo shuffler started to well up in my mind, but I stifled it. I had a hard time waddling down the hall to my bedroom.

The bed groaned under me as I sat on it, and then laid on my back with my knees up. I had to call Sherri and let her know I was back. When I was done, I might call Brandon. Sherri answered on the first ring.

"Where the hell have you been?"

"Asleep mostly," I said.

"Jesus, I wish I could say the same thing."

"Yeah, sorry, I sort of checked out there."

I could tell she was being delicate with me because she didn't curse me out or accuse me of being a bitch. She just wanted to know what had happened in the office with the cop and what I knew about Willie.

"I thought you'd been arrested until the rumors about Willie started going around," she said.

I told her everything that happened in the office, everything that Officer Rey told me, and about the note. When I was done, Sherri was silent on the other end.

"That stupid asshole," she said finally. "God, what was he thinking? And what was up with that snatch of a mom?" I could tell she was being careful not to blame me. That was okay because I was blaming myself. I said so.

"Bull," she said. "No matter how much he liked you, that's no reason to go and off himself. That's the kind of crap that happens in a, I don't know, a freaking Shakespeare play. No, Courtney, you aren't allowed to take the blame for this one."

I was touched. I really thought she might agree with me once I said I felt guilty. She must have really thought it wasn't my fault. She knew the situation better than anyone. If she didn't blame me, maybe I could let myself off the hook a little bit about it.

She kept going off about how much she missed him and how mad she was at him for killing himself. It just didn't make sense to her. Through it all, I picked up that she was at least a little mad at me for not being around the last few days. She'd wanted someone to talk to and I wasn't there. She didn't really have anyone else she could confide in.

"Hey," I said, interrupting another tirade about how dumb Willie was. "I'm really sorry I wasn't there for you to talk to. I couldn't handle it very well and it never occurred to me that you wouldn't be able to handle it, either."

"Why, because I'm dead inside or something?"

"It's not that and you know it," I said. "It's just that you're so tough."

"That's me," she said, "Miss Tough Girl."

"I just thought . . ."

"What?"

"I just thought that maybe you didn't like him as much as I did," I said, and winced as I said it. "Because of the way you would ride him about stuff."

She was silent again. I knew she was still there because I could hear her breathing.

"Someone needed to," she said. "Someone needed to kick his ass so he'd get out of that goddamned house and do something with himself. If I was hard on him, it's because I wanted him to be better. I wanted him *to want* to be better."

"Oh," I said.

"I don't wish I'd been easier on him. I *do* wish I'd told him more that I liked him. I'm really going to miss him."

"Me too."

We spent about a half-hour talking about all the stuff we'd done with Willie and funny things he'd said—intentional and otherwise. By the end, we were both crying again. Sherri cried! I never thought I'd live to see it again since she seemed to give it up in the seventh grade.

We made a plan for her to pick me up the next day since I'd decided to go back to school.

"Prepare to be the center of attention," she said, "though I'm sure no one will actually act like they're checking you out."

I groaned. I knew what she meant. I'd seen it in action before. I'd just never been its target. The whole school could sometimes come together and focus on one person without ever saying a word to them. I got a small taste of that on Monday as I walked down the hall with my dad. It would totally suck, but I could deal with it.

"Thanks for the warning," I said.

"Are you going to call Brandon?" Sherri asked.

"What?" I asked. "Why would you ask me that?"

"Because he's been asking me about you. He's worried about you. It's sort of sweet while also being annoying."

"I don't know," I said, "I think maybe I should tell him to give me some distance. Take a break from him for a while until I get my head back together. The situation with Willie has me all sorts of messed up."

"Don't do that," she said quickly.

"What are you talking about?"

"I'll deny saying this if you ever mention it to someone else," she said. "Brandon doesn't seem that bad. For a jock. And he likes you. *And* he had nothing to do with Willie's . . . death. So don't push him away."

I sat there in shock. Was she sticking up for Brandon? Even more, was she telling me to see him? I didn't know what to say.

"Besides," she went on, "it would really suck to be alone right now when you have a chance not to be. You know?"

"Yeah," I said, "I do."

We said good night and hung up. I immediately dialed Brandon's number.

And got his voice mail. Of course. I left a message telling him I'd be back at school tomorrow and that I was looking forward to seeing him again. I apologized for not being around for the last few days. I hoped he'd understand. I hung up.

I did a couple of hours of homework and then, despite having slept for three days straight, I went back to bed.

CHAPTER FOURTEEN
Jane Austen's Most Delicate Creation

The next morning at breakfast, I got a taste of what the rest of my day would be like. Dad and Bev hovered over me, quick to step in if they thought I needed something, all of it in a way meant to keep me unaware they were there. Holy shit, it was annoying.

At one point, I sat there eating some pancakes my dad made—from scratch! They kept asking if I needed anything, if everything tasted good, if I needed more orange juice. I dropped my napkin and nearly bumped heads with Bev when she swooped in to pick it up. Because, apparently, I was incapable of picking it up myself due to my grief. I felt like Jane Austen's most delicate creation. I fumed at being treated like such a baby. Then I accidentally knocked my OJ over and sent it spilling across the table. Dad and Bev moved in like a pair of firemen at a really big . . . fire. Dad grabbed paper towels, Bev wielded her napkin, and something in my brain broke.

"I can clean up a mess on my own," I said, pushing my chair away from the table more forcefully than I meant. My plate of half-eaten pancakes clattered and the fork fell on the floor. They both stopped and looked around, guilty, unsure what to do next.

"I know you guys want to help make my day easier. All

you're doing is driving me nuts." I sopped up the OJ with paper towels I tore out of my dad's hands.

"We're just trying to help," Dad said. I didn't look up from the juice because I didn't want to feel sorry for him. I was too busy feeling sorry for myself.

"I know, Dad, and I appreciate it," I said. "It's just too much." I stopped and stood up. I threw away the paper towels, then ran water until it got warm and wet a kitchen rag. "I just want things to be normal," I said finally.

"Courtney," he said, "things *aren't* normal."

"No," I said, "they're not. They really suck, but we can *act* like they're normal, right?"

"I don't know if that's the healthiest thing right—"

"Sure we can," Bev said, giving me and Dad this little smile. "For a while, anyway. You gotta face reality sooner or later, though, hon."

I felt big with liking for Bev right then. I thanked her and looked at Dad for his reaction.

"We will need to sort this out eventually," he said. "Yes, for now we can let it lie."

"Thanks, Dad." A car horn saved me from any more discussions about my feelings. I looked at the wet rag in my hand. "I guess I do need help," I said, feeling stupid. "Can one of you finish cleaning this up? I have to go."

Dad chuckled as he took the rag from me. The chuckle could best be described as "sardonic."

I gathered up my stuff from my room and headed out. I found myself really scoping out the path from the house to the car as I left. There's only one tree in the yard and it's as big around as my wrist, so not many zombies could hide behind it. Regardless, I was feeling extra paranoid. Apparently I took too long for Sherri's liking because she laid on the horn after a few seconds. She made a hurry-up gesture with her free hand.

"What the hell were you looking for?" she asked as I climbed into the car. God bless Sherri. I could always count on her to not spare my feelings. "Did what Willie did to himself make you go simple?"

"What does that mean?" I asked as she screeched the tires and pulled away.

"Just don't let it get to you," she said. "What happened to him happened because he wanted it to. It's not like he's dead because of some random attack."

"No," I said, "but we've seen more of those, right? There was that old lady, and Crystal and I got attacked up by the reservoir." I didn't bring up the pregnant shuffler who came for me mostly because I was trying my best to suppress that memory.

"There are always attacks," Sherri said. "Just like there's always car wrecks or drug overdoses or cancer." She fell silent and I thought we were done talking for a while. Then she started up again and her voice sounded quavery.

"Look behind all the trees you want," she said, "don't go out after dark, travel in groups. None of it would have saved Willie from himself."

I could see tears welling up in her eyes, which took me by complete surprise. I started to reach out to touch her arm, then I stopped.

"Are you okay?" I asked.

She looked at me, her eyes red. She didn't answer. Instead she turned back to the road, laid on the horn, and screamed at the top of her lungs. For block after block she screamed and screamed, until her voice petered out to nothing and then she'd take a ragged breath and do it again. The whole time she pushed down on the horn.

I just stared at her, a little scared, mostly sad. I had no idea losing Willie would affect her like that.

We came to a red light and she finally stopped honking and screaming. She put her head down on the steering wheel.

"It's all just so stupid," she said.

I didn't say anything. I couldn't think of anything *to* say.

She sat up and looked at me with red-rimmed eyes. "Sometimes I feel like doing something stupid."

"If you kill yourself, I will be totally pissed at you," I said. "I'll tell everyone at your funeral that you had sex with Coach Santori and you offed yourself because he wouldn't leave his wife for you."

She barked a hoarse laugh at that, which was good, I guess. The car behind us honked because the light had turned green. Sherri automatically flipped the guy the bird and peeled away through the intersection.

"I wouldn't kill myself," she said. "Not that kind of stupid."

"Then what?"

She shrugged. "I'll think of something," she said.

We reached the school and performed the required security ritual. She parked and we climbed out of the car. I stood there for a minute looking at the school, watching the kids file in. Each one of those kids held a judgmental look or thought for me and soon they'd have a chance to give it to me. Jesus, I sounded maudlin.

I shouldered my backpack. Sherri just nodded and we walked toward the school together. When it was time to part, we said our good-byes.

"Don't decide to do anything *too* stupid," I said.

"And don't you pussy out and let 'em see you cry," she answered.

I turned and joined the flow of kids going in through the school's main entrance. I heard the ebb and flow of conversation change around me. Little eddies of whispered accusations swirled around me. I made a promise to myself, almost a mantra.

I will not pussy out.

I will not pussy out.

The day turned out to be not as rough as I feared. I got a lot of stares and the whisper brigade was in full swing, though it didn't feel like it carried the malevolence I expected. At lunch, Sherri told me that the school grief counselor had been running interference for me; she'd been spreading the word about what happened. So the folks in the hall weren't suspicious or angry, they were sympathetic. Which was almost worse.

It became apparent after lunch that the hardest part of being in school would be avoiding the grief counselor. Ms. Bjorn had done her bit by getting people off my back, now she could do me a favor and do the same herself. I had a lot of near misses as I saw her standing near my locker or in the halls along the path I used to get to class. I might talk to her next week. There was no way I wanted to pow-wow with her just then.

I made it through the day without having to talk to her. I also went all day without seeing Brandon. He didn't even come and join me and Sherri at lunchtime, which I really thought he would. I knew at least that I'd see him in Journalism.

Except that I didn't. The room fell silent when I entered. I ignored them for the most part and scanned the room. No Brandon. He must have been behind me. I found a seat and watched the door for when he came in. My view was blocked by Phil standing in front of me. Besides Sherri, he was the first person to actually walk up and speak to me.

"I heard what happened," he said. As socially awkward

as ever. I paused for a second to see if he'd say he was sorry about it, or that I was brave for coming to school. Nothing.

"Yeah," I said, "it really sucks. I wish Willie had reached out to me."

Then he looked confused. He really had no idea what I was talking about. After a second, I could see a light go on inside his head and he nodded.

"Right," he said, "your friend killed himself. I forgot."

Forgot?

"That's not what I was talking about," he said.

I shook my head bewildered. This conversation was becoming downright Kafkaesque. "Okay," I said, "what *were* you talking about?"

"I heard Crystal Beals talking a few days ago about you guys being attacked by zombies," he said. "She told how you fought them off—killed a couple." He stood there nodding.

"Yeah?" I said.

"That's just pretty freaking cool, is all," he said. "I had no idea you had it in you."

Again, I shook my head in bewilderment. "Thanks," I said.

"I drew a cartoon of you as a badass zombie killer," he said, and he looked proud—of himself or of me I have no clue. "I submitted it for the paper. Mrs. Johnson killed it. Too raw or something. You want to see it?" He inclined his head toward his desk where I saw a manila folder stuffed full of drawings.

"Maybe some other time," I said. Read: *Never, not ever, you freak.*

Mrs. Johnson came into the room and asked everyone to take their seats. Phil nodded down at me. "Any time," he said, "catch you later." And he went over and slouched behind his desk.

Mrs. Johnson caught my eye and gave me one of those sad-smile, head-dip things that means a person is really sorry for what you're going through.

"Hey," she said, "welcome back, Courtney."

I gave her a quick smile that I meant to look brave and then willed her to please ignore me. Which she did, thank God.

Fridays are the day when Mrs. Johnson meets with the paper's designers and paste-up starts. That leaves the rest of us to work on stories or, as was the case with most of us, to goof off and talk. I found Elsa and asked her what was up with Brandon.

"I think he's meeting with some recruiters from different colleges," she said. "The coaches set it up for all the juniors. He said yesterday that he called and left you a message. Did you not get it?"

I could have smacked my head. Instead I just turned and walked away. I knew that Brandon left me a bunch of messages. I never got around to listening to them. I assumed they'd all say the same thing. Man, I needed to have a better relationship with my phone.

I dug it out of my bag and went off to a quiet corner of the room. I could have mapped the progress of the news about what happened just listening to those messages. His first message sounded confused; he'd heard about me being taken out of class and wanted to know what was up. In the next, he sounded a little panicky. He'd just heard that I got led out of the school in cuffs by a cop. He called me after he talked to Sherri the first time. She'd also heard the rumor about me being arrested but didn't know why.

"She said she thinks she knows what's going on, but she won't say," he said. "Why would she think you could be arrested?" He sounded confused and scared. Oh, Christ, I felt sick to my stomach. Even though she hadn't done it to be mean, Sherri had let the cat out of the bag. There was no way Brandon wouldn't bring up what she'd said. I needed to figure out what I was going to tell him the next time I saw him. I was suddenly grateful he wasn't in class that day.

The next message was after he'd heard what had really happened. He was really sorry; he felt bad for me and told me to call if I needed to talk. Then there were a couple more like that. Finally he called right before I got out of bed last night telling me he wouldn't be in school and why. Then he said I could call him later tonight if I wanted. He sounded sort of pathetic. Now on top of everything else I was feeling, I also felt guilty for not getting back to him. How many bad feelings can someone feel before they just plain overload? I thought I was about to find out.

I wasn't actually ready to talk to him yet. I decided to text him instead. Texting is, of course, the coward's alternative to calling. It's the modern equivalent of the passive-aggressive Post-it note. Even if someone texts you back right away, you can pretend you didn't get it until you're ready to deal with it.

> Working 2nite. Will call you 2morrow. Promise.
> Everything is OK.

That last bit was a lie. I figured it was a harmless one, though. Maybe if he thought everything really was okay he wouldn't try to contact me until the next day and I'd be able to figure out what to tell him. Maybe I was just kidding myself.

I moved back over by Elsa. She'd been joined by a few other kids. I sat on the periphery and listened, not feeling like joining in. Not feeling like much of anything, really.

★   ★   ★

I hesitated bringing up Brandon's phone message to Sherri. I knew it had the potential to explode and I didn't feel like us not talking again. I had to say something, though. Keeping quiet about it was just dumb and would probably cause more problems.

Sherri drove me to my house after school. She was also going to drive me to work after I changed my clothes.

"So, I don't want this to turn into a thing," I said. "I thought I should tell you that I got a message from Brandon pretty much telling me that you told him about my side job."

"Hmm," was all she said. A sly look told me she wasn't going to let this go too easily.

"You know what I'm talking about," I said. I could already feel my pulse getting quicker. "I just wanted you to know I knew."

"Now you know I knew you know," she said. "What of it?"

I didn't say anything.

"Uh-huh," she said. "So what are you going to say to him?"

"I won't talk to him until tomorrow at the earliest," I said. "I'll figure out something by then."

"I'm sure you will," she said.

Later she sat on my bed while I changed into a plain tee and my Dickies work pants. She leafed through a comic I'd left on the floor.

"We should hang out tomorrow," she said without looking up from the comic.

"Maybe, I said, "I have something I have to do during the day."

"Are you seeing Brrraaa-aannn-donnn," she said it in sing-song.

"No," I said.

She looked up from the comic. *The Invisibles,* I noticed. That's a good one.

"What?" she said.

I heaved a sigh. "I have to go see Buddha tomorrow," I said. "Also, I need a ride."

Her eyes flicked down and I know she was looking at the drawer where I stashed my money. I thought about how it was Willie who built the false bottom in the drawer. I frowned. I wonder what other cool junk he would have built if he were still alive.

"What?" I asked her.

"You've just got huge balls on you," she said. "I'm sort of impressed."

"Well," I said, "Willy was going to give me a ride, but . . ." I let it hang in the air.

"I'm glad you stopped before you said it's what he would have wanted," she said. "Because I would have done my best to hurt you." She heaved a monumental sigh and went back to reading her comic. "Fine. I'll take you, but you'll owe me."

I stopped myself from smiling or gloating.

"Thanks," was all I said.

I gave myself a once-over in the mirror. I was as ready as I was going to get.

"Okay," I said, "let's hit it."

As we drove to the Bully Burger, we talked about crazy things Willie had said or done in our presence. Like the time he rode his bike off the roof of his house and into a huge rhododendron that his mother loved more than her kids. He could hardly walk straight for a week. He thought it was the funniest thing ever. Telling stories like that was a good way to pass the time, and it helped me feel not so angry at him. When I got to work I felt this funny combination of happy and sad. Bittersweet I guess you'd call it.

As I walked up to the front doors, I wondered if I'd ever feel just one thing again or if every good feeling would be wrapped up with a bad one.

"Never mind me," I said to myself under my breath as I walked into the store. "I'm just busy having a pity party."

CHAPTER FIFTEEN
Mija

A lot of people drove away from the Bully Burger very pissed off that night. I had to tell them I wasn't holding and wouldn't be until the next week. To add insult to injury, I made them pay for food that they didn't really want and probably couldn't eat if they were jonesing for some Z. I built up a pretty hefty karmic debt standing in the drive-thru window. On top of everything else, I guess I could take it.

When I first got to the store, I thought Mr. Washington was going to send me home. He'd heard from some of my coworkers what had happened. Despite being a running dog of the capitalist et cetera, he's a pretty decent guy. I assured him I was up to covering my shift.

"You want to take a break, you let me know," he said with a wink. "I'll make one of these slackers take the window." This earned me reproachful glares from everyone in ear shot.

It was fairly busy for a Friday night. The front gate stood open most of the time, letting the steady stream of traffic in and out of the lot. Chacho stood out there since the boss was on-site. He watched the entrance for any uninvited guests. Chacho's a big guy and under all that armor I could tell he was sweating like a pig. I felt sorry for him.

I also knew that Mr. Washington would go home soon and that Chacho could come inside and strip that shit off.

We had so many cars coming and going I didn't even notice when Brandon walked into the store until he stood at the counter waving at me like a little kid. I became very aware of the other Bully Burger employees looking at me as I waved back at him. A tiny wave, from the hip. Very little wrist movement.

He leaned over the counter. "Hey," he said, "can you take a break for a minute?"

I hadn't been expecting this. I looked around and caught the boss's eye. I asked if I could take a break and he said sure. He put the headset on himself to cover me and he looked annoyed as the first customer off the bat must have ordered a Whopper.

"Where do you think you are, son?" he demanded. "We don't serve that crap here!"

He shot me a "What the hell are these kids on?" look and then turned back to the register. What were these kids on, indeed? It was a good question.

I took off my shirt of many colors and threw it on the counter in back before stepping into the dining room. I found myself caught up in a hug. I panicked for a second because it was so unexpected. Then I relaxed a bit and just went with it. After a second Brandon pulled away and gave me one of those sad smiles—God, I was really tired of that look.

I stole a quick glance over at the front counter. Ashley looked pissed as she stared right us. No doubt an evolutionary response to two disparate social circles colliding. I blew her a kiss and let Brandon lead me to an empty table.

He sat across from me and leaned forward to talk in a low voice. He still had that damned expression plastered on his face.

"Are you okay?" he asked.

"I'm better now," I said. "I'm sorry I checked out. I guess finding out about Willie really sucked it out of me."

"No fooling," he said, "I know what that's like."

"You do?"

"Sure, when I went to Whitaker one of my best friends killed himself."

"I never knew that," I said. "I'm sorry."

He shrugged. "It's okay," he said. "It *did* take a long time to get over it. I realize now that there wasn't really anything I could do to change his mind."

Ugh. "How did he do it?" I asked.

He'd looked far away for a second. "Oh, yeah. Well, you know how everyone has at least one gun in the house nowadays?"

"Yeah," I said, getting the picture.

He spread his hands. *There you go,* the gesture said.

"Anyway," he said, "I'm glad you're doing okay. I'm sorry about your friend. It really sucks."

"It really does," I agreed.

"I was freaked out there for a while when it first happened," he said, and I squirmed in my seat. "Especially when Sherri thought you might have been arrested." He paused for a second and looked at me, smiling. "Why would she have thought that?"

The conversation had taken a weird, and seemingly practiced, turn. Which annoyed me.

"Listen, Brandon," I said, "my break time in a booth in the Bully Burger really isn't where we should be having this conversation."

"Where, then?" he asked.

I tried to keep my face blank as I regarded him. His smile faltered and I couldn't tell what was beneath it. Anger, concern, something else?

"Maybe tomorrow," I said. "Maybe we can talk tomorrow. Would that be okay with you?"

"Hey," he said, "I'm sorry to come on so strong. I'm, I
don't know, concerned. You know?"

"Sure," I said. He still sounded angry at being put off.

Mr. Washington's voice drifted into the dining room.
"Why the hell is everyone ordering a Whopper? Is this
some kind of stupid prank?"

"I should get back there," I said.

"Okay," he said, "can I call you tomorrow?"

I told him he could and he hugged me again before he
left—a quick one this time.

As I walked into the kitchen, Ashley glared at me as I
went past.

"What was that all about?" she asked.

"What," I said, "you've never seen a girl and her sex
slave?"

I relieved Mr. Washington before he dragged some
poor, unsuspecting drug addict through the drive-thru
window.

Even though I was allowed to clock off at the end of the
night after I counted my till, I felt generous and decided
to help the closing staff clean up. I did the dining room
pretty quick—wiped down the tables and chairs and swept
up. Carol, the gal washing dishes that night, would mop
out the whole restaurant last thing after everyone left. I
milled around looking for something else to do and Mary
Kate asked if I'd take out the dining room garbages. I
wrinkled my nose and she heaved a dramatic sigh.

"If you don't want to be helpful, you can just have a seat
next to Chacho," she said, and pointed at him. He just
grinned at us from behind his magazine. He's not an employee of the store, he works for a private security place,

and because of that, he didn't have to clean. Something he liked to remind us of. As I stood there thinking about it, the prospect of sitting with Chacho and watching the other suckers clean up sounded good. I felt the need to be nice, however, so I gathered the trash.

The garbage at a fast-food joint is the worst. All that processed, fried, greasy food makes for one stinky mess. Then people throw their sodas on top of that and, even after just an hour or so, the trash liner is filled with this co-agulated mess that smells a lot like vomit. Woe be unto you if you get any of that shit on you. It's like a portable version of the Bog of Eternal Stench.

I yanked one can out of its little house and pulled it over to the other bin. Took that liner out and threw it into the first can. Thankfully neither was very full so I could do this; otherwise I'd have to make two trips to the Dumpster—and the Dumpster smells even worse than the trash cans.

I wheeled the can out the side door. I patted my pocket on the way to make sure I had my keys on me. That late at night the doors lock behind you automatically and it's a huge pain in the ass waiting to be let back in, especially since letting you in seems to be pretty far down on everyone's list of priorities.

"Courtney!" Chacho yelled at me from behind the counter. "I have to talk to the boss for a minute. Wait for me to go out with you." He turned and walked toward Mr. Washington's office.

I thought about waiting, but then decided to screw it. I'd be done and back before Chacho was finished. I pushed open the door and stepped out.

It felt nice to be outside after being in the grease pit for six hours. I took a deep breath and let it out slowly. As I exhaled, I heard something shift and fall back by the

Dumpsters. It startled me, but I didn't think much about it—whoever threw out the trash last had probably done as sloppy a job as I was about to do.

I wheeled the can back that way and then stopped again. Had I heard something else? I stood there straining to listen. All I could hear was my own accelerated heartbeat. The gated area where the Dumpster and the incinerator lived was set off from the store; it sat in the back of the lot, about twenty or thirty yards away. That night, all of a sudden, the distance seemed to grow longer and longer as I looked at it.

And then, *ugh,* a rat skittered out from under the fence and made a beeline for the back of the parking lot. Disgusting.

A loud metallic snap behind me made me scream and jump about ten feet in the air. Mary Kate stood at the drive-thru window and glared out at me.

"How long are you gonna milk this, Courtney?"

"Go screw, you cow," I yelled back at her. I heard hysteria creeping into my voice. "You scared the crap out of me."

"Whatever," she said. "Just get back in here." She slammed the window shut.

I flipped her the finger even though she was already gone. Fear was replaced with me being really pissed off. I grabbed the trash can and nearly tipped it over as I yanked it behind me. After the can was righted, I pulled it behind me more gingerly. I muttered to myself as I dragged it toward the Dumpster. I wanted to hold on to my anger because I knew what would replace it once it dissipated.

When I reached the shed, I noticed that its large double doors were ajar. The same hypothetical lazy employee I'd imagined earlier didn't just leave a mess in the Dumpster that would later settle, they'd also forgotten to close the doors all the way. Right. I craned my neck in various positions to try to see anything in there that might be, you know, deadly. It was too F'ing dark to make out anything.

As I saw it, I had two choices. One, stand there until MK, or her evil twin, yelled at me again or, two, just open the door and see that there was nothing there.

Quick as I could, before I could think my way out of it, I grabbed the edge of the nearest door and flung it open.

And *a pair of zombies came lunging at me!*

I stared into the ravaged face of the one on the left and my mind went blank, as empty as his freaking eye socket.

Then the rotten-meat smell hit me.

I screamed and backpedaled as fast as I could. I forgot about the trash can behind me. Me and it went over backward—fast-food trash went everywhere—and I found myself sliding around in a pile of congealed grease and soda. If I hadn't been scared out of my damned mind, I would have puked my guts out.

I slipped on the ground as I tried to stand. The two shufflers came at me, their mouths gaping. They'd have been salivating if they were still alive. I finally got my feet under me and was about to sprint back to the store when I heard more shuffling behind me. I shot a look in that direction and a third zombie was coming up fast on my blind side. If I hesitated much longer, she'd be right on top of me.

I backed away as fast as I could without slipping in the filth again. That meant putting more distance between me and the store. Between me and safety. This was *no bueno*.

My brain went into overdrive and, at the same time, I couldn't think what to do. It felt like I was stepping on the gas while the car was in park. I started to find myself caught in this loop where I wondered if I knew them. They all looked to be my age. Two boys and a girl. One of the boys and the girl looked like preppies. Nice clothes before they were ravaged, a popped collar on the boy. But the other guy was a definite grunge head. They all looked freshly dead. Lots of flesh on their bones still—in fact, I didn't see any obvious chew marks on the grunge dude. You know, there's no way these three would have hung out in life. Now here they were. Zombification had brought them together. It was like an after-school special directed by Wes Craven.

I became aware that as I was wasting time thinking of this inane crap, I kept backing away from the three of them. I just got farther and farther away from the store. I needed to do something. *Anything!*

"Hey, you guys!" I screamed at them. "That doctor guy says you can communicate. Or we can communicate with you, or something." And, so help me, they stopped and just looked at me. For about a second. Then they started their slow walk to what they saw as a mobile feast.

"You guys don't want to do this," I said. "You don't have to eat me. Jesus, I bet you'd have liked me when you were alive . . ."

The chain-link fence stopped me from going any farther. Oh, my God, I was so screwed. The trio got closer and closed ranks. If I was going to do something, it had to be right, no-shit, now.

I decided on screaming. I let out a high-pitched cry as loud as I could and hoped the people in the store, especially Chacho, heard it. Again the zombies stopped for a second. Almost like they were waiting to see if anyone would answer. Then they started toward me again. No one from inside came to my rescue.

Right, I had to save myself. I braced myself against the fence and took a deep breath. I tried to clear my mind and not think about what I was set to do.

I launched off the fence as hard as I could and ran right

at those undead assholes. I gave a battle cry as I did it to psyche myself up.

I aimed for the space between the preppy boy and girl. The boy got his hand on my upper arm. I wrenched myself away from him and he lost his grip. Thank God for the fact I was covered in greasy shit. I started running again, I couldn't lose momentum. When the girl lunged at me, I dipped down and shoved her like I'd first learned playing field hockey back in middle school. She sprawled on the pavement. I kept running and I was clear of them. I let out another shout and made a beeline for the restaurant. I ran smack-dab into the locked door. Damn. The folks inside just stared at me and went back to what they'd been doing.

It felt like I moved in slo-mo as I dug the keys out of my pants pocket. Why did I wear such tight pants? It felt like I could barely get my stupid hand in there. The grease made it hard to grip the keys. I glanced over at the shufflers— the girl was back on her feet and the boys were making steady progress toward me. I did my best to ignore them so I wouldn't panic again.

The key finally slid into the lock. I gave it a turn and threw the door open and bolted inside. The first thing I saw was an empty seat where Chacho should be.

I heard someone call from the back, "Jesus, Courtney, what's your—"

"Where is Chacho?" I screamed at no one in particular.

"Have you been rolling in the garbage back there or what?" I didn't look up to see who was talking to me. If I knew for sure who it was, I'd probably kill them later.

Chacho's stuff sat next to his seat. He must have still been in the boss's office. *Great timing, Chacho.* I rushed over and threw the helmet on my head. Then I grabbed up the shield and the baton and I ran back outside. I heard someone yelling that I couldn't take that stuff. I ignored them. No one was going to tell me what to do just then.

Only about thirty feet separated me and the boys. I closed it quickly as I gave my *Braveheart* yell again. Since I had more room to maneuver, I dodged to their left at the last minute and swung the baton at the preppy boy's head. But my aim sucked and I hit him in the shoulder.

While he recovered, I charged the grunge shuffler with the shield held up between us. I hit him with enough force to knock him down and was just able to not fall on my ass. With him down and the girl still lagging behind, I had the preppy boy to myself.

I turned to face him and held the shield up like I'd seen Chacho do a bunch of times. I circled him to the left and when he lunged at me, I dodged to the right and swung the club right at his melon. That time I connected and I nearly dropped the baton as the shock of it traveled up my arm. The kid's head busted open like over-ripe fruit. It was disgusting. He fell down and didn't look like he'd be getting up.I stood there for a second to admire my handiwork.

"Courtney, goddammit!" someone shouted at me from the store. Chacho stood in the open doorway and pointed off to my right. The grunge zombie crawled on hands and knees to get at me. I was dimly aware of Chacho running back inside the store for something.

My first inclination was to boot the kid in the head and see if I could actually knock it off his shoulders. I reconsidered because I had my Chucks on and I could see him just biting through them, so I settled for swinging away with the baton like a kid at tee-ball.

It took three good swings before his head finally caved in and he fell on his face.

I immediately turned to face the girl. She was just a few

feet away. I planted my feet underneath me and got ready to take a swipe at her. Then I noticed Chacho standing next to me and he had something in his hands.

An ungodly boom sounded as he leveled his shotgun and pulled the trigger. The zombie chick flew through the air and landed a few feet away from us.

"What in the hell is wrong with you, Courtney?" Chacho looked so pissed, like I've never seen him before. But every time he breathed out, his lips flapped and for some reason that struck me as really funny. I tried to hold it back, but I started giggling. Chacho looked even more mad and that made it even funnier. Pretty soon I laughed out loud and then tears were running down my face because of it. I knew everyone was watching me through the store's plate-glass windows. I still laughed like it was the funniest thing in the world. I started to worry that I wouldn't be able to stop—maybe I'd really gone around the bend. Jesus, maybe I was crazy and I'd start to think everything was funny. Napalmed babies, burning churches, hordes of zombies; all of it was fodder for chuckles when you're insane.

Everyone stood at the big window looking out at me and Chacho. They all looked horrified. Except for Phil. He stood there looking basically emotionless, like always, but then he gave me a thumbs-up. Why? Because I'd killed a bunch of zombies on my own or because I was losing it? That made me laugh even harder.

Chacho grabbed me by my shoulders and gave me one big shake. My head whipped back and forth and if it weren't for him holding on to me, I would have fallen to the ground. I stood there, stunned, just looking into his eyes. He'd gone from angry to worried in the space of a few seconds. That, more than anything, got me to stop laughing. I started crying instead. Not the great racking sobs I'd gone through when I heard about Willie's death. Just a soft, hopeless crying.

Chacho pulled me close. I guess he didn't care that I was covered in Bully Burger trash. He whispered softly to me in Spanish. I couldn't understand a word and it felt so nice, so soothing. Actually, I did catch one word, *mija*. "My daughter." I cried a little harder then. Everything felt hopeless. Everything felt like it always did.

CHAPTER SIXTEEN
The Girl in the Backseat

Because being covered in zombie gore was sort of an occupational hazard, Chacho kept spare sets of clothes in his rig. While he dragged the bodies back to the incinerator, I changed into a set of coveralls that would have fit about three of me. I did what I could to make them stay on my body. Rolled sleeves and pants legs at least meant you could see my hands and feet. I cinched the waist with a belt borrowed from Mary Kate and I got some flip-flops from her evil twin, Ashley. It was really quite attractive in a postapocalyptic sort of way. The clothes I'd been wearing earlier went in the incinerator, too.

Mr. Washington left after asking me a bunch of questions. I think he was mostly worried about whether or not I would sue him because the store's security guard was in his office at the time of the attack. After I convinced him I didn't even know how to contact a lawyer, he went home, still muttering to himself. I'm sure he had nightmares about lumbering liability suits that night.

Everyone else finished cleaning up while I sat with my back to them and stared off into the distance. This crazy idea was running around in my head and I wanted to think it through.

Chacho sat a couple of tables away and picked up his magazine again. I turned to face him.

"You should come sit over here," I said.

He set down his magazine, heaved himself out of his seat, and sat across from me in the booth. He didn't say anything, just waited for me to talk. Man, I liked him so much.

"So, I'm having this crazy thought," I said.

"No shit." Deadpan.

"Funny. Listen: the way those zombies came at me. Two hiding in the Dumpster area and one trying to flank me. That was a trap."

Chacho nodded slowly. "Yeah," he said, "that *is* crazy."

"Cha-*cho*." I hated it whenever I whined, but I couldn't keep it out of my voice. "C'mon, man, what else would you call that? A classic pincer move."

"Now you're General Patton. I don't know about battle tactics, but I do know—from experience—that zombies aren't aware enough or smart enough to plan traps."

"Maybe it's not smarts," I said.

"What, then?"

"I don't know," I said. I strained for an analogy that would work. "Okay, you know the way some animals work together to do stuff. Even *insects* can work in groups. Would you call those creepy ants in South America smart?"

"No, I wouldn't," he said. "I also wouldn't say that what happened tonight is evidence the zombies are working together."

I sat there fuming. I thought if anyone would believe me, it would be Chacho.

"Oh!" I startled him, which was pretty funny. "The reservoir," I said.

"What reservoir?" he asked.

"You didn't hear what happened to me at the reservoir last weekend?" His expression was all the answer I needed so I launched into the story of me and Crystal being attacked by three zombies. A pair on one side and a single from the other.

"Tell me that's coincidence, Chacho."

He scratched the stubble under his chin while he thought about it. "Something happening twice isn't exactly a trend," he said. "I admit that it's weird, but that's all it is. Weird."

I sat back in the bench and pouted. Chacho is like special-forces guy. How could he not see it as plainly as I did? Maybe because he wasn't the one who had been attacked. Even if that's what it was going to take, I didn't want it to happen. Besides Sherri, Chacho was the coolest person I knew. Cool or not, I was still mad at him, though.

"You can go back to your booth," I told him.

He chuckled. "Yes, ma'am."

Screw him. I crossed my arms and slumped down in the bench. People were going to be sorry when a huge wave of highly coordinated ninja zombies swept across the face of the earth.

The next thing I knew, Chacho shook me awake. I'd fallen asleep on the bench. My body felt achy as I stood up. I wasn't sure if it was from sleeping on the bench or laying into those zombies earlier. I worked the kinks out as I stumbled to Chacho's work SUV. Besides me, that night he carried the twins home, too. The rig had two rows of seats behind the driver. I took it as a bad sign that they huddled together in the very back, probably to facilitate better whispered bitchiness. Hell, let them talk about me if it meant I got to ride shotgun.

They fell silent when I first climbed into the cab. After a beat, I heard whispers and suppressed giggles. Being a better person than them, I ignored it.

Chacho climbed in a couple of minutes later. He scoped out the girls in the backseat and then whispered, "What the hell?" I just shrugged.

"You live closer to the store," he said to me. "You also live just a few blocks away from me so it'd be cool if I could take you home last. You mind?"

I shook my head. Just then, talking seemed like way too much effort. I sometimes forgot that Chacho lived in my 'hood. I'd see him out at, like, the grocery store and, instead of the gray overalls, he'd have on jeans and a T-shirt. Usually his kid, a little boy about five or six, was with him. It was like running into one of your teachers outside of class, except that I'd never seen any of my teachers kill a bunch of the undead.

We drove farther south on Commercial and then entered a gated community to our left. We weren't far from Brandon's subdivision. The guards at the gate eyed me and Chacho suspiciously. Then he saw the girls in the back and waved us through. As we meandered through the streets, the twins' whispers and giggles became louder. Chacho glanced at me and then he reached over and flipped on the stereo. Latin-tinged hip-hop came out of the speakers. I usually didn't like anything even resembling rap. This, however, was pretty cool. I wondered who it was, but didn't ask.

We stopped in front of a huge house. It looked like my place could fit in their living room. Ashley told me one time, or maybe it was Mary Kate, that the only reason they worked was because their dad thought they needed to learn what it felt like to be one of the common people. Ugh.

Chacho idled at the curb while the twins disembarked. When Chacho called good night to them, they had a real giggle fit, nearly fell over each other as they staggered up the walk. Even though there was zero possibility of their being attacked by zombies—damn it all—Chacho stayed parked until they were safely inside. Then we glided back onto the road.

We were nearly back to the neighborhood's gates when

I felt like I could talk to Chacho. Having the twins in the back had been a real mood killer.

"How many zombies have you killed?"

"A lot," he said. "I think you're gonna catch up pretty quick the way you're going."

The guards already had the gates open for us when we got to the security checkpoint.

"How many really?" I asked.

"What's this about?"

"Where were you when the dead returned?"

We were at the stop sign, waiting to make the turn onto the main road. He stopped long enough to give me a once-over.

"Again," he said, "what's this about?"

"Just curious," I said.

I sat up and turned down the music. Down, not off. I liked the way the rhythm matched my heartbeat. Or maybe my heartbeat matched the rhythm.

"It seems like anyone older than me, you know them for longer than ten minutes and you hear the story about where they were. I've never heard yours, that's all."

He didn't answer and, after a little while, I figured he wasn't going to. Which was fine; I didn't want to harp on him and piss him off, I really was just curious.

"Baghdad," he said. He stared straight ahead.

"Like, in, uh, Iraq?" I asked.

"Yeah, Iraq," he said. He paused, checking his mirrors and changing lanes. "I was stationed there when I wasn't much older than you."

I scanned my memory banks for what I knew about that from my different Civics and History classes.

"Holy crap," I said. It didn't really seem like enough. It was all I could manage.

"Right." Chacho nodded slowly as he pulled off Commercial and toward my neighborhood. "We'd been killing people there for a couple of years at that point. Hussein had been killing his own people for even longer than that before we showed up. There were dead people everywhere."

I thought he was going to keep going on. He didn't.

"What was it like?" I prompted.

His hands gripped the steering wheel so tight I heard the hard plastic squeaking. "What am I supposed to say to that, Courtney? It was bad? It sucked? It was a living nightmare?

"I never thought I'd get out of there. I literally gave up hope of getting out alive. That's the hardest part. If the Army hadn't come to airlift us out when they did, I would have just given up."

We stopped. I looked at my comfortable little house. I felt so stupid for bringing this up.

"Sorry," I said, "I was just curious . . ."

"I know."

There wasn't anything else to say, so I opened the door to get out of the truck.

"Hey," Chacho said. I closed the door again.

"I don't know what you're going through," he said. "I do know you need to figure that shit out. You're starting to look like me back when I gave up."

I swallowed hard. "What should I do?"

"Hell if I know," he said. "Just do it quick. Talk to your dad. He's some kind of shrink, right?"

"Yeah, some kind."

"Well, there you go. Damn, I could have used a doctor. I didn't get myself together until my wife threatened to divorce my ass."

"Maybe I should get married so my husband can threaten me."

"There's no boys around you worth getting married to," he said.

"Well, Brandon seems to be interested in the position now . . ."

"Like I said," he said, "no one. You should get on inside." He pointed out the window. "Looks like someone's waiting for you."

My dad stood in the open doorway and he waved. I turned back to Chacho and smiled. It felt weird, having some clue of what he'd been through, and knowing he cared enough about me to tell me to get my act together.

"Thanks," I said.

"You'll be okay," he said. "Just gotta figure some stuff out."

I nodded like I believed it would be as easy as he made it sound, then I got out of the rig and walked toward the house where my dad waited for me.

It was just him, too, which I liked. Bev wasn't bad; I just craved time alone with Dad. She had to work late and he'd told her that he'd see her tomorrow.

"You should have told her to come over after," I said. "I'm going to bed soon anyway."

"I'll see her tomorrow," he repeated.

He asked me how my day was and I told him as much as I could about school and work. I didn't tell him about the zombie attack. He knew something had obviously happened since I came home wearing Chacho's clothes. I made up a hilarious story about dumping garbage all over myself. Okay, maybe not hilarious, but he laughed and it kept him from delving any deeper into my admittedly thin story. Sometimes I wondered if Dad just didn't want to see that I was spreading the bull pretty thick.

I used up all of our hot water showering the various forms of gunk off my body and out of my hair. I stood under the hot water for as long as I could massaging the knots out of the muscles in my arms and back. I didn't feel clean when I was done, really. I got into my boxers and T-shirt and thought I would go right to bed. Dad was still up when I got out of the bathroom.

I stayed up with him for a while. He popped popcorn and we watched some late-night TV. Dad laughed at all the crappy jokes the host of the show told so maybe he really did think my story was funny, too.

After saying good night and getting ready for bed, I closed my bedroom door and pulled the drawer with a false bottom out of my dresser. I counted the cash I had stashed there one more time and sorted out the money I owed to Buddha, and set some aside to use during the trip to see him the next day. That money went into my backpack where I could easily get at it and the other money went back into the drawer.

The tally from my half-year of illicit activity came to nearly $60,000. I know Sherri wanted me to quit, but if I could keep this up until I graduated next year, I'd have enough for a year of school in New York, two if I made the money stretch. And I could make it stretch. I mean, I'd gone this long without spending any of that money on clothes or video games or any of the dumb stuff that other kids wanted. I had a goal and I was going to meet it.

I considered going online, but it felt like all I would see were sites where I used to chat with Willie, so I decided to go to bed. I lay there in the dark concentrating on what I should tell Brandon tomorrow when I saw him. That was a trick my Calculus teacher taught me. If you have a problem you can't solve, think about it as you go to sleep and in the morning you'll more than likely have the answer. Believing in that little bit of wisdom was as close as I came to a religion.

I thought on it as hard as I could, trying not to picture the worst-case scenario as I did it, and I drifted to sleep.

*   *   *

I rode in the front seat of the land boat, Willie beside me at the wheel. He looked good, maybe better than he ever had when he was alive. So, call it a win–lose situation. The moon and stars hid under a blanket of clouds and the boat's headlights seemed barely able to penetrate the darkness. I could only see a few feet ahead of us as we barreled along.

He took his hands off the wheel to light a cigarette. The car seemed to drive itself around a sharp bend in the road. I found this sort of comforting.

Willie blew a stream of smoke out the window that was rolled down about halfway.

"You need to stop worrying about that jock asshole." He placed his hands back on the wheel and jerked hard to make us swerve into something I hadn't seen was there. There was a huge thump and it flew over the car and was gone. That was a zombie, right?

"You need to worry about yourself."

"Worry about what?" I asked. When had Willie started smoking? Was that something you did after you died to kill time?

"You know what's coming, girl." A voice from the backseat. Professor Keller rode behind me. Normally, I'd have lowered the sun visor and looked at the person in the backseat through the vanity mirror. This time I knew that I didn't want to see what was back there.

"What do you mean?" I asked. "What's coming?"

"Zombie-ism in popular culture has been used to represent any number of social ills." I guess I wasn't going to get a straight answer from the prof. "Fear of disease, the rise of the military-industrial complex, rampant consumerism."

"Do you know what I need to worry about, Willie?" I

shrugged forward, lifting my back away from the seat. I felt sure that at any moment the professor's hand was going to creep over and grab my shoulder.

"In almost every iteration, however," the guy in the backseat went on, "zombies are used to represent a loss of individual identity and an envelopment by the mind of the mob." Now it sounded like he was talking around a mouth-full of something. I'd started to smell something, too. Like rotten meat.

I turned to talk to Willie, to beg him to answer me, please. I could barely see across the seat to where he sat. He was one indistinct shadow amid even more darkness. I couldn't even make out the glow of his cigarette. As soon as I turned my eyes from the road, we hit something else, the car shuddering with the force of it.

I turned back to the road and I tried to squeeze my eyes shut; I knew there was no way in hell I wanted to see what we hit next. But I couldn't. I couldn't shut my eyes, I couldn't turn my head. I had to watch the road.

"Please," I shouted, "would someone tell me what the hell is about to happen?"

"You know what's about to happen, Courtney." A new voice came from the backseat, a girl's voice. One that I knew but couldn't place. Who was it? "Things are about to get pretty hairy for you."

That smell was getting worse. Now, in addition to that, there were these *sounds* coming from the backseat. Smacking, tearing, like someone was eating a really sloppy meal. Meat, I kept thinking of meat.

Suddenly I could see farther down the road than I'd been able to. Someone stood there in the middle of it and refused to move. I couldn't tell who it was and I wanted to wake up before I figured it out.

"Oh, look," said the girl in the backseat as we rushed at

the lone figure in our path, "there's the last member of our little group. You should scoot over and make room, Courtney."

I started to scream because Willie wouldn't slow down and, as she laughed, I knew who the girl in the backseat was.

The clock read just a little after 1 a.m. Oh, my God, I'd only been asleep for an hour. I lay there in the dark trying to catch my breath, trying to convince myself that I wasn't still in the dream. Still, I pulled my feet away from the edge of the bed and tucked the blanket under them. I imagined that would be protection against anything on the floor that might want to reach up and grab me.

The dream scared the crap out of me for no reason I could pinpoint. Earlier that night I'd faced real live zombies. So why would a conversation scare me so much? Why was my brain so weird?

I was positive I'd never get back to sleep that night, but I finally drifted off as the sky started to lighten outside my window.

CHAPTER SEVENTEEN
Confused with a
Chance of Angry

I woke up feeling hungover. Which really sucked because, you know, I didn't drink the night before. I tried to rub gunk out of my eyes and stopped when pain shot up both my arms. It felt like I'd spent the last day doing chin-ups or something. My back wasn't much better.

I sat up as gingerly as I could. I suddenly felt like that guy Sam Jackson played in *Unbreakable*—the one with glass bones. Oh, man, this sucked. Maybe Dad had some pain pills I could bum off him. I'd tell him I hurt from the fall I took—which might be partially true.

Unfortunately Dad was nowhere to be found—no note or anything, either. What was he doing being gone so early in the morning? Then I saw the clock in the kitchen. It was almost noon. I'd slept for like twelve hours! He was probably out with Bev. Or maybe he was at his office—he sometimes had office hours on the weekend so students would have an easier time speaking with him. I could have called him, but it just didn't seem like that big a deal. Maybe I'd call if I couldn't find any painkillers anywhere.

There were none in the hall bathroom cabinet. Even though I didn't think there would be any, I still looked just in case. Dad had his own bathroom so I figured I'd go there next.

It felt weird going into Dad's room without asking. We

have a rule about always knocking and respecting each other's privacy. But he wasn't around to ask, so I figured I didn't really have a choice.

Dad's room was as neat as mine was messy. No clothes on the floor, bed made, books stacked neatly. It's kind of gross. He had the curtains wide open and the sunlight flooded in. I went into the bathroom and opened his medicine cabinet. All I found was shaving cream, toothpaste, and various powders and creams that made me question if I ever wanted to accept a hug from him again. No prescription drugs that would help with my back, though. Unless lowering my blood pressure was the ticket.

I knew that Dad had some Percocet somewhere. About six months before, he'd had his last two wisdom teeth pulled and the dental surgeon gave him a prescription. He barely took any because he's Mr. Stoic. I was positive he'd have kept them around. He can't get rid of anything that might be useful later on.

I knew from some earlier, possibly illicit, snooping that Dad has a drawer where he keeps things he doesn't want me to know about. Mostly it's a collection of the tamest porn I have ever seen. Seriously, it's nothing you wouldn't see in a Victoria's Secret catalog. That's also where he keeps files on his students-slash-clients if he has to bring work home. If he had prescription-strength painkillers in the house, that's where I'd find 'em.

Little twinges of guilt pricked at me as I knelt down on the floor and opened up the bottom drawer to his dresser. It squeaked loudly. I stopped what I was doing and listened for my dad, my heart pounding fast. Stupid, I was being stupid. I knew for a fact that my dad wasn't even home. I could fling the whole dresser to the ground and he'd never know.

I pulled the drawer open and it groaned in protest.

A single layer of underwear lay on the top of the

drawer. Grimacing while I did it, I moved those aside and exposed a small stack of 80s-era *Playboys*. I tried not to judge how well-thumbed the magazines were. Taking those out, I uncovered a small tin box. The pills had to be in there. Before I went digging for them any further, I stopped and wondered how smart a move this was. Would Dad know how many had been in the bottle? And if he did, would he wonder how one or two, or more, managed to make their way out? I decided that if he noticed, he'd be too embarrassed to ask me about it, so I went for it.

I took the top off the box and there was the bottle of pain pills. Right next to a baggie of weed. I laughed out loud and took the baggie out of the tin. The thought of my dad sparking up just would not compute. There was a small glass pipe in the baggie, too, and, somehow, it was easier to see Dad with a pipe than to imagine him rolling a joint. Maybe he and Bev got high before they did it. I started laughing all over again.

But my laughter choked up when I saw what was underneath the bag of weed. A small, two-ounce Ziploc full of black powder lay in the bottom of the tin. My mouth dried up and I felt an icy throbbing in my stomach as I set the bag of weed down and picked up the smaller baggie. I turned it over and over, squeezed it with my fingers through the plastic. There was no way this was happening. Why did my dad have a bag of Vitamin Z in his god-damned drawer of naughty pleasures?

But I knew why he had it. He had it for the same reason that everyone I ever sold this stuff to had it. My body couldn't decide if it wanted to puke or cry. I hoped it wouldn't decide to do both at once. Vitamin Z was for hop-heads like the losers I sold to every night at the Bully Burger. People who had nothing in their lives. Stupid losers who couldn't feel anything unless they were stoned out of their minds.

Tears fell down my cheeks and into the box. I swiped at my face with my sleeve and then started wiping out the box with the tail of my shirt. I put everything back just the way I found it—I didn't even take any pills. There was no way in hell I wanted my dad to know that I'd been in here and seen this. Anyway, the pain in my arms and back didn't seem to bother me anymore.

As I slid the drawer closed, the doorbell rang and I nearly jumped out of my skin. I wasn't expecting anyone to come over. No one just dropped by. When you might run into a pack of zombies every time you turned a corner, you tended to make sure the person you wanted to see was home before you got in your car.

I closed the door to Dad's room and ran down the hall to open the front door. Brandon stood there with his arms crossed. He looked huffy, put out. Not a good look for him; it did weird things to his forehead.

"Are you ready to tell me what's up?" he said, and then he really looked at me. I probably looked like shit. Tears and snot streaming down my face. I was obviously in the middle of crying. Brandon looked confused; his arms dropped from across his chest and he just generally softened. A crying girl is like kryptonite to any boy who's still a virgin.

"Hey," he said, "what's wrong?"

"Nothing," I said. "Why are you here?"

"Oh, um, I just wanted to come and . . . talk to you? You know?" He was so concerned for me, it made me angry, made me want to punch him in the face. I swallowed that down and opened the door for him to come in.

"Grab a soda out of the fridge," I told him. I turned away and walked toward the bathroom. "I'll be right back."

I washed my face, scrubbed it really hard with some of

my dad's apricot facial goop. Did you know that they put ground-up walnut shell in it? It's really good if you want to wash your face and punish yourself all at the same time. Multitasking.

As I put the towel back on the holder, I grabbed my makeup bag. I decided to make Brandon wait for a while before I came out. He'd either be gone or totally mad when I got out. Either of those was fine with me.

A layer of foundation, blush, lipstick. I applied mascara, super-thick and clumpy. Last, I put on a thick-ass amount of eyeliner. The more I put on, the more it looked like some superhero's domino mask. I liked that—the mask. I made it even thicker. When I was done, I stood and looked at myself. I didn't look like myself—a stranger stood in front of me. I smiled and the person across from me did, too. She had bright red lipstick smeared across her teeth. Perfect.

I stopped one last time before I left the bathroom. Why was I doing this? Brandon was out there, and he was confused about what was going on and that made him angry. Why was I trying so hard to push his buttons? Maybe because I could. I wanted to be in control of the situation—any situation—for once. And if things got out of hand with Brandon out there, I think I'd be okay with where it led.

I took a deep breath.

Brandon started talking as soon as I opened the door to the bathroom. "What were you doing in there? You've been in there for, like, half an hour!"

He shut up as soon as he saw me and shifted uncomfortably in his chair at the kitchen table. He looked confused. I sat across from him and smiled, showing him my teeth. I reached over and grabbed his soda, brushing his hand as I did it. He recoiled away from me and looked down at his hand like it was dirty now or something. I took a sip of the soda and replaced it. A big ring of red lipstick stood out on the can.

It felt like I was working some kind of magic spell. If I could sap Brandon's anger and focus, I could bolster my own confidence. I didn't think it was going to work.

"What did you want to talk to me about, Brandon?"

He swallowed hard. He kept his gaze right on my eyes.

"I want to know what Sherri was talking about the other day," he said. "Why did she think you might be arrested?"

He didn't sound angry anymore. He also didn't sound confused or disoriented, either. I was screwed.

"Who the hell knows what Sherri was thinking," I said. "I know she's my friend, but she can be pretty out there sometimes."

He narrowed his gaze at me and lowered his head a little. He actually blushed. "You're lying," he said softly.

I clenched my jaw. I hated being called a liar. Even when I was lying.

"I don't know what Sherri was talking about," I said. "I don't know what else to tell you."

"You could have told me this last night," he said, his voice soft. "There was no reason to put me off until today."

"We're not supposed to talk to friends when we're on the clock," I said quickly. Probably too quickly. Shit. It seemed like last night I had decided to tell him, I just hadn't decided how to do it. Why was I lying now? I was getting angry. At myself for the lies I was slinging, and at him for making it necessary.

He just sat there shaking his head back and forth.

"Listen, Brandon . . ."

"I was really starting to like you."

"What does that mean?" I leaned forward and looked right in his face. He avoided my eye. He just looked down into his lap. His hands played idly with the soda can. I realized he hadn't taken a drink since I'd given it back to him.

"Brandon?"

"I don't care how terrible you think it is," he said, quiet. "I just thought we were starting to like each other. Trust each other." He looked up at me. I'd expected tears. Instead he looked calm and defiant. "I can't like you or trust you if you're going to keep lying to me."

I swallowed hard. This was it. This was when I needed to man up and tell him the truth.

"There's nothing to tell," I said. "If Sherri was here, she'd tell you the same thing."

He lowered his head again. I was about to start trying to convince him again when the doorbell cut through the silence.

"Who the hell . . . ?" I whispered as I got up and went to the door.

Big as shit, Sherri stood out on my front step. Didn't people call before coming over anymore? What happened to common courtesy? She started laughing as soon as she caught sight of me.

"Holy crap," she said. "Excuse me, Taylor Momsen, is Courtney home?"

"What are you doing here?" It would be fair to say that I screeched at her.

"I thought we said we were gonna hang out together," she said, and made air quotes. "And stow the attitude, okay? It's out of character and not very believable."

I leaned in and whispered. "Can you please just go?" I asked. "Like right now?"

"Hi, Sherri." Brandon was right behind me.

I slumped against the door. "Why don't you come in-side?" I said to Sherri. Then, as she was walking past me, I whispered right in her ear, "You inconvenient skank."

She just sashayed into the house and smiled brightly. If Sherri was a comic book character, she'd be Loki. She really took a lot of joy in spreading chaos wherever she went.

She sat down at the kitchen table, patted the seat next to her, and smiled up at Brandon. Looking huffy, he did as she wanted. I just stood there with my arms crossed and my bottom lip protruding about a mile.

"So what were you two talking about?" God, I hated her right then.

Brandon looked up at me and waited for me to say something. They both *just sat there* and stared at me. Those jerks.

"I sell drugs."

My mouth fell open. Had I said that? It must have been me—neither of them had opened their mouths. Was that possible?

Sherri did a double take, completely taken by surprise. That felt good, I have to admit. At least this afternoon wouldn't be a complete loss. But it was Brandon's reaction that concerned me. He sat there for another moment, studying me. He looked away. Oh, God, could he not even look at me now?

"Is that all?" he said.

I decided I needed to sit down. Sherri looked confused with a chance of angry. She glared at me for a second like I'd done this somehow.

"That's all you have to say?" she demanded.

Brandon shook his head and then took a sip of his soda. He didn't seem to care about the lipstick marks anymore.

"You know that, like, half the kids I know sell pot,

right?" he asked. "Ken Leung has been selling pot and speed since junior high! Hell, *I've* sold pot before."

"Wait a minute," I said, "if this doesn't faze you, then what did you think I'd done?"

"I don't know," he said. "Since you weren't talking to me, I guess my brain leaped to the worst-case, you know, situation."

"Scenario," I said.

"Selling drugs isn't the worst-case?" Sherri said. She still sounded like she couldn't get her bearings.

"No, I guess I thought maybe she, you know, had something to do with her friend's death. Your friend, too, I guess."

I felt suddenly queasy. There's no way he could know I felt partly responsible for Willie's suicide. I don't know what my face did, but Brandon got really serious really fast.

"You didn't, did you?" he asked. "Have something to do with him dying, I mean. Like he didn't overdose or anything?"

"Oh, Christ," Sherri said, and she stood fast and knocked the table. "I cannot believe you're okay with this."

"What?" Brandon asked.

"Sherri thought you were going to be disgusted," I said. *So did I,* I thought. I didn't know how to feel now that he seemed okay with it. Was that creeping sensation in my gut disappointment?

"Why would you think that?" Brandon turned in his seat to look at Sherri.

"Never mind."

"No, really."

"Really," Sherri said. She kept her back to us. "Drop it." It looked like she was studying a photo of me and my parents. From back in the day when Mom was still around, obviously.

"Sure," Brandon said. He turned back around and rolled his eyes at me. I ignored him.

"I know what stupid thing I want to do," Sherri said, her back to us still.

"What are you talking about?" I asked.

She turned to face us. I thought maybe she'd been crying or at least holding back tears, instead her eyes were totally clear.

"The other day," she said, "I told you I wanted to do something stupid. I just didn't know what. Remember?"

"Yeah," I said. It had been just yesterday, so of course I remembered.

"Well, I figured out what stupid thing I want to do."

"What?" I asked. I didn't like where this was going.

"I want to go in with you when you go to see Buddha," she said, "and I want to get high while we're there."

"What the hell?" I asked. "Five minutes ago, you thought I was a lowlife for selling this stuff and now you want to get high?"

She came and sat back down.

"You've told me that you were curious about it before and you told me if you ever did it, it'd be with him because he's the only person you'd trust not to kill you, right?"

" 'Kill you'?" Brandon asked. He looked freaked out. "We are just talking about reefer or cross-tops or something like that, right?"

Sherri gave him a withering look. "No, Nancy, we're not. Our little Courtney sells Vitamin Z. Still think it's no big deal?"

He gave me a questioning look. I ignored him.

"I'll ask you again," I said to Sherri. "What's this all about?"

She sat back and looked really tired. More than that, really. Defeated. Like she felt she couldn't go on anymore. She actually gave me a little smile.

"I want something that will make me forget everything that's going on. Alcohol doesn't do that. Weed doesn't do it." She shot a look at Brandon. He stared into the open soda can and didn't see it. "But I've heard from people who've taken it that Vitamin Z does. I want that right now."

I'd heard the same thing from a couple of people. Mostly at parties. For some reason talk at our parties always included a lot of discussion about what sort of excesses people had experienced, either drugs or booze. The folks who'd done Z would say they couldn't explain it to you, you'd have to try it for yourself. While they were on it, though, they felt completely gone from the world. They always had this sort of scary, faraway look in their eyes when they talked about it. It was a look I usually associated with religious nuts.

"I don't like it," I said.

"Tough titties," Sherri said. "If you want a ride out there today, I'm going in with you." Normally she'd smile when she said something like that. A mean smile, but still. This time she was totally serious.

"Brandon, tell her this is nuts," I told him.

"You guys shouldn't go by yourselves," he said. "I should go, too."

I felt like I was going crazy. Or everyone else was crazy and I was still holding it together. Somewhere along the line, all control over the situation had slipped out of my hands. Really, I should have been used to the feeling. At least Sherri was looking smug again—we were back on familiar ground there.

"You want to go, too," I said.

"You're going to go visit a drug dealer," he said. He said

it the way you'd tell someone with a stick of dynamite to step away from the open fire. "It'll be dangerous, Courtney."

"I've been going to see this guy twice a month for more than a year now. By myself. I think we'll be fine."

"Well, I still want to go."

I was about to keep arguing. Sherri cut in.

"You should let him come," she said. "If nothing else, we can take his truck. It's a lot nicer ride than my POS car."

"This is crazy," I said. "It's bat-shit stupid is what it is." I felt desperate. No matter what either of them said, or how casual they both seemed to be taking it, I knew for a damned fact it was going to end badly. But I guess that was never enough reason not to do something.

"Why not?" I said, invoking the *Wild Bunch* mantra again. Hey, things worked out for them, right?

I got up from the table and headed down the hall.

"You two stay here," I called over my shoulder.

"Where are you going?" Sherri asked.

"To wash this crap off my face," I answered. "There's no way in hell I'm going to see Buddha made up like this."

CHAPTER EIGHTEEN
Counting Coup

We got through the freeway checkpoint with no problems. The guards acted all soldierly when we first pulled up—standing at attention and weapons at the ready, like that. Then they saw me in the passenger seat and they relaxed.

"Hey, Courtney," a guy named Winton said. He's a black guy only two or three years older than me and he acts like he's all worldly. Based on his accent, I'd say he was from Georgia—I'd never bothered to ask him. "This your boyfriend?"

I felt Brandon tense beside me.

"No," called Sherri from the backseat. "*I'm* her *girlfriend*!"

Winton looked a little shocked. Then a crooked smile broke out across his face and exposed a gold tooth. "Sweet," he said. "I thought so . . ." He shouldered his rifle. "ID, Miss?"

I don't know why we had to go through this every time. I handed him my student ID. Tucked behind it I'd folded five twenty-dollar bills. One for each of the guys at the checkpoint. Buddha arranged for all of this, though I had to pay them out of my share.

Winton counted the money and then showed me that gold tooth again. "Everything looks in order, Miss." He pulled back the sleeve on his right arm and checked a big ol' military watch. "I've got thirteen-twelve right now. Our boy in Portland will open up the road block at Exit Six-B at fourteen-hundred sharp. It'll stay open for a half-hour. Okay?"

"Just like we always do it, Private."

He laughed. "Now I know why you never give me any play," he said, and he peered at Sherri in the backseat.

"Yeah," I said as Brandon put the truck in drive, "that's why."

They pulled the Humvee out of our way and Brandon accelerated onto the freeway.

Road trips were usually a lot of fun. This one not so much. I sat and stewed, pissed off that I'd allowed myself to be pressured into letting the two of them come along *and* wondering what I would tell Buddha when he opened the door and saw Brandon and Sherri following me around like puppies I'd picked up in the Safeway parking lot. Brandon was trying to act stoic and tough—supposedly for my sake. Sherri sat in the back plotting her self-destruction.

"Can I ask you a question?" Brandon asked.

"It's obvious you can," said Sherri from the backseat. "The question is, may you?"

Brandon looked surprised and a little confused. I suppressed a grin. Who knew Sherri paid attention when I corrected her grammar?

"What?" I asked.

"Why do you sell drugs?"

"What do you mean?" I asked. Brandon kept his eyes on the road.

"I mean, it's not like you're spending the cash on stuff," Brandon said. "At least, nothing obvious. You don't have a car, no flashy phone, no designer clothes."

"You don't like what she's wearing?" Sherri asked. "I think she's very stylish."

"What I'm saying," said Brandon through teeth that were ever so slightly gritted, "is that I can't figure out what you're doing with the money you're obviously making."

"I'm saving it," I said. I felt my cheeks grow flush and hated that I had that response.

"For . . . ?" Brandon prompted.

I shot a glance back at Sherri. She just stared back. Waiting.

"When I finish school, I'm going to move to New York and go to school at Columbia," I said. "I'm going to eventually get a doctorate in epidemiology from the Mailman School there."

"New York is closed," Brandon said.

"The Army'll open it in time for me to go."

"Why New York?" Brandon asked.

"Good question," said Sherri.

"There are places all over that study the spread of disease," he went on.

I heaved a huge sigh. I told very few people my plan because even to me it sounded a little crazy. Crazy or not, however, it was the plan.

"My mom studied at the Mailman School," I said. "A couple of years before the dead came back, she dropped out."

"Did your mom die in the zombie attacks?" Brandon asked.

"No," I said, "but sometimes I think she should have. She screwed off to Seattle with some douche when I was a kid."

Brandon took his eyes from the road long enough to give me a look.

"I don't understand," he said.

"My mom was studying at the Mailman Center," I said. "She might have been the one to discover a way to stop the spread of zombie-ism. But she quit, just like she quit my family. Well, I'm going to go there and finish what she refused to."

The road noise seemed really loud, and none of us spoke to replace it.

Brandon finally cleared his throat and said, "That still doesn't make any sense to me, Courtney."

My heartbeat quickened. I sat forward and stared out the windshield. I didn't want to look at him just then.

"OHSU, right here in Oregon, just up in Portland," he said, "they're doing research into whatever spreads the zombie virus. Why not just go there? Why pin your hopes on such a long shot? Why risk jail and your whole future on something that may never happen?"

"Let's change the subject," I said. I wanted to scream, to lash out and punch Brandon as hard as possible. I just sat there.

"Even if they open New York, and the . . . whatever center," Brandon went on, "what makes you think you'll be accepted?"

He waited for me to answer, which I refused to do.

"I think Courtney said to change the subject," Sherri said. I heard the ice in her voice. She may think my plan is crazy, and that the way I'm going about funding it is wrong, but I was still her friend and she had my back. Thank God.

"Right," said Brandon. "I'll shut up."

None of us said anything for a while. I mean, what was there to say?

"Will you at least put some music on?" I asked after a few miles. The silence was killing me.

The Pixies came over the speakers as he flipped on the

CD player. Good, I could do with some thrashing guitar, and Black Francis's screaming fit my mood.

"Jesus," Sherri said from the backseat, "could we have some music from this century?"

Brandon pressed buttons until he found something Sherri could live with.

We'd been on the road for about thirty-five minutes, which felt about right since we'd just hit the Tigard exit. We had another fifteen or so to go. When you're traveling north, Tigard is where you first see the wall. Right after the dead came back, the government decided they were going to build a wall around the greater Portland area. You know, seal the suckers in so they couldn't get out and spread their disease. I don't think the wall even got half-built. There are sections of it all around the city. There are also gaps all along it, too, so it's pretty worthless. It's like the fence around the school on a huge scale. But along that stretch of freeway, both sides of the road were lined with twelve-foot-tall concrete slabs. They wanted to keep the roads safe to encourage highway travel and shipping. It was two in the afternoon and we were the only car on the road, so I don't think it worked the way they planned.

As you motor along I-5, the freeway rises up and crosses the river from the west side of Portland to the east. When it does, you can finally get a look at the city. The buildings along the waterfront are all rotting and falling apart. It's sad, really. I guess Portland used to be pretty dank back before the zombie infestation. It was no New York, but what is?

As we drove past, I saw what looked like a bunch of people strolling up and down the Esplanade. Looking closer I saw that it was zombies milling around. They were the reason the city was closed off, and why the people who lived on the east side of the river had blown up all the bridges that connected them to the other side.

Speaking of the people, I could see some cars and trucks—trucks mostly—parked along the water on the east side. Guys with rifles stood out there aiming across the river at the zombies. Every once in a while, there'd be a popping sound and a puff of smoke, and then a zombie across the water would fall down or not. It seemed like an interesting way to kill time.

We drove past that scene, and Brandon exited I-5. We looped around to our left and we were on the 405. We drove west for just a few minutes. I told Brandon to start slowing down and pretty soon I told him to get off the freeway. A Hummer was parked next to a dismantled barricade. I saw a soldier sitting behind the wheel, and I waved as we drove past. He totally ignored me. From there, I directed Brandon through the twisty streets to a spot where we could park.

Buddha lived on the west side of the river, where all the zombies were confined. His apartment building sat at the foot of the West Hills, tucked behind the baseball stadium and just a couple of blocks from the Max light rail line. It would have been a really desirable location if it wasn't for all the undead strolling through the streets.

We parked in a tree-lined cul-de-sac up a hill from where the apartment sat, the branches overgrown and making the whole street shadowy and spooky despite the fact that it was the middle of the afternoon. We climbed out and Brandon got into the back of his truck to grab a shotgun from the gun rack.

"You should leave that," I said.

"Are you crazy?"

"First, let's stop questioning my sanity for the rest of the day, okay?" I said, and Brandon turned an appropriate shade of crimson. "Second, Buddha won't really appreciate you showing up at his front door with a loaded shotgun—he's funny that way. Finally, fire that thing and you'll attract every shuffler in a half-mile area." We stood there for a minute while he thought through it.

"I don't like it."

"You don't have to," I said. "You can stay in the truck and wait for us if you want." I felt mean saying it. There was just no way I wanted him taking the boom stick along with us. Finally he shrugged and put the shotgun back and closed the truck's door. He dug the key fob out of his pocket and pointed it at the truck.

"Don't lock it." Sherri stood with her hands in her pockets. She looked down the street toward where we would be headed in a second.

Brandon shot an exasperated look at me.

"We may need to get back into it in a hurry," I said. "Also, zombies won't be interested in jacking your stereo."

"Fine," he said, and walked toward me. He scuffed his shoes along the ground as he did, like now that he felt put upon, his feet were too heavy to lift all the way.

We walked along side by side by side, Brandon between me and Sherri.

"I'm usually not so lame," he said to me.

"I'll take your word for it," I said. I thought I'd whispered my response. Sherri laughed out loud, though, so she'd obviously heard it. Brandon's cheeks went a deeper shade of red. Oops.

"Listen," I said, "there's gonna be nothing to worry about, okay? I've done this a hundred times before."

"Twice a month for a year?" Brandon asked. "I thought you were in AP Math."

"Are you sure there's nothing to worry about?" Sherri asked.

We had just crested the hill and I looked down the street. About a million zombies milled around in front of Buddha's building.

"Huh," I said. I really didn't have anything else.

"We need to get out of here before they notice us," Brandon said. I was really glad he was the first one to say it.

"Oh, Princess," Sherri said, "do the zombies scare you?"

"Of course they do," Brandon said as loud as he dared. "They scare *all* sane, normal people. There's no way we could get past them all."

Sherri smiled. A sly, I've-got-an-idea type of smile.

"What?" I asked.

"You know what."

"No, really, what are you thinking, you moron?" I demanded.

"Just think about it some more."

I looked down the hill at the shufflers mingling around in front of the building. Studying them, I realized there weren't as many as I first thought. Some clumps of zombies gathered here and there. For the most part, they shuffled around in singles, bouncing off each other like flesh-eating pinballs. What could Sherri be thinking about, and how could I know what it was? It must be something we'd both already seen or done, right? As soon I thought that, I knew what she meant. I started to smile myself.

"Okay," said Brandon, "now it's my turn to ask what you're thinking."

"Counting coup!" Both Sherri and I said it in unison.

"Counting what?"

"Someone didn't pay attention in History class," Sherri said in a singsong voice.

When Sherri and I were in sixth grade together, we did a unit on American Indians in our History class. We both became fascinated by everything Indian. We made ourselves headdresses, we ate trail mix—the closest we could come to pemmican—we slept outside in a makeshift teepee every chance we got even though it was April and it rained almost every day that month. But the thing we loved the absolute most was the concept of counting coup.

Indians used to go into battle and, sure, they killed a ton of whites (not enough, apparently), but one of the things they'd do that they thought was really badass was to run up to their enemies and touch them—either with their hands or with a stick—and then run away. They wouldn't kill, or even hurt them. Just touch and then scamper away. That earned them bragging rights. Like, "I was so close to that dude, I could have totally smoked his ass, and I *didn't*. That's what a bad MF'er I am!"

I explained all of this to Brandon and he stood there looking at me like I was crazy.

"You don't get it," Sherri said to him.

"I get it," he said. "What I don't get is why you'd bring it up right now."

"Because it's something Sherri and I used to do with zombies," I said. "When we were younger."

"It's something you used to do?"

"Yeah," Sherri said, "we'd find a group of shufflers and we'd run through them and touch one or two. They're so slow and stupid that if you do it right, you'll be past them before they even notice you."

He looked like he was going to throw up. "You're kidding me."

"Don't be a dick, Brandon," Sherri said.

"Sherri, cut it," I said. "Brandon, we have to get around those zombies, right?"

He nodded slowly, like he was trying to convince himself that wasn't the case.

"Right. Well, running through them has a couple of purposes."

"Like what?"

"One: it gets us past them a lot quicker. If we tried to sneak around them, it'd take us a couple of hours to work our way through to Buddha's apartment, and we'd still have to get through them anyway. Second: it helps you not be so afraid of them. The adrenaline kicks in, your senses sharpen."

"Sharp senses," Sherri agreed.

"You get this amazing rush and then, when you're past them, you wonder what ever made you afraid of them." I could feel myself smiling at the memory of Sherri and me doing this. It wasn't a regular thing. We'd only done it a dozen times or so since we'd been allowed out by ourselves.

"This is so stupid," Brandon said.

"That means you've decided to do it," I said. All of my anger at him from earlier had died down. It wasn't gone completely, but I could ignore it at least. Quick, before I was able to convince myself not to, I leaned over and kissed his cheek. "You're going to love it!"

It looked like that had been the right move. He blushed like crazy, but he looked determined now. He started to jump up and down and take really deep breaths. That must have been some sort of football player psyche-up thing. Whatever it took.

Sherri rolled her eyes at me and made kissy lips. I was grateful she didn't say anything.

"Okay, gang, listen up," I said, and then I told them the plan for getting into Buddha's building. We needed to start out silently, no yelling, or screaming, as the case may be. The zombies couldn't know we were there until we were actually running through them. We couldn't bunch up, but we had to stay together, too, since we'd have to get inside the lobby. I had a key card and it would be best if we all got there at the same time so we could all go inside together. Once we were in the lobby, we'd be safe. The glass was all reinforced and the shufflers wouldn't be able to break it. Once we all piled into the elevator, they'd stop trying to get inside.

"The elevator works?" Brandon asked.

"There's a generator in the basement. Everyone ready?" We all were or, at least, we said we were.

"Let's wild-bunch it," I said, and we started off.

At first we all jogged along. Easy, like we were starting our morning run or something. But the steep hill made it easy to gain speed. That was good, I wanted a lot of momentum by the time I hit the first of the zombies. Halfway down the hill, and I could already feel my heart beating against my chest and my breath was starting to burn. Too soon. I stopped breathing through my nose and started gulping in air through my mouth. It sounded ragged. I stole quick glances to the side to make sure we were still grouped together. Sherri was a little behind me and Brandon was a little ahead.

Another few yards and we'd be in the knot of undead. Sherri, behind me, was the first one to let out a whoop. A high, piercing war cry. I thought maybe she did it to help ease the pain in her lungs—if she was feeling anything like I did, anyway. I let out a high screech.

Brandon hit the first zombie, a shoulder check that knocked the damned thing off its feet and sent it flying. He gave out this guttural shout that scared me more than the zombies did. He barely slowed down as he kept running toward the building.

I was a lot less effective. I reached out and slapped the back of the nearest zombie, a girl. I felt something give way underneath her clothes. I tried hard not to think about it. I gave an out-of-breath cry and kept going.

I heard Sherri laughing a few paces behind me and then I started laughing, too. I threw my whole body into the next zombie, a guy who had just started turning around.

He fell into another UD and they both biffed it. I laughed harder.

I stopped laughing when I saw Brandon standing next to the entrance. He pointed at the door to Buddha's building, which stood wide open. I didn't slow down, waved him on.

"Get inside," I tried to yell. I could barely get my breath.

I glanced back at Sherri. She was practically running up my ass, so I gave it all I had to stay ahead of her.

Brandon was pissed. He dodged inside the lobby right ahead of us.

We all stopped short. Four zombies stood between us and the elevators. The smell of rotting meat was heavy in the small space. I immediately got goose bumps up and down my arms.

"No way!" Sherri yelled between gasps.

"Close the door," I panted.

"Close it?" Brandon asked. Then he saw what I saw. The zombies we'd run through were converging on the building. If we didn't close the doors, we'd have a lot more than four zombies to worry about.

Sherri pulled the door closed and we heard the electronic *snick* of it locking. One problem down. Next problem: The four shufflers in the lobby were onto us.

Brandon drove his shoulder into the nearest one, a rotting old man in a cardigan. The left arm of the sweater hung empty. The zombie duffer hit the ground and there was an audible cracking sound and he laid there without moving. Sweet! Brandon then picked up a lobby chair and he started swinging it around like Conan in a furniture store.

"Press the button for the elevator!" he screamed at me and Sherri because, to be honest, we were just standing there gawking at the show he was putting on.

A really fresh zombie, he looked relatively clean and I didn't see a bite mark on him, stood in the back of the room, near us and the elevators. He seemed to watch everything we were doing. As creepy as the undead are, thinking he might be watching us and planning something was off the creepiness charts.

Brandon was beating up the other two zombies with his chair. I looked around for something to hold off Genius Zombie and spotted a fire extinguisher. I hoped it still worked. I took it off the wall and started edging closer to the shuffler. I followed the instructions printed on the extinguisher and got it ready to fire.

"Sherri," I called over my shoulder, "get ready to rush the elevator."

"Ready when you are."

When I was just a few feet away, the thing lunged at me, like it had been playing dead or something. He was so fast I almost forgot I had the extinguisher in my hands. I pressed the lever and a thick cloud of white chemicals shot right into the thing's face. It stumbled past me, blind, and I took a swing at it with the heavy metal cylinder. My timing was off and I barely connected with its back. All I did was send it crashing into one of the walls.

Brandon was done with his two zombies—they were on the floor, their heads broken open—and came to help me. The last zombie moved faster than anything I'd seen before. He must have been really fresh. He hit the wall and rebounded like nothing happened. He turned on us, snarling and swiping at us. Brandon held him back with the raised chair.

Behind us I heard the elevator bell ding and Sherri yelled out, "It's here!" The bell got the shuffler's attention, too, and he lunged in that direction. Brandon leaped forward and actually trapped the thing against the wall in the legs of the chair.

"Get in the elevator now!" he screamed at me, and I did what he said.

Sherri was already in there, huddled against the back wall trying to make herself as small as possible. I scooted in next to her.

"Get ready to press the CLOSE DOOR button." Brandon yelled. I remembered hearing once that the CLOSE DOOR button doesn't actually do anything, elevator makers just put it in there because people like to press it; they'd complain if it wasn't there. I did not bring that up to the guy currently holding off a snarling, flesh-eating monster.

"Come on," I said.

I could tell it was taking everything Brandon had to hold the zombie against the wall. His arms strained and his cheeks were a really frightening shade of red. As soon as I told him we were ready, he nodded and I heard him count to himself, psyching himself up.

"One . . . two . . . ," he took a deep breath, "three!" He whipped the chair away and then, as soon as the zombie lunged forward, he pushed the chair legs right into the thing's face. The zombie stumbled and Brandon used that momentum to throw it to the floor. Then he hightailed it to the elevator.

I started pressing the CLOSE DOOR button like a freaking lab rat looking for a fix and Brandon sprinted through the slowly closing doors and nearly crushed Sherri in the process.

It felt like the doors barely moved. Glaciers moved faster. I could see beyond the doors as the zombie threw the chair off him and then got to its hands and knees. I swear to God the thing shook its head like it needed to clear it, and then it looked up at us and snarled, pissed. It got to its feet and stood there for a second and bellowed at us. I nearly jumped out of my skin. I'd never heard a zombie make a noise like that. Then it charged.

It hit the doors just as they closed and for a second I thought the stupid things were going to open. Then I felt the elevator shudder as it started to rise. I let out a breath I didn't know I'd been holding and I slumped back against the wall. I took a minute to try to get my heart rate back down.

We were all silent as we rode up. Finally Brandon looked from me to Sherri and asked, "You know what would make counting coup more fun? A *shotgun!*"

Our laughter sounded forced and almost like screams. We had to laugh, though—if we didn't we'd probably start crying or maybe just lose it altogether and go catatonic. Our laughter faded away and we rode the rest of the way up in silence. The elevator bumped to a stop on the penthouse level. We collected ourselves as best we could.

As we walked into the short hallway outside Buddha's apartment, Sherri said to Brandon, "Okay, Captain Kickass, you can hang out with us anytime you want."

He looked weirdly proud at that.

"Ditto," I said.

The hallway outside the apartment had only two doors, one on either side. Back in the day there had been two apartments on this floor. Since Buddha became the sole occupant, he knocked out the walls and now lives in one huge apartment. It's pretty badass.

Brandon and Sherri stood behind me as I stopped in front of one of the doors. I was having second thoughts about this, then I guessed we'd come this far. Too late to start being smart about things.

I went ahead and knocked.

CHAPTER NINETEEN
Vitamin Z

Buddha opened the door and a big grin broke across his craggy face. "My favorite mule!" he said, and then he saw Sherri and Brandon and he put the grin back wherever it came from. "And who do we have here, Courtney?"

"Can we come in, Buddha? We just had to deal with a bunch of zombies down in the lobby."

"Son of a bitch!" He turned and stormed off. The door stood open so I shrugged and marched in. I figured he'd have closed it if he wanted us to stay out. When I was inside, I turned to see my lame-o friends still standing in the hallway. I waved them in and gave them my best eye roll.

Deeper into the apartment, I heard Buddha screaming at someone. He must have been on the phone. He had some of his goons living in the apartments below his, and there was a chemist or two in a lab he kept on a lower floor. He never liked to have any of them come up to his personal apartment.

"Wow, now I want to grow up to be a drug dealer," Sherri said as she and Brandon followed me into the living room and sat on couches. I knew what she meant. Buddha had every wall he could knocked down, and then he filled the place with all the cool art and furniture he could get his goons to scrounge up. I heard that armed parties of them went through all of the abandoned houses in the hills behind the apartment complex right after the city forced their owners to evacuate.

"Is it a problem that we're here?" Brandon asked. We still heard Buddha yelling at someone on the phone from the other room—his bedroom, the one enclosed space on the whole floor.

"Too late to do anything about it now," I said.

The bedroom door opened and Buddha came out. He's tall, like six-five, and really thin. Wiry, you know. He looks like some of the wrestlers at school, though none of them have a full-on ZZ Top beard and long flowing hair—and it's gray, almost white. He looks kind of crazy in a good way. As he walked, he pulled his hair back and tied it with something.

He walked over to a bar near the kitchen area and poured himself a drink. "That's the third time in about two weeks that one of those assholes downstairs forgot to close and lock that door right." He stood with his back to us. "I've got a bunch of guys going downstairs to clean up whatever's left behind. Sorry you had to deal with it."

He brought his drink over to where we were. He sat next to me, across from Brandon and Sherri, and put his feet up on the glass coffee table between us. He threw his arm around me.

"I wasn't expecting you to have an entourage," he said.

"These are friends of mine," I said.

"I hoped you weren't bringing in some strangers off the street." He took a swallow of the amber liquor. "Do these friends have names?"

"Sherri and Brandon." Sherri gave a tiny wave.

"Great."

"They call you Buddha, right?" Brandon asked.

"Yep."

"But that's not your name, right? That's a nickname."

"You're a sharp one," Buddha said, still grinning. "Ma and Pa Schreibstein did not name their baby boy Buddha. But it's what you can call me."

"Why 'Buddha'?"

"Brandon, what the hell?" I asked. I didn't understand why he was pushing this.

"It's okay," Buddha said, and he patted my knee to reassure me. I saw Brandon bristle at that. "Why Buddha?" he asked, and leaned forward. "Well, it was given to me by my friends when I was younger."

"Yeah, but why?" Brandon asked again, despite my trying to will his damned head to explode. "There's always a reason for the nicknames people give out."

"You're right," Buddha said, "sure. Well, I guess there's only two reasons someone could get the nickname 'Buddha.' One, you are a serene, peaceful person who'd never hurt a soul, just like the Bodhisattva. Or, two, you're not."

When he spoke next, he tapped a gnarled finger on the glass of the tabletop. "Which do you think was my case, son?" Buddha leaned back and spread his arms along the back of the couch. "So, why'd you bring your friends, Courtney?"

I pulled the envelope with his money out of my bag and handed it to him. "First things first, I guess."

He took it from me and got up. He headed back to his room. "Get everybody some drinks. I'll be back in a minute."

As soon as the door clicked shut I turned on Brandon. "What is your problem?" I hissed at him.

"What?" He had the balls to look innocent.

"Getting into a pissing contest with him about his freaking nickname? What is that?"

"I was just curious."

"That stuff about his nickname," I said as I stood up, "that's true. I've heard stories from his guys about him."

"He doesn't scare me," Brandon said.

"Then you're way dumber than I thought," said Sherri, "and that's pretty dumb."

I stomped over to the bar and fished some sodas out of the mini-fridge. Brandon refused to look me in the eye as I walked back to the couch and sat down. Which made me even madder because I was trying to give him my best glare the whole time. I set my soda down next to me on the couch and handed one to Sherri. I took the last can and shook it for a good while before I handed it to Brandon. Sherri snorted laughter. Brandon just looked at the can for a second before he said, "You know, no matter how bad you shake them up, if you just let modern Coke cans sit for about ten seconds, they won't spray." And he set his can down on the table.

"Just stop being a dick," I said to him.

Buddha came back into the room and sat down.

"Thanks, Courtney," he said. "So, what was the other reason you came over today?"

I didn't answer. I found that when it was time to actually come right out and say it, I couldn't ask him to get us high. I'd made a point of never using up to this point. Part of it was that a lot of people said using Vitamin Z just once could make you an addict—in public, I told everyone I thought that was bull. The truth was that I really did believe it. The other part was that I thought people who did use were huge F'ing losers. Everyone I'd ever sold to looked like scum and trash to me. I never felt bad that I was selling them this potentially dangerous drug because I didn't care about them at all. So, given that, how the hell was I supposed to ask Buddha to fix us up?

I looked at Sherri. She avoided my eyes. No help there even though it was her idiot idea. I could feel Buddha staring at me. I cleared my throat.

"We want to know if you'll get us high," Brandon said.

I looked up and he was looking right at me. "With the Vitamin Z."

Buddha looked slowly from Brandon to me. "Is that right, Courtney?" he asked. When I nodded, he said, "I have to admit that that surprises me. I thought you were dead set against it." He scratched his head. "You know, time was I required my sellers to get high with me. But, like I said, I was a different creature then. So, I'll ask again: Is this what you want?"

I nodded. "Yeah," I said.

Buddha didn't answer for a while. Again he looked back at Brandon and I wanted to scream at him, *Stop looking at him, this was my decision!* But I kept my mouth shut.

"Right," Buddha said quietly, and stood up. "If you'll excuse me, I have to go into my room again." He walked away, then stopped. "I'll bring a pipe, okay? None of you look like you'd be very needle-friendly." And then he disappeared into the room and the door closed behind him.

"It is what you wanted, right?" Brandon asked.

"Of course it is," I snapped at him. I wasn't done being mad at him yet.

"Just checking."

"I'm having second thoughts," Sherri said.

"It's probably a little late for that," Brandon said, and just then I really hated him. Hated how calm he was, hated how he didn't seem afraid of Buddha like he should have been. I hated him because he was there in Buddha's apartment with me. No one I liked should ever have been in there.

"It feels too late for a lot of stuff," I said. Even as I said it, I regretted it. It felt petty and too dramatic. Neither of them reacted, probably too wrapped up in their own worries and fears to notice I was a lame-ass. So, that was good.

Buddha came out again and headed over. He had a small

box in one hand and a big brick-shaped thing wrapped in plastic in the other. He handed me the brick as he sat down.

"For you," he said. "'Cause I might forget once we get going."

I hefted the bulk of Vitamin Z in my hand. This brick would probably earn me another $5,000, even with what I owed Buddha and other operating expenses. I stowed it away in my bag.

Buddha opened his box. It was felt-lined and inside was a metal pipe, a tiny bag of Z, and a pretty big bag of weed. He set everything on the table and then opened the bag of pot.

"Marijuana?" Brandon asked. "Are we gonna smoke that first?"

"Smoke 'em together," said Buddha as he loaded a hit into the pipe. "Some people smoke it straight, but they're pretty far gone. Junkies who can't get a hit otherwise. Get it?"

Brandon nodded. "Is it really made out of zombie brains?"

"You sound nervous, all these questions." He didn't look up from what he was doing.

Brandon swallowed hard and nodded. "I guess I am. I heard using just once can make you addicted."

"That's really rare," I said. I hoped I didn't sound too much like I was trying to convince myself.

"That's right," Buddha said as he went back to loading the pipe. "You're both right. It happens. It's rare, but it happens." He zipped up the bag of pot and set it in the box, then he took up the bag of Z and popped it open. He took just a few grains and sprinkled them on top of the weed in the pipe. "And to answer your original question: Yep, it's made out of actual zombies' brains. Before you ask, it's also true that some addicts who die of overdoses come back as zombies." He held the pipe out to Brandon. "Wanna take the first hit?"

Brandon just sat there and didn't make a move for the pipe. I told myself that if he refused, I'd refuse, too. I'd tell Buddha that we'd made a mistake and no hard feelings. I knew Buddha liked me and that he wouldn't hold it against me. I had my new supply of Z, there was no real reason for us to stick around. All Brandon had to do was turn down the pipe and we could leave.

Brandon reached out and took it out of Buddha's hands. My heart sank. "Where's the fire?" he asked.

"Oh, right," Buddha said, and he dug a battered old Zippo out of his pocket.

I turned away as Brandon took the lighter and raised the pipe to his lips, so I didn't see him take a hit, but I heard his explosive cough a few seconds later. Buddha chuckled. "Open up that Coke and take a swig," he said. "It'll help the burn in your throat."

There was the pop/fizz sound of the can being opened and then Brandon's cough subsided a little. Sherri took the next hit; she handled it better than Brandon, holding the smoke for a good fifteen or twenty seconds before she let it out in a thick stream.

Then it was my turn. I picked up the pipe in my left hand, the lighter in my right. I was about to light it up when Buddha stopped me.

"Let me charge that up." He took a few more grains of Z and sprinkled them on top of the charred pot. "Okay, go for it."

Brandon sat back on the couch, his arms relaxed at his sides. He smiled at me and his eyes were already glassy. Sherri wouldn't look at me; she stared at a string of hair she held in front of her eyes and twirled. No help from either of them. So I forced a smile, took up the pipe, and took a big toke. I'd smoked pot a few times, and this was just like that—the harsh, acrid smoke attacking the back of my throat. There was something else to it, too. A sweetness flooded my tongue. All I could remember was reading once that human flesh smelled sweet when you cooked it. I started to gag, which triggered a cough. I held it together and kept most of the smoke in my lungs.

Even before I exhaled the whole hit, I felt a pleasant coolness spreading through my brain. It started in the back of my head—in my lizard brain—and it crept like fog up to the front. My mouth was instantly dry and I immediately picked up my own soda after I handed the pipe and lighter off to Buddha.

He took a large pinch of black powder out of the bag and grinned at me as he threw all of it on top of the cinder in the pipe. I smiled back and surprised myself because I could tell it was a genuine smile. All the anxiety I'd felt before melted away. My body relaxed, too, molding itself to the couch. It felt good.

Buddha sucked on the pipe, a startling sound because he sucked so long and deep. My lungs ached a little thinking about it. Then he let fly with a monstrous stream of smoke. He looked like a dragon—it went on and on. When he was finally done, he set the pipe and lighter on the table and grinned at me again.

"It's nice to see you relaxed, Courtney," he said. "You're usually so uptight all the time." He put his hand on my knee and rubbed his thumb around in a little circle. It felt nice.

"Hey," Brandon said, "that's my sort-of girlfriend you're groping, Buddha." But there was no anger in his voice. He wore a dopey grin and could barely lift his arm to point at us.

Buddha laughed and raised his hands in mock surrender. "Right," he said, "right. We need some music." He stood up and walked over to the stereo. He didn't wobble at all. I knew that if I stood up just then, there was a good chance I'd fall flat on my face.

"This is nice," Sherri said, and she finally smiled, too. "This isn't so bad."

"This?" Buddha asked. "This is just the pot. Give it a few minutes and you'll feel the Z kick in." Brandon and Sherri nodded in unison at that and I noticed after a second that I was doing it to. I laughed out loud and they both giggled, although I'm sure they had no idea why.

Music came out of the speakers and I immediately stopped laughing. I sat up and found Buddha over by the stereo.

"I know this!" I shouted at him. "Chacho played this in his truck the other night."

"Big Star," Buddha said as he walked back to the couch. "This 'Muchacho' has good taste."

I stared at him with my mouth wide open. I could feel the gears in my brain spinning at a million miles an hour. None of the gears would catch. Goddamn that pot for making my fuzzy brain even fuzzier. Buddha was looking at me now, a little worried. I think he could tell there was something going on with me. It was something he said. Just a minute ago.

"That's it!" I yelled. Buddha sat back away from my explosion. "Muchacho!"

"Muchacho what?" he asked.

"Muchacho . . ." I searched my memory. Nothing. "Shit," I said, and sank back to the couch.

The other three laughed. Maybe at me, maybe about something else, I didn't know. I worried at the fact that I couldn't follow the thread of a minute-long conversation. Was that the pot or the Z? I don't think pot had ever affected me like that.

I blinked my eyes and looked around the apartment. Then I blinked some more.

"Did someone turn down the lights?" I asked.

"Oh, yeah," said Sherri. "It's getting dark."

Brandon looked around. He alternately blinked and opened his eyes as wide as he could.

"It's not dark," he said. "There's something about the color."

Buddha nodded. "Get ready, kids, here it comes."

"What is this?" Sherri demanded.

But I never heard if Buddha answered her.

The world is gray.

The four of us are the only spots of color and we're quickly fading. I stand and it's a struggle. My arms and legs don't want to work right. I feel an itch that wasn't in my body. An idea grabs me and won't let go.

"I need to get downstairs."

I think the others will argue with me, but only two of them stand, ready to join me. The old one with a beard stays and waves us on. He cackles and mutters to himself.

We head out the door and to the elevator. It takes all three of us to figure out pushing the button to operate the thing. It's only the call of the others outside that can get us to concentrate enough to figure it out. After an eternity, the doors slide open and we stumble inside. We stare at the buttons on the control panel for a long time before the boy bellows and stabs at one of the buttons with a jerking motion of his arm. I hope it's the right button.

The doors open onto an empty room. It smells of gunpowder and meat. There was violence here recently and it makes me salivate despite my dry throat. Beyond the room, through the window, I see the others. The mass of our kind gathered in the streets. All I want in the world is to be with them.

We run across the room and throw ourselves at the window.

Why can't we get to them? The girl manages to throw herself against the door in such a way that it opens and she falls out. The boy and I see the opening and we follow her.

As soon as we exit the room, as soon as we're out on the street, all sense of "I" and "me" is gone. In its place is left "us" and "we." We are absorbed into the mass of our own kind. Everyone so different but all the same. We feel the comfort of losing our selves. We are lost in an ocean of the group's thoughts. "Hunger." And beneath that, we feel or hear something else, something more. We're not far enough gone yet to sense it properly.

A misshapen face, nose and cheeks missing, eyes milky, stands inches away from us, staring, sensing we are different. But even we are gray, no trace of pink, of color. The face sniffs us, deep chuffing noises, and then moves on. We are the same and so it has no interest in us.

We move through this colorless world, fascinated with the feeling of belonging. We are lost within a mass of others just like us. We've never felt so free.

But still, there are the nagging voices, just out of range of our sensing. And, slowly, the realization of hunger. It starts as a feeling—remote— in our stomachs. Soon it's all we can think about. Our hunger consumes us.

We wander aimlessly through the gray landscape, bumping into the others like us, choosing turns at random. Searching always for what can sustain us.

As we stumble down an alley, drawn by the smell of rotting meat—one of us fed here a while ago—we hear something and stop. Something new has come to us. Behind the Dumpster, something radiates. As we walk closer, we see a shimmering flash of color against the wall. The hunger, already more than we could bear, spikes and we're driven forward.

An animal yowls at us as it darts farther down the alley. For a moment, we stop and watch it. The cat, alive, pulses with color, stands out in this monochrome world like a flare in the darkness. It's so easy to track. We run as fast and as well as we can after it.

We slow as we reach the dead end where the animal has trapped itself. We spread out. We can't let it escape. Nowhere else to go, it arches its back and growls at us—a hissing, snarling sound deep in its throat.

As we approach it, our hands outstretched, an idea comes to us. This feeling, it's not just hunger. We are dazzled by the sight of it, its color and vitality, the life it contains. What we feel is love. We love it and its life so much that we have to have it be a part of us. The thought of letting it go and not having some tiny portion of its life inside of us is unthinkable.

It tries to find a way through our collective grasp. There's no way out. Finally, there's no other option, the creature leaps forward, claws exposed, and it's a whirlwind of slashing legs and biting teeth. It doesn't matter. We love it so much, we'll accept its punishment. The injuries are a small price to pay to possess it.

Several of us have our hands on it and we are all desperate to have it to ourselves. It comes apart as we fight over it, and still it screeches as we open our mouths wide and let its blood, its life and vitality, flood our mouths.

And then there's blackness.

CHAPTER TWENTY
I'm Sure She's Fine

I came to because the sun shone right in my eyes. I squeezed them shut even more tightly than they'd been. It didn't help. I rolled from my back onto my side and reached for a pillow to throw over my head. That's when I noticed I wasn't in my bed. Instead of my worn cotton sheets, I felt grass underneath me. I opened my eyes and propped myself up on my elbows. Sunlight flooded into my head, which I thought was going to explode.

I immediately lay back down as a headache the size of a rottweiler jumped up and down on my skull. I fought off a wave of nausea. Why was I outside? Why did my mouth feel like it was lined with fur?

I became aware of a loud snore beside me. Moving my head as little as possible, I rolled over to see Brandon there on the grass beside me. I chanced a look down, my head throbbing the whole time, and I laid back, relieved that we both still had our pants on.

When I rolled over, I'd pinned my left arm under my body and I became slowly aware that it hurt. A lot. I raised my body up and pulled my arm out from under me, wincing as it scraped against the ground. Three deep gouges ran up and down my arm, each one filled with dried blood.

What the hell?

I struggled to remember what happened the night before that could account for this. My mind came up empty. Actually, it felt like it might stay empty for the rest of eternity, which would be fine with me if the pain in my head would just stop.

"Brandon," I hissed, and stopped to squeeze my eyes shut again. Speaking brought a new wave of agony and nausea. I blindly reached out with my left hand and hunted around until I found him next to me. I groped my way up his body until I had hold of a lock of his hair. Then I yanked it for all I was worth.

He jerked away from me and yelped, "Hey!" Then there was silence for a while. "Oh, Jesus," he said.

"Yeah," I said, "so you're awake?"

"I am now." His voice sounded thick with phlegm and he coughed, and then he moaned. "Where are we, Court?"

Court? Even in my diminished state, I knew that that particular bud would need clipping. "I was hoping you could tell me, *Brand*."

"Why are we outside? Where's my truck?"

"These are all excellent questions." I'd planned to say something else, too. Something really scathing. Nothing would come to mind. "I wonder if Sherri is feeling like crap right now, too. I mean, I *hope* she is since this is her fault."

Brandon didn't answer. I heard him moving around and decided to take a chance and open my eyes to see what was up. I winced away the pain of actually taking in the world. Brandon had sat up. He slowly looked all around us.

"Where *is* Sherri?" he said.

I sat up as fast as I dared—which wasn't very fast—and my head swam anyway. Tiny black dots floated in front of my eyes until I squeezed them shut. Once the feeling passed I opened them again.

We were in a pasture bordered on one side by a split rail fence and on the other three by rows of some sort of trees. What they were, I had no idea, I'm not a tree expert. A few cars buzzed by on the road beyond the fence.

"There's your truck," I said to Brandon.

"That's good. I'm glad we didn't walk all the way here."

"Yeah, driving while we were blacked out is so much better," I said. "But where's Sherri?"

Brandon just shook his head. He looked really far away and he had a dopey grin that irritated me.

"What's up with your arm?" he asked.

I looked at it again.

"I don't know, scratches I guess."

"Scratches?" The dopey grin was gone, replaced by a look of concern. Hungover concern.

"Down, boy," I said. "If these were zombie scratches, I'd already be, you know . . ."

"I guess."

I poked around in my mouth with my tongue again. There was something in there. I finally reached in and dug around with my fingers. I pulled something out and looked at it. It looked like I had a bunch of hair in there. What the hell? I threw it away in disgust.

"We have to go look for Sherri," I said. "Why aren't you concerned about where she is?"

I took out my phone and dialed her number. It went right to voice mail. I hung up without leaving a message.

"Sherri's fine," he said. "She's probably at Buddha's place, or she woke up in a field like we did." He looked around, like maybe Sherri was going to spring up out of the grass.

"That's not good enough!" I shouted. "We need to look for her." I felt so scared I could barely think. The only thing that made sense was to try to find Sherri.

"Okay," Brandon said. He did an impersonation of a

reasonable person, but I could see anger creeping in at the edges. "Where should we start? Buddha's place?" He stopped and looked around. "Where is that, do you think?"

"I don't know."

"That's right, Court, you don't know. I don't know." He stopped and scooted close to me. It felt like he was about to reach out for me, but maybe he thought better of it. "We'd just be running around, burning gas and making ourselves crazy. The best thing we could do is head home and wait for her to call us. The moment she does, I'm in my truck so I can pick her up." He gave me a sincere smile that made me want to punch him in the junk. "Believe me, she'll be okay."

"What if she's not okay?" I asked.

"Jesus," he said, "you worry too much."

I worry too much about my friend who went missing while we were stoned out of our heads on a drug made from zombie brains. A friend who was the main course for a bunch of shufflers for all I knew.

"Take me home," I told him, and slowly managed to stand up. The ground seemed to roll gently beneath me as I walked toward the truck. It was like the one time I was on a boat. I didn't like it.

Brandon caught up to me and he took my hand in his. I let him because it helped steady me.

"I'd drive you home if I knew where we were."

"We'll figure it out on the way."

"What's all over your face?"

"I don't have a mirror, jackass."

He turned his head this way and that and squinted at me. "It looks like either your lipstick got smeared all over your face . . ."

"Or . . . ," I prodded.

"Or, I don't know, blood maybe?"

I stopped. Something nagged at me. Something from last night, and then the fact that I had hair or something in my mouth.

"Oh, shit," I said, and I started to retch. I didn't even try to hold it back. I just wanted it out of me. I fell to my hands and knees as I heaved up everything in my stomach. The pain in my head shot from "dull ache" to "drum circle" in nothing flat. Brandon backpedaled away from me and fell on his ass.

"What's going on, Courtney? Are you okay?"

I waved him away. He let me finish without talking to me again. When I was finally done, I grabbed up a fistful of grass and wiped my mouth as well as I could.

"Do you remember a cat?" I asked. "From last night?"

"Maybe? Why?"

"I remember a big group of us cornered it in an alley . . ." My voice trailed off. I tried to think of some other explanation and came up empty.

"What is it, Court?"

"Don't call me that anymore! I hate that shit—shortening people's names. We're not in an episode of *Friends*, okay?"

"Okay, just tell me what's going on."

"I think I ate a cat last night," I said. I whispered it. Brandon sat forward and I know he was about to ask me to repeat myself. Then he got it. His eyes widened. He opened his mouth to speak. Nothing came out.

"Yeah," I said. "If I hadn't just puked, I think I'd be sick." I could barely remember the specifics. All I could recall with any clarity was the feeling of belonging and how incredible it was. But I could bring to mind enough flashes to know that I'd helped kill and eat that poor cat. I wanted to be sick all over again, maybe forever. I'd never killed anything that wasn't already undead. Oh, God, I didn't even kill spiders—I scooped them up and put them outside. How could I have done this? All because of that stupid drug.

Did other people on Z kill animals? Had they ever killed other people? I shoved the thought away for now.

"Do you have any water in your truck?"

"I should have some bottles in there, yeah." He stood and held out his hand to help me up. My head actually felt better since I'd been sick. Yea, vomiting. He took my hand again and we started back toward the truck.

"Do you think that's where you got those scratches?" He examined my arm.

"It must be," I said. "Which is fine, that cat deserved to scratch the hell out of me."

"It wasn't you," Brandon said, "it was the drugs."

"That's bull, Brandon, and you know it. *I* chose to take the stupid drugs. *Me*."

He didn't answer. When we climbed over the fence, Brandon opened the truck and found a bottle of water for me. I used it to wash my face off and then to rinse out my mouth. He held out a second one for me and I drank that one down. I immediately felt better when I drank it. I just didn't know if I deserved to feel better. I thanked him and climbed into the truck. I just really wanted to get home. I wanted to see my dad.

"Shit," I said under my breath.

"What is it?" Brandon asked as he got us onto the road and started driving in the direction we'd been facing.

"My dad is probably freaking out."

I found my phone in one of my jacket pockets. I expected to see a zillion messages. There was just one. I pushed the RETRIEVE button and listened.

"Hey, Courtney, it's Dad. I just wanted to touch base and let you know not to stay up waiting for me to get home. I'm going out with Beverly and we'll more than likely go back to her place after. There's a lasagna in the fridge and a twenty on the counter in case you need anything. Call me if you need to. I'll see you sometime tomorrow. Love you. 'Bye."

I stared at my phone for a long time. I felt like it had betrayed me. Or Dad had. Someone sure had. Maybe me.

"Everything okay?"

"Everything's great," I said. "Where are we?"

"I think we're actually somewhere around Silverton. I saw a marker and we're on Two-thirteen. If I keep driving this way, I'll run into Silverton or Salem. Either way, it won't take too long to get you home."

I didn't say anything. I just sat back and crossed my arms over my chest. I wanted to have a world-class sulk.

I tried calling Sherri again. I just got her voice mail. "Call me," was all I said when I got the beep. I settled back into the seat.

It turned out we were headed toward Salem and would be home in twenty minutes or so. I fought with myself the whole way there. I kept telling myself that Sherri was fine; she'd probably made her way home the way Brandon and I had made our way to that field. I'd hear from her later. Other stuff worried me, too. The fact that my dad wasn't home, hadn't been home, really irked me. I told myself that it chapped my hide because he was being totally irresponsible to stay out all night when he had a teenage daughter at home. He should be there for me when I needed him! That wasn't it or, at least, that wasn't all of it. A big part of it was that I wanted him to know I'd been out all night and to be furious and demand to know where I'd been. I wanted him to do all the things Dad had never done—I wanted him to goose-step back and forth in front of me and send me to my room without any dessert.

I wanted him to get out of me what had just happened.

Why did I want to get caught? It was freaking dumb to

think that would make things better. I mean, I'd probably lose all the money I'd earned over the last year. That meant bye-bye New York, or anywhere else cool, after I was finally done with school. More than that, I could end up going to jail. They'd probably make me tell them about Buddha. How long would I last in jail once Buddha figured out it was me that got him arrested? No, telling anyone, my dad included, was not the way to go. I needed to stop being all passive-aggressive with myself. If I wanted to stop selling drugs, I should man up and just stop. I totally could anytime, too. As soon as I had another few thousand, I would stop.

I heaved a big sigh and sank even farther into the seat.

"I'm sure Sherri's fine," Brandon said. He gave me quick concerned glances as he drove.

I forced a smile. "Thanks. I'm sure she is, too." It was easier to lie than it was to tell him that I was worried. But just hearing him mention her name made my heart beat harder.

We drove on for a minute before he cleared his throat. I thought maybe he wanted to turn on the radio or something.

"What is it?" I asked.

"I just wanted to ask you about last night."

"What about it?" I asked.

"Did you like it?"

"Did I like it?" I repeated. I couldn't believe he was asking that. "Brandon, last night, while under the influence, I ate a *kitty*!" I was sitting up by then, practically shouting right in his ear. When I was done, I scooted as far away as possible—right up against the door. My head throbbed again and I savored the feeling.

"Yeah," he said nearly whispering. "I mean except for that."

I felt my jaw fall open. I rubbed my face. He was serious. "Except for the part where I killed and consumed a small animal, did I have a good time? Is that what you're asking?"

"Yeah."

"Yes, Brandon, except for that, I had a lovely evening."

He nodded, this weird, convulsive head movement. "Sure," he said. "Sure."

"I get the feeling you want me to ask you how you liked it, Brandon." He shrugged in this really unconvincing way. "Okay, so how'd *you* like it?"

A huge grin consumed his face. "Oh, my God, Courtney, I *loved* it. I thought it was incredible. I mean, when was the last time you felt free of all the clutter inside your head?"

"Eyes on the road," I said as we started to drift into the oncoming lane.

"Right, sorry. I mean pot and beer will help your problems seem not so bad, but they're always still there, right? Last night I felt like . . . I felt like not me. It was amazing."

"What problems?"

He looked confused. "What?"

"You said pot helps you not care about your problems. What problems?"

"What, I'm not allowed to have problems?" The grin was gone, replaced by an ugly scowl. He hunched over the steering wheel and refused to look my way. "I guess only *you're* allowed to have problems, right?"

I ran my hand through my hair. I didn't want to deal with this right now. "Sorry. You have problems. The Z helped you forget them. Go on."

"It didn't help me forget them," he said. "While I was on it, my problems didn't exist. Dude, I felt like *I* didn't exist."

"And that was good?"

"You took it, too," he said. "You tell me."

I remembered the feeling of giving myself up, losing my identity and becoming a part of the mass mind of undead outside Buddha's apartment. It had felt good at the time. Now I wasn't so sure.

"Maybe," I said.

"Bullshit."

"Don't tell me what I think, Brandon," I said. Junior Timothy Leary let it drop.

I tried to close my eyes, but every time I did, I saw Sherri in any number of horror-movie scenarios. Each one involved zombies feasting on her guts as she screamed and screamed. Keeping my eyes open became the order of the day.

We finally pulled up alongside my house.

"Thanks for the ride," I told Brandon as I climbed out.

"Sure," he said. "Hey, let me know when you hear from Sherri."

"Do you really care?"

The look he gave me wasn't anger or anything I'd expected—it was hurt. *Oh, shit.*

"Sorry," I said. "Discovering I killed a small animal can make me a real bitch. Of course I'll let you know."

"Okay," he said, and I closed the door before he could say anything else. The truck pulled away as I opened the front door to the house. I gave thanks that the curtains were still drawn—of course they were, Dad hadn't been home all night!—the dark felt good on my eyes.

I went into the kitchen and drank about a gallon of water. I knew that I should take a shower and wash out the scratches on my arm or, at the very least, brush my teeth. I felt like ten pounds of crap crammed into a five-pound bag. Somehow, I bypassed the bathroom, went right to my room, and collapsed onto the bed. I tried Sherri's phone and it went to voice mail. I asked her to call me as soon as she could, then I let the phone drop to the floor.

I fell asleep thinking of all the different ways Sherri might have died.

CHAPTER TWENTY-ONE
Darth Vader Is Your Dentist

Sunday passed in a cone of dread-filled silence. I jumped at every sound, waiting for Sherri to call me. I kept dialing her—like every five minutes—but it immediately went to voice mail. Until I got a robot voice telling me the mail box was full. After that, I had no choice but to call the landline at her house and risk speaking to the mutants that passed for her parental units.

The phone rang more than half a dozen times and I was about to hang up, but then someone picked up.

"What?" A woman's voice. Sherri's mom.

"Hi, Mrs. Temple," I said. "May I speak with Sherri."

"You could if I knew where she was," she said, and I heard her draw on her cigarette.

"So she's not there right now?" I asked. I fought to keep my voice calm.

"This is Courtney, right?" she asked. "Jesus, Courtney, I think the last time I saw her was . . . what, *Thursday night*." Another draw on her cancer stick and this time I heard her exhale. "You don't know where she's got off to, do you, Courtney?"

"No, Mrs. Temple," I said, and, for once when I was asked that question, I didn't have to lie when I answered.

"Yeah, well," Mrs. Temple said sounding philosophical, "I'm sure she'll come home when she gets hungry."

"Yeah," I agreed, and forced a chuckle. "Well, if you see her, please tell her I called."

"Sure," Sherri's mom said. "If you see her, tell her it'd be great for her to put in an appearance around here. The lawn needs mowing."

I promised I'd do that and hung up. It took all my strength not to pick up the phone again and call Brandon. I wanted to demand he take me back to Portland so we could look for Sherri, but I knew what he'd say to that and part of me knew he was right. Where would we even start looking?

I had to have faith that Sherri would just show up soon and laugh at me for worrying about her.

"Jesus," I could hear her say, "you are such a virgin."

I needed to take my mind off the situation—as if that were possible—and decided the best way to do that was some busy work.

After I showered and got dressed, I broke open the cellophane brick Buddha had given me and a million little Ziploc baggies fell out. I put those away and put some aside to take with me to work the next time I was on at the Bully Burger. I felt like a hypocritical shit packaging up more Z, but I still needed to sell it and pay Buddha for the stuff.

Dad finally came home and he and I seemed to avoid each other. I knew why I was doing it—I was still in shock a little bit from what happened Saturday night. I had no clue what his deal was, though. I'd walk into rooms that I thought were empty and find him in there muttering to himself. When he noticed I was there, he'd smile at me, kind of embarrassed, and then he'd make some lame excuse about forgetting something in another room. His behavior was slightly bizarre and creepy. To be honest, I was too wrapped up in my own head to ask what was up with his.

The one conversation I had with him was to arrange for a ride to school on Monday since I didn't know if and when Sherri would be back. Dad mumbled that that'd work, we'd just have to go earlier than I was used to. After that we retreated to our rooms and didn't talk for the rest of the day.

I caught up on homework and trolled the Internet for a while. It had been days since I'd looked for news about the Army retaking New York. I resisted looking it up then. I convinced myself a long time ago that the longer I waited to look at the news, the better chance that it'd be good when I did. I knew it was stupid and I also believed it to be true. After I exhausted the wonders of the world wide web, I turned in to bed early.

My phone rang sometime in the middle of the night. All I knew was that it was dark outside as I unwrapped my blankets from around my legs. Dad must have forgotten to turn on the air-conditioning because I was sweating like a pig. After groping around long enough that I thought I was going to miss the call, I found the phone and flipped it open.

I must have said something understandable because after a second, Sherri's voice came through the speaker. "Come outside, Courtney."

"Sherri?" I was wide awake. "Where've you been?"

"Just come outside, shithead," she said, "and bring your gun."

"My pistol?"

"Just do it." And the line went dead.

I clicked on the light and hunted up clothes. I found my pistol laying on top of my nightstand, which is weird because I didn't remember taking it out of my bag before I went to sleep. I picked it up and headed out into the hall.

I paused as I passed my dad's room. Something inside

the room scratched on the door. I knew that it wasn't my dad. I knew my dad was in there and that whatever scratched at the door had killed him. The scratching became more insistent, nearly a pounding. I tightened the grip on my pistol and thought about throwing open the door and shooting whatever was in there. I knew Sherri was waiting for me. The thing would wait. I'd be back.

I had to shield my eyes from the glare of the sun. When had it become daytime? Before my eyes adjusted, I started hearing things. Moans and footsteps, shuffling. I knew what would be there once I could see again. Zombies, hundreds, maybe thousands, crowded the streets. They pushed against the fence that surrounded our yard, but none of them tried too hard to get in. Looking up and down the street, I saw that ours was the only yard the shufflers hadn't gotten into. I heard far-off screams, maybe two or three streets away. It didn't bother me. Then I smelled rotting meat behind me and I knew who was there.

"Took you long enough to get out here."

"Hi, Sherri," I said, and I turned. This time I wasn't afraid to confront her. Most of her face was gone. How she was able to talk, I'm not sure. One milky eye squinted at me. "I think you need a new moisturizer."

"Very funny," she said, and the one side of her face that was still attached pulled back into a smile. "You're gonna need your sense of humor soon, *culo*."

"Oh, yeah?" I asked. I planted my hand on my hip and tried my best to look bored. For a second I felt like I was outside myself and watching this scene. I liked this new me, this unafraid me. I hoped I'd keep it up.

"Hell, yeah," Sherri said.

Clouds covered the sun and the day darkened and grew cold. Then I heard something from a long way off—a kind of roaring sound. I knew what it was. It was the zombie from the lobby of Buddha's building. The one that seemed faster and smarter than a zombie should. It was out there, a long way off, and it was coming for me.

"Laugh it off, girl. I'm here to tell you some important shit."

No. It was all too much. I knew I was dreaming. Knew it. I hated it. I refused to play along. I sidestepped around Sherri and headed back toward the house.

"Sorry, Sherri. Whatever you have to tell me is going to have to wait."

But as I got to the front door, I heard that scratching sound again. The one I'd heard coming from Dad's room. Whatever had been in there had gotten out. I made a small mewling sound in the back of my throat. This wasn't fair.

I turned and Sherri stood where I left her. The super-zombie gave another roar and now it was much closer, maybe only a couple of blocks away. Beyond Sherri, the horde of zombies still clogged the streets.

No way was I going to let some monster hunt me down; I was going to go to it and face it. I gripped the pistol more tightly, then I marched past Sherri and threw open the gate that stood between me and the zombies on the street.

"I could have told you how to make it through what's coming," Sherri said behind me.

I wanted to say something clever and mean. Nothing came to mind. Instead I waded into the sea of monsters. They let me pass at first, taken by surprise at my boldness, maybe. But then they started to clutch at me as I strode past. Panic set in then—the dream wasn't doing what I thought it would. By then I was too deep into the mob. There was nowhere to go. They had me. I screamed, sure I'd wake myself up before they could do me any real harm. I kept thinking that until their teeth tore into my flesh.

★ ★ ★

My dad stood over me, shaking my shoulder.

"Hey," he said, "I thought you were going to get up early. We have to leave in a few minutes."

I did my best to pull myself out of the dream and into real life. It was slow going. I faked a smile and told him I'd be ready before he knew it. When he left, I pulled on my standard uniform—one of the benefits of wearing practically the same thing every day—and then ducked into the bathroom to wash my face. After that, I just grabbed my bag and was ready to go.

The ride in with my dad was probably the longest of my life. I had all of this stuff I wanted to either tell him or ask him—my worries about Sherri and what happened Saturday night and wanting to know what the hell he was doing with Z in his drawer, for starters. I'm sure he had things he wanted to tell me or ask me, important stuff. But we passed the whole ride saying stupid, meaningless crap to each other. "Anything exciting happening at school today?" "Nope." "Hey, can we have stew for dinner tonight?" "Don't see why not." *Ad nauseam.*

The school has a turnaround area that's patrolled by guards with assault rifles for parents who are dropping off their kids. Dad let me out there and we said really lame good-byes and he took off as I was walking through the gate to the school yard.

I kicked myself for not talking to him about anything meaningful, and for not at least saying a real good-bye. Sometimes when I'm being mopey and dramatic, I tell myself stuff like *Well, that might be the last time you see him.* Even if I totally know that's not the case, it's just me trying not to act like I'm in a freaking soap opera.

The whole day passed in this sort of fugue state. Sometimes I'd realize I was sitting in, like, AP English, and I'd have no memory of leaving AP History. Half the time I was really only aware of worrying about Sherri, the other half I wondered why Brandon hadn't sought me out to talk to me.

As I walked down the hall, my attention was caught by one of the gazillion posters advertising the end-of-year dance that was happening this week. I was offended by their forced joyfulness. The theme this year was "Make It Last Forever!" Ugh. Having a dance in the climate at the time? The theme should have been, "Masque of the Red Death." Not that any of these melon-heads would get it.

At lunch, I sat outside by myself on the bench that was farthest from the school. All my food tasted like wet card-board, which was, I admit, a step up from what it usually tasted like. I ate mechanically—put food in my mouth, chew, swallow, repeat. I just needed to fuel my body so I could move on to the next thing.

When I finished eating I went over my Trig home-work. Normally as entertaining as talking to a jock, this time I lost track of the time. I think I also didn't hear the bell that ends lunch. When I looked up, I noticed that the last of the other kids was now trooping back to the build-ing. I wondered if anyone had tried to get my attention and call me back.

I stuffed my book and notebook back into my bag and I was getting ready to go in when I saw something out past the fence. I started walking that way. I stole a quick look up at the two guard towers that command the back field. I didn't see anyone. A state-mandated nap break, no doubt.

Near where I saw the zombie kid a few days ago, there was definitely someone or something standing out there again. Maybe some of his little zombie friends missed him and had come looking for him. Sorry, little dudes, I think some fascist with a scoped rifle sent your friend to a farm where he could run around and play with other shufflers.

I stopped a couple of feet away from the section of single-layer fence and stood there peering out at the figure in the trees. It was smallish compared to the other zombie, so I guessed it was a girl. I was trying to psychically will her to step out where I could get a better look at her when she actually did what I wanted and emerged from the shadows. I was amazed and proud of the powers of my mind for a whole couple of seconds.

Until I noticed it was Sherri.

I fell against the fence and caught myself from hitting the ground by lacing my fingers through the chain-link. I felt sick to my stomach as I watched her walk closer. I tried to convince myself that it wasn't her but there was no way it could be anyone else. Unlike in my dream, her face was fine. In fact, she looked like she hadn't been touched. Her clothes were intact, even if they were filthy, and I couldn't see any bites or scratches on her.

She walked toward me. My heart beat faster because I thought she must be alive, but as she got closer, I knew I was wrong. Her skin was ashen, her eyes sunken and glassy. Then she opened her mouth and hissed at me and black fluid dripped down her face.

The image of her went blurry as I started to blink away tears. She stopped just a little way away from the fence. I stood and took an involuntary step away from her, hating myself as I did. A long, soft moan escaped her lips.

"Oh, Jesus, Sherri," I said. "Oh, I'm so sorry. We should have never gone to Buddha's. It was stupid and I knew it. I should have said no." She didn't respond, just stood there panting, watching me like a cat watched a mouse.

A sob escaped me and I wiped at my eyes. I wanted to turn away from her, to get her out of my sight. I needed to call her parents. As shitty as they were, they needed to know what happened to her.

I was just about to turn when an idea came to me. Despite the revulsion I felt when I looked at her, there was something I had to try.

"Sherri," I said, "Sherri, if you're still in there, I know you'll hear me and be able to answer." I waited and got no reply. "Listen, can you tell me what it's like? Is it like when we took Z? Does it hurt?"

She took a step forward. She opened her mouth like she was going to start speaking.

"Cor . . . ," her voice rattled out of her throat.

"Yes," I sobbed. "It's me, Courtney!"

Sherri looked right at me and something passed between us, some connection or understanding. Then her eyes went blank again.

"Cor . . . ," She said again. "Cor!" The sound became a roar and she threw herself at the fence. Her mouth opened wider and wider. It looked like a snake dislocating its jaw to swallow a rat.

"No, don't," I moaned. I stepped back from her.

With her mouth opened wide, Sherri pressed her face against the chain-link fence. She started to work her jaw up and down.

"Stop it." My shoulders shook as I held back a sob. "Please, stop it."

When biting through the fence didn't work, she started to rub her face back and forth against it, working her jaw the whole time. The fence was acting like a cheese grater, gouging bits of flesh out of her face.

This couldn't get any worse.

Then, of course, it did.

As Sherri pressed herself against it, the fence lurched forward. I jumped back in surprise and then noticed that the concrete moorings stuck in the ground were barely half a foot deep. She gave it another shove and the fence moved again.

"Stop it, Sherri," I said. "Don't do this. It's me!"

With one last push, the fence fell inward to the ground and Sherri rode on top of it. I had to run backward to avoid being caught underneath it and I tripped over my own stupid feet as I went. I landed hard on my tailbone but didn't take any time to nurse my sore ass. Sherri was already scrambling toward me over the fallen fence and she was closer than I would have guessed possible.

I meant to tell her to stop again, to beg and reason with her. What came out when I opened my mouth was a scream that burned my throat. I just kept on screaming as I pushed myself backward as fast as I was able, my mind blank except for the thought that I wasn't going to get away. Sherri was crawling faster than I was.

I finally found my words, or word—I just started screaming, "Stop, stop, stop!" Over and over again. Not that it did any good. Sherri was practically on top of me and I decided to stop crawling and got ready to use my energy to kick her as hard as I could. I cocked my knee and got ready to kick her in her stupid, mauled face.

Just as her hand wrapped around my ankle, the top of her head exploded in a black mist. She managed to pull herself forward once more before she fell forward and stopped moving. That's when I heard the warning klaxon coming from the guard towers.

I jerked my leg away and stood up. I started to walk back toward the school and saw two of the stupid little golf carts the guards use rolling toward me. A ride back to the school sounded good at this point. Also, a chance to lay down, and be given super-strength sleeping pills, please.

I was pretty surprised when the carts stopped about ten yards away, the guards got out and three of them pointed their assault rifles at me. The fourth guard kept his hand on his side arm and started pointing to the ground with his free hand.

"Get down on the ground!" he yelled at me.

"It's okay," I said. "I'm fine."

"Get on the ground. I will not tell you again!" I noticed that he had unsnapped the strap that held his pistol in its holster.

I got down on my hands and knees and he yelled at me to lay down flat and put my hands over my head. What the hell? I'd just survived a freaking zombie attack and these guys were going Rambo on me.

I saw a couple pairs of shiny, black boots come into view.

"What's going on?" I asked, and I was annoyed at how shaky my voice sounded.

"Did the zombie scratch or otherwise hurt you?" the guy yelled at me. He was like a foot away and he still felt the need to yell. It came to me that these guys were probably all hopped up on adrenaline *and* they were pointing weapons at me. I was in really deep doo-doo.

"No," I said, trying to be calm, trying to smack them in the face with my total badass serenity. "I'm not hurt."

Another voice cut in, high-pitched and way too excited. "Look at these scratches on her arms! Did that thing do this?"

That totally blew my cool. "It was a cat! A cat did that!"

"You just need to lay there until Health Services comes for you."

The guard tower klaxons had cut off by then and far off I heard a new siren. I knew that would be the HS ambulance. I raised my head enough to see that a pretty big crowd had gathered out by the school. They were all gawking, trying to figure out who was being held down by four rent-a-cops.

The HS ambulance pulled right onto the lawn and made ruts all along its path. I thought how the custodians were going to be pissed and I felt a giggle rise up in me. I stifled it. The last thing I needed in this situation was to lose it.

Three people in Tyvek Hazmat suits climbed out of the truck. They also wore full-face respirators, and I couldn't see any sign of humanity behind the mirrored faceplates. They stood and talked with one of the guards. Then they went back to the truck and brought out a stretcher and something else before coming over to me.

"Will you roll over, please?" one of them asked, and I did. "We want you to slide onto the stretcher, please, then we're going to put these restraints on you."

One of the HS guys held a confusing tangle of leather straps with padded cuffs. I think the guy could tell that was freaking me out, because he quickly followed up with, "Don't worry, it's just procedure. We'll let you out once we get to the hospital."

I know he meant that to reassure me. Coming from that mask, however, it was like finding out Darth Vader is your dentist and he just told you, "This won't hurt a bit."

But I did as he asked and scooted my body up onto the stretcher. The guy with the harness moved in, and so did one of the guards—covering me, I guess. The dude with the harness knew what he was doing because in less than a minute, my wrists and ankles were secured to the rails of the stretcher. Once I was strapped in, they extended the thing's legs and wheeled me toward the ambulance.

As we bumped along the grass, I heard a voice calling out my name again and again. I lifted my head as much as I was able and looked out toward the crowd. Brandon stood there, separate from the rest of the kids. He had his hands cupped around his mouth and he was trying to get my attention.

"Call my dad!" I screamed. "Call my dad!"

Then they hit the bumper of the truck with the stretcher, which threw my head back. They slid me into the ambulance, and two of the guys climbed in behind me as they shut the doors. A few seconds later, the engine rumbled to life and we took off across the grass.

"I'm going to take some vital signs from you, okay . . . ?" one of the guys said to me. I knew he was fishing for my name.

"Let me alone," I yelled at top volume. Then I just started to scream. My best friend was dead on the football field and I was being abducted by men in black. I was officially losing my shit.

I felt a searing pain in my right arm and stopped screaming long enough to look down. One of the EMTs had stuck me with a syringe. I wanted to start shouting about this new indignity, but I suddenly felt like it didn't matter. I felt like I was falling down a hole and everything that mattered was still up on ground level.

At that moment, falling down was the best feeling I'd ever had.

CHAPTER TWENTY-TWO
The Spider-Man of Inappropriate Conversational Gambits

The only time I visited anyone in the hospital was after my mom slipped a disk falling down in our house. It was because of that injury that she started doing Pilates to try to feel better. That, of course, is where she met her douche bag instructor and then decided to abandon her family and run away to Seattle. Anyway, when she was in the hospital, they stashed her in a big room with three other patients. It didn't matter if you pulled shut the little "privacy curtain," you still heard the other people's conversations, TVs, or snores. I remember at the time that it was super-annoying.

But I'd have given anything to have a few other people in the room with me as I came to, strapped to a bed in a darkened space. That prick of an EMT had lied to me.

Once I was awake, only two people ever came in to see me. At least, I think there were only two people that came in—both wore the same type of Tyvek environmental suits and full-face respirators that the EMTs had. One was a nurse who looked at all the monitors hooked up to me and the other stood by the door with a hand on his side arm. I guessed they came in once an hour to do their thing. I tried to speak to them the first couple of times they came in. They never responded. I gave up after a while.

In between their visits—visits I started looking forward to even though they ignored me completely, which made me feel like I was right back at school—I just lay there in the dark, trapped with my feelings. I kept seeing Sherri. Her as a zombie, her trying to eat me, her with the top of her head flying off. I was almost constantly in tears, which really sucked because I couldn't wipe my eyes or my nose with my arms strapped down.

Around what I guessed was bedtime, they gave me some sort of sedative. Any other day and I'd have really enjoyed it. That day it just kept me in this half-awake state where I kept hallucinating. I kept seeing zombies out of the corner of my eye. When I turned to focus they were gone. At one point, I noticed that Willie was standing next to my bed. I tried really hard to apologize to him, but I had a hard time making my tongue work right. The next thing I knew, he'd been replaced by the girl in the bikini from the reservoir. After that it was just a retelling of *A Christmas Carol* with one ghost after another.

My dad was in my room at one point, too, and I was convinced I'd stopped tripping and that he'd come to get me out. Then his face melted off. My screams must have been pretty annoying. The nurse and guard came into the room then and the nurse gave me another shot. That one knocked me out but good. I remembered having time to be grateful.

When I came to, the guard sat in a chair by the door. They'd opened the blinds on the window and sunlight streamed into the room. I blinked against the light and then rubbed my eyes. Then I stared at my arms like I'd never seen them before. I turned to the guard.

"When'd they take off the straps?"

He stood up and opened the door. "The doctor is going to want to see you," was all he said to me, and then he left and closed the door behind him.

It only took the guard, the nurse, and a tall, old guy a couple of minutes to come back to the room. I spent most of that time just moving my arms and legs. It felt good.

The doctor smiled at me when he walked in, but it wasn't a real smile. His eyes didn't really change. He smiled the way some people ask, "How are you?" Like it was a social nicety. He flipped open a chart and looked at it for a minute. The nurse was also out of the environmental suit. She was a pretty Latina. Older, like fifty or something. She gave me a real smile. The doctor spoke to me without looking up from the chart.

"Do you often take drugs, Miss Hart?"

"Why are you asking me that? I thought you were just watching me to make sure I wasn't going to turn into a zombie."

"We were observing you for signs of zombification," the doctor said, and he was still looking at his chart. "Part of that process is to do blood work and look for the presence of the zombie virus. We didn't find it. We also did a tox screen and we found modified cocaine in your system. I think the name on the street is 'Vitamin Z,' right? I'd guess that you'd taken it sometime within the last seventy-two hours."

"Will you look at me when you speak to me?"

He looked up from his chart, uncertainty in his eyes. He probably wasn't used to being spoken to like that by patients. I didn't really care, though; I didn't like him all of a sudden and I wasn't going to hide it.

"So, how often do you use, Miss Hart?"

"That was the first time. On Saturday night." I fought hard not to lower my eyes or sound apologetic.

He made more notes. "It *is* my business, Courtney," he said, and I sat up straighter. I hadn't said it was none of his business. I got the sense he'd rehearsed this little play once or twice before he came in to see me. I also didn't like him calling me "Courtney." When people like him start calling you by your first name, it's usually a sign of trouble. "The hospital has to decide whether or not to report this to the police. We have to report it to your parents, of course." And then he looked up from the chart and he smiled for real this time.

Asshole. I kept my face neutral. He went back to his chart.

"Anyway," he said, "if you'd been infected during your attack, you'd have exhibited signs by now, so we're going to release you to the care of your"—he flipped over some pages—"your father."

"Great. Thanks, doc."

"One last thing, Courtney. A couple of your fellow students reported that it looked like you'd been trying to *speak* with the zombie before it attacked you. Why would you be doing that?"

That stung. I thought about Sheri getting high with me and how things turned out for her. Something wanted to click in my brain because of that thought, but the more I tried to latch on to it, the faster it receded. I let it go for now.

"Can I get dressed now?"

He gave me that smile again. "Of course. Your father should be here any minute. The nurse will show you where you can find your clothes."

He and the guard cleared out, leaving me alone with the nurse.

"Don't worry about him," she said as soon as the door closed. "You've heard that joke about doctors?"

"Which one?" I asked.

"What's the difference between God and doctors?"

I smiled. "What?"

"God doesn't think he's a doctor."

I knew I liked her.

★ ★ ★

The hospital had washed my clothes and now they smelled like industrial-grade cleaner. Not exactly spring fresh. Whatever, it was nice to be out of the backless gown—and out of the restraints, come to think of it. I could scratch being tied up off any list of possible fetishes.

The nurse walked down the hall with me and pointed me in the right direction as she went off to do some Florence Nightingale stuff.

I found the family lounge where I expected my dad was waiting for me. What I didn't expect was for Brandon to be there, too, holding a huge bouquet of Mylar balloons. He sat right next to Dad. They were *talking to each other.* Seeing him threw me. The memory of Saturday night came flooding back on a wave of resentment for him. If he'd just said something, stopped us, Sherri would still be alive. Then I had to admit that I could have stopped it, too. Hell, I could have not been selling Z, right? None of this was Brandon's fault—that was a little fantasy I'd have to give up on.

Still, why the F was he here with my dad? Part of me wanted to crawl back to the hospital room and tie myself to the bed before they noticed I was here. Best just to get it over with. I cleared my throat.

They looked up and they both broke into smiles. I didn't buy Dad's, though. I wanted to ask him what was up. Then Brandon was mauling me like a big, friendly dog. He wrapped me in his arms and pressed his face into my hair. Dad smiled more genuinely then, so I decided I could let myself ease into the hug a little. I'll admit that it was nice.

When the hug broke up, Brandon took a step back and gave me one of those "you are so brave" smiles. His eyes may have been a little moist.

"I was so worried about you," he said.

"I'm sorry," I said. I couldn't think of anything else to say.

"I heard you'd been attacked by a zombie and I just—I don't know, I freaked out a little. I'm glad you're okay."

He hugged me again.

"Okay," I said. "Thanks." *You know who that zombie was, right?* I wanted to ask him. I kept my mouth shut.

Brandon stepped back when my dad stood up and opened his arms for me. I stepped into the embrace and pressed my face into the hollow of his neck. We didn't say anything for a long time and just stood there. He smelled like Old Spice and just a hint of sweat. It felt really good. Holding him made it easy to ignore everything that had happened and everything that was going to happen. There should be stores where you can walk in off the street and get a hug and then go on about your business. It would make life easier.

Dad pulled away finally and rubbed my back. He gave me that same sad smile and then looked over at Brandon who was standing there so patiently with his dopey grin and his bunch of balloons.

"I hope you don't mind that I invited Brandon to come with me," Dad said. "He called the house asking about you several times so, I figured . . ." He trailed off.

"No, it's great." I smiled at Brandon. "I'm glad you're here."

"These are for you," Brandon said, and handed me the balloons.

"You shouldn't have gone to any trouble." Sixteen years of politeness training at the hands of my dad sometimes made me say things I didn't believe.

"Yeah, well, it was no trouble. There's a guy in a coma down there who won't miss them."

"So sweet." I gave him a nod, acknowledging the joke. "Really, thanks."

"Brandon asked if he could drive you home," my dad cut in.

"Oh, that isn't a good idea?" I couldn't keep the question out of my voice.

"I told him it was fine with me. But only if he drove you straight home, and if it was okay with you."

Brandon was assaulting me with that grin and those teeth. God, the ability to hypnotize their prey must be an inherited trait in WASP families.

"S-sure," I said. "I guess I'll see you at home in a few minutes?"

Dad kissed my forehead. "Yeah. Drive safely."

"I will, sir," Brandon said. "I always do."

Sir? If I hadn't just been released from the hospital following a zombie attack, I'd feel like we were in a 1950s educational film about etiquette. Dad gave me a wave and headed off toward the parking lot. I let it go.

"Let's go," Brandon said, and he took my arm. This was getting to be too much. I let him lead me down the hall in the opposite direction from my dad. The balloons he gave me kept bumping into stuff as we went. Carrying them along felt weird. Some other girl who wasn't me could pull it off. Maybe I could "accidentally" let go of them once we got outside.

He led me to his truck and opened the door for me.

"Want me to help you up?"

"You know, I was in the hospital for observation, not because there was anything *wrong* with me."

"Right. Sorry."

Damn. "No, listen, Brandon, I'm sorry. It's just been a stressful few days, you know? Having shit heaped on me like that tends to make me a bitch."

"It's okay." He gave me a weak smile.

"Not really. Thanks, though, for—you know, for everything."

"You're welcome, Courtney."

"Okay," I said, "now help hoist me up there before someone tells us to get a room."

Once we were both in the truck, Brandon navigated out of the parking lot and got us pointed toward home.

"It's good to see you again," Brandon said.

"You said that."

"I know, but it's true. What was it like?"

"Do you know who the zombie was that attacked me?" I asked. I really hadn't meant to say that. Brandon looked at me like I'd just booted his puppy into traffic.

"I know it was Sherri," he said. "I'm sorry."

"You are sorry," I repeated.

"Jesus Christ, Courtney! What do you want me to say? Is there anything that would make it better?" His cheeks were red. I couldn't tell if he was mad or embarrassed.

"Yeah, well, she wanted to do something stupid. Mission accomplished."

We drove to my house without speaking after that. I guess I kind of burst his bubble. Which I hadn't meant to. It's sort of my superpower. I'm like the Spider-Man of inappropriate conversational gambits.

When we parked on the street in front of my house, Brandon said, "I really am sorry, Courtney. I'm sorry about Sherri. I know you two liked to egg each other on, but I know you liked her, too. I hate that she died. I feel responsible for it. At a bunch of points, I could have said something or I could have stopped it, and I didn't. I'm sorry that I was so weak." Tears welled up in his eyes. He really looked like he was in pain.

I knew it wasn't his fault; I could have told Sherri no when she said she wanted to go with me to Buddha's. I knew it was a world-class bad idea. But I just let her ride over me and went along with it. Now I had tears in my eyes.

"Jesus," I said as I swiped them away with my sleeve, "it's like she's giving us a guilt trip from beyond the grave. Listen, you can let yourself off the hook. I'm more to blame than you are. I need to figure out a way to make it better, okay?"

"What does that mean?"

"How the hell should I know?" I asked. "Despite my grade point average, I'm starting to figure out that I'm not all that bright."

He chuckled and then so did I. I almost laughed but stopped myself. I wondered if I'd ever laugh again.

"You'd better go," Brandon said. "Your dad is watching us from the front porch."

And there he was. I suddenly felt a huge surge of love for my dad. There he stood with his pot belly, his shorts with sandals and black socks, and his worried eyes, and I loved him.

"Yeah," I said, "I'd better."

"Can I call you later?" Brandon asked.

"If you called me later, I'd answer the phone."

I climbed out and quickly got into my yard and closed the gate. I went and stood beside Dad while we watched Brandon drive away.

"He seemed nice," Dad said.

"If you like that sort of thing."

"You seem to like that sort of thing. You almost looked happy."

He wore that same sad smile that he'd shown me in the hospital.

"I'm happy," I said. "Usually. Just not lately."

"You want to go inside and rest?"

"I got plenty of rest being tied to my bed for a day and a half."

"Maybe we should go get something to drink and you can tell me everything that happened to you."

I grimaced. I said that sounded like a good idea.

The whole story took more than one soda to tell. After our second can, Dad ran and got some takeaway chicken and I kept going. With some judicious editing, of course. I wanted to tell my dad everything that was going on, but I hadn't decided how to frame it yet.

After I was done and we were wiping grease from our mouths and fingers with lemon-scented moist Towelettes, my dad sat back and rubbed his noticeably larger belly.

"That's quite a story, Courtney," he said. "There's one thing I still don't understand."

"What's that?" I'll admit that chicken thighs and mashed potatoes had lulled me into a false sense of security.

"How did Vitamin Z get into your system?"

And all of that delicious fried food plummeted to the pit of my stomach like so much concrete. A million lies ran through my brain. I could deny it and try to say the hospital had been wrong. To be honest, it just felt like too much effort.

"They told you about that, huh?"

"It's their legal responsibility to tell me."

I drew a deep breath, unsure how to go on.

"Courtney, did you get it out of my dresser?"

I had to think long and hard about what he'd just said. I opened my mouth a couple of times. I couldn't make my voice work.

"I know you were in my dresser," my dad went on after I didn't say anything. "Isn't that right?"

I nodded.

"And I assume you saw the packet I had in there?"

"Yeah."

"Did you take some of it?"

I shook my head.

"Then where?" he asked.

I realized too late that I could have totally said I got it from him and all of this would have passed. I'd still be in trouble, but that would have been offset by Dad's guilt in giving drugs to his little girl. I dimly remembered that the day before yesterday I'd wanted to come clean with my dad and tell him everything about my selling drugs. But the thought of how much trouble I faced suddenly put all of my intentions into doubt. I swallowed my guilt.

"Courtney?"

"Well, Sherri—"

"Oh, *Sherri,*" my dad said as if just invoking her name explained every bad thing I might have ever done. I suddenly felt flush with anger.

"What does that mean?"

"You got the drugs from Sherri, right?"

I sat there and seethed, hurt by my dad's dislike and distrust of my best friend. My dead best friend.

Not that it would hurt her feelings if I played along. Would it?

"Courtney?"

"That's right," I said. I couldn't look him in the eyes as I spoke. It felt like I was killing Sherri all over again.

Dad just sighed and nodded his head, as if all of his worst suspicions about Sherri had just been confirmed. I sat across from him feeling like the smallest piece of crap in the world.

I was so awash in guilt that I'd almost forgot to bring up something that had been bothering me for days.

"So, can I ask where the, um, the drugs in your room came from?"

Dad hefted a huge, Charlie Brown–worthy sigh. He stared at his hands for a little while before looking up and answering.

"I should start by telling you that I'm not seeing Beverly anymore," he said.

That subject change nearly gave me whiplash. "Okay," I said. "What does that have to do with the Vitamin Z?"

"Well, Beverly brought it here."

"*She* did?" I asked. I know I couldn't keep the disbelief out of my voice. "Why would she do that?"

"She *said* that she found it on a student she had caught doing something or other." I could tell that he didn't believe that story. "She said that she wanted us to try it. She had done it—only a couple of times, she said—with her ex-boyfriend and had really liked *doing stuff* while she was high."

"Doing stuff?"

"Sex," Dad said.

Ugh. I should have stuck with the euphemism.

"I told her I was uncomfortable with it and wanted time to think about it. I convinced her to leave it here with me while I thought about it." He gave me that same sad smile. "I didn't have to think long about it. I broke up with her on Saturday and I flushed it down the toilet."

"What did Bev say?"

"Let's just say she wasn't very happy with me." He gave me a more genuine smile. "But what was she going to do? Report me to the police?"

I agreed and then Dad's smile evaporated. He put his hand on mine. "Courtney, I have to apologize."

"For what?"

"For bringing someone into the house and into our lives who would have anything to do with drugs like that."

My face burned. "But, I . . ."

"That's different, I think. I'm concerned and, I have to say it, disappointed. However, I feel like you were led astray, and I'm assuming it was an experiment. One that you won't repeat after seeing the horrible results."

I nodded.

"But Beverly was an adult who'd clearly made a decision to let drugs be a part of her life. There's no way I could continue to see her under those circumstances. I hope she gets help, I told her as much. Until she does, though, I'll have nothing to do with her."

"You wouldn't have anything to do with anyone who," I hesitated, "had anything to do with drugs?"

"No, I wouldn't," Dad answered flatly. "And neither should you."

I felt sick to my stomach. If my dad knew what I'd been doing for the last year, he'd hate me. He'd probably throw me out of the house.

"I'm sorry, Dad," I whispered.

He hugged me as well as he could while sitting. I felt his warmth and smelled his scent, a smell so familiar I could pick him out if I was blindfolded, and I started to cry. I cried because it felt like I'd just lost something that I couldn't ever replace. The worst part was that I'd lost it because of my own stupidity.

"It's okay, Pumpkin," Dad said as he stroked my hair. "Like I said, I know you were experimenting. It's scary to me and I know you won't do it again. I'm just glad nothing happened to *you*."

Meaning he was okay with something bad happening to Sherri?

He held me for a long time until I got over my crying jag. After that we talked about what we were going to do about my mistake. How we'd make sure it didn't happen again. We never talked about punishment in my house; we always talked about correcting behavior. My dad wanted me to talk to the school's counselor about what had happened. He was going to try to keep a better eye on me and my whereabouts until I'd shown I could be trusted, and I was expected to come home directly from school at least for the next week. I didn't point out that this wouldn't be a problem since both my friends with cars were now dead. When all was said and done, I felt like I got off lighter than I deserved. Of course, I didn't ask for more punishment.

It was late by that time and he asked if he could go to bed, or if I wanted him to stay up and talk some more. I said I should be getting to bed, too, and we both headed off in that direction. I stopped to wash my face. It seemed like I was doing an awful lot of crying before bedtime lately. I decided then and there that I was going to cowboy up and stop crying all the damned time. Then I did my nightly routine and went into my room.

I should have just climbed into my bed, but I decided to do one last thing. I started up my computer. It had been days and days since I'd checked on news from New York. The last few days had been so wretched that I knew—just *knew*—that there had to be some good news about the Army reclaiming Manhattan. It was like the universe owed me one.

I brought up my favorite news website, and sure enough, there was something: GOVERNMENT INDEFINITELY SUSPENDS PLANS TO RECLAIM NYC. I stared at the headline for an eternity and it just refused to make sense. Why had I been selling Vitamin Z? Why had I been planning to get out of this horrible goddamned town? New York and the Mailman School both felt like stupid pipe dreams. Maybe Brandon had been right about that. I'd been going along like I deserved all these great things to happen to me, and now . . . The universe was telling me I deserved something, all right.

I powered down the computer and crawled into bed.

So much for my promise to not cry so much.

CHAPTER TWENTY-THREE
A Cocktail Dress?

I thought my dad was going to ask me if I wanted to stay home from school that day considering, you know, that I'd just been through some unspeakable trauma. That would give me the option of either saying no, I didn't want to go and having a day off, or I could be stoic and brave and fight through the tears and go. But all he did was call me to breakfast and tell me I had to hurry if I wanted a ride with him. Was this tough love because I was a reforming drug addict? If it was, I didn't like it.

I threw on my skinny jeans, black tee, and Dr. Martens. I decided to skip breakfast in favor of putting on my makeup. I was applying the last of my eyeliner when Dad said we had to go. He frowned at me as I walked out of the bathroom, but he didn't say anything. Maybe he had meant to cover new hygiene and appearance guidelines at our little confab last night.

We didn't talk much on the way, and when he dropped me off he reminded me to either arrange for a ride home—directly after school—or call him and he could come get me.

"I love you, *too*, Dad. I'll *miss* you."

"Don't be a smart-ass," he said. "I love you, we just need to establish some rules is all."

"Rules good. Girl bad."

He threw me a courtesy laugh. "The girl's not bad, and we want to keep it that way."

He drove away and left me at the mercy of my classmates.

All of whom were pretty awful. No one even attempted to hide the fact that they were staring at me. I felt like a walking freak show. I'd survived a zombie attack from my former best friend. I'd been carted off tied to a stretcher—at gunpoint! Jesus, I might as well be wearing mourning weeds and rending my hair.

And people didn't whisper so much as *stage whisper*. I heard lots of speculation about how Sherri got turned into a zombie. Or what she had been doing right before being attacked. It ran from not-far-off-the-mark—"I heard she was on some drug-fueled rampage and just ran straight at a group of zombies," a wide-eyed freshman reported to her friends—to the completely ridiculous—a senior football player told his teammates that he had been the last boy to be with her before the accident. They all nodded appreciatively because they'd cracked his code and had figured out what "been with" meant in this situation.

I did my best to keep my head down and pretend I didn't hear anything. If high school had declared majors, ignoring hurtful comments would have been mine.

Brandon and I ate lunch together in the cafeteria. He left his table full of cronies, which was actually really nice of him. They all craned their necks to watch him walk over and sit down next to me. I wondered about the loss of social standing hit points he took every time he was with me. I reasoned that he had plenty to spare and shouldn't worry too much.

He bumped my shoulder as he sat. "How are you?"

Dealing with a ton of guilt and remorse would have

been the correct answer, but sometimes honesty has no place in normal conversation. Instead, I shrugged as eloquently as I could.

"Yeah, I guessed," he said. "I've been hearing all kinds of stupid rumors today about you and Sherri. There wasn't much of that while you were gone."

"I guess people were saving it up for me personally," I said. "They're all so considerate."

"Ignore them. People have to talk about someone, it just happens to be your turn today." He looked extremely sage for someone with a zit on his chin.

"It's been my turn a lot lately," I said. "Has it ever been your turn?"

He thought about it for way too long.

"Forget it," I said.

"No, wait, I've got it!" He looked super-excited to have come up with something. "Once in third grade—"

"Seriously? Third grade?"

"Once in third grade, I fell off the jungle gym and broke my arm. It hurt so bad that I peed my pants. For years—*years*—afterward, people would talk about the time I peed myself. I'd remind them why and they'd all sort of go, 'Oh, yeah, that was awful,' and then go back to laughing about my pee-pee pants."

I was smiling even though a story about him breaking his arm shouldn't have been funny.

"That really happened?" I asked.

"Ask any number of people on the playground at Englewood Elementary that day."

"I don't think I can date a boy who pissed himself."

He got a sly look on his face and grinned. "Are we dating?"

I took an involuntary deep breath. "Was it a little bit of pee, or was it a gusher? Like did you get anyone else wet?"

"You're not going to answer my question?"

"Well—"

I became aware of people snickering at the next table over. Tracy Magaw and her ilk were sneaking glances at us—at me, then turning to confer and laugh. Suddenly my lunch tasted like cardboard.

"Why don't we go outside where there's fewer . . ." Brandon spread his hands to take in all of humanity.

"Sure," I said. We picked up our trays and left the cafeteria.

I laughed when we got outside. Brandon looked at me like I was deranged.

"Well, at least now they're fixing that damned fence!"

A crew worked out at the broken section of fence installing a new run. A new *double* run. A squad of shotgun-toting guards watched the tree line while the crew did their thing.

"Whatever it takes, I guess," I said.

"Yeah," said Brandon as we sat down at one of the tables. "The rumor going around is that the school is super-nervous because they left that fence unfinished for so long. I think they worry that your dad is going to sue. You know, my dad has a great lawyer, maybe your dad should call him."

"Jesus, if that isn't romantic, I don't know what is," I said.

"Yeah." Brandon gave that a halfhearted laugh. "Hey, I'm really sorry about everyone staring back there. People can suck sometimes."

"It's okay," I said. "I mean, yes, people do suck. I guess I'll have to accept that for a little while. At least until summer. Then I'll have three months where I never have to see these d-bags and maybe they'll all forget about it."

Brandon sat up—I think the accurate term would be he

"perked" up—and he started talking excitedly. Unfortunately, he had just taken a bite of his sandwich and I got covered in a fine mist of half-chewed tuna.

"Sorry. Sorry," he said, and picked bits of lunch off me. "You saying about the end of year reminded me. I'm going to have an end-of-the-year party."

"When?"

"Well, seeing as next week is the end of the year, I thought that would be a good time to do it."

"Smart-ass."

He grinned and generally looked really satisfied with himself. I'd have to watch that. I couldn't let his ego grow out of control. Generally, I think that tending a boy's ego is a lot like growing a bonsai tree. You're constantly pruning and cutting and making sure it's exactly the size and shape you want. Bear in mind I'd never had a boyfriend. It's just what I'd picked up in the school yard.

"And about the party," I told him, "I'm not sure. I'll have to ask my dad and he may not be all that keen on letting me out of his sight."

"What's up with your dad?"

I told him about the blood tests the hospital ran and what they found swimming around in mine. The hospital had informed my dad of my extracurricular activities, of course. His eyes went wide at that point and I assured him that his name had never come up during any of the talks between me and my dad. He relaxed at that. I went on to explain how my dad had me on a short leash for the time being, so the party might be a tall order.

"Maybe if you asked him?" Brandon prodded.

I shrugged. I didn't know how I felt about a party. I leaned toward "not." The last time there'd been anything like partying, I'd gotten drugged out of my head—literally—and then Sherri—I cut off the thought.

"Is it going to be at your place?" I asked.

"It's going to be at my dad's cabin."

I stopped. *No way*. He couldn't be that dumb, could he?

"Is this the cabin by the reservoir?" I asked. He nodded rather than talk around another mouthful of food. "The same cabin where we, you know, got attacked by a bunch of zombies, right?"

"It was only three," he said.

"Three too many, Brandon! How do you know it won't happen again?"

"It won't," he said emphatically. "It so won't. The sheriff up there did a sweep of the area after . . . you know, what happened. They cleaned out a bunch of shufflers."

Cleaned out. That's a nice euphemism for killed. I wondered if zombies had their own euphemisms. Maybe eating someone's brain was "going off my diet."

Brandon put his hand on mine. I'm sure he meant it to be reassuring. "It'll be totally safe up there, Courtney."

I extricated my hand from his. I felt a pang when the smile fell away from his face.

"Well, whatever, I'll have to ask my dad before I can make any plans." Now I was banking on the fact that my dad was still in Great Santini mode and wouldn't let me out of the house. Which was fine with me. I really didn't want to go to a party in monster-infested woods, and this way Dad would be the bad guy.

"Yeah, ask him," Brandon said. "It's, like, a week and a half away. He can't stay mad at you that long, right?"

"Mad at me" was an interesting way to describe being concerned about the fact that his daughter might be a junkie. Anyway, I sort of hoped he could stay mad that long. I didn't say that, obviously.

My answer at least made Brandon happy. He remained Mr. Smiley through the rest of our lunch. After we were done and had gathered up our stuff, we walked back to the building. We separated in the main hall and I was just about to leave when he stopped me.

"Did you notice?"

"Notice what?"

"Did you notice that I didn't press you to answer the question I asked at the start of lunch?"

I had to think back. What had he asked me? Oh, shit, he'd asked if we were dating. It took an effort not to slap my forehead.

"I did notice, and it's great," I said. "Could you keep being great and not press me for an answer?"

"Sure," he said, and his smile only slipped a little bit. "I'm not a complete jerk, you know."

"I never thought you were a *complete* jerk, Brandon," I said.

"Right. Well, I'll see you in last period."

"It's a date," I said. I made my fingers into imaginary pistols and shot at him. Then I quickly turned and wondered what the hell I had just done. I walked away as quickly as I could. Maybe I was lucky and he thought it was some kind of Tourette's outburst.

Later that day, I got to Journalism class before Brandon. I sat down next to an empty chair and put my bag there so he'd be able to sit with me.

As I unpacked my bag, Phil walked over to me. He stood there, silent, until I acknowledged him.

"Hi, Phil."

"Hey," he said. He held out a folded piece of paper to me. I took it and set it on my desk. "I was sorry to hear about Sherri. I don't think she was all bad even though she was kind of mean to me."

"Thanks."

"Are you okay?" he asked, and the question took me by

surprise. Except for Dad and Brandon, no one had asked that.

"I'm doing okay, Phil. Thanks for asking." It barely felt like a lie.

He looked at me for a second like he didn't believe me, then he pointed to the paper he gave me.

"That's for you," he said. "I hope you like it."

He turned and went back to his seat at the back of the class.

I unfolded the heavy paper, almost like construction paper except that it was bright white and it felt really smooth to the touch. I gasped a little when I saw what was on it. Phil had drawn a really beautiful pen-and-ink portrait of Sherri. I'd seen a bunch of Phil's comic strips and this was nothing like those. The style he used on those was scratchy, lots of pen lines, and (I realized) intentionally dirty. This was so clean and there were no extra lines. It reminded me of Hergé, the artist who drew *Tintin*. Phil made Sherri look really sweet, except for this curl on her lip that made her smirk. It completely captured what she'd been like in real life.

Tears welled up in my eyes. Who would have thought that Phil, the ogre we banished to the back of the Bully Burger every chance we got, would do something this expressive and vulnerable—let alone that he would give it to me?

"Are you okay? What's that?" Brandon moved my bag and sat next to me. He turned in his seat and glared back at Phil. "Did he say something to you?"

I wiped my eyes and handed over the drawing. "No, he asked if I was okay, and he gave me this." Brandon took the drawing and looked at it—glanced at it, really—and then handed it back.

"That's cool," he said.

Cool? What the hell was that? I glared at him. He wasn't

looking, so it was wasted. I turned back and caught Phil's eye. I mouthed "thank you," and he gave me a curt nod.

I turned back around and tried my best to concentrate on class. Instead, I found myself staring down at Phil's drawing again and again.

Brandon gave me a ride home after school. We didn't speak much. I mostly sat as far from him as possible and sulked. He looked confused about why I was giving him the silent treatment, which may have been unfair but it suited me just fine.

When we pulled up to the sidewalk outside my house, Brandon asked me, "So, you'll ask your dad about the party next week?"

"I *said* I would, okay?"

"Okay," he said. He looked like a puppy that I'd smacked on the nose. Seeing him act so weak and vulnerable triggered something in me. It made me want to be cruel to him, to hurt him and drive him away. I gritted my teeth.

"I'd better get out of here."

"Sure. I'll see you tomorrow," Brandon said.

I didn't answer him. It didn't seem like something that needed an answer right then. I retreated inside where there was no one for me to be mean to but myself. I immediately went into the bathroom and washed my face. I was just going to splash it with cold water, then I saw what that did to my eye makeup, so I decided to go whole hog and scrub it. When I was done, I stood looking in the mirror for a long time. My face was all scrubbed and new pink. I felt like I didn't recognize myself. Then I wondered where all of this Sylvia Plath angst was coming from.

I wished that Sherri were there to talk to. She'd have whipped me into shape. She'd have said something funny and just this side of devastating. She'd have said it with a smile so it would have been okay. It would have been cool if Willie were there, too. Even if he'd have been stealing glances at my ass. Hell, as far as I know, he's the only boy who ever looked at my butt with anything like longing before Brandon came along. I missed his dumb jokes and his sweetness. I missed my friends. It was that simple, I guess. Without them, I didn't really feel like me. I felt like I was going to become someone else without them around to help guide me, and I didn't know if I'd end up liking the person I'd become.

I did homework until Dad got home. Mostly I reviewed notes for all my classes since we had finals at the beginning of next week. Even with all the shit that had been going on in my life, there was no way I was going to allow myself to flunk any of these tests.

Dad got home and brought a pizza and salad with him. It struck me every once in a while how few meals I ate that had been cooked in my house. I think normal families ate home-cooked meals. At least, that's what I'd read in a magazine once. Probably *The Watchtower* . . . So maybe that meant my family wasn't normal. Not a big revelation there, I suppose.

Dad grilled me about my day. I didn't mention the drawing of Sherri that Phil had given me, knowing how he felt about her. He told me about his day and an awkward run-in with Bev. Apparently all the security guards there were acting like snots toward my dad since the two of them broke up. Dad didn't take it seriously, though it made me really mad.

While we were cleaning up our few dishes, I cleared my throat and said, "So, Brandon is having a party next week to celebrate the end of the school year and he asked if I wanted to come." Dad didn't say anything for a long time, so I rushed to fill in the silence. "I told him I was grounded and probably couldn't come, so it's not a big deal if you say no."

"Brandon?" Dad asked. He scratched his chin. "I don't see why not, as long as you keep to the conditions of your grounding until then."

What. The. Hell? It was okay for me to blow off my punishment because it was Brandon throwing the party? It wasn't computing somehow. What, exactly, had Brandon said to my dad as they waited for me in the hospital?

"I'll want to talk to his folks first," Dad went on. "Make sure there will be supervision and all. Okay?"

"Um, sure," I said. "Okay." Even though it didn't feel okay. It felt like when I was waiting for Brandon or Sherri to back out of smoking the Vitamin Z at Buddha's place. I had wanted Dad to say I couldn't go so I could tell Brandon sorry without feeling like a bitch. Once again my dad's ability to be reasonable had let me down. But when my dad turned to look at me, I forced a smile that must have looked natural.

Later that night, I was reading some comics in bed, trying to get to sleep, when Brandon called. I considered letting it go to voice mail. I decided to bite the bullet and answer it.

"Hey, how are you?"

"I'm okay," I said.

"That's good. You seemed sort of, I don't know, *down* earlier."

I think he meant to say I seemed like a grade A snatch. "Being back at school was hard. I'm sorry I took it out on you," I told him.

"You didn't. Don't worry about it."

"Sure," I said.

"I was just calling to ask, you know, how you're doing,"

he said. "But I also wanted to see if you'd talked to your dad about the party."

I told him that I had, in fact, talked to my dad, and that, miracle of miracles, Dad had said *yes,* but he'd made it clear that I had to be on my best behavior between now and then or else the deal was off.

"That won't be a problem for you," Brandon said, "you're always on your best behavior."

I let that lie hang in the air for a while, then I mentioned that my dad wanted to talk to his dad so he could be sure of some stuff. Brandon said that would be no problem and he gave me his dad's personal cell phone number. That's how he said it, "My dad's personal cell phone number." Like as opposed to the number for his dad's cell phone caddy.

"Great," I said, "my dad will call your dad, there will be many reassuring statements made, and then I'll see you at your little soirée."

"Hey, do you own a cocktail dress?" The question came so seemingly free of context that it took me a moment to recognize that Brandon had actually spoken English to me and that he was awaiting a coherent answer.

"A cocktail dress?" I paused as if I had to really think about this. My closet had *so many* delicious treasures hidden within it. Was a cocktail dress one of them? "No," I said.

"Well, I was thinking that the party should be formal— it keeps everyone from getting too out of control when they're all dressed up."

There was a pause as I wondered exactly how I was supposed to respond.

"Uh-huh," I said finally.

"I was wondering if you'd let me buy you one."

"Buy me one? A dress?"

"A cocktail dress."

"Right," I said, "a cocktail dress. I think that might be a little weird, Brandon."

"Would it?"

"Yes," I said, "it would. It really would."

"Why?"

"I don't think we're at a place where I'd be comfortable with you buying me something like that," I said. Then quickly followed up with, "Or *anything*! We shouldn't be buying each other anything just yet."

He accepted that, and I convinced him that I'd be able to buy my own dress. I thought of the drawer-full of ill-gotten money I had stashed. I could spare some of that for a dress for a party, right? It wasn't like I was going to be using it to travel to, say, *New York,* any time soon. I convinced him that I'd buy my own dress, and that I needed to get off the phone and go to sleep.

Before I hung up, he asked if he could give me rides to and from school since I didn't have one otherwise. I thought of the awkward ride with my dad earlier and I let myself be convinced pretty easily. He was unreasonably happy about the prospect of driving back and forth to my house for the next week and a half. I certainly wasn't going to burst his bubble.

"Okay," he said, "I guess I'll let you go to sleep. Good night."

"You, too. Good night."

I was about to hang up, when I put the phone back to my mouth and said, "Brandon?"

"Yeah?"

"Thanks."

"For what, exactly?"

"Being nice? Not an ass? I'm not sure, just thanks."

He laughed. "Yeah, okay. You're welcome."

We said good night for real and I was about to turn off the lamp beside my bed, but I got up instead.

There was something that'd been nagging at me for a while. I went to my desk and fired up my laptop. After it came to life, I opened Gmail and started a new message.

To: Rjkeller@ucdavis.edu [I found his e-mail address once when I Googled him.]
Subject: New mutants?

Dear Professor Keller,
I'm writing to you because I saw you on a talk show a little while ago and what you had to say really caught my interest. I know you don't know me, but I hope you won't throw away this e-mail without reading it. I'm a sixteen-year-old high school junior in Salem, Oregon, and I've been having a lot of run-ins with zombies. That's nothing special, right? Everyone has run-ins with zombies, but I've noticed something different about some of the shufflers lately.

I went on to tell him about the speedy zombies I'd encountered and how they seemed to coordinate attacks. As quick as possible, I mentioned the episode at the beach and out behind the Bully Burger. I finished by saying I hoped he's get better soon and that news of his attack had really upset me.

I started to close out the window when a chime told me I'd received a new e-mail. My heart thudded in my chest when I saw that it had come from Professor Keller. But then I felt deflated when it turned out to be an out-of-office reply.

I crawled into bed and tried to swallow my disappointment. At least I'd reached out to the guy. I drifted off imagining scenarios where Keller regained consciousness, immediately checked his e-mail, then wrote me back. We got together and figured out a way to stop zombie-ism forever. And I got to move to New York. I knew it was a fantasy, but it made me happy.

I slept better that night than I had in a long time.

CHAPTER TWENTY-FOUR

My Little Fantasy Cocoon

Without Sherri and Willie in my life, the days took on a sort of sameness they never had before. Wake up, go to school, deal with the shit you found there, go home or go to the job. Over and over. Hardly any laughs or surprises. Even if some of those surprises had been vicious verbal attacks, it was better than the boring-ass routine I found myself locked into. Now all I had to look forward to was the occasional shuffler encounter.

That Friday night at work I told all the people who wanted Z that I was out and would get to my supplier—*supplier*, not *dealer*—soon. There was a lot of grumbling, but no one yelled at me. No way could I sell any black powder then, not so soon after Sherri OD'd. But I knew that my get-out-of-town stash would need to be fed before too long and I'd have to start selling again soon.

A few things stood out the next week—I mean on top of the general excitement everyone felt about the end of the year being so close. As summer approaches, it starts to feel a lot like the end of *The Lord of the Flies*. Minus the pig's head on a stake. So far, anyway. On Monday I had my first of two meetings with the school's counselor, Miss Bjorn. You know, I get that she has a thankless job, trying to get a bunch of hormonal teenagers to open up about all the crap in their lives. But, seriously, no, thank you.

Opening up about my emotions runs counter to every les-
son I'd ever learned in my career as a teenage girl.

Ms. Bjorn's office was small, even by teachers' standards,
and crammed with papers and books everywhere. I
thought she might have a couch in there. That would have
been a physical impossibility. She had to clear off a chair
for me to sit in. Then she completely scuttled any chance
I would tell her the truth by telling me that if I related any
illegal activities to her as part of our discussions, she was
obligated to report those matters to the authorities. Read:
If I mentioned the fact that I sold drugs, I would be arrested so fast I'd be knocked out of my Dr. Martens. So
that meant I delivered a highly sanitized version of the
truth. I lied.

Since The Man already knew I'd smoked Vitamin Z, I
let that into the narrative. When she asked where I got it,
I swallowed my guilt and said that Sherri had it. I knew
the police would look for her, find out that she had been
turned into a zombie and then killed, and they wouldn't
be able to look any further. Miss Bjorn took this in and
then spent the rest of the hour asking why I'd felt com-
pelled to take such a dangerous drug. How do you answer
a question like that, even when you're trying to be honest? *Well, on one hand there's the peer pressure, and on the
other, I'm almost terminally bored in this stupid town.* I mumbled something about feeling stifled by society's expecta-
tions, et cetera.

I got out of there with an assignment to journal about
how all of these events made me feel. "Write a letter to
the you you want to be in ten years and relate this episode
to that self." I've always *hated* referring to things that happen in life that way. *Episodes.* Like, my life may be crappy,
but it is not as crappy as some reality TV show. For one
thing, it generally has better dialogue. My next meeting
with her was going to be Friday of that same week, so I

could mostly forget about it for the next three days, and then I'd be free of her for the whole summer.

After that, I got on my game face and tackled my finals—yes, I can make sports analogies. Actually, I sleep-walked through everything but AP Chemistry. That one had me sweating a little, but I was pretty sure I nailed it. Yay, me.

The last thing that stuck out of the sameness of the week was that Dad gave me permission to go looking for a dress with the closest thing I had to a friend nowadays, Elsa Roberts. I tried to suppress the feeling that I was shopping for a new best friend to replace Sherri at the same time I was hunting for a dress.

Dad actually tried to force me to take some money for the dress. I was able to convince him that I'd saved enough from working at the Bully Burger to afford it on my own.

Elsa and I went to a shop in downtown Salem called Cherry Redd. I'd considered some of the usual suspects like Macy's and whatnot, and dismissed them. Those places just seemed so square. Cherry Redd was a place where you could buy formal wear with some flavor. Elsa wrinkled her nose as soon as we walked into the store. The shopping experience consisted mostly of me trying on various things and Elsa sitting outside the changing rooms shaking her head slightly saying, "I don't know, Court-ney." Basically, it was all left up to me. I chose what the shop called a "Heartbreaker sweetie satin dress," in red, and a crinoline to go underneath it. Black pumps and a lit-tle clutch purse brought the total up to just under $300. Elsa's eyes went big when I pulled out a wad of bills and peeled off a bunch of twenties. I gave her a meek smile and hoped she wouldn't ask how I'd earned so much working at a fast-food joint.

Afterward, Elsa wanted to go and get a coffee or some-thing. She was ready to see this stereotypical girls' outing through to its bitter conclusion, apparently. I wanted to go to one of the cool, local coffee shops that dot downtown. She didn't like any of those places so we ended up at Starbucks. The zombie invasion disrupted whole ways of life and killed millions, but it couldn't shut down crappy, corporate coffee. I doubt even a nuclear strike from orbit could do that.

Elsa ordered some dessert-y monstrosity with syrups and cream and whipped topping. It must have had coffee in it because she ordered it decaf. When it was my turn, I ordered a large black coffee and the guy behind the counter got all superior and looked down his nose at me. But he didn't give me any backtalk with my java.

We sat out on the sidewalk and watched the traffic pass by. The occasional National Guard Humvee with a roof-mounted turret gun drove by. I didn't know why they still patrolled downtown; it had been years since any shufflers had made it that far into the town.

"So, you're going to Brandon's party on Saturday?" Elsa asked me.

"I am; that's why I needed the dress and stuff. What are you wearing?"

"I'm not wearing anything."

"*That* is a bold choice," I said.

"I mean, I'm not wearing anything *to the party*." She paused and took a sip of her drink. She came away with a glob of whipped cream on the tip of her nose. "I wasn't invited."

It took a moment for that to register. "What do you mean, you're not invited?"

"I didn't make the cut, Courtney. It's no big deal."

I reached out and dabbed at the cream on her nose. She withdrew and got it herself.

Didn't make the cut? That made no sense. Brandon

seemed really friendly with her the other week when we were working on that news story together. I told her that.

"The party is just for him and his friends. He may have been nice to me when we were working together, but that's just called 'manners.' It doesn't make us best friends. Or friends at all."

"Well, I think that's stupid." I said it loud enough for some people walking past to stare at us. "Want me to tell him to invite you?"

She said, no, that was okay. She was going to a party at Carol Langworthy's which would be low-key and, somehow, fun.

"Wait a minute," I said, "Carol is having a party? Why didn't I know about it?"

"Because everyone knew you had been invited to Brandon's. Why would they bother once you'd already got asked by the prince to the ball, you know? You should probably get used to it. No one can live in both worlds."

I sat there and thought about that for a while. I liked it less the more I thought about it. So, just because I started to become friendly with Brandon—and I wouldn't even say that I was part of his world yet, it wasn't like all his friends had welcomed me with open arms—that meant that I had to give up being friends with all of my old crew? What utter bull. Then I realized that I had done it myself before. Like with Crystal. Once she got on the cheer leading squad, we stopped asking her to do stuff. It wasn't out of spite or anything. I remember reasoning that if she had a choice between hanging out with the cool kids and hanging out with *me*, well, I know who I'd have chosen. Only I didn't want to make that choice now that I had to.

I wished Sherri had been around to talk to about this.

I let out a huge, world-ending sigh.

"I know," Elsa said. "It really sucks. I have to admit that

I was surprised when you asked me to come with you to-day."

"I guess someone forgot to forward me the memo on my upgraded social status."

She took another sip of her drink, careful to keep her nose out of it this time.

"Well, I'm glad you asked me along," she said. "It proves you're not a total bitch yet."

"Not yet," I said. It sounded hollow, and neither of us even smiled at that statement. We parted ways pretty quickly after that.

I still couldn't go out other than work and school—and the odd shopping spree, apparently—but I talked to Brandon every day. My dad allowed me to use the phone as long as I had all of my homework done, which had never been a problem for me.

That night I called Brandon and told him about buying a dress for his party. I left out the part about me discovering the fact that I'd been canonized by his little circle. He was super-excited about the party and reported to me that my dad had called his dad and that all the dads were now in agreement about how the party would be conducted and supervised. Brandon thought it was a hoot that my dad was so concerned about all of this.

"Well, just look at it from his point of view," I said. "As far as he's concerned, his little girl is one toke away from becoming a crack whore."

"And the truth is so much worse!"

What can only be described as a pregnant pause filled the space between us.

"I was just joking," Brandon said. "Because, you know, you sell the drugs."

"I got it."

"Shit. I put my foot in my mouth, didn't I?"

"No," I said. "No, every girl likes to hear that she's worse than a crack whore."

A big exhalation of breath came from the other end of the line. "Maybe we can pretend that I just had, like a stroke, or a sudden bout of retardation."

Now he was making retarded jokes. Great. "That sounds fine to me," I said.

"I'm really sorry; I didn't mean it like that."

"I guess I'm just sensitive," I said. "But you're forgiven as long as we drop it right now."

"Is that supposed to be some kind of punishment?"

"Don't push it."

He stopped and told me about his preparations for the party instead. Many of this developments were "sick," "diesel," and "off the chain." I did the telephonic equivalent of nodding along without paying too much attention. You know, I said, "uh-huh," "wow," and "great" at regular intervals. After a while, I told him I had to get off the phone so I could write up my journal entry for my meeting with Miss Bjorn the next day.

"What are you going to write?"

"I'm treating it like a creative writing assignment," I said. "It'll be a short story featuring a main character who happens to share my name. It's like Paul Auster." The silence on the other end told me Brandon didn't know who that was. Since I wanted to get off the phone, I didn't bust his balls about it.

I actually did write my assignment for the meeting. To avoid getting caught in a lie, I stuck to the truth as much as possible. But that still meant an awful lot of lying. I had to say that Sherri supplied the drugs, that I didn't know where she got them—since I would never in a million years mention Buddha—and I had to leave Brandon out of it.

I'll admit that by the time I was done, I was miserable. Was that Ms. Bjorn's intention? To destroy me emotionally? Well, mission accomplished. I felt like I'd been doing a pretty good job of hiding myself from any emotions about Sherri, and about Willie, and dealing with the counselor made me face all of this garbage. But, really, what was the use? Being all weepy about it wasn't going to bring either of them back. Confronting your emotions was pretty worthless in my opinion.

After I wrote my essay for Miss Bjorn, I felt like I should go to bed. I just lay there forever, staring at the ceiling. Writing that stupid thing for her had brought up all of these goddamned feelings even though it was half-lies. Jesus, why didn't I just go ahead and write the truth? Oh, right, because I'd go to jail and Buddha would have me killed by some bull dyke while I was there. Still, I didn't know what to do with all of this *sadness.*

I sat up in bed, my heart pounding, because for just a second—literally, just a *second*—I thought about all of the Z I had stashed in my room and the way it had made me forget everything that was going wrong in my life while I had been on it. I shook my head, trying to clear it. There was no way, with a capital "N," I was going to take that crap again. The fact that I had even considered it freaked me out. Okay, I hadn't considered it. I'd just thought about it. It had crossed my mind. Still.

I needed to put as much distance between me and the Z as I could right now. I got out of bed and I snuck down the hall and through the living room. I opened the front door and sat down on our little concrete stoop—it's just two steps and a "porch" that's like four feet square. The night wasn't too hot and there was a nice breeze. It seemed to clear my head. I sat there a long time just looking at my neighborhood in the dim light. It was pretty. I was fairly sure that those were the only circumstances under which my 'hood could look nice. I wrapped my arms around my knees and lowered my head on top of them. I felt like I could go to sleep right there with all of that sweet air moving around me.

Then I heard the sound of breaking glass a long way off and a dog started barking. It sounded blocks and blocks away. It really bothered me. It was like a sound of the real world intruding on my little fantasy cocoon. The dog's barking became more and more insistent. It made me think of that old lady we found after she got killed. I didn't want to be thinking those thoughts right then. Or ever, really.

I got up and went back into the house, making double-damn sure to lock the door and bolt. I went down the hall and into my room just long enough to grab my blanket and pillow. I carried them into the living room and lay down on the couch.

"Good night, Sherri," I said to the darkness. "Good night, Willie. I hope you guys are happy wherever you are. Happier than you were *here,* anyway." I felt sort of silly talking to them like that, even though it felt good, too. So I decided to cut myself some slack and just run with the good feelings. It's not too often I can do that. Maybe I was making progress after all.

Friday passed by like a dream. The last day of school is always a pain in the ass and exciting all mixed together. I didn't even have any tests that day. If it hadn't been for my appointment with Miss Bjorn, I might just have skipped. As it was, we didn't do anything in any of my classes. All the finals had already been graded, all the assignments and extra-credit turned in. We'd be mailed our final report cards over the summer. I'd already asked all of my teachers for my grades so I knew I'd aced them.

The meeting with Miss Bjorn went as I expected. She

read over what I'd written and we spent the hour talking about it. Sometimes she gave me this look like she was skeptical. Since she couldn't look into any it, she just let it slide.

When we were done, she told me that she hoped I'd consider seeing another therapist over the summer and that I'd keep seeing her once the school year got started again next fall.

"Sure," I said, "I'll think about it." There was a snowball's chance in hell I'd actually consider either of those things, though she didn't need to know that. I didn't want to hurt her feelings. I mean, I'm not a *psychopath*.

When I left Miss Bjorn's office, I went right into the end-of-year rally. The rally is a ploy to get people not to skip the last day of classes. Mrs. Ibrahim comes out and gives a motivational speech, then coach Amara introduces the football team's starting lineup for next season.

I became unreasonably excited when he said, "At quarterback, Brandon Ikaros!" and Brandon came running out in his letterman jacket and blinded everyone in the bleachers with his smile.

The team stood and waved at us all and absorbed our adoration for five minutes or so while the girls from the new cheer leading squad—Crystal was named captain!—danced around. It was very bread and circuses.

Once the representatives of the ruling elite—in whose numbers I could now count myself, apparently—walked back into the locker rooms, the lights dimmed and Mrs. Ibrahim walked to center court as a screen lowered from the ceiling. The crowd grew silent and I felt my heart thudding in my chest. We'd all been through enough of these rallies to know what was coming.

"I hate to end the school year on such a down note," Mrs. Ibrahim said, "but we have to acknowledge the students we've lost over the year, including two whom we've lost very recently, Sherri Temple and William Luunder."

Photos of those students who were either confirmed dead or just missing flashed on the screen while dramatic music played in the background. I think it was something from *The Lion King*. Sherri and Willie were last. On the left side of the screen was a photo of Sherri culled from her one appearance in the *Quotidian*. Her mouth was open, eyes half-closed, and she was in the process of shoving a piece of pizza in her maw. Under the photo was her name and the years she was alive. Next to that photo was Willie's information. Where there should have been a photo of him was the text: *No Image Found*. They couldn't find one photo of him? Why didn't they come to me and ask for one—someone had to know we were friends. Goddamn these people. All of them! I was surrounded by people giving polite golf claps over a pair of dead kids they'd never cared about when they were breathing!

I gathered my stuff and stormed off the bleachers and into the bathroom. I locked myself in a stall and concentrated on fighting back the tears. But that was a losing bet, so I just let go. I sat there on the toilet crying over my dead friends until the rally was over. Then I got up, washed my face, and went to find Brandon so he could take me to work.

As he drove me, he was *stoked*—his word. He kept yelling, "I'm stoked!" over and over again during our ride to the Bully Burger. Apparently he was in this state not just because summer was starting, but also because he was going to have the "sickest party ever" the next day. I tried to go along and ride the wave and be excited for him. After what happened in the gymnasium, I wasn't really feeling it. But either I did a good job faking it or he was too

wrapped up in how very awesome the situation was to notice my lack of enthusiasm.

When he dropped me off, he asked if I needed a ride
home. I told him no, that Chacho would drive me. It was
his job and all. That was fine since he had to go out to the
cabin with Ken to finish getting it together. He'd see me
the next night.

"I hope you're ready to have your mind blown with
happiness," he told me just before he pulled away.

I was so ready for that.

Once I got inside and changed into my uniform, I went
into the back and found Phil. He stood over the sink
cleaning the dishes that had been dirtied during prep. His
ears were covered with these big, bulky headphones, the
cord to which snaked down his back and into his pocket.
I said his name a couple of times. He didn't hear me. I finally had to poke his shoulder.

He spun around like he'd been bitten. His eyes were
wild there for a second until he saw it was me, and then
he calmed down.

"Hey," he said. "I didn't see you."

"Obviously. How are you?"

He blinked at me and then quickly looked around the
room. Maybe he thought our conversation was the preamble to something bad. A trap, a prank, something. Once
he decided that nothing awful was too likely to happen, he
relaxed. He reached down and switched off his mp3
player.

"I'm okay. How are you?"

"I'm good," I said. "Listen, I just wanted to thank you
for that drawing of Sherri you gave me. It was pretty kickass."

He nodded. "Yeah, it turned out well."

I didn't really know what else to say, so I smiled and
started to turn to get back to the front of the store.

"Hey," he said, and I turned back. "I heard you're going to Brandon Ikaros's party out at the reservoir."

"Yeah," I said. Was he going to try to wrangle an invitation? It hadn't been that nice a drawing.

"Is that a good idea?"

"What do you mean?"

"I mean, you already got attacked out there once." He shrugged.

"No, the sheriff cleared it out after that. They said they'd make extra patrols. You know?"

"Sure," he said. "As long as you feel safe." He reached down and clicked on his mp3 player and turned around to keep washing dishes.

I stood there for a second before I figured out that I'd pretty much been dismissed. I turned and walked out of the back and over to the register. What the hell was he thinking, treating me like that? Apparently he didn't get the memo about my hierarchical upgrade, either.

I put it out of my head as best I could. I checked to make sure my apron pocket was full of baggies of Z, and it was empty. Shit, I'd forgotten to stock up my supply before I came to work. I remembered holding the bag full of Z this morning, but I guess I put it back without getting any out. If I kept this up, I'd never get out of this burg.

I sighed, put on my headset, and gritted my teeth. Then I welcomed my first customer of the night.

CHAPTER TWENTY-FIVE
Classic Horror Movie Setup

I felt like sort of a tool because when it came time to get ready for the party on Saturday, I had to actually go on YouTube and look up videos that explained how to apply makeup. Pretty girl makeup, not the type I usually do. I thought about calling someone for help and I couldn't come up with anyone. Elsa was out for obvious reasons. Ditto every other girl I knew. I didn't know any popular girls well enough yet to call and ask for help. Especially because they'd probably think I was special if I needed assistance with something like my freaking makeup. For the time being I was on my own.

I searched a long time to find a video featuring someone who didn't look like a total skank, and then even longer to find someone who didn't make me want to murder her because she was so F'ing stupid. The world of makeup tutorial videos is apparently a serious business. You can learn how to apply cosmetics for any number of social situations and ethnic profiles. It was sort of fascinating. I thought that maybe next year when I was in my college prep Psychology class, I might delve into this whole phenomenon. For the moment, however, I chose "elegant makeup" by a chick who called herself MissFactor99 and got to work.

MissFactor99 made everything seem so easy and never

once implied that at some point I would want to kill my-self with the goddamned mascara applicator. Two hours and innumerable face scrubbings later, however, that's where I was. I was about to give up and go au natural when it just sort of fell together. One minute I was Miley Cyrus after a bender, the next I was Audrey Hepburn. Okay, not Audrey Hepburn, but I looked damned good. I sat back and admired myself for a few minutes and then it struck me that I hadn't built in time to do anything with my hair. I refused to cry as it would ruin all of the work I'd just put into my face. I finally just sort of threw my hair up into a bun–like thing and called it good. I hoped that my face would distract from the rest of my head area.

Compared to the rest of the preparations, getting dressed was a snap. I mean, I've worn clothes before, and every-thing was fairly intuitive. After I was dressed, I stood and looked at myself in the full-length mirror that hangs on the back side of my door. I had a hard time believing it was me. I'd never looked anything like this. For God's sake, the dress gave me *cleavage*. I opened the door and called down the hall for my dad.

I heard him coming and he made some joke about how long I'd been locked in my room and sending a rescue party. Typical dad "humor."

Just as he was about to enter my room, I called out, "Okay, close your eyes." He stopped walking and did as he was told. "I want your honest opinion of how I look, okay?"

"Of course."

"No, you have to be honest. I don't have the capacity to gauge how I look, so you have to be totally, brutally honest. Even if I look like shit."

"Courtney, your language."

"Promise!"

"I promise I'll tell you you look like crap," he said.

"Funny. Right. Open your eyes."

He did and he looked at me for a moment and then he sort of slumped against the door frame. His mouth opened once or twice and nothing came out.

"Is it bad?"

"Pumpkin, it's . . . No. You look great."

"Really?" I asked. Skepticism seemed the most prudent course.

He straightened up and took a couple of steps into the room. He made a twirl motion with his finger and I spun around for him. He smiled a little and shook his head.

"I just never expected to see you looking like this. It's a long way from jeans and a flannel."

"It is. But it's okay?"

He didn't say anything for a minute, just looked at me.

"Can I ask you a question?"

"Sure."

He nodded his head and collected his thoughts. He looked like he was really choosing his words. "You look *so* different than your normal self. Are you happy with how you look?"

"I think I look pretty good, I guess. So, yeah."

"Hmm. Maybe what I should have asked is, 'Are you happy with *why* you've made such a drastic change?' "

I had a weird fluttering feeling in my stomach. What was this? Why wasn't my dad happy about this. I would have guessed he'd always wanted a daughter who looked like, well, a *girl*.

"I don't think I know what you mean," I said.

"You're doing this because of Brandon, right?" he asked.

"I thought you liked Brandon," I said.

"I like him fine," he answered. "That's not the point. Are you happy making such a big change for *any* boy?"

"It's just one night, Dad. Just one party."

He nodded again. "Of course. I just . . . If you were going to make changes in your life, I'd hoped you make them because *you* want to, and not because of anyone else."

"He's not Professor Higgins, Dad, and I'm not Eliza Doolittle."

He laughed at that. "You certainly aren't," he said. "I just love the hell out of you, Courtney, and I want you to be happy."

I wasn't sure where this emotional stuff was coming from.

"I love you, too, Dad. And I'm reasonably happy."

He shrugged. "Sometimes that's all you can ask." He kissed the top of my head.

A car honked outside and we both looked toward the street.

"That'll be Crystal," I said. "She's giving me a ride since Brandon and Ken are busy out at the cabin getting stuff ready."

"Have your phone?" Dad asked. I nodded. "Emergency cash?"

"Check."

"Your, you know." He cocked his finger and thumb in the shape of a pistol.

"Yep."

"Condoms?"

"Dad!" He just gave me a look. "I can say with ninety-nine percent certainty that I will not be needing condoms tonight."

"It's that one percent of uncertainty that worries me."

"I won't need them," I said. "And if I do, I'll make him get some. Or them. I hear the whole football team will be there, so . . ."

"How was I blessed with such a funny daughter?"

We walked down the hall and into the living room. I

grabbed my wrap off the back of the couch and opened the door to leave. Before I did, I turned and kissed my dad on the cheek—smeared lipstick be damned!

"Have fun," he said.

"I'll try. Thanks."

He smiled at me and I hurried across the yard, through the gate and into Crystal's waiting VW Rabbit. She smiled and told me I looked great as I climbed in. I told her the same thing, which was the absolute truth. She looked like a model in an orange dress that was so tight I wondered how she moved her legs enough to work the car's pedals. I noticed that the dress also had long sleeves. She made a *pfft* noise and waved away my compliment. We both waved at my dad as we pulled away onto the street and headed out to the cabin.

Crystal and I ran out of conversation long before we got to the cabin. Mostly we just stared straight ahead and listened to music. Every once in a while, one of us would say that we liked a band that came on the radio. This sparked a conversation lasting about half a minute or so— did the other one agree? Had we ever seen them in concert? Were all the band members still alive? Then we'd fall back into a really uncomfortable silence. It reminded me of the last time I saw my mom, minus the preamble of screaming and reproachful tears.

As we rode along in silence, I started to feel—I don't know—a presence. I kept hearing Sherri's voice ring through my head. "I hope you have fun at your party, Courtney. I mean, I'm having a blast being worm food. Except, maybe, I think they cremate zombies, right? Flames are cool, too." I actually looked over my shoulder at the backseat a couple of times, but of course there was nothing there. Crystal finally asked me if everything was okay.

"I'm great," I said. Crystal was nice enough to let it slide.

So much for telling my dad I was happy earlier. For the rest of the ride, I resisted looking behind me and tried to ignore Sherri's voice.

My sense of relief at seeing the cabin was Bible-sized. We parked in back, right next to Brandon's truck. I admired his Benelli shotgun again for a second before heading inside.

Brandon and some of his pack had strung up white Christmas lights everywhere inside. I could tell it was going to be really pretty once it got dark enough to justify turning them on. The kitchen table groaned under the weight of about a million bottles of liquor. Crystal took one look at the bottles and shook her head.

When we walked into the living room, the boys who were hanging the last of the lights all stopped and shouted out their hellos to Crystal. For me they just kind of glowered and gave me slow-motion bro nods. You know, the kind you do just with your chin. Great. Either they all hated me, or they couldn't remember my name.

Brandon came out from the back of the cabin carrying an empty box. He still wore jeans and a T-shirt. He spotted Crystal and jerked his head back at the rooms behind him.

"Hey, Ken is in my room."

She walked past him and he took a step into the living room and then stopped. He smiled when he saw me.

"Jesus, Courtney, you look great!"

"You should try to sound less surprised when you say that."

"You've got to know it's a big change," he said.

I couldn't think of any way to argue that, so I changed the subject. "What's in the box?"

"Nothing yet," he said. "I'm going to fill it with anything too breakable or steal-able and then stow it away. You know what these parties can be like. I don't want my dad freaking out afterward."

"Say, speaking of your dad, he's okay with the frat boy shrine in there?" I hooked a thumb over my shoulder in the general direction of the booze in the kitchen.

"Well, it's not like he knows about it."

I thought about that for a second while he went around the room picking up trinkets and putting them in the box.

"Wait," I said after I'd finally processed it. "Isn't your dad gonna, you know, *see* all the booze?"

All of the boys stopped what they were doing again, looked at one another, and laughed. What was the joke? I didn't like that it seemed to be me.

After they all calmed down, Brandon said, "Of course he's not going to be here. Like he doesn't have anything else better to do than watch after all of us."

"But he told my dad . . ."

"That's what he tells uptight parents who call him. But he doesn't show up here. He trusts me."

So Brandon's dad lied to my dad about chaperoning the party. He doesn't really come to these things because he trusts Brandon. Brandon exercises that trust by buying up all the booze in the state for his little shindig to serve to his underage friends. That was all just *sweet*.

"Was he lying about the extra police patrols tonight?"

"Are you still worried about that?" he asked. He had the gall to look incredulous.

"*Yes,* Brandon. Yes, I am still very worried about that."

Brandon shot a look at one of his friends. It must have taken all of his strength not to roll his eyes.

"Okay. Sorry," he said, and I could tell he wasn't really. "Yes, there will be extra sheriff's patrols tonight. Okay?"

"Yes, thank you." All I could do was wonder if he was

really telling the truth. Oh, God, I felt like a pain in my own ass. I just needed to let it go and trust him.

He hefted the box. "I'm going to take this in the back. Then I'm going to get dressed, okay?" Then, to the group of guys still milling around the living room he said, "We'd better all get ready. People will be here soon.

"I'll be right back, okay? Make yourself a drink," he said to me, then turned and disappeared into the back of the house and all of his friends did the same. That left me all alone and unsure what to do with myself. So, of course, I did like he said and got a drink.

I was on the couch sipping a Red Bull and vodka and leafing through a copy of *Architectural Freaking Digest* when Brandon finally emerged from the back. I had to admit that he cleaned up nice. He wore a navy, single-breasted suit with a skinny black tie. He looked like the youngest cast member of *Mad Men*. I threw the magazine on the coffee table and whistled a wolf call at him. He stopped in his tracks and looked down at himself.

"Really?" he asked. "I look okay?"

I tried to figure out if he was serious. Did he really not know that he was good looking? I gave him the benefit of the doubt because he was a boy. "Yeah," I said, "you look good."

He smiled and looked at himself again. "Thanks. I had to step it up a notch so I looked okay next to you."

Again I could detect no trace of sarcasm in that statement. I stood and walked over to him, grabbed his hands, got up on tiptoe, and kissed his cheek.

"Thanks," I said.

"If that's the reaction they get, I'm going to be slinging compliments left and right."

"It only works when they're sincere," I said.

"You think I'd compliment you and not mean it?"

"We should get you a drink," I said.

"Sure," he said. "Yeah, before everyone else shows up."

"Too late, Romeo." One of his friends had come from the back of the house and stood in front of the picture window in the living room. He finished tying his tie as he spoke. "It looks like the first group is here, man."

Brandon went to the window.

"We're on," he said. Then he winked at me. "Show-time!"

It felt like I was attending two parties simultaneously. Throughout the night, any time Brandon was nearby, his friends were bright and funny and they acknowledged the fact that I was a living organism sharing the space with them. When he wasn't there, not so much. It took me a little while to clue in to that fact, though, because I am apparently developmentally challenged where social situations are concerned.

After everyone arrived, I stuck close to Brandon's side. He greeted everyone and made sure they knew where the booze and snacks were located—though, to be honest, everyone behaved as if they'd been to the cabin a million times and they knew where everything was. Brandon introduced me to everyone. Which was funny because I'd known most of these people since kindergarten. Everyone smiled and greeted me like it was the first time they'd ever laid eyes on me. I played along and didn't bring up things like, for instance, the time Kimmy Parnell barfed all over herself at my sixth birthday party and had to go home in hysterics. I just smiled and waved and said things like, "How *nice* to meet you!"

That was strange enough. The real weirdness started after we'd all been standing around talking. Brandon told a story about some amazing football exploit of his and everyone laughed and said how diesel it had been to be there. I said I was sorry I missed it and everyone jumped in and told me how great it had actually been—even though I was standing there and had just *heard for myself* that it was utterly amazing. Jessica Lyman actually put her hand on my shoulder and said, "Girl, you should have been there."

Then Brandon had to go locate some more chips or something. He gave me a little squeeze and told me he'd be right back. I watched him walk away and when I turned back I noticed that everyone we'd been talking to had splintered off into little groups and none of those groups included me. I thought that maybe I was being paranoid—something I'm prone to at parties—so I walked up to one of the groups and tried to muscle in on their confab. I was given the big ol' cold shoulder. I tried it twice more and got the same reaction.

When Brandon returned, I was part of the group again. Even if I didn't already have a finely honed awareness of personal rejection, I would know I was being snubbed. The worst part was that I couldn't even complain to anyone about it. If Sherri was with me, we could go stand in the corner, glower at the mean kids, and talk about what total bitches and assholes they all were. I couldn't even talk to Brandon about it.

Finally I just got to the point where I would wander off whenever Brandon left and I'd look at the paintings on the walls, the books on the shelves, or whatever. I'd only go back to whatever group Brandon was talking to when he returned.

I sort of wished the phantom Sherri voice would come back so I'd have someone to talk to.

During one loneliness interlude I stood there studying the titles of the books on a shelf that was sort of hidden, and I was practicing my telekinesis by willing everyone in the cabin except for me and Brandon to burst into flame.

I had my back to the room so I couldn't see anyone and there was music blaring. I still heard the murmur of conversation and every once in a while the sound of laughter rose above the noise. Each shrill exclamation of joy felt like a rusty nail being driven into my soul.

A hand touched my shoulder and I spun around to find Brandon there, his brow creased with worry.

"You okay?" he asked.

"Super. How could I not be?"

He frowned at me and then he got this weird look on his face—like he had a secret.

"Hey, you should come with me."

"Where?"

He didn't answer; he just grabbed my hand and walked through the crowd. I let him lead me away and I couldn't help noticing that several girls made a point of making eye contact and glaring.

What is this? I wondered as he led me down the hall and into one of the back rooms. His room by the looks of it. Posters for the Portland Trail Blazers and swimsuit models decorated the walls. He led me in, closed the door, and then sat me on the bed. Then it hit me, *My God, he wants to have* sex! Suddenly it felt like I didn't know how to sit—cross my legs, or not? I didn't know what to do with my arms and I was breathing too fast. I didn't even think I wanted to have sex.

"Hold on," he said to me, and then started to scrounge through a drawer in his dresser. Looking for condoms, I supposed. After a minute he stood up, turned, and held his hands out to me. He held a Ziploc sandwich baggie. Were his condoms in there? I took the bag and looked at it. Inside were three smaller bags. Inside each bag was a finely granulated black powder. Vitamin Z.

"What the hell, Brandon?"

"I thought we could have some later. You know, after most of the crowd thins out."

"Are you kidding me?"

He looked confused. "You don't want to?"

Suddenly I knew exactly what to do with my body. I stood up and threw the baggie to the floor.

"Well, the first time *was* great since I ate a freaking cat and my best friend died." I retreated from him when he took a step toward me. "I can't believe you went out and bought this and thought I'd want to smoke it with you."

"It's not a big deal, Courtney."

"Not a big . . ." And I stopped. A really terrible idea floated into my head. "Have you smoked it again since last Saturday?"

"Just once with Ken."

I backed away from him toward the door. He stooped to pick up the bag. I was so pissed. Pissed at him, at me, at a world messed up enough to think up making a drug out of a goddamned *zombie brain*. Especially me for selling that shit, even though I didn't bring that up to him.

"Jesus." It was all I could think to say.

He sat on the bed pouting, staring down at the baggie he held in his hand.

He looked up. "If it's so freaking evil, why are you still selling it? Or have you stopped since the last time I saw you?"

"Congrats on scoring that debate point." I turned and walked out the door. I stormed down the hall. I needed to find Crystal. I'd demand that she take me home. I almost stopped and went back to scream at him that I had not, in fact, sold any more black powder.

When I got to the living room, I scanned the faces there. I couldn't see Crystal. It was the same thing in the kitchen. Once I was in there, I decided that I couldn't stay in the house for another second without screaming and going crazy.

I burst out the back door into the dark and relative quiet outside. A slight breeze came in off the reservoir and added a chill to the air. I knew I'd get cold soon. For now, it felt great. I walked over to a small shed that stood about forty feet or so away from the house, and I slipped around to the back side. I didn't want to be found too easily. *If* someone came looking for me, that is.

I leaned against the wall of the shed and felt the rough boards through the thin material of my dress. I took a few deep breaths, trying to clear my head. What was Brandon thinking? After everything that had happened, how could he go and bring some Z to his damned party? And what was so terrible about his life that he needed to get high and forget it? It made absolutely no sense.

Deep down a voice whispered that it was my fault. *I* had dragged him along to see Buddha. *I* had been the reason he hadn't refused the pipe when it was offered to him. He hadn't wanted to lose face in front of *me*. That was right, wasn't it?

I heard a rustling in the woods in front of me and I held my breath and tried to listen. Soon my lungs ached and I couldn't hear anything because of the sound of blood pounding through my ears. I let out the breath and stood, ready to run. My hand curled around the butt of the revolver in my purse.

Two figures came out of the bushes right in front of me, and I nearly blew the heads off Phil and his buddy, Cody. When they saw me, Cody gave me a goofy smile and a wave. Phil just looked at me, as if he was assimilating my existence into his worldview.

"Hey, it's that chick we saved," Cody said.

"Hi, Courtney," Phil said.

"Hi, Phil. And no one saved my ass," I said to Cody.

"If you say so." Cody peered around the shed to look at the house. "They look like they're having a good time. This is pure horror movie fodder, man."

I ignored him for the moment and took in their outfits. They were dressed a lot like they were the last time I saw them—camouflage pants and shirts, homemade weapons, face paint.

"What the hell are you guys doing out here? Did you ride your bikes out here?"

"Hell, no," said Cody. He was still scoping out the house.

"Cody borrowed his mom's car. It's parked down by the road."

"Okay, that answers one of my questions."

Phil looked me in the face and blinked a couple of times. I got the sense he was trying to decide whether or not to let me in on their little plan. Finally, he looked over at Cody and then back at me, and his shoulders seemed to relax a little.

"We're here in case there's trouble."

"Trouble."

"Classic horror movie setup," Cody repeated. He grinned and he snapped his fingers compulsively. He was afraid or keyed up on adrenaline—hopefully just adrenaline. "A bunch of teenagers in a secluded area—where there's *already* been a zombie attack—partying. The last thing anyone expects is some kind of trouble. Bam!" He punched the wall of the shed and I felt it shake against my back. "The time is right for a brain buffet."

"That's great, *Edgar Frog,* except that this isn't a movie."

Cody looked confused. "What the hell did you call me?"

"Lost Boys," Phil said. "I get the reference. It's funny." It occurred to me just then how rare it was for Phil to display any emotions. It was kind of weird. "Though they were dealing with vampires."

"Sure, but you get the sentiment."

"Right. You think we're nuts. I get it."

Cody went back to checking out the house. Phil joined him, peering over his shoulder. The breeze finally got to me. I wanted to be done with this little farce and inside.

"This is stupid, guys," I said. "It's not a movie, and there aren't going to be any zombies."

"Then what are those?" Phil asked, and he pointed with his nail-studded baseball bat.

CHAPTER TWENTY-SIX
As We Hurtled Forward

"**W**hat?" I walked around behind Phil and looked over at the house. At least a dozen zombies emerged from the tree line and approached the front. I couldn't see any walking up to the side of the house that faced the beach. I wouldn't be surprised if there were some there, too. I bet they were everywhere. *Oh, no.* I whipped around and looked into the forest behind us.

"Me and Cody were just back there," Phil said. "No undead. I think it's too overgrown for them."

"Oh, man, what are we going to do?"

"Do you have your phone?" Phil asked. I nodded, too horrified by the thought of so many zombies to actually speak. "Call someone in the house, let 'em know what's going on. We'll try to help out here."

"I wasn't expecting so many, dude," Cody said. There was the unmistakable edge of panic in his voice.

"Just more to kill," Phil answered.

I rummaged through my purse and got my phone out. I found Brandon in my contacts—I still hadn't added him to speed dial—and pressed the CALL button. It rang and rang. I thought it was going to go to voice mail and I would have to leave the most messed-up message in history when I heard Brandon pick up on his end. I had to hold the phone away from my ear because the music was so loud.

"Court?" He yelled into the phone. "Where are you, I've been looking for you."

"Brandon, there are zombies headed toward the house!" I sort of stage-whispered because I didn't want to attract the attention of any of the UDs.

"What? I can't hear you over the music. Zombies?"

I yelled into the phone, "There's a bunch of zombies attacking you, goddammit!"

From the house there came the sound of breaking glass and then a scream. The music cut out and there was a lot of shouting.

I hung up the phone. "I think they know now," I told the boys.

"What next?" Cody asked. Phil hefted his bat in response.

"Bullshit," I said.

They both looked at me.

"Against that many zombies, with *those*. You guys will last about ten seconds."

"What do you suggest?"

"The cars parked on the other side of the shed."

They exchanged a look. "Do you want us to drive out of here? 'Cause we're not doing that," Phil said.

"No, asshat. Brandon has two shotguns in his truck. I think some of the others did, too."

"Niiiice," Cody said.

"I say we round them up and then take them inside to help defend the cabin," I said.

"You want to fight your way *into* a house that's besieged by the walking dead?" Cody asked. He looked like I just suggested kicking him in the junk for funsies.

"There are no zombies at the back of the house," I said. "It won't be much of a fight."

Phil thought about it for just a second. "Okay," was all he said.

I kicked off my shoes and walked gingerly over the crushed gravel. We went around to the other side of the shed and scoped out the vehicles parked there. A couple dozen cars and trucks lined up along the front of the shed, including Brandon's bit of overcompensation. We darted out together and each went to a different vehicle. I opened the door to an old Toyota truck. It had a gun rack with a pump shotgun in the back window. I snatched it up and looked around for shells. I couldn't find any. Phil and Cody met up with me and we checked in to see how we'd done. We were like the world's most dangerous group of trick-or-treaters. Phil had another standard pump shotgun, a couple boxes of shells, and a couple of pistols. Cody shrugged at us.

"No guns in the first car. I found a duffel bag, though."

Phil wandered off to the next car in the line.

"That's good, we can carry what we find in that," I told Cody.

As silently as we could, we went through all of the cars. Finally, I sneaked over to Brandon's truck and tried the door. No luck, it was locked. I looked up at the house as I heard more shouts. Even more zombies swarmed around the cabin. Some of the zombies seemed to be moving awfully fast. *Damn.* I heard the *pop pop* of a handgun. Okay, they had some protection in there. They could use more.

"Oh, my God!"

I spun around at the sound of Cody's exclamation. He and Phil stood on the other side of the car admiring something.

"What is it?" I whispered.

Phil held up a rifle that looked like it could kill you just by looking at it.

"What the hell is that?" I asked.

"AR-fifteen," he answered, "and about a million clips for it. Who's car is this?"

"I think it's Ken's," I said.

"I have a newfound respect for him. What's in the truck?"

"There are a couple of shotguns in here, but it's locked."

"Not for long," Phil said, and smiled for maybe the first time ever. As he walked over to me, he reached around to his back pocket. He pulled out a Leatherman and opened it to the screwdriver. He motioned for me to step back.

I said, "I get the Benelli."

"You can have it," he said. "I have this." He brandished the machine gun.

I stepped away and he put the tip of the driver in the center of the window. He applied pressure and the window shattered inward. Then the truck's alarm started screeching.

We all froze. I checked out the zombie's reaction to this. A bunch of the speedy zombies were running at us full-tilt and a few of the regular flavor were lumbering behind them.

"Kill the alarm!" Cody had one of the shotguns pressed against his shoulder. He looked like he was going to lose his cool soon.

I threw open the truck door, crawled inside, and scrambled over the seat into the back. A boom sounded right next to the truck followed by a series of bangs and another boom. I guess the zombies had reached Phil and Cody.

I got the shotguns off the rack and turned to throw them into the front of the cab. Before I could do that, one of the zombies flung itself into the truck and lunged at me. I batted at it with the double-barrel and dropped the Benelli. It swiped at me and I avoided it by pressing myself back against the seat. Then I swung the butt of the

shotgun into its face and drove it away. That gave me
enough room to swing the barrel around and point it in
the thing's face.

"Choke on this," I said, and pulled the trigger.

And nothing happened. It wasn't loaded. Why couldn't
I hook up with a boy irresponsible enough to go around
with loaded guns in his truck? The thing lunged again and
I used the shotgun to keep it at bay. Then I started screaming.

After a second, I heard footsteps on the gravel outside,
and the *pop pop pop* of machine gun fire filled the cab and
nearly deafened me. Despite that, it was pure joy watching that monster fly into pieces.

Phil opened the mini-door in the back of the truck, and
over the ringing in my ears I heard him ask if I was okay.

"Peachy," I shouted. "There's no goddamned ammo."

Phil rooted around on the floorboards and under the
seats. After a second he struggled with something and then
stood and pulled out a big ammo box. He opened it and I
saw it was stuffed with shells.

"Gimme some of those," I said, and I fed eight shells
into the automatic shotgun.

I heard Cody's boomstick roar to life again and then I
heard him yell something at Phil that I couldn't quite
make out. Phil looked me right in the face to make sure
I'd hear what I needed.

"Cody says we have to move," he said. "The shufflers
are just about on us." He helped me out of the truck.

Cody was reloading so Phil took out the couple of shufflers closest to us, dropping them with impressive effi-
ciency. He might have been a little scary, but I liked how
he got stuff done.

"What's next?" I said as Phil slammed another clip into
the rifle and put a round in the chamber.

"We walk to the house, I guess," he said. "Stay together, like in a little circle. Watch each other's backs. Sound good?" Cody nodded, then he looked at me. "Ready?"

"Why not?" I said.

We did like Phil said. They let me take point so I wouldn't have to walk backward. We crawled along to make sure we didn't get separated. A zombie diverted its course to come at us and I pulled the trigger. The recoil nearly broke my shoulder. The zombie was nice enough to fall to the ground and not get up again.

I heard the boys firing their weapons, too. I figured as long as I kept hearing that, we'd be safe and we'd make it. The cabin got closer and closer. Now there were more zombies, both shufflers, and runners. The runners were the worst. You wouldn't know they were even aware of you and then all of a sudden they'd turn and be right on top of you. I pulled the trigger more out of instinct than anything. The worst part was that they didn't really look like zombies. No chew marks, no herky-jerky movements. Something tugged at the edge of my awareness, but then I lost it as I had to kill a new shuffler.

Even though it wasn't far from the shed to the cabin, we had to stop three times so we could reload. I never let the monsters get close enough to touch me and I was still covered in a lot of gore from their exploded heads. If I'd had time to think about it, I'd probably have puked. *I'll never get this dress clean,* I thought and I made a sound that was half-laugh, half-hysterical scream.

"Keep it together!" Phil yelled.

We got to the back door and I saw it was barred by a table or something. I banged on it with the butt of the shotgun.

"Let us in," I yelled. "It's me, Courtney!"

"No way!" A boy's voice. "We can't open it. I'm sorry."

"Are you freaking kidding me?"

And then I heard another voice. "Courtney?" It was Crystal. "Get out of the way, asshole, and get that table out of there. Open the stupid door!"

Phil and Cody fired off a volley of rounds as the folks on the other side of the door took down the barricade. Finally it opened. I'd never been so happy to see a bunch of jocks. The three of us ran inside and the folks who opened the door got it closed again and the table propped against it. The four kids, Crystal and three boys, took us in with sunken, too-wide eyes. I'm sure we looked the same to them.

"Where's Brandon?"

"In the living room, I think," Crystal told me.

"Give them a shotgun," I said.

"Shotgun?" one of the jocks asked.

"We come bearing gifts," Cody said, and dug a shotgun out of the duffel and then Phil scooped some shells out of the ammo box.

We trooped into the living room to see what was what out there.

Brandon was helping to hold things against the window. Tables, bookshelves, anything solid. Three or four boys to each of the two big windows in the living room, and two held an upturned couch across the door. Shattered glass and blood stained the carpet around the windows. All of the girls at the party and a small group of boys huddled in the center of the room. A couple of the girls whimpered every time a zombie thudded against the barricades. It took all my strength not to tell them to shut the hell up.

The group on the floor saw us first and looked around to see if maybe we'd brought reinforcements. Sadly, it was just us. When Brandon saw us, he called for one of the boys to come replace him at the window.

He gave me a quick hug, then stopped when I didn't return it. It wasn't exactly the time for a Nicholas Sparks moment. He backed away and his glum expression changed when he saw what we were carrying.

"Oh, my God, you guys. This is so awesome!" He picked up the double-barrel shotgun that had been in the back of his truck. He cracked it open and loaded it. "This makes me feel a lot better." I was just glad that he didn't want the shotgun I'd picked for myself.

"We need some sort of plan," Phil said. "Has anyone called the police?"

"Natalie did," Brandon answered, and pointed to a girl in the group on the floor. "Service out here is really shitty. She barely got a signal and she could barely hear them on the other end."

"I don't know if they heard me," a girl with long black hair and a big gash in her cheek said. Blood flowed down her neck and stained her white dress red. "I don't know if any help is on the way."

"You're bleeding," I said. "Did a zombie get you?"

She shook her head.

"Flying glass," Brandon said. "They took us by surprise and grabbed three kids on the porch before we knew what was going on. I guess that's why you called, right?"

"Yeah," I said.

There was a thump and the boys nearest the door scrambled to make sure the table they held up stayed in place. A girl screamed and Natalie shushed her and held her close.

"We need to get out of here," Phil said.

"To where?" the screaming girl demanded. "We're safe in here! There's no way I'm going out there!"

"Hush, Cass," Natalie said.

"She has a point," Brandon said. "Where would we go that's safer than where we are?"

"Everyone's parked out on the side," Phil said. "Get to the cars and leave this place behind."

"That's suicide," Cass said. "You can go suck it if you think I'm leaving here."

"We can do it," I said, and all eyes were on me. "We can do it the way Phil, Cody, and me moved across the yard. People with guns on the outside and everyone else in the center. Like the Spartans, right, but with better firepower."

"No way," Cass said, and I was tempted to walk over and smack her. "There's no way that'll work, and why is anyone listening to these three outcasts anyway?"

"Hey," Cody said. "I haven't even said anything."

"It could work," Brandon said.

"What are you talking about?" Cass shrieked.

"We need to get out of here," Brandon told her. "Those things already got three of us. Stick around here and who knows how long we'll last."

"I'm not going out there," she said, her jaw set. I'm sure she was going for defiant. She came off more like a petulant kid.

"Then you can stay here," Brandon told her. No one, not even Cass, argued with that.

"We should hand out the guns, all gather in the living room, and then get going," I said.

"And make sure everyone has their car keys," Phil put in.

"Right. Where's Ken?"

"Him and some others are in the back bedroom; it's the only room back there with a picture window like these."

"It's been pretty quiet back there for a while," Natalie said. She stood up and looked through the weapons. She chose a little automatic Beretta. I was about to ask if she knew what to do with it when she removed the clip, checked the load, replaced it, and slid back the receiver to put a round in the chamber. "I have one just like it in my glove box. Hey, this may be mine," she explained when I gawked at her.

"Can we be best friends?" I asked her.

"If we get out of this alive, we'll talk about it," she said, and grinned. "For now, let's go get the boys out of the back."

As we walked down the hall, Brandon started getting everyone to their feet and making sure folks knew where their car keys were.

"Don't forget Crystal and them in the kitchen," I said to him. He nodded.

I caught up to Natalie, who stopped to wait for me.

"This is some kind of crazy, huh?" she asked. "The zombies and all?"

"I guessed it would happen."

She laughed. "And you still came out here anyway. Stupid or macho?"

"A little of both, I guess."

"Yeah," she said as we reached the door at the end of the hall. "I think we'll be friends for sure." She opened the door. Hands reached out of the darkened room and grabbed her. She screamed and I threw myself back against the wall to avoid the zombies' clutching hands. Natalie screamed and fired the Beretta. There were too many of them for it to do any good.

I screamed, too, and raised the shotgun. I could hear steps coming quickly down the hall toward me. I couldn't fire, I'd hit Natalie. She screamed again and a zombie reached deep inside her abdomen.

I pulled the trigger. The first shot hit her dead in the chest and she stopped resisting the monsters. I kept pulling the trigger. It seemed no matter how many times I fired into the room, no matter how many of the assholes I killed, more kept coming. There was a click as I pulled the trigger on an empty chamber.

Brandon stood beside me then. He screamed into my ear, asking what was going on. Then he looked into the room and saw that it was filled with the monsters. Saw Natalie and saw that Ken and the others must be dead. He fired his own gun, let loose with both barrels. I ran forward and pulled the door shut. It shook as the undead on the other side threw themselves at it.

"They were waiting for someone to open the door," I said to no one in particular. "They planned another freaking ambush."

"We need to get out of here," Brandon said.

We ran back into the living room.

"Where's Nat?" Cass asked.

Brandon shook his head and the girl broke down in tears. He asked one of the boys who didn't rate a gun to help her.

I grabbed more shells out of the ammo box and loaded the shotgun. We were going through the ammo too fast. We needed to move out now or things were going to turn really ugly. Uglier than they already were. Brandon was about to call to the crew in the kitchen that it was time to go when Phil interrupted him.

"Brandon, is this place insured?"

"What? Why are you asking that?"

"Is it?"

"Yeah, I guess."

Phil slung the AR-15 over his shoulder and walked over to the fireplace at the end of the room. Over the mantel were two oil lamps. He took both and walked to the near end of the hall. He hurled one of the lamps down the hall where it smashed against the wall.

"Hey!"

Phil took a lighter out of his pocket, lit the second lamp, and then threw it after the first. The whole back of the hallway filled with flames. The heat reached us just a second later.

"That back room is filled with zombies," Phil said. "I don't want them coming out behind us."

Brandon didn't say anything. He didn't look too happy, either.

"As soon as I tell the guys in back to go, drop your stuff from the windows and get in the circle," I told the guys at the windows. I turned to a couple of kids manning the front door. "Then you guys open the doors. The people with guns go out first and clear the porch, then everyone else comes out behind us and we move as a group toward the cars."

"I still don't know why we're listening to her," Cass said.

"That's why you don't have a gun," Brandon said to her. "Let's go," he yelled to the people in the kitchen.

After a pause, there was the sound of them dropping the table, the sound of splintering wood, and then the *boom boom boom* of gunfire. The four of them came running in a second later.

"We'd better go," Crystal said. She stopped and surveyed the faces in the room.

Crystal said, "Ken?"

No one said anything. She figured it out.

The guys at the windows dropped the tables and bookshelf and ran to join us. The two guys at the door let their bookshelf drop and did the same. There was a pause before the door burst open and a zombie ran in. Phil opened up with his rifle and the thing flew out again. Then the debris in front of the windows was pushed in and monsters started climbing in. Four of us—Brandon, Cody, a kid I didn't know, and me—rushed out onto the porch and let loose with our guns. The others stayed inside and took care of any zombies that made it in either through the windows or the kitchen.

It only took a few seconds to clear the porch and we called the others out. We gathered outside and started down the wide steps to the sandy lawn.

"Stay close together," I yelled as we started to slowly move toward the cars. The cars were maybe twenty yards away. We moved so slowly it felt like we weren't making any progress.

I saw that the whole back of the cabin was on fire. I hoped Phil was right, I hoped a ton of zombies were caught in the blaze.

The whole world narrowed down to those cars. Get to the cars. Whenever a zombie popped into view between them and me, I pulled the trigger. My arm ached like it was going to fall off from the recoil. Once again I heard the click as I fired on an empty chamber. I was almost relieved to not feel the kick of the shotgun.

"I need to reload," I said.

"Me, too," said someone else.

There was too long a pause before I heard Cody's voice. "We're out of shells."

"Jesus," Cass said, her voice high and keening. "We're all dead. This was such a *good* idea!"

"Someone had better shut her up," I said. I was tired of being understanding and sympathetic.

"We just need to keep moving," Brandon said. I could tell he was trying to keep the panic out of his voice.

Phil was apparently the only one with ammo left. The assault rifle kept up a steady chatter that almost drowned out the fact that we were all arguing ourselves to death.

"We need to head back," Cass insisted.

"We can't go back, you stupid skank," I shouted. "The damned house is on fire!"

"And whose bright idea was that?"

We had beaten back the zombies as we walked along and fired at them. Now they lurched closer and closer. It made me crazy angry to see our doom walking slowly toward us while we stood still *talking.* There was no way Phil could keep them off of us. Then I noticed that there were too many of the monsters between us and the cars.

"We need to use our guns like clubs," I said. "We might be able to fight them off. We need *to move,* dammit!"

"Wait," Brandon said. "What's that?"

Then I heard it. Sirens, and not too far off. Natalie's phone call must have gone through. I would have breathed a sigh of relief if I didn't have to get busy beating zombies to death with the butt of my shotgun. Thank God we'd killed most of the runners or else we would have been toast.

As we kept at it, the sirens got louder and we could see the red and blue lights strobe through the trees as the police came up the twisty driveway.

I heard a scream behind me. I had to ignore it because I had troubles of my own. I started swinging the gun like a club. My lungs hurt as if I'd been running all night long and I worried I was going to lose my grip on the gun because my hands and upper arms were covered with black zombie gore. Just when I thought I couldn't go on anymore, I heard the first of the shots. A zombie stumbling toward me fell as the top of its head peeled off. I looked up and saw a squad of police in riot gear and armed with automatic weapons slowly advancing through the mass of zombies. That was the good news. The bad news? We were in their line of fire.

"Everyone get down!" I yelled as I dropped to the grass. I hoped everyone heard.

I spent the next eternity or so lying on the ground, covering my head and hoping the SWAT guys reached us before the oncoming horde of zombies. I lost all sense of time because the only thing I heard was the sound of rifle shots, and it started to mesmerize me. After a while, I was aware that someone stood over me. I opened my eyes to see a pair of combat boots. I looked around and saw that the line of cops had reached us and were now breaking to walk around us.

A second line of cops came up behind the first and started looking after us.

"Stay down for the time being," a cop yelled at us through his helmet's visor. "We have medical teams on the way. They'll assess you before we move you out of the area."

It occurred to me that they were less worried about whether or not we were okay, and more concerned if any of us had been infected. I was positive I was going to have to spend a few more days under guard at the hospital. Not to sound shallow, but none of this was my idea of a great kickoff to the summer.

The medical guys showed up a few minutes later and did triage on all of us. I was relieved that they cleaned up my arms and face and said I was good to go, no hospital for me.

The cops gathered up those of us who didn't have to go to the hospital. Only three kids had to go. Two because they'd possibly been bitten or scratched by a zombie and one, Cody, because an overzealous jock had clubbed him in the head when they were both going for the same zombie. The rest of us were given blankets and cups of coffee while we were told to wait. Coffee! Like the zombie invasion is sponsored by freaking Starbucks or something.

I sat on the tailgate of a truck next to Phil, sipping my java, not saying anything. Just listening to the dwindling sound of gunfire as the police cleaned up the last of the zombies. That's where Brandon found me. He came up and gave me a big hug.

"I'm really glad you're okay," he said into my hair as he hugged me. I was mostly worried he was going to spill my drink all down my front. After everything we'd been through, the last thing I needed was a scalding burn on my temporary cleavage.

After he pulled away, I said, "Brandon, I think we should talk."

"Sure," he said.

"Why don't we go over . . . ? Well, anywhere else." I gestured toward Phil.

We walked a few feet away. With nothing between us and the burning house, the flames warmed the night air. I wouldn't need my blanket for long in the heat. I wondered if anyone had called the fire department.

"What's up, Courtney?" Brandon asked.

No way to sugarcoat it.

"I can't see you anymore."

His mouth fell open. "What?" he demanded. "Is this because I had the party out here after you said I shouldn't?"

"No," I said, then corrected myself. "Yes, but not totally."

"Not totally? Then why?"

"Look at me, Brandon," I said. I spread my arms. "This dress, my makeup, my hair. I didn't do any of these things because I wanted to, I did them because I thought *you'd* like them."

"I do like them."

"Not the point. I was trying to change to get you to like me. Look at me—I feel like freaking Sandra Dee in reverse."

Brandon looked confused. "Sandra who?"

"It's from *Grease,*" Phil piped up from the tailgate of the truck. "It's good, even though it has a lousy message. You should watch it."

I turned and glared at him. I said, "Some privacy, Phil?"

He slunk away to where most of the others were gathered.

"So, that's it?"

"Also, your friends don't like me." He opened his mouth to interrupt. I steamrollered over him. "They don't, Brandon. Trust me. I don't want to leave the few friends I have left because I've gotten an unexpected bump in social status. And . . ."

"What?"

"It's the Vitamin Z," I said. "I really don't like that you and Ken were doing it after the experience we had."

"That is so hypocritical," he said, his face flushed. "I can't take it, but you can sell it." He pitched his voice low so that, hopefully, none of the cops milling around would hear.

I was expecting that. "You know what? You're right." He looked so hurt and angry and confused, I wanted to do something to try to comfort him. I didn't, though. It would just make things even worse later. "I've been a hypocrite and I've been really stupid and selfish. Well, I'm going to stop. I decided that I'm not selling anymore."

"You had some sort of what, epiphany, while you were slaying zombies tonight?" he asked.

"I've been thinking about it for a while, I guess. I hadn't been selling it since last week, but I've decided to make it permanent. Yeah, tonight made it all come together," I said.

We stood there in the glow of his dad's burning cabin, undead bodies scattered around and police questioning our friends. I couldn't have asked for more in the teen-romance department. I felt bad that I was doing this to him now, but I thought it was best to just be done with it.

"Does it help if I say I'm sorry?"

"Not really. No."

"That's what I thought."

I can't believe I'm saying this—I was actually saved by the police. An officer walked up to us. He'd just removed his helmet and his head steamed in the cold night air.

"You Brandon Ikaros?" he asked. "It's your dad who owns this place?"

"Yes, sir."

"Want to come this way? We have some questions. It won't take long."

Brandon followed the guy away. I waited to see if he was going to glance back at me. Because, you know, I like to torture myself. He didn't. Which broke my stupid heart.

I found Phil. He and a boy I didn't recognize stood together and talked about the assault rifle that Phil had used—and that the police had taken away from him. They were apparently bonding over weapons of all sorts. I tugged on his sleeve to get his attention.

"Can you drive me home?" I asked. "I mean, assuming you got the keys from Cody."

"Sure," he said. "As soon as the police get our contact info, they said we can go. I guess they'll be calling everyone in the next day or two to ask what happened."

I looked around at the mess. "Seems pretty obvious."

Phil just shrugged. "We can find an officer and give him our info."

We found a cop and he wrote down everything he needed. He said we'd get a call tomorrow to schedule a time to go to the police station and answer some questions. I heard a few kids complaining about it. I didn't mind. I figured it was the best possible circumstances under which I would visit a police station.

The police made me give them their blanket back. Phil actually took off his jacket and put it around my shoulders as we walked. Cody's car was a battered old station wagon. It looked totally unsafe. I thought about going back to see if anyone else could give me a ride. I was so damned tired, though, that I just climbed in. After everything else that had happened that night, I figured I was charmed.

Phil steered down a narrow dirt road toward the highway. We rode on in silence for a while. I didn't want that. I needed noise, music, something. I went to turn on the radio and found a gaping hole full of wires where it should be.

"Seriously?"

"Cody bought a new stereo a while ago and ripped out the old one before he made sure the new one would fit."

"Well, that just seems like the perfect capper to the evening."

"It was an interesting night," Phil said. He said it so seriously that I burst out laughing.

"Was that funny?"

"The fact that you don't know that it was funny, makes it *really* funny." He smiled, just a fast smile—there and gone. "You should smile more often."

"Should I?"

"Yeah," I said. "You're cute when you smile."

He just nodded his head slowly and blinked a couple of times. Same old Phil. "Maybe I'll find some reason to start doing it more often," he said.

"Yeah," I agreed, and I turned to look at the darkened road that we were driving down. The headlights could barely cut through the darkness. If you didn't know better, you might think that the world didn't exist beyond the reach of the headlights and it was being created one second at a time as we hurtled forward.

"Something's bugging me," I said.

"What's that?" Phil asked.

"The zombies."

"No crap," he said.

"No," I said. "Not all of them. Just the runners."

"The fast ones?" Phil asked. "Yeah, those guys were murder."

"Where'd they come from?" I asked. "Why were there so many of them? And why'd they look like they hadn't been chewed on?"

"Good questions," Phil said. "What are the answers, Nancy Drew?"

"You just made a cultural reference," I said, and he smiled again. "I don't know, but I feel like I know the answer. I just need to put it all together." I also noticed, though I didn't mention it, that Phil was the first person to not call me crazy for talking about the new runners. Another point in his favor.

The hum of the tires on asphalt started to lull me to sleep. My defenses were down. That's my best guess for why I said the next thing.

"Can I ask you a question?" I asked.

"Yes," Phil said.

"Say someone had a plan," I started, and I laid out my grand scheme for him—New York, the Mailman Center, all of it. And then I told him why I wanted to do it. I left out how I planned to finance the operation.

He didn't say anything for a long time, and I braced myself for the worst.

"It's good to have a goal," he said.

"That's it?" I asked.

"What else?"

"Most people think I'm crazy when I tell them my plan," I said.

He frowned a little, then went back to his usual poker face.

"Why would you give a damn what anyone else thinks about it?" he asked. "It's your plan. If it's crazy, you'll figure it out. But watching you handle yourself the last few days . . ." He shrugged. "I can't imagine anything will stop you."

I stared at him in amazement. I wasn't used to feeling gratitude toward one of my peers and I didn't know what to do with it.

"Thanks," I said.

"You bet."

I turned to look out the window. Trees barely visible in the darkness flashed by. I smiled, sure he couldn't see it.

We fell back into a comfortable silence. Just like in Crystal's car, I became aware of Sherri's voice again in the back of my mind. This time she was laughing at me because I'd let my guard down with Phil, and because I'd decided to play detective. I figured that was okay, I probably deserved her laughter.

But I knew I'd figure it all out and get the last laugh.

Score One for Me

Dad took the news of the zombie attack relatively well. I mean, sure, he stormed up and down the living room and swore that he was going to sue Mr. Ikaros into the poorhouse. But I say he took it relatively well because when you compare it to how he reacted when I told him I'd been dealing drugs for nearly a year, he'd been a peach about Mr. Ikaros.

He stopped, became absolutely motionless, but his face grew this really frightening shade of red.

"What did you say?" he asked. His voice was brittle like cracked glass.

"I wanted to tell you sooner," I said. It sounded lame even to me. "But it's not the easiest . . ."

"Drugs? What sort of drugs?"

"Vitamin Z," I whispered.

And then he did the very worst thing I could have imagined. He just sort of crumpled into a dad-shaped ball on the couch. He wouldn't even look at me. His disappointment hung in the air like a fart in church. I would have taken him screaming at me any day.

He was silent and still for a long time, minutes, before I built up the courage to say anything.

"Dad?"

"Are the drugs in the house now?"

I told him they were.

"Show me."

He stood up and led me to my room. I knelt down and pulled out the drawer with the false bottom and showed him my stash. He held the brick of Z in one hand and a gallon-size Ziploc stuffed with cash in the other.

"What were you planning to do with this?" he asked. "Why would you ever need this much money?"

"I was going to use it to get out of town and pay for college."

I guess that you could technically describe the sound he made as a laugh, but it sounded more like a bark or a rough cough.

"Can you get a college degree in jail?" he asked. My heart sank. Was my dad really going to turn me into the cops? "Maybe they have correspondence courses . . ."

"Dad?"

He muttered to himself, I didn't catch all of it, but I'm pretty sure he wondered where he'd gone wrong.

"We have to get rid of this," he finally said loud enough for me to hear it.

We flushed it all down the toilet. It was only afterward that it occurred to me that we probably killed every fish in the Willamette River. I didn't mention that to Dad.

He made it clear that I'd be spending the summer under close supervision. "House arrest" may have been the term he used. And it was a given that I no longer worked at Bully Burger. Which, really, was fine with me.

Dad took the brick of money into his room saying we'd figure out what to do with it later. We went to bed that night with a lot of stuff unresolved—how would I work things out with Buddha? How would Dad keep an eye on me while he was at work? But I knew that we'd talk it all out—talk and talk and talk—over the coming days and weeks.

I turned off my lamp and settled down to a long night of not sleeping when there was a knock at my door.

"Come in," I said, and Dad opened the door. He stood in the doorway, lit from behind by the hall light and casting a long shadow into my room.

"Courtney," he said, "even when I'm angry at you, I still love you very much." That was something he'd been telling me forever. It was easier to believe when he was mad at me because of a broken window or a missed curfew. I had a hard time accepting that he loved me now that I was a proven menace to society.

I wanted to diffuse the tension in the room. I struggled to think of something funny to say.

"Do you?" I asked.

"Yes," he said. "I think that when we make mistakes, when we lose our way, that's when we need the love of others the most."

"Thank you, Dad. I love you, too."

"Okay," he said, "get some sleep."

He left, shutting the door behind him.

I cried myself to sleep that night, but it felt like a release, it felt like something I'd earned.

There was a minor sensation in the local news about the attack. Apparently a lot of people had suspected that zombie attacks were on the rise, and that the zombies themselves were different now—that they were working together in groups, for a very deadly example—this was the first concrete evidence anyone had that it was so. And what was up with some of them being faster and more aggressive?

Even though Professor Keller was still in a coma, I sent him the articles. I'm sure he'd have a science boner over it when he woke up. Hell, he might even come here to study what happened. Maybe he'd be able to come up with a way to help the Army clear the shufflers out of New York. I was still clinging to my hope that I'd get out of Dodge someday.

My dad didn't have to worry about Mr. Ikaros getting his. The parent of every kid at the party, and a lot of people besides, were calling for his head on a stick. Especially since some kids died during the attack. People were making it out like Mr. Ikaros practically invited every shuffler in the county to come to a teenage smorgasbord. One of the national networks came down and ambushed him outside of his work, shoved a mic in his face, and asked him how he felt being as evil as Hitler and Lord Voldemort combined. Mr. Ikaros turned beet red and could barely catch his breath. I seriously worried he might have a heart attack right there.

I felt so bad that I thought about calling Brandon to see how he was doing. I stopped myself. It sucks when simple kindness seems like a bad idea.

I started spending every day at my dad's office. Which answered how he planned to keep an eye on me while he was at work. I read and worked on my laptop. My dad gave me the task of researching drug-prevention charities. And that answered what we'd be doing with the money I'd earned over the last year. Maybe "earned" isn't the right word.

After he was done at work, he drove me over to the Bully Burger. He sat in the parking lot while I went inside to hand in my uniform and tell Mr. Washington he'd have to find a new drive-thru register monkey.

Chacho was in a chair reading his newspaper, so that meant that Mr. Washington wasn't around. I guess I could resign to Chacho as well as I could to anyone. I set the bag with my stuff on the table in front of him.

"What's this?" he asked. He pawed through the bag.

I motioned with my head out to the parking lot where my dad sat glaring into the store.

"I'm not going to be working here anymore," I said. "My dad decided it'd be for the best."

"Uh-huh," Chacho said. He looked me over. "You okay? You seem different.

"I've just been through a few things this last little bit."

"I heard," he said. "You're like the Terminator for zombies is what I heard."

I laughed. "When you say I seem different, how do you mean that?"

He studied me. He frowned really deeply, too deeply to be real, and he stroked his chin.

"Relaxed," he said. "You look relaxed, maybe on your way toward being happy. I'm not used to it. You took my advice and you're getting squared away."

I laughed again and he smiled at me.

"Well, I think you better get used to it," I said. "Me being happy, and all."

He nodded, smiling. "If you say so, *chica*."

I thought about the hard and shitty stuff ahead of me. Telling Buddha I wouldn't be selling for him anymore. Oh, right, and I needed to pay him for the drugs currently swirling around in the river. And I still needed to settle things with Dad. That was just for starters. I knew I'd be miserable while I was going through all of it. Then I thought about when I had all these awful tasks behind me.

I bet that I'd feel free.

"Hell, yeah, Chacho," I said. "Get used to it for sure."

"Okay, Courtney," he said. "Listen, you need anything, you give me a call. You're one of the good ones."

Rather than tell him how wrong he was about me, I asked him if Phil was working tonight.

"Naw," Chacho said, "he quit, too. I thought it might have had something to do with you."

"Not me," I said. "It must have been his own bonehead idea. Well, I'll see you around, Chacho."

"I hope so," he said.

I didn't bother to say good-bye to anyone else.

Later that night, or early the next morning if you want to be technical, I woke to the sound of pebbles hitting my window. My first thought was that it was zombies and I grabbed my pistol. Then I got my head together and realized I was in the middle of a teen romance cliché instead.

I opened the window and Phil stood out there in his combat gear. He held some papers in his hand.

"Hey," he whispered.

"Hey."

"I heard you quit the Bully Burger."

"Wow," I said, "news travels fast."

He shrugged.

"Chacho told me the same thing about you," I said.

"Yeah, I got a better deal at the Cinema."

"Nice," I said. "You'll look good in the corporate-mandated vest."

"The pay is better and I won't be running a deep fat fryer," he said.

"There is that," I said. I realized he was still just standing there. "Want to come in?"

"I better not," he said. "Cody's waiting to go on patrol." He pointed off toward some bushes by the chain-link. Sure enough, there was Cody, all done up in camo, too.

"Hey, Cody," I whisper-shouted. "You feeling better?"

He gave me a thumbs-up.

"How come you quit?" Phil asked.

The question caught me off guard a little.

"What?" I stammered. "Oh, I'll tell you later. Okay?"

"Sure," he said. "Hey, I have something for you," he said. He handed the sheet of paper to me.

Actually, it was two sheets, one on top of another with a hinge made out of masking tape, like a cover. I switched on the lamp and opened it. It was a drawing of me. The style was somewhere between the realistic drawing of Sherri that he'd done and his usual cartoony stuff. It was me holding a shotgun in one hand, the barrel resting against my shoulder. Smoke came out of the barrel. I had one foot planted on the head of a fully dead zombie. I had on the outfit I'd been wearing on Saturday night. There was some decorative stuff behind the main image and it sort of made me think of old Norman Rockwell paintings. The thing that totally got me was my expression. I had a sneer/smile that didn't make me look too mean. I looked like a complete badass, like I could take anything that came my way.

I set the drawing down on the table.

"Come here," I said. He got close and I leaned out the window and threw my arms around his neck. I felt his body go stiff and he never relaxed. He must have hated it, so I let him go after a minute.

"Thanks, Phil. I really like it. If, you know, you couldn't tell."

"I'm glad. It was fun to draw."

"You said you had another one of me, didn't you?"

"Yeah."

"I'd like to see it," I said. "Maybe I could see all your drawings?"

A smile, unsure at first and then bigger, spread across his face. I could have been mistaken, but I think he blushed a little. I had been right the other night. He *was* cute when he smiled.

"Are you serious?" he asked.

"Of course."

"Yeah, that'd be great."

"You know what else?" I asked. Phil recognized it for a

rhetorical ploy and didn't answer. "I think some night I'd like to go out with you and Cody. On patrol."

"Yeah?" he asked again.

"Yeah."

"That'd be great," he said. "You'll be a badass zombie slayer."

"I'll do my best," I said. "It might be a while, though. I'm sort of in hot water with my dad."

"Why's that?" he asked.

"I'll tell you another time."

Great. Another thing to add to my ever-growing list of things to do.

"Okay," Phil said. "Well, we'd better get to it."

"Kick some zombie butt," I said. "Don't die."

"Never," he said.

He hopped over the fence and the two of them took off into the night. How weird was my life that I accepted that as normal? And that I knew I'd be joining them sometime soon? Would I really be as badass as Phil thought? I hoped so because I'd spent a good part of my life avoiding being eaten by shufflers.

It was true that I'd been through a lousy few days, and that there was more lousy ahead of me, too, but I knew that things would get better. Hell, even though they looked bad on paper, I knew I was still better off than I'd been. I wasn't selling drugs, I wasn't lying to my dad anymore, and my dad didn't hate me because of it.

No matter how rotten things got in the next little while, I knew they'd pass. I knew that they'd get better. I knew that I'd *make* them better.

So, score one for me, I guess.

ACKNOWLEDGMENTS

It feels like the biggest cliché in the world to say that no one writes a book in a vacuum, but it's true. My friends Michael Lane and Julian Cautherley first gave me advice about the story back when I thought it would be a comic book, and I bet they don't even remember it. Scott Wolven was the first person besides me to read the finished manuscript. He then gave me the courage to wrestle the damned thing into submission via rewrites. Kate Erickson and my wife, Melissa Kreutz Gallardo, helped me to polish it further.

I'd be a jerk if I didn't mention a few people who read early chapters and gave me encouragement to carry on. So, thanks to Nancy Holder, David Anthony Durham, and Michael Kimball—all had advice for me at the early stages of this book's life. All of them are also, not coincidentally, faculty members at the Stonecoast MFA program. Further, they are all working writers (as is Scott Wolven) whose works you should hunt down and shove in your eyeballs.

Huge, Grand Canyon–sized thanks to my agent, Ann Collette, who saw potential in the manuscript when I wasn't too sure about it myself. I'll never forget her first words to me. We were in a cramped room full of soon-to-be MFA graduates waiting to speak to a real live agent for the first time. After I introduced myself and told her which sample I'd submitted to her, she spread her arms and said, "Come to Momma!" I knew right then she was the agent for me.

Thanks, too, to my editor, Michaela Hamilton. Never

underestimate how much a good editor can help you shape a novel.

This may seem strange, but I need to give a shout out to Salem Cinema in Salem, Oregon, and its owner, Loretta Miles. During most of the book's writing, I was a stay-at-home dad who worked part-time at the Cinema. I'm guessing that more than half of the first draft was written in the down time after movies started up. An aspiring writer might do worse than a part-time job at a cool, indie movie theater owned by an equally cool, indie lady.

Finally, thanks to my parents, neither of whom lived to see this book's publication. They seemed to not really understand my compulsion to write, but they never actually discouraged me, and even seemed hopeful that I'd succeed.

The zombie wars continue . . . and Courtney continues
to fight!

Don't miss

ZOMBIFIED

Coming from K-Teen in 2015.

Keep reading to enjoy a preview chapter . . .

CHAPTER ONE
Do Me a Favor in Return?

From the top of some hill I didn't know the name of, the whole of Salem spread out before me. I thought I might puke.

The day before my senior year starts and here it is my first time out of the freaking house all summer without my dad in my back pocket—except for some late-night vigilante shenanigans that Dad didn't know about—and where does my buddy Phil decide to bring me? To gaze upon the town I can't wait to escape. Needless to say, Phil is not Casanova. On the plus side, he could probably have told me who Casanova was. I think.

I closed my eyes and drew a deep breath. Jesus, I was acting like a grade-A bitch, even if it was only in my head. I opened my eyes and tried to see our hometown in a more positive way. Obviously Phil liked staring down at it, so I wanted to get in sync with him.

The Willamette River glittered in the sun, cutting Salem off from West Salem. The one surviving bridge was covered in traffic—the other bridge had been blown up years ago in the first days after the dead came back. Downtown was dominated by the capitol building, the Gold Man shining on top. There was the courthouse, a few churches, a big bank or two, all of it dotted with parks and clumps of trees.

Nope, it didn't do it for me. The smell of old cigarettes didn't help much. Whoever owned this car before Phil had been a heavy smoker and we couldn't get rid of the stench. If Phil noticed my deep dislike of this little excursion, he didn't let on. But then Phil seems not to catch too many social cues. It's simultaneously cute and infuriating.

"Why did you bring me out here?" I asked.

Phil slowly blinked his eyes. A tic of his. He has brown hair that's too long and gets in his face. A sharp chin. Good lips and nose, too. I used to think he was plain looking. When I caught myself remembering that, I blushed and mentally backed away from the thought the same way I would back away from a dog that might be dangerous. Again, he didn't seem to notice.

"I thought you'd like it," he said. He shrugged. "I like it."

I decided to change the subject.

"How's the movie theater?" I asked.

"Good," he said. "I like running the projector. It's old and needs constant repair. It's fun." He smiled and I wondered again how I'd ever thought he was plain.

"Have you been by the Bully Burger lately?" he asked. We used to work there together until we both left for different reasons.

"Nope," I said. "I haven't been back since I quit. What's up?"

"I was in there a few days ago," he said. "Chacho said someone was looking for you."

"Oh, hell," I said. "It wasn't Brandon, was it?" Brandon had been a boy I was falling for at the end of last school year. Before everything went to hell, that is.

"I don't think so. No one knew this guy's name."

"Did one of the Olsen twins see him?" The twins weren't really named Olsen, but they were for-real named Mary Kate and Ashley. No, seriously. "Did they at least describe him?"

"No," said Phil. "And I didn't ask Chacho what the guy looked like."

"How is Chacho?" I asked. He was the security guard at the Bully Burger, and the only cool adult I knew.

"He seemed okay, I guess," said Phil with another shrug.

"That's good," I said, but my mind raced for a while, wondering who'd been asking about me. You wouldn't know it to look at me, but a number of unsavory characters might actually be hunting for me.

"Can I ask you something?" Phil asked.

"You can ask."

"What's up with you and Brandon?"

This threw me. I wasn't expecting Phil to be aware of anything going on in my social life.

I shrugged.

"You two seemed to be an item last year," he said. *An item?* Was Phil a character in a *Sweet Valley High* novel? I let it slide. "And then you weren't, and now you act weird whenever his name comes up."

I slid down in the front seat of the horrible old Ford Taurus Phil had bought over the summer. The cracked leather creaked and made fart noises. I always knew that I'd have to talk about Brandon with Phil at some point. I was just lucky that he hadn't asked me before now.

"Can we get out of the car?" I asked. "Get some fresh air?"

"Is this some sort of stall tactic?" he asked.

"Only sort of," I said. "Mostly I want some fresh air." The stale cigarette smell really was getting to me.

Rather than answer, Phil opened his door and climbed out. I did the same but, as I got out, I grabbed my bag and started rummaging through it.

"What are you looking for?" he asked as he squinted at me through the windshield.

"My gun," I said. Technically, it's a revolver.

"Are you planning to shoot me?" he asked. It took me a second to realize he'd made a joke. They were pretty rare, coming from him.

"Ha," I deadpanned. "I just want to be ready for any uninvited guests." I grabbed the pistol and stood, tucking it into my waistband.

He looked around us. We'd parked at the end of a dead-end street on top of this hill. There were a few houses on either side, all of them surrounded by chain-link fencing, and a few trees.

"I don't think there are gonna be any zombies around here," he said.

"Yeah, well," I said, "the last time I thought I'd have a zombie-free evening with a group of friends, I had to deal with a whole army of the suckers." At Brandon's year-end party a couple months ago, we'd been attacked by the zombie equivalent of the Golden Horde. That was one of the reasons I'd stopped seeing him. But just one.

He sat on the bumper of the car and I did the same. I waited for him to ask me again, before realizing he wasn't going to. He seemed happy just to look out over the city I wanted to get out of so badly. I considered not talking, not bringing it up again, but worried what the consequences of that would be. I couldn't figure out how Phil was doing such a number on my head; was it sorcery?

I noticed that he was sort of gesturing in the air with his hands, another tic. Little movements like he was conducting a symphony or something. I thought about his hands and what they'd feel like on my skin, then put that thought away. Now wasn't the time.

"As preface to this whole story," I said, keeping my eyes forward, definitely not looking at him, "I just want to say that I don't do it anymore."

"Ominous," Phil said. "Do what?"

"I used to sell drugs," I said. "For, like, the last year that I worked at the Bully, I was selling Vitamin Z out of the drive-thru window."

I waited for a response, but Phil stayed silent. It didn't feel judgey. And, as a girl raised in the American school system, I know judgmental. I decided I could go on.

"I never tried it myself," I said, "until I did. Just once." I glanced at Phil and he nodded slowly. "Brandon was with me. And Sherri." Sherri had been my best friend since birth, and she'd worked at the Bully Burger with me Phil and me. "While we were high, we got separated from Sherri. The next time I saw her, she was a zombie."

"The whole episode freaked me out something fierce. I decided to stop selling, and definitely decided I'd never do Z again."

"I had no idea that's how Sherri died," Phil said. I searched for some hint of what he was thinking, but his voice was a monotone. "You never told me."

"There was never a good time to bring it up," I said, and cringed. Jesus, I could be pretty lame.

"And now this thing with Brandon," Phil said.

"And now this thing with Brandon," I agreed. "He kept on going with it. He had some at his end-of-year shindig and wanted me to smoke it with him. That was right before the zombies made their grand entrance."

Phil nodded. He'd been there for that part. Not as a guest of the party. He'd just shown up in case there was trouble of the undead variety. Because he really likes to kill zombies and he was pretty sure they'd be showing up like ants at a picnic.

"And he'd smoked it once or twice before that night, too."

"Why?" Phil asked.

"He said it made him forget himself," I said. "Not just his troubles, but himself. He liked that, I guess."

Phil cocked his head and looked at me. "Why did you sell Vitamin Z?" he asked.

I felt a little ember of resentment start to glow in my chest. My fallback position whenever I'm put on the spot is to get angry and let my inner bitch off her leash, but I knew that wasn't fair to Phil. He deserved some answers. I took a deep breath and did my best to grind out that fire.

"I needed it to fund my plan," I said. My plan to get the hell out of Salem, move to New York City—if the Army ever reclaimed it from the zombies—attend Columbia University, and find a cure for the zombie plague.

I braced myself for him to be horrified. Or at least mildly grossed out. What I wasn't prepared for was him taking it in stride.

"I'm not surprised you don't want to see him anymore," he said. "Especially since Sherri died because you guys gave her Vitamin Z."

I took a deep breath. No one else had blamed me for Sherri's death and what Phil said pushed all of my defensive buttons. I took another deep breath and decided to let it slide.

"That's it?" I asked him. "Nothing about me selling it?"

"You stopped selling it after that, right?" he asked. "After you figured out it was bad mojo?" I nodded. He shrugged. "I've done too many dumb things myself to start judging people."

"Are you Christian?" I blurted out. It would explain why he wouldn't want to judge me. And it would explain why, after months of going out on zombie patrol, he hadn't made one attempt at kissing me. Or even copping a feel. I'd briefly considered that he might be gay, but my sexuality-detecting equipment wasn't picking up any fabulous signals. It occurred to me that this was actually the first time we'd hung out together in a non-zombie-killing capacity. I liked it, but I wish we'd decided to do

something—anything—else. We could have gone somewhere private, just as an example. . . .

He looked confused. "No, I'm not. Would it matter if I
were religious?"

"No," I lied. As much as I like to be open-minded,
churchy-Joes rub me the wrong way. It's something I
needed to work on, okay? "I'm just trying to figure you
out."

"My aunt says, 'that way leads to madness.' " He said it
without a smile—smiles from him are rare—but he didn't
seem sad about it, either.

"Your aunt seems to have you pegged," I said.

A grin almost played across his lips.

His lips.

Man, I needed to get a grip. I stood up and checked that
the pistol was still firmly in place.

"Let's go for a walk."

"Where?" Phil asked.

I pointed past the end of the street. Where the pavement ended, a small foot trail led down into some trees.

"Maybe we can get a better look at this beautiful city of
yours," I said.

"Sure," he said. "Let me get my bat out of the trunk."

I thought about that for a moment. His bat is of the
ordinary baseball variety—wood and about yea long—
except that it had nails pounded through it and was covered in the gore of about a hundred undead. It occurred
to me I'd never seen it in full light. I didn't think I wanted
this to be my first time.

"Why don't you leave it?" I asked. "If we run into trouble, I have this." I lifted up my shirt to show him the pistol and exposed a good portion of my belly, too. Not that
he seemed to notice.

"Okay," he said, barely glancing at me. "You want to go
down first, or me?"

I stifled a bunch of lame double entendres and said, "Let me." Maybe I'd at least find a zombie who found my body appealing.

I started picking my way down the path, which was steeper than it had appeared from up on the street. A few times my feet tried to get out from under me, but I never actually fell on my ass. So, points to me, I guess.

Once we got down about six feet or so, the ground flattened out a little and I became less worried about falling off the hill. But the trees were a lot thicker and closer than they'd appeared from up above and I started worrying about new stuff, i.e., shufflers deciding I looked like a tasty snack.

Phil skidded the last foot or so and he grabbed me to stop himself from falling. His hand slipped around my waist and he left it there for a second after he got himself righted. My heart started to thud in my chest and all thoughts of the undead went right out of my head. I felt like the heroine in a Regency novel that featured monsters, as dumb as that sounds.

"Sorry," Phil said.

"No problem." I looked out at the city. Being a few yards closer to it didn't make it any prettier. So much for my brilliant ideas.

"Let's go down here," Phil said as he started walking. "I think there are some big rocks we can sit on." He paused and grinned at me. "The better to enjoy the incredible view."

"More jokes," I said. "You're like a junior Dane Cook."

"I hope I'm less douche-y."

I didn't answer that and just followed him. We found the rocks pretty easily. Big, flat stones that jutted out of the dirt. They were probably part of the mountain we were crawling all over. It felt good to sit in the sun with a boy I was starting to like. I warned myself that this was only the second time I'd been through this, and the first time—with Brandon—hadn't turned out well. It wasn't that I didn't trust Phil, it was that I didn't trust myself.

We sat there without talking for a while and then, as I'm prone to do, I started mentally picking at something Phil had said earlier.

"What dumb things?" I asked, picking up on what he'd said in the car.

He stared out at the city and frowned.

"Too soon," he said.

"When?" I prodded.

He turned toward me. "I'm not sure. But I'll know when it's the time. If it ever is."

"And you expect me to be satisfied with that answer," I said, teasing him.

"You don't have a choice," he said, serious as a heart attack. This wasn't a side I'd seen of him before. I knew he was sort of distant, but I wasn't really prepared for defensive. He seemed almost like a real boy at this point.

The sun was behind us, but it must have started to set because we were in shadow by then and the air was getting cooler. I rubbed my arms when goose bumps sprang up on them.

"Maybe we should head back to the car," I said. "I've had enough of this scenic beauty for a while."

"Okay," said Phil. He stood and turned back the way we'd come, and then he froze. "Oh," he said.

I didn't need to ask.

A zombie stood right on the path that led back to the car. Of course. She wasn't all chewed up and bloody, but her gray skin and the black slime that oozed out of her mouth were good indicators of what we were dealing with. I took a second to admire her Smiths T-shirt. It was the MEAT IS MURDER one. How's that for irony? She looked like she was our age, maybe a little younger, and used to be pretty. I guessed that maybe West Salem High was missing a cheerleader.

We stood there for a minute, all three of us. She made no attempt to come at us, and we weren't exactly ready to rush her. I started to look around because the last few times I'd had run-ins with some shufflers, they'd been traveling in packs. But if there were others with her, they weren't coming out to play.

"Courtney," Phil shout-whispered at me.

"What?" I said.

"Don't you have a gun in your pants?"

No, I'm just happy to see you, I thought and grinned despite the situation. I was so scared I felt a little giddy. But he was right, I did have a pistol. I slowly snaked my right hand across my belly and under my shirt. Finding the pistol, I wrapped my hand around it, careful to keep my finger off the trigger so I didn't shoot myself in the gut when drawing it out. Just as slowly, I moved my left hand up and grabbed my shirt. I took a deep breath, let it out, then simultaneously lifted the shirt and drew the pistol.

Which stuck in my waistband!

I was so confused, I almost shot myself. Looking down to see what was going on, I heard the zombie snarl. The gun's sight had snagged on something, but I couldn't tell what.

"Courtney!" Phil shouted.

I looked up to see the dead girl charging me. Yanking the gun free, I felt a searing pain on my belly. Then she hit me like a freaking undead linebacker. We both went over and she landed on top of me. I let go of the gun to grab her arms and keep her off me.

The bitch was inches from my face, snapping her jaws and drooling black goo all over me. I was trying to keep the ooze from getting in my mouth and my arms were already shaking with the effort to keep her up.

"Philip," I screamed, "grab the gun!"

I didn't hear him respond. Where the hell was he? I knew I couldn't last much longer. A whimper escaped my throat and I cursed myself for that. There was no way I wanted to go out crying in front of a goddamned zombie.

Just then something flew across my body and knocked the dead girl off of me. Phil had tackled her and was now wrestling on the ground with her. He'd ended up on top, but I could tell that he couldn't let her go or try to get away without the risk of getting bitten. At least she wasn't leaking zombie tranny fluid all over him.

Despite just wanting to curl up into a ball, I got up on my hands and knees and started searching for the gun. Rocks and other junk dug into my knees and the palms of my hands as I probed under bushes and scanned the area. I didn't see the damned pistol anywhere.

"Courtney!"

Phil was now lying flat on his back, the dead girl contorting every way she could to try to get her teeth into him. His eyes bulged, his face and neck were a scary shade of red. I knew he wouldn't last much longer. Screw the gun.

I found the biggest rock I was able to palm. It felt good in my hand—jagged and heavy. I scrambled over to where Phil tangled with the zombie, stopped, and raised the rock high in the air. Phil's eyes turned toward me and something like relief washed over his expression. If this were a movie, this would be the point where I said something ironic, but I couldn't think of anything.

"Do it!" Phil screamed.

The dead chick turned to look at me and hissed through blackened teeth.

I brought the rock down with all my strength right on her nose. I felt more than heard the sickening crunch of her nose caving into her face, then more black ooze squirted from the wound. She screamed and let go of Phil to clutch at it. She fell over backward as Phil bucked her off him.

I immediately collapsed onto her chest and, with my free hand, pushed her arms out of the way. She looked up at me with one ruined eye and I almost hesitated because of what I saw there. Almost. Instead, I brought the rock down on her face and felt/heard another crack. Then I did it again, and again. I lost track, but soon the crack was replaced with a sucking, squelching sound.

I felt fingers close around my wrist as I raised the rock again. Phil stood over me, his blank expression taking me in, then looking toward the zombie's busted gourd.

"Okay, Courtney," he said. "She's done."

"I should have let you bring the bat," I said. The last few words came out strangled because I started to cry. I was only marginally less embarrassed to cry in front of Phil than I had been about squirting a few in front of the shuffler.

Phil pulled me off of her and helped me walk back to the rocks. We sat there for a few minutes while I got myself together and the last of the sunlight disappeared.

"We need to get out of here," Phil said. "Just in case there are more."

"My gun."

"You can buy a new one," he said. "C'mon."

We made our slow way back to the car. My knees were killing me, and something happened to my hip that I was just starting to feel. Also, I had a deep gouge across my stomach where the pistol's site scratched me. After a lot of tripping and sliding, we made it up the steep embankment and over to the car.

I sank into the seat and tried to ignore the pain. Phil flipped on the dome light and we examined each other for gouges and bites. None that we could see. There wasn't much we could have done at that point if there were any. We'd be zombies before we could get to a hospital.

We sat back down and Phil started the car. Elvis Costello, Phil's favorite, came pouring out of the speakers. As Elvis sang about the terrible state of the radio, I sat there thinking about how earlier I'd been fantasizing about Phil's hands on me. Well, he'd just pawed me all over, and I couldn't think of anything less sexy.

"Thanks," he said, "for saving me. I wasn't going to last much longer."

"You bet," I said. "Do me a favor in return?"

"Anything," he said.

"Never bring me to this place again."

"Done," he said.

He put the car in reverse and turned around.

We didn't talk. What can I say? Killing undead teenagers always make me feel somber. I thought about what I saw in the dead girl's eye right before I hit her with the rock. Usually the word used to describe a zombie is "lifeless," right? But she'd shown some spark, some hint of recognition that threw me for a second. I couldn't tell you what that meant, or why it was there, but something about it made me shiver.

"You cold?" Phil asked. "Want me to turn on the heat?"

"No," I lied. "I'm fine."

And we drove off toward whatever the new school year had to offer.

GREAT BOOKS, GREAT SAVINGS!

When You Visit Our Website:
www.kensingtonbooks.com
You Can Save Money Off The Retail Price
Of Any Book You Purchase!

- **All Your Favorite Kensington Authors**
- **New Releases & Timeless Classics**
- **Overnight Shipping Available**
- **eBooks Available For Many Titles**
- **All Major Credit Cards Accepted**

Visit Us Today To Start Saving!
www.kensingtonbooks.com

All Orders Are Subject To Availability.
Shipping and Handling Charges Apply.
Offers and Prices Subject To Change Without Notice.